Albert Harkness

A New Latin Reade

Albert Harkness

A New Latin Reade

ISBN/EAN: 9783337332778

Printed in Europe, USA, Canada, Australia, Japan

Cover: Foto ©Andreas Hilbeck / pixelio.de

More available books at **www.hansebooks.com**

A

LATIN READER,

INTENDED AS A

COMPANION

TO THE

AUTHOR'S LATIN GRAMMAR.

BY

ALBERT HARKNESS, LL. D.,

PROFESSOR IN BROWN UNIVERSITY.

REVISED EDITION, WITH EXERCISES IN LATIN COMPOSITION.

NEW YORK:
D. APPLETON AND COMPANY,
1, 3, AND 5 BOND STREET.
LONDON: 16 LITTLE BRITAIN.
1881.

A

LATIN READER,

INTENDED AS A

COMPANION

TO THE

AUTHOR'S LATIN GRAMMAR.

WITH

REFERENCES, SUGGESTIONS, NOTES AND VOCABULARY.

BY

ALBERT HARKNESS,

PROFESSOR IN BROWN UNIVERSITY.

REVISED EDITION.

NEW YORK:
D. APPLETON AND COMPANY,
1, 3, AND 5 BOND STREET.
1881.

PREFACE

THE object of the present revision is to adapt the Reader to the Revised Edition of the author's Grammar. Accordingly, all references are made to that edition.

But, in connection with this special object, it has been thought best to give the whole work a somewhat careful revision. Various slight changes have, therefore, been introduced in different portions of the volume. In Part First a few sentences and constructions, deemed too difficult, have given place to others, which will be found, it is hoped, better adapted to the wants of the learner.

The method of instruction adopted in the series of Latin text-books to which this volume belongs requires that the Reading Lessons should be accompanied by regular Exercises in translating English into Latin. Ample provision is made for such exercises in the author's Introduction to Latin Composition, which is intended to be put into the hands of the pupil when he begins the Reader, and to be used in weekly lessons throughout his entire preparatory course. That, in general, such exercises should form a regular progressive series, and be published in a separate volume, scarcely admits of a doubt; but, for the accommodation of certain schools, in which a large proportion of the pupils pursue the study of the Latin only a very limited time, it has been deemed advisable to insert Part First of the Latin Composition in a special edition of the Reader. This arrangement will furnish such schools the full benefit of an elementary drill in Latin Composition, without involving the necessity of procuring a separate work upon that subject. The special edition will be entitled the "Reader with Exercises." The title of the regular edition will remain unchanged.

PROVIDENCE, *December* 15, 1874.

PREFACE.

THE Latin Reader now offered to the public is intended as a companion to the author's Latin Grammar. It comprises Reading Lessons, Suggestions to the Learner, Notes, and a Vocabulary.

The Reading Lessons are abundantly supplied with references to the Grammar, and are arranged in two parts.

Part First presents a progressive series of exercises illustrative of grammatical forms, inflections, and rules. These exercises are intended to accompany the learner from the very outset in his progress through the Grammar, and thus to furnish him the constant luxury of using the knowledge which he is acquiring. They have been carefully selected from classical authors.

Part Second illustrates connected discourse, and comprises Fables, Anecdotes, and History. The Anecdotes have been selected from various classical sources; the other portions have been derived chiefly from the Lateinisches Elementarbuch of Professors Jacobs and Döring, though, in the Grecian History, Arnold's Historiae Antiquae Epitome, founded upon the work of Jacob and Döring, has furnished a few extracts. The Historical selections were, with a few exceptions, derived originally from the Latin historians Eutropius, Justin, and Cornelius Nepos.

The Suggestions to the Learner are intended to direct the unskilful efforts of the beginner, and thus to enable him to do for himself much which would otherwise require the aid of his teacher, and to do easily and pleasantly much which would otherwise be difficult and repulsive. They aim to point out to him the *process* by which he may most readily and surely reach the meaning and the structure of a Latin sentence, and then to teach him to embody that meaning in clear idiomatic English. Experience has abundantly shown the need of some such directions. The beginner's first efforts to solve the problem presented by a Latin sentence are too often little better than a series of unsuccessful conjectures, while his first translations are purely mechanical renderings, with little regard either to the thought of his author or to the proprieties of his mother tongue.

The Notes aim to furnish such collateral information as will enable the learner to appreciate the subject matter of his reading lessons, and such special aid as will enable him to surmount real and untried difficulties. Grammatical references can be employed only to solve grammatical difficulties; and, though for this purpose they are absolutely invaluable, it is yet a mistake to suppose that they can ever supply the place of commentary.

In the Vocabulary, the aim has been to give to each word the particular meanings which occur in the reading lessons, without omitting, however, its essential and leading signification.

At the solicitation of many eminent classical Professors and Teachers, the author has it in contemplation to publish an Introduction to Latin Composition, consisting of two parts, the first intended for the beginner, and the second for the more advanced student. Accordingly, the present work has been made simply a Reader, and all Exercises in writing Latin have been reserved for a future volume.

With this statement of the design and plan of the work, the author commits it to classical instructors, in the hope that, in their hands, it may render some useful service in the important work of classical instruction.

PROVIDENCE, *Aug.* 21*st*, 1865.

CONTENTS.

PART FIRST.

GRAMMATICAL EXERCISES.

	PAGE
Nouns	1
Adjectives	3
Pronouns	4
Verbs	5
Syntax of Nouns	9
Agreement of Nouns	9
Nominative	10
Vocative	10
Accusative	10
Dative	13
Genitive	16
Ablative	19
Syntax of Adjectives	26
Syntax of Pronouns	26
Syntax of Verbs	28
Agreement	28
Indicative	28
Subjunctive	29
Imperative	35
Infinitive	35
Gerunds and Gerundives	37
Supines	39
Participles	39
Syntax of Particles	40

PART SECOND.

LATIN SELECTIONS.

		PAGE
Fables		41
Anecdotes		45
Roman History		52
Period I. Italian and Roman kings		52
II. Roman Struggles and Conquests		58
III. Roman Triumphs		65
IV. Civil Dissensions		72
Grecian History		80
Period I. Grecian Triumphs		80
II. Civil Wars in Greece		84
III. Graeco-Macedonian Empire		89
Suggestions to the Learner		99
Notes		109
Latin-English Vocabulary		139

EXPLANATIONS OF REFERENCES AND ABBREVIATIONS.

THE reference numerals in the Latin text, and in the Suggestions, refer to the author's Latin Grammar, the Revised Edition.

In the Notes and Vocabulary, the Arabic numerals refer, when enclosed in parentheses, to articles in this work; and, when not thus enclosed, to articles in the Grammar.

Roman numerals refer to the Suggestions.

The following abbreviations occur:

adj........	adjective.	lit	literally.
adv........	adverb.	m	masculine.
comp......	comparative.	n	neuter.
conj.......	conjunction.	part........	participle.
defect.....	defective.	pass........	passive.
dep........	deponent.	plur. *or* pl....	plural.
f..........	feminine.	prep	preposition.
impers....	impersonal.	pron	pronoun.
indec	indeclinable.	subs	substantive.
interj.....	interjection.	superl......	superlative.
irreg.......	irregular.		

PART FIRST

GRAMMATICAL EXERCISES.

---•••---

NOUNS.

Definition, Gender, etc.—39-42; 44-47.

First Declension.—48.

Note.—Before reading the Latin Exercises, the pupil is expected, in every instance, to learn carefully those portions of the Grammar which are embraced in the large type of the sections designated.

1. 1. Ală, alā, alae,¹ alam, alārum, alis, alas. 2. Victoriă, victoriā, victoriae, victoriam, victoriārum, victoriis, victorias. 3. Causae, fortūnae, portae. 4. Causā, fortūnā, portā. 5. Causam, fortūnam, portam. 6. Causārum, fortunārum, portārum. 7. Causis, fortūnis, portis. 8. Causas, fortūnas, portas.

Second Declension.—51.

Rule II.—*Appositives.*—363; 352, 2.

2. 1. Domĭnus, domĭni, domĭno, domĭnum, domĭne, dominōrum, domĭnis. 2. Gener, genĕri, genĕro, genĕrum, generōrum, genĕris, genĕros. 3. Servi, anni. 4. Puĕri, socĕri. 5. Agri, magĭstri. 6. Templi, belli. 7. Servis, annis. 8. Puĕro, socĕro. 9. Agrōrum, magistrōrum. 10. Templa, bella.

---

¹ When the same Latin form may be found in two or more cases, the pupil is expected to give the meaning for each case.

11. Lucus, stellă. 12. Luci, stellae. 13. Lucum, stellam. 14. Luco, stellā. 15. Lucōrum, stellārum. 16. Lucis, stellis. 17. Lucos, stellas.

18. Dionysius tyrannus.¹ 19. Dionysio tyranno. 20. Dionysium tyrannum. 21. Tulliă regīnă. 22. Tulliae regīnae. 23. Tulliam regīnam. 24. Puer Ascanius.

THIRD DECLENSION.—CLASS I.—57–61.

RULE XVI.—*Genitive.*—395.

3. 1. Princĭpis, princĭpum. 2. Dux, duces. 3. Regem, reges. 4. Regis, milĭtis. 5. Regi, milĭti. 6. Rege, milĭte. 7. Reges, milĭtes. 8. Regum, milĭtum. 9. Regĭbus, militĭbus.

10. Virtus regis.² 11. Virtūtes regum.² 12. Vindex libertātis. 13. Vindĭces libertātis. 14. Nepotĭbus regis. 15. Virtūte regis. 16. Virtūte milĭtum.

17. Belli causă. 18. Belli causas. 19. Victoriă regis. 20. Victoriae regis. 21. Gener judĭcis. 22. Sapientiă judĭcis. 23. Regis filiă. 24. Tulliă, regis filiă.

THIRD DECLENSION.—CLASS II.—62–64.

RULE XXXII.—*Cases with Prepositions.*—432–435.

4. 1. Nubi, nube, nubium. 2. Hostem, hostes, hostĭbus. 3. Carmĭna, carminĭbus. 4. Consŭlis, passĕris. 5. Consŭlum, passĕrum. 6. Consulĭbus, passerĭbus. 7. Leōni, virgĭni. 8. Leōnes, virgĭnes. 9. Patrem, pastōrem. 10. Patres, pastōres. 11. Opus, corpus. 12. Alam avis. 13. Custōdes urbis.

14. Cicĕro consul.¹ 15. Cicerōnis consŭlis. 16. Cicerōnem consŭlem. 17. Nepos consŭlis.² 18. Nepōtes

---

¹ See Grammar, 363.   ² 395.

consŭlis. 19. Nepŏtes consŭlum. 20. Pater judĭcis.
21. Patres judĭcum. 22. Patrĭbus judĭcum.
23. Post Romŭli mortem.' 24. Apud Herodŏtum,
patrem historiae. 25. Ad virtūtem. 26. Ante lucem.
27. Contra natūram. ˉ28. Sermo de amicitiā.' 29. Pro
patriā. 30. Sine labōre. 31. In amnem.' 32. In bello.'

FOURTH DECLENSION.—116.

5. 1. Fructūs, cornūs. 2. Fructĭbus, cornĭbus. 3.
Cantum, currum. 4. In currum. 5. In curru. 6. Solis ortus. 7. Ab ortu ad occāsum. 8. Ante solis
occāsum.

FIFTH DECLENSION.—120.

6. 1. Acies, aciem, aciēi. 2. Diēi, faciēi. 3. Rei.
spei. 4. Diem, faciem. 5. Rem, spem. 6. Die, facie.
7. Re, spe.
8. In aciem. 9. In acie. 10. Facies urbis. 11.
Spes fortūnae. 12. Contra spem. 13. Sine spe.

ADJECTIVES.

FIRST AND SECOND DECLENSIONS.—148–150.

RULE XXXIII.—*Agreement of Adjectives.*—438.

7. 1. Servus bonus. 2. Servi boni. 3. Servo bono.
4. Servum bonum. 5. Serve bone. 6. Servōrum bonō-
rum. 7. Servis bonis. 8. Servos bonos. 9. Regīnā
bonā. 10. Reginae bonae. 11. Regīnam bonam. 12.
Regīnā bonā. 13. Regīnārum bonārum. 14. Regīnis
bonis. 15. Regīnas bonas. 16. Exemplum bonum.
17. Exempli boni. 18. Exempla bona.

1 432, 433.   2 432, 434.   3 435, 1.

19. Puer pulcher. 20. Puellă pulchră. 21. Tectum pulchrum. 22. Pŭěri pulchri. 23. Puellae pulchrae. 24. Tecta pulchra.

25. Verǎ amicitiǎ. 26. Gladius longus. 27. Magnǎ gloriǎ. 28. Spes falsǎ. 29. Siue magno labōre. 30. Modius aureōrum annulōrum.

THIRD DECLENSION.—152-158.

8. 1. Dolor acer. 2. Sine dolōre acri. 3. Dolōres acres. 4. Hostis crudēlis. 5. Hostem crudēlem. 6. Hostium crudelium. 7. Hiems glaciālis. 8. Hiěmem glaciālem. 9. Carmen dulce. 10. Carmĭna dulcia. 11. Innumerabĭles fabŭlae.

COMPARISON OF ADJECTIVES.—160-162.

9. 1. Triumphus clarus. 2. Triumphus clarior. 3. Triumphus clarissĭmus. 4. Triumphi clari. 5. Triumphi clariōres. 6. Triumphi clarissĭmi. 7. Vir fortis. 8. Vir fortior. 9. Vir fortissĭmus. 10. Sapiens vir. 11. Sapientior vir. 12. Sapientissĭmus vir. 13. Fortissĭmi vǐri. 14. Fortissimōrum virōrum multitūdo. 15. Perītus dux. 16. Peritissĭmi duces. 17. Bella funestissĭma.

PRONOUNS.

CLASSIFICATION AND DECLENSION OF PRONOUNS.—182-191.

RULE XXXIV.—*Agreement of Pronouns.*—445; 445, 1.

10. 1. Mei. 2. Tibi. 3. Inter se.[1] 4. Ad te. 5. Pro nobis. 6. Post me. 7. Ante nos. 8. Patriǎ meǎ.[2] 9. Nostrǎ patriǎ. 10. Magister tuus. 11. Tuǎ mens. 12. Nostri milĭtes. 13. Nostrae amicitiae.

---

[1] 432.   [2] 438, 1.

14. Ad salūtem vestram. 15. Ad vitam suam. 16. Hic' vir. 17. Haec urbs. 18. Hoc regnum. 19. Hujus viri. 20. In hac urbe. 21. Haec regna. 22. Illi viri. 23. Pro illis viris. 24. Ante hunc diem. 25. Sub hoc rege. 26. Pastor illīus regiōnis. 27. Idem locus. 28. In eundem locum. 29. Circa eandem horam. 30. Id tempus. 31. Ab ipsā natūrā. 32. Ii ad quos.' 33. Quae civĭtas ? 34. Ab alĭquo. 35. Faustŭlus quidam.

VERBS.

INTRODUCTION.—192-197; 199-203. ·

VERB SUM.—204.

RULE III.—*Subject Nominative.*—367.

RULE XXXV.—*Agreement of Verb with Subject.*—460.

RULE I.—*Predicate Nouns.*—362.

11. 1. Aristīdes' justus' fuit.' 2. Justus * est.' 3. Justus erat. 4. Justi sumus.' 5. Justi fuerāmus. 6. Justi erĭmus. 7. Justi simus. 8. Justi fuissēmus. 9. Cato sapiens erat. 10. Sapiens fŭerat. 11. Sapientes erĭtis. 12. Sapientes fuistis. 13. Sapiens es. 14. Sapientes este. 15. Lex brevis est. 16. Lex brevis esto. 17. Leges breves sunt. 18. Leges breves sunto. 19. Ego consul' fui. 20. Cicĕro consul fuit. 21. Cicĕro consul fŭerat.

FIRST CONJUGATION.—205, 206.

RULE V.—*Direct Object.*—371.

12. 1. Amat, amant. 2. Amābat, amābant. 3.

---

* *Justus* agrees with the pronoun *is*, he, the omitted subject of *est.*

     ¹ 438, 1.   ⁴ 438.   ⁶ 460; 460, 2.

     ² 445.   ⁵ 460.   ⁷ 362.

     ³ 367.

Amavĕrat, amavĕrant.   4. Amavĕrit, amavĕrint.   5.
Amet, ament.

6. Laudat, laudātur.   7. Laudant, laudantur.   8. Lau-
dābat, laudabātur.   9. Laudābant, laudabantur.   10.
Laudet, laudētur.   11. Laudent, laudentur.

12. Oratiōnem¹ laudo.   13. Oratiōnem laudāmus.
14. Oratiōnes laudabĭmus.   15. Oratio laudātur.   16.
Oratiōnes laudantur.   17. Virtūtem amātis.   18. Virtūtem amabĭtis.   19. Virtus amātur.   20. Virtus
amāta² est.   21. Ego patriam liberāvi.   22. Patriam
liberavērunt.   23. Patria liberāta est.   24. Ancus urbem ampliāvit.   25. Marius fugātus² est.   26. Fugāti
erant.   27. Socrătes accusātus est.

SECOND CONJUGATION.—207, 208.

13. 1. Moneo, moneor.   2. Monēbam, monēbar.
3. Monēbo, monēbor.   4. Moneam, monear.   5. Monē-
rem, monērer.   6. Monui, monuĭmus.   7. Monuĕrat,
monuĕrant.   8. Monuĕris, monuerĭtis.   9. Monuĕrim,
monĭtus sim.   10. Monuissēmus, monĭti essēmus.
11. Monēte, monentor.

12. Terrēbat, terrebātur.   13. Terrēbant, terreban-
tur.   14. Terrēret, terrerētur.   15. Terrērent, terreren-
tur.   16. Terrĭtus sum, terrĭti sumus.   17. Terrĭtus es,
terrĭti estis.   18. Terrĭtus est, terrĭti sunt.

19. Gloriam¹ veram² habes.   20. Gloriam habēbis.
21. Equĭtes gladios habēbant.   22. Gladios habuērunt.
23. Gladium habuisti.   24. Homo habet memoriam.
25. Cum Romānis⁴ pacem habuĭmus.   26. Pacem habue-
rāmus.   27. Pacem habebĭmus.   28. Cyrus omnium in
exercĭtu⁵ suo milĭtum nomĭna tenēbat.

---

¹ 371.   ⁵ 438.   ⁶ 435, 1.
² 460, 1.   ⁴ 432, 434.

THIRD CONJUGATION.—209, 210.

RULE LI.—*Use of Adverbs.*—582.

14. 1. Rego, regor. 2. Regĭmus, regĭmur. 3. Rĕgit, regĭtur. 4. Regunt, reguntur. 5. Rege, regĭte. 6. Regendi, regendo. 7. Rectus eram, recti erāmus. 8. Spero, pareo, duco. 9. Speras, pares, ducis. 10. Sperāmus, parēmus, ducĭmus. 11. Sperābam, parēbam, ducēbam. 12. Sperābant, parēbant, ducēbant. 13. Sperāvi, parui, duxi. 14. Speravĭmus, paruĭmus, duxĭmus. 15. Speravērunt, paruērunt, duxērunt.

16. Deus omnem hunc mundum regit. 17. Deus mundum semper[1] rexit. 18. Deus mundum regēbat. 19. Deus mundum reget. 20. Cicĕro ad Attĭcum[2] scribit. 21. Ad te saepe scribam. 22. Cicĕro multos libros scripsit. 23. Ad amīcum de amicitiā[3] scripsi. 24. Librum de senectūte scripsĕrat. 25. Quid dixisti? 26. Nihil dixi. 27. Quid dixistis? 28. Multa de amicitiā dixĭmus. 29. Haec recte dixistis. 30. Hic liber ad te scriptus est.

FOURTH CONJUGATION.—211, 212.

15. 1. Audiēbat, audiēbant. 2. Audiebātur, audiebantur. 3. Audiam, audiēmus. 4. Audiar, audiēmur. 5. Audīvit, audivērunt. 6. Audītus est, audīti sunt. 7. Audivĕram, audiverāmus. 8. Audītus eram, audīti erāmus.

9. Sperat, paret, ducit, scit. 10. Sperant, parent, ducunt, sciunt. 11. Sperābat, parēbat, ducēbat, sciēbat. 12. Sperabāmus, parebāmus, ducebāmus, sciebāmus. 13. Sperābo, parēbo, ducet, sciet. 14. Tullus bellum finīvit. 15. Bellum finivĕrat. 16.

---

[1] 582.　　　[2] 433.　　　[3] 434.

Bellum finītum est. 17. Hic dies Graeciae libertātem
finiet. 18. Cives templum custodiunt. 19. Templa cus-
todiēmus. 20. Templum custodīte. 21. Brutus Macedoniam custodiēbat. 22. Hanc provinciam custodīmus.
23. Hoc audivǐmus. 24. A vobis audīmur.

VERBS IN IO, THIRD CONJUGATION.—221–223.

`16. 1. Romāni urbem capiunt. 2. Urbes capiēbant.
3. Urbem capiēmus. 4. Haec urbs capiētur. 5. Urbes
capientur. 6. Regǔlus captus est. 7. Milǐtes arma ca-
piunt. 8. Scipio Carthagǐnem cepit. 9. Praefecti regii
Eretriam cepērunt. 10. Regis pater fugit. 11. Fugiē-
bat. 12. Lacedaemonii fugiunt. 13. Fugērunt. 14.
Xerxes in Asiam fugěrat.

DEPONENT VERBS.—225–230.

17. 1. Coriolānus populātur agrum[1] Romānum. 2.
Pyrrhus Campaniam depopulātus est. 3. Milǐtes agros
depopulabantur. 4. Hoc facǐnŭs rex mirātur. 5. Hoc
mirāmur. 6. Puer laudem merētur. 7. Laudem mere-
ris. 8. Laudem merentur. 9. Gloria virtūtem sequǐtur.
10. Ascanium secūtus est Silvius. 11. Justitiam sequǐ-
mur. 12. Justitiam sequēmur. 13. Cum Scipiōne honōrem partīmur. 14. Id opus inter se partiuntur.

PERIPHRASTIC CONJUGATION.—231, 232.

18. 1. Virtūtem laudatūri sumus. 2. Virtus laudanda est. 3. Quid laudatūrus es ? 4. Bonitātem laudatūrus sum. 5. Omnia[2] sunt laudanda, quae[3] conjuncta cum virtūte sunt. 6. Quid vituperandum est?
7. Omnia sunt vituperanda, quae cum vitiis conjuncta

---

[1] 371.   [2] 441.   [3] 445.

sunt. 8. Gloriam veram habitūrus es. 9. Gloriam veram habitūri sumus. 10. Cicĕro ad Attĭcum scriptūrus erat. 11. Epistŏla scribenda est. 12. Orātor audiendus est. 13. Senatōres Cicerōnem auditūri erant.

SYNTAX OF NOUNS.

AGREEMENT OF NOUNS.

RULE I.—*Predicate Nouns.*—362.

19. 1. Mercurius *nuntius* erat. 2. Furius *consul* erat. 3. *Homo* sum.[1] 4. Bacchus erat vini[2] *deus.*[3] 5. Somnus est *imāgo* mortis. 6. Historia *testis* tempŏrum habētur. 7. Historia *magistra*[4] vitae habētur. 8. Socrātes *parens* philosophiae dicĭtur. 9. Brutus *homo* magnus evasĕrat. 10. Nos *causa*[5] belli sumus. 11. Nautius et Furius *consŭles*[6] erant.[7]

RULE II.—*Appositives.*—363.

20. 1. Dionysius *tyrannus* expulsus est. 2. Demarātus, regis *pater,* fugit. 3. Apud Herodŏtum, *patrem* historiae, sunt innumerabĭles fabŭlae. 4. Hannĭbal Saguntum, foederātam *urbem,* expugnāvit. 5. *Themistŏcles*[8] veni ad te. 6. Cato littĕras Graecas *senex*[9] didĭcit. 7. Junius aedem Salūtis, quam *consul* vovĕrat, *dictātor* dedicāvit. 8. Socrătem, sapientissĭmum[10] *virum,* Athenienses interfecērunt.

---

[1] 460, 2.	[4] 362, 1, 1).	[7] 363, 2.
[2] 395.	[5] 362, 1, 2).	[8] 363, 3.
[3] 51, 5.	[6] 463, II.	[9] 162.

NOMINATIVE.

RULE III.—*Subject Nominative.*—367.

21. 1. Cuncta *Graecia* liberāta est. 2. *Patria* mea est mundus. 3. *Paulus* consul[1] regem ad Pydnam superāvit. 4. *Philosophia* inventrix legum fuit. 5. Omnium malōrum *stultitia* est mater. 6. Non[2] omnis *error* stultitia est. 7. Quot *homĭnes*,[3] tot *sententiae.*

VOCATIVE.

RULE IV.—*Case of Address.*—369.

22. 1. Disce, *puer*, virtūtem. 2. Tu, mi[4] *Cicĕro*, haec accipies. 3. Te, *Minerva*, custos urbis, precor ac quaeso. 4. Audīte, *judĭces*. 5. Disce, *puer*, virtūtes. 6. *Amīci*, diem perdĭdi. 7. Conservāte, *judĭces*, hunc homĭnem.

ACCUSATIVE.

RULE V.—*Direct Object.*—371.

23. 1. Accēpi tuas *epistŏlas*. 2. Labor *omnia* vincit. 3. Anĭmus regit *corpus*. 4. Nostra *nos* patria delectat. 5. Miltiădes totam[5] *Graeciam* liberāvit. 6. Sophŏcles *tragoedias* fecit. 7. Studia *adolescentiam* alunt, *senectūtem* oblectant. 8. Romŭlus *Romam* condĭdit. 9. Avaritia *probĭtātem* subvertit. 10. Virtus conciliat *amicitias.* 11. Virtus *amicitiam* gignit.

12. Vestri patres eam *vitam*[5] vixērunt. 13. Mirum *somnium*[5] somniāvi. 14. *Pacem*[7] desperāvi. 15. Se-

---

[1] 368.	[4] 185.	[6] 371, 1, 3).
[2] 582.	[5] 151.	[7] 371, 3.
[3] 460, 3.		

quăni Ariovisti *crudelitātem*[1] horrēbant. 16. *Brutum* Romānae matrōnae luxērunt. 17. Milĭtes invādunt *urbem.*[2] 18. *Aciem*[3] circumvenērunt. 19. Caesar *agrum* Picēnum percurrit. 20. Periculosissĭmum[:] *locum* sum praetervectus. 21. Germāni *flumen* transiērunt.

RULE VI.—*Two Accusatives—Same Person.*—373.

24. 1. *Cicerōnem* universus popŭlus *consŭlem* declarāvit. 2. Romŭlus *urbem Romam* vocāvit. 3. Fecit *herēdem filiam.* 4. Socrătes totīus[4] mundi *se civem* arbitrabātur. 5. Cato *cellam* penariam rei publĭcae nostrae, *nutrĭcem* plebis Romānae *Sicĭliam* nomināvit. 6. Praesta *te virum.* 7. Senātus *Catilīnam hostem* judicāvit. 8. Senātus *Paulum consŭlem* creāvit. 9. *Socrătem* Apollo *sapientissĭmum*[5] judicāvit. 10. *Mesopotamiam fertĭlem* effĭcit Euphrātes. 11. *Tiresiam sapientem* fingunt poētae. 12. *Polycrătem felĭcem* appellăbant.

RULE VII.—*Two Accusatives—Person and Thing.*—374.

25. 1. *Te* tua *fata* docēbo. 2. *Hoc me* docuit usus, magister[6] egregius. 3. Fortūna belli *artem victos*[7] docet. 4. Augustus *nepōtes* suos *littĕras* docuit. 5. Antigŏnus *iter omnes*[8] celat. 6. *Pacem te* poscĭmus. 7. Boeotii *auxilia regem* orābant. 8. Cato interrogātus est *sententiam.* 9. Marcius omnes *artes* edoctus fuĕrat. 10. *Auxilium a Caesăre*[9] petiērunt. 11. *Te illud*[10] admoneo. 12. *Te id* consŭlo. 13. Hannĭbal nonaginta

---

[1] 371, 3. [5] 373, 3. [9] 441, 1.
[2] 371, 4. [6] 363. [10] 374, 3, 3).
[3] 162. [7] 575. [11] 374. 5.
[4] 151.

B

*millia*¹ pedĭtum *Ibērum*¹ traduxit.   14. Belgae *Rhenum*¹ transducti sunt.

RULE VIII.—*Accusative of Time and Space.*—378.

26. 1. Servius Tullius regnāvit *annos* quattuor² et³ quadraginta.   2. Appius Claudius caecus *annos* multos fuit.   3. Quaedam bestiŏlae unum *diem* vivunt.   4. Dionysius quinque et viginti natus *annos* dominātum occupāvit.   5. Caesar duas fossas quindĕcim *pedes* latas perduxit.   6. Milĭtes aggĕrem altum *pedes* octoginta exstruxērunt.   7. Arăbes gladios habēbant longos quaterna *cubĭta*.   8. Urbs quinque diērum *iter* abest.

RULE IX.—*Accusative of Limit.*—379.

27. 1. Cicĕro *Athēnas* venit.   2. Regŭlus *Carthagĭnem* rediit.   3. Hannĭbal *Capuam* concessit.   4. Cicĕro maxĭmum numĕrum frumenti⁴ *Romam* misit.   5. Dionysius navigābat *Syracūsas*.   6. Curius elephantos quattuor *Romam* duxit.

7. Aurum *domum*⁵ comportant.   8. Ego *rus* ibo.⁶ 9. Veni consŭlis *domum*.   10. Verres *Delum* venit. 11. Pausaniam *Cyprum* misērunt.   12. Hannĭbal *in hiberna*⁷ *Capuam* concessit.   13. Legiōnes *ad urbem* addūcit.   14. Darīus *in Asiam* rediit.

15. Consŭles *Romam* redībant.   16. Cicĕro *domum* redĭĕrat.   17. Consŭles *in Graeciam* venĕrant.   18. Publius Scipio *in Hispaniam* missus est.   19. Cives *rus* fugient.   20. *In Etruriam* missus erat.   21. Tullia *in forum* properāvit et regem salutāvit.

---

¹ 374, 6.   ⁴ 395.   ⁶ 295.
² 174.   ⁵ 379, 3 ; 119, 1.   ⁷ 379, 4.
³ 308, 310, 1.

RULE X.—*Accusative of Specification.*—380.

28. 1. Equus tremit *artus.* 2. Aenēas¹ caedit nigrantes *terga* juvencos. 3. Hannĭbal *femur* ictue cecĭdit.
4. Hannĭbal *anĭmum* incensus est.
5. Haec vis valet *multum.*² 6. Haec vis *idem* potest.
7. Nervii *nihil* possunt. 8. Thebāni *nihil* moti sunt.
9. *Quid* hostis potest? 10. *Quid* venisti? 11. *Quid*
pl̄ura³ dispŭto?

RULE XI.—*Accusative in Exclamations.*—381.

29. 1. O praeclāram *vitam!* 2. O *spectacŭlum* mi-
sĕrum! 3. O *tempŏra,* o *mores!* Senātus conjuratiōnem
intellĭgit, consul videt. 4. O *vim* maxĭmam⁴ errōris!
5. O *clementiam* admirabĭlem!

DATIVE.

RULE XII.—*Dative with Verbs.*—384.

30. 1. Non *scholae,* sed *vitae* discĭmus. 2. Omnes
homĭnes *libertāti* student. 3. Germāni *labōri* ac *duritiae*
student. 4. Ego *philosophiae* semper vaco. 5. *Pietāti*
summa⁵ tribuenda⁵ laus est. 6. Non solum *nobis* divĭtes
sumus, sed *libĕris, amīcis,* maximēque *rei publĭcae.*

7. *Philosophiae* nos tradĭmus. 8. Graeci homĭnes
honōres tribuunt iis *viris,* qui tyrannos necavērunt. 9.
Non placĭdam *membris* dat cura quiētem. 10. Omnes,
quum valēmus, recta consilia *aegrōtis*⁷ damus.

---

31. DATIVE OF ADVANTAGE AND DISADVANTAGE.—385.
—1. Probus' invĭdet *nemĭni.* 2. Homĭnes *homĭnĭbus* prosunt. 3. Nocet *altĕri.* 4. Consulātus meus placuit
Catōni. 5. *Diōni* crudelĭtas tyranni displicēbat. 6.
Themistŏcles persuāsit *popŭlo.* 7. *Parti*' civium consŭ-
lunt. 8. Milĭtes non *mulierĭbus,* non *infantĭbus* peper-
cērunt. 9. Nemo liber est, qui *corpŏri* servit.

32. DATIVE WITH COMPOUNDS.—386.—1. Pelopĭdas
omnĭbus affuit *pericŭlis.* 2. Natūra *sensĭbus*' ratiōnem
adjunxit. 3. Leges omnium' salūtem singulōrum' *salūti*
antepōnunt. 4. Parva *magnis* saepe' conferuntur.'
5. Hannĭbal terrōrem injēcit *exercitui* Romanōrum.
6. Aristīdes interfuit *pugnae* navāli apud Salamīnem.
7. *Consiliis* interdum obstat fortūna. 8. Homĭnes *homĭnĭbus* plurĭmum' et prosunt et obsunt. 9. Consŭles
libertāti suas opes' postferēbant.' 10. Bona existimatio
divitiis praestat. 11. Tu virtūtem praefer' *divitiis.*
12. Quidam succumbunt *dolorĭbus.* 13. Neque deĕro'
neque superĕro' *rei publĭcae.*

33, DATIVE OF POSSESSOR.—387.—1. Fuēre *Lydis*
multi reges. 2. Non semper idem *florĭbus*'⁰. est color.
3. Est honos *eloquentiae.*

34. DATIVE OF APPARENT AGENT.—388.—1. *Caesări*
omnia erant agenda. 2. Diligentia colenda est *nobis.*
3. Multa videnda sunt *oratōri.* 4. *Cui* non sunt haec
audita ?

35. MISCELLANEOUS EXAMPLES.—1. Haec sententia

' 441.	⁵ 582.	⁹ 133, 1.
² 385, 3.	⁶ 292, 2.	⁹ 288.
³ 386, 1.	⁷ 380, 2.	¹⁰ 83.
⁴ 441, 1.		

consŭli placuit. 2. Romŭlus civitāti profuit. 3. Civcs legĭbus parēbant. 4. Vobis summam[1] laudem tribuĭmus. 5. Darīus, rex Persārum, Graecis[2] bellum intŭlit. 6. Leonĭdas se[3] perĭcŭlis obtŭlit.

ᴚᴜʟᴇ XIII.—*Two Datives—To Which and For Which.*—390.

36. 1. Virtūtes *hominĭbus decŏri* sunt. 2. Virtūtes *hominĭbus gloriae* sunt. 3. Probĭtas est *omnĭbus*[4] *amōri.* 4. Crudelĭtas est *omnĭbus odio.* 5. Virtus neque datur *dono* nequc accipĭtur. 6. Pausanias, rex[4] Lacedaemoni-ōrum, venit *Atticis auxilio..*

7. Hoc *vitio mihi* dant. dabis, quod tu ipse fecisti? *castris praesidio* relinquit. locum delegērunt.

8. Idne[4] *altĕri*[4] *crimĭni* 9. Caesar legiōncs duas[4] 10. Hunc *sibi domicilio*

Rᴜʟᴇ XIV.—*Dative with Adjectives.*—391.

37. 1. Verĭtas *mihi* grata est. 2. Gratissĭmae[4] *mihi* tuae littĕrae[10] fuērunt. 3. Patria *Cicerōni* erat caris-sĭma. 4. Id *Deo* est proxĭmum,[11] quod est optĭmum.[12] 5. Minĭme[13] *sibi* quisque notus cst. 6. *Morti* nihil est tam simĭle, quam somnus.[14] 7. Homĭnum *genĕri* cultūra agrōrum est salutāris. 8. Belgae proxĭmi sunt *Germānis.* 9. *Iis,* qui vendunt, justitia necessaria est. 10. Pax *nobis* omnĭbus fuit optabĭlis.

Rᴜʟᴇ XV.—*Dative with Derivatives.*—392.

38. 1. Esto obtemperatio *institūtis* populōrum.

---

[1] 163, 3.   [6] 346, II. 1.   [11] 166.
[2] 384, II.   [7] 441, 2.   [12] 165.
[3] 448.   [8] 175.   [13] 305, 2; 165.
[4] 441.   [9] 162.   [14] 417, 1.
[5] 363.   [10] 132.

2. Insidiae *consŭli* non procedēbant.   3. Convenien꞉er *natūrae* vivĭmus.   4. Philosŏphus *sibi* constanter convenienterque dicit.

GENITIVE.

RULE XVI.—*Genitive with Nouns.*—395, 396.

39. 1. Piĕtas fundamentum¹ est omnium *virtūtum.* 2. Ira est initium *insaniae.*   3. Sapientia est *rerum* divinārum et humanārum scientia.   4. Nona *diēi* hora erat.

I. SUBJECTIVE GENITIVE.—1. Vultus sermo ' quidam² tacĭtus³ *mentis* est.   2. Nostri milĭtes impĕtum *hostium* sustinuērunt.   3. Themistŏcles non effūgit *civium* suōrum invidiam.   4. *Ventōrum* pater regit navem.   5. *Singulōrum* facultātes divitiae¹ sunt *civitātis.*

II. OBJECTIVE GENITIVE.—1. Crescit amor *nummi.* 2. Anĭmi morbi sunt cupiditātes *divitiārum, gloriae, voluptātum.*

III. PARTITIVE GENITIVE.—1. Justitia nihil expĕtit *praemii,* nihil *pretii.*   2. Conon *pecuniae* quinquaginta talenta civĭbus suis·donāvit.   3. Permagnum pondus *argenti* fuit.   4. Socrātes *omnium* ³ sapientissĭmus⁴ judicātus est.   5. *Gallōrum* omnium fortissĭmi sunt Belgae. 6. Ubĭnam *gentium* ⁵ sumus?   7. Satis *eloquentiae* ⁶ fuit, *sapientiae* parum.

IV. GENITIVE OF CHARACTERISTIC.—1. Tarquinius fratrem habŭit Aruntem,⁷ mitis *ingenii* juvĕnem.

---

¹ 362.   ³ 396, III. 3) (2).   ⁵ 396, III. 4) (2).
² 438; 438, 1.   ⁴ 162.   ⁶ 396, III. 4) (1).
                                        ⁷ 363.

2. Athenienses belli ducem¹ elĭgunt Perĭclem,¹ spectātae *virtūtis* virum.² 3. Classem³ septuaginta⁴ *navium* Athenienses Miltiădi⁵ dedērunt.

V. GENITIVE OF SPECIFICATION.—1. *Cyri* nomen⁵ accēpit. 2. Quid sonat vox *voluptātis ?* 3. Virtūtes *continentiae, gravitātis, justitiae, fidei,* omni honōre⁶ dignae sunt. 4. *Germaniae* vocabŭlum recens est. 5. *Domĭnĭ* appellatiōnem semper⁷ exhorruit Augustus.

RULE XVII.—*Genitive with Adjectives.*—399.

40. 1. Avĭda est *pericŭli* virtus. 2. Haec aetas *virtūtum* ferax est. 3. Conscia mens *recti* famae⁸ mendacia⁵ ridet. 4. Romāni appetentes¹⁰ *gloriae* atque¹¹ avĭdi *laudis* fuērunt. 5. Multi *contentiōnis* sunt cupidiōres¹² quam *veritātis.* 6. Epaminondas fuit perītus *belli, veritātis* dilĭgens. 7. Conon prudens *rei* militāris erat. 8. Socrătes se omnium *rērum* nescium¹³ fingit. 9. Themistŏcles peritissĭmos¹⁴ *belli* navālis fecit Athenienses. 10. Homo *ratiōnis*¹⁴ est particeps. 11. Plena *errōrum* sunt omnia. 12. Omnes *virtūtis* compŏtes¹⁵ beāti sunt. 13. *Viri*¹⁶ propria est fortitūdo.

RULE XVIII.—*Predicate Genitive.*—401–403.

41. 1. Damnatio est *judĭcum ;* poena, *legis.* 2. Imbecilli *animi* est superstitio. 3. Xerxis⁵ classis mille et ducentārum *navium* fuit. 4. Claudius erat *somni* brevissĭmi. 5. Permagni *momenti* est ratio. 6. Temerĭtas

---

¹ 373.	⁷ 582.	¹² 162.
² 363.	⁸ 395.	¹³ 373 ; 373, 3.
³ 384, II.	⁹ 371, 3, 1).	¹⁴ 399, 2, (3).
⁴ 176.	¹⁰ 575 ; 353.	¹⁵ 157, 2.
⁵ 371.	¹¹ 587, L	¹⁶ 399, 3, 3).
⁶ 419, IV.		

est florentis ¹ *aetātis;* prudentia, senescentis. 7. Praeda parvi *pretii* fuit. 8. Thebae ² *popŭli* Romāni factae ³ sunt. 9. Voluptātem virtus *minĭmi* ⁴ facit. 10. Divitiae a me ⁵ *minĭmi* ⁶ putantur. 11. Nulla .possessio *pluris* ⁵ quam virtus aestimanda est. 12. Vendo meum frumentum non *pluris,* quam cetĕri. 13. Mentīri ⁷ non est *meum.* ⁶ 14. *Tuum* est mihi ⁴ ignoscĕre.

RULE XIX.—*Genitive with Certain Verbs.*—406–408.

42. 1. *Eōrum* miserēre,¹⁰ qui¹¹ in miseriis¹² sunt. 2. Anĭmus memĭnit¹³ *praeteritōrum,*¹⁴ praesentia cernit, futūra praevĭdet. 3. Reminiscĕre pristĭnae *virtūtis* Helvetiōrum. 4. Deōrum¹⁵ immortalium *beneficia*¹⁶ recordor. 5. Oblīti sunt *injuriārum.* 6. Habētis ducem memŏrem *vestri,* oblītum *sui.*¹ 7. Aliōrum vitia cernit, obliviscĭtur *suōrum.* 8. *Flagitiōrum* suōrum recordabĭtur. 9. Planci *merĭti* recordor.

10. Magni¹⁷ *rei* publĭcae intĕrest. 11. Illud *Cicerō-nis* maxĭme interfuit. 12. Hoc regis nihil¹⁷ intĕrest. 13. *Scipiōnis* meminĕrat. 14. *Sui* oblītus ĕrat. 15. Miserentur *sociōrum.* 16. *Atheniensium* maxĭme interĕrat.

RULE XX.—*Accusative and Genitive.*—410.

43. 1. *Te* vetĕris *amicitiae* commonefacio. 2. Tiberius *judĭces*¹⁸ *legum* admonēbat.

---

¹ 575.	⁷ 549.	¹³ 297, I.
² 131, 1, 2).	⁸ 404, 1.	¹⁴ 575; 295, 2.
³ 279; 294.	⁹ 385.	¹⁵ 45, 6.
⁴ 403; 165.	¹⁰ 271, 2.	¹⁶ 407, 1.
⁵ 414, 5.	¹¹ 445.	¹⁷ 408, 3.
⁶ 165, 1.	¹² 435, 1.	¹⁸ 93.

3. *Te* convinco non *inhumanitātis* solum, sed etiam [1] *amentiae.* 4. Fannius *Verrem* insimŭlat *avaritiae* et *audaciae.* 5. Cicĕro *Verrem avaritiae* coarguit. 6. Orestes accusătur *atricidii.* 7. Nicomēdes *furti* damnātus est.

8. Nonne [2] *te* misĕret *mei ?* 9. Num [2] hujus *te gloriae* paenitēbat ? 10. *Me* non solum piget *stultitiae* meae, sed etiam pudet. 11. *Me* civitātis *morum* [2] piget taedetque. [4]

ABLATIVE.

RULE XXI.—*Ablative of Cause, Manner, Means.*—414.

44. I. CAUSE.—1. Caesar *beneficiis* ac *munificentiā* magnus habebātur, *integritāte* vitae, Cato. [5] 2. Quidam *vitiis* suis gloriantur. 3. Gubernatōris ars *utilitāte*, non *arte* laudātur. 4. *Avaritiā* et *luxuriā* Romāna civĭtas laborābat. 5. Nimio *gaudio* paene [6] desipiĕbam. 6. Adolescentes senum [7] *praeceptis* gaudent. 7. Laetus *sorte* tuā vives sapienter. [8] 8. Campāni fuĕrunt superbi *onitāte* agrōrum.

II. MANNER.—1. Miltiădes summā [8] *aequitāte* res Chersonēsi constituit. 2. Athenienses *vi* summā proelium commisērunt. 3. Sidĕra [8] *cursus* suos conficiunt maxĭmā [10] *celeritāte.* 4. Athenienses *cum silentio* [11] audīti sunt. 5. *Cum virtūte* vivĭmus. 6. Pausanias epulabātur *more* Persārum.

III. MEANS, INSTRUMENT.—1. Servius Tullius *virtūte*

---

[1] 587, I. 5.	[5] 367, 3.	[9] 84.
[2] 346, II. 1.	[6] 582.	[10] 165.
[3] 83.	[7] 66.	[11] 414, 3.
[4] 587, I. 3.	[8] 103, 3.	

regnum tenuit. 2. Nemo fit¹ *casu* bonus. 3. Avărus
anĭmus nullo satiătur *lucro*. 4. Trahĭmur omnes *studio*
laudis.² 5. Magnos homĭnes *virtūte* metīmur, non *for-*
tūnā. 6. Dido³ vitam suam *gladio* finīvit. 7. *Voluptāte*
capiuntur homĭnes, ut *hamo* pisces.⁴ 8. Minuuntur atrae
carmĭne curae. 9. Boni nullo *emolumento* impelluntur
in fraudem.⁵

IV. Agent.—1. Alcibiădes erudītus est *a Socrăte*.⁶
2. *A Deo* omnia⁷ facta sunt.⁸ 3. Sacra *ab Numā* insti-
tūta sunt. 4. *A multis*⁹ ipsa⁹ virtus contemnĭtur.

RULE XXII.—*Ablative of Price.*—416.

45. 1. Ego¹⁰ spem *pretio* non emo. 2. Vas Corin-
thium magno *pretio* mercātus sum. 3. Viginti *talentis*
unam¹¹ oratiōnem Isocrătes vendĭdit. 4. Si prata *magno*
aestĭmant, quanti¹² est aestimanda¹³ virtus? 5. Fanum
pecuniā grandi vendĭtum est. 6. Otium non *gemmis*¹⁴
venāle est.

RULE XXIII.—*Ablative with Comparatives.*—417.

46. 1. Vilius argentum est *auro, virtutĭbus* aurum.
2. Lux *sonĭtu* est velocior. 3. Amōris simulatio pejor¹⁵
est *odio*. 4. Nihil est veritātis *luce* dulcius. 5. Nihil est
ratiōne melius.¹⁶ 6. *Lacrĭmā* nihil citius arescit.
7. Tullus Hostilius ferocior quam *Romŭlus*¹⁶ fuit.
8. Sol major¹⁶ est quam *terra*. 9. Natūra nihil habet

¹ 294.	⁷ 441, 1.	¹² 402, III. 1.
² 396, II.	⁸ 294; 294, 2.	¹³ 232.
³ 68.	⁹ 452.	¹⁴ 416, 1, 4).
⁴ 367, 3.	¹⁰ 446.	¹⁵ 165.
⁵ 435, 1.	¹¹ 175.	¹⁶ 417, 1.
⁶ 414, 5.		

praestantius quam *honestātem.*[1] 10. Timoleon sapientius[2] tulit[3] secundam fortūnam quam *adversam.* 11. Major famae sitis est quam *virtūtis.*[1]

RULE XXIV.—*Ablative of Difference.***—418.**

47. 1. Patria mihi[4] vitā meā *multo* est carior. 2. Pompeius *biennio* major fuit quam Cicĕro.[1] 3. Hic locus aequo *spatio* ab castris[5] Ariovisti et Caesăris abĕrat. 4. Numa Pompilius *annis* permultis ante fuit quam[6] Pythagŏras. 5. IIomēri[7] etsi incerta sunt tempŏra, tamen *annis* multis fuit ante Romŭlum.[8]

RULE XXV.—*Ablative in Special Constructions.***—419.**

48. I. UTOR, FRUOR, ETC.—1. Multi *beneficio* Dei perverse utuntur. 2. *Recordatiōne* nostrae amicitiae[9] fruor. 3. Commŏda, *quibus* utĭmur, a Deo[10] nobis[11] dantur. 4. Lux, *quā* fruĭmur, a Deo nobis datur. 5. Virtūtis munĕre functus sum. 6. Solus potītus est *imperio* Romŭlus. 7. Numĭdae plerumque *lacte*[12] et *carne*[13] vescebantur.

II. FIDO, CONFIDO, ETC.—1. *Prudentiā consiliō*que[14] fidĭmus. 2. Quis aut corpŏris *firmitāte* aut fortūnae *stabilitāte* confīdet ? 3. Juvĕnis nitĭtur *hastā.*

III. PLENTY AND WANT.—1. Abundārunt[15] semper *auro* regna Asiae. 2. Capua fortissimōrum virōrum *multitudĭne* redundat. 3. Antiochīa eruditissĭmis *homi-*

---

[1] 417, 1.	[6] 523, 2, 2).	[11] 384, I.
[2] 582, 305.	[7] 395.	[12] 74.
[3] 292.	[8] 432, 433.	[13] 72, 3.
[4] 391.	[9] 396, II.	[14] 587, I. 3.
[5] 434.	[10] 414, 5.	[15] 234.

nĭbus affluēbat.   4. Nihil honestum est quod [1] *justitiā*
vacat.   5. Nulla [2] vitae pars vacat *officio*.   6. Nunquam
eminentia *invidiā* caret.   7. Magna negotia magnis *ad-
jutorĭbus* egent.   8. Deus *bonis* [3] omnĭbus explēvit mundum.   9. Hectŏra [4] *vitā* spoliāvit Achilles.   10. Caesări
tradĭta urbs est, nuda [5] *praesidio*, referta *copiis*.   11.
Virtūte multi [6] praedĭti sunt.

IV. Dignus, Indignus, etc.—1. Virtus *imitatiōne*,
non *invidiā* digna est.   2. Quam multi indigni *luce*
sunt, et tamen dies orĭtur. [7]   3. Sapientia *eo* contenta est,
quod adest.   4. *Intelligentiā* vestrā frētus sum.

V. Opus and Usus.—1. *Magistratĭbus* opus est.   2.
Multis [8] *duce* opus est.   3. Nihil [9] opus est *simulatiōne*.
4. *Navĭbus* consŭli usus est.   5. Quantum [10] argenti [11] est
tibi opus ?   6. Nobis exempla permulta opus sunt.

Rule XXVI.—*Ablative of Place.*—421.

49. 1. *In Italiā* bellum fuit.   2. Haec ab Romānis
in Graeciā gesta sunt.   3. Iphicrătes *in Thraciā* vixit.
4. Caesar *ab urbe* proficiscĭtur.   5. Darīus *ex Asiā* in
Eurōpam [11] exercĭtum trajēcit.   6. Talis *Romae* Fabricius, qualis Aristīdes *Athēnis* fuit.
7. Tarquinius Superbus mortuus est *Cumis*.   8. Numa
Pompilius *Curĭbus* habitābat.   9. *Syracūsis* est fons
aquae dulcis, cui [12] nomen Arethūsa est.   10. Demarātus,
Tarquinii regis pater, fugit Tarquinios [13] *Corintho*.   11.
Haec *terrā marī*que [14] gesta sunt.   12. Conon plurĭmum [15]
vixit *Cypri*, [16] Timotheus *Lesbi*.

---

[1] 445.	[6] 268, 2.	[11] 435, 1.
[2] 151.	[7] 419, 3.	[12] 887.
[3] 441, 1.	[8] 380, 2.	[13] 379.
[4] 68.	[9] 419, 3, 2).	[14] 422, 1, 1).
[5] 438.	[10] 896, III.	[15] 380, 2; 165.
		[16] 424, 1.

Rule XXVII.—*Ablative of Source and Separation.*—425.

50. 1. Praeclārum *a majorĭbus* accepĭmus morem.[1]
2. Hoc *a senĭbus*[2] audivĭmus. 3. Disce, puer, virtūtem
ex me, fortūnam *ex aliis.* 4. Collatīnus *ex urbe* migrāvit.
5. *Jove*[3] nate, Hercŭles, salve.
, 6. Abstĭnent *pugnā.* 7. Lacedaemonii de diutĭnā
contentiōne destitērunt. 8. Zama quinque diērum iter[4]
ab Carthagĭne abest.]9. Ariovistus millĭbus[5] passuum
sex *a Caesăris castris*[6] consēdit. 10. Tu, Jupĭter, Catilīnam *a tectis* urbis, *a moenĭbus, a vitā fortunis*que civium omnium arcēbis. 11. Dionysius tyrannus *Syracūsis*
expulsus est. 12. Aristīdes nonne[7] expulsus est *patriā* ?
13. Themistŏcles imperātor bello Persĭco *servitūte* Graeciam līberāvit. 14. Robustus anĭmus omni est liber
curā et *angōre.*

Rule XXVIII.—*Ablative of Time.*—426, 427.

51. 1. Augustus obiit[8] sexto et septuagesĭmo aetātis
anno. 2. Socrătes suprēmo[9] vitae *die* de immortalitāte
animōrum multa disseruit. 3. Timoleon proelia maxĭ-
ma [10] natāli *die* suo fecit omnia. 4. Quā *nocte* natus est
Alexander, *eādem* Diānae Ephesiae templum deflagrāvit.
5. Solis *occāsu* suas copias Ariovistus in castra reduxit.
6. Nemo mortalium omnĭbus *horis* sapit.] 7. Laelius
sermōnem de amicitiā habuit paucis *diēbus*[11] post mortem Africāni. 8. Roscius litem[12] decīdit abhinc *annis*
quattuor. 9. Carthāgo septingentesĭmo *anno* postquam
condĭta erat, delēta est.

---

[1] 83.	[5] 378, 2.	[9] 163, 3.
[2] 66.	[6] 132.	[10] 165.
[3] 66, 3 ; 425, 3.	[7] 346, II. 1.	[11] 427.
[4] 378.	[8] 295, 3.	[12] 82, 6.

Rule XXIX.—*Ablative of Characteristic.*—428.

52. 1. Caesar Procillum, *summā* [1] *virtūte* adolescentem, ad Ariovistum misit. 2. Aristotĕles, vir [2] *summo ingenio, scientiā, copiā*, prudentiam cum eloquentiā conjunxit. 3. Cato *singulāri* fuit *prudentiā* [3] et *industriā*. 4. Appius homo fuit *summā prudentiā, multā* etiam *doctrīnā*. 5. Hannibālis nomen erat *magnā* apud omnes *gloriā*. 6. Agesilāus *statūrā* fuit *humĭli* et *corpŏre exiguo*. 7. Caesar fuit *excelsā statūrā, colōre candĭdo, nigris ocŭlis*.

Rule XXX.—*Ablative of Specification.*—429.

53. 1. Sunt quidam homĭnes [4] non re, sed *nomĭne*. 2. *Doctrīnā* Graecia Romānos et omni litterārum *genĕre* superābat. 3. Mardonius, *natiōne* Medus, a Pausaniā [5] fugātus est. 4. Helvetii relĭquos Gallos *virtūte* praecēdunt. 5. Ancus regnāvit annos [6] quattuor et viginti, cuilĭbet [7] superiōrum [8] regum belli pacisque et *artĭbus* et *gloriā* par.

Rule XXXI.—*Ablative Absolute.*—430 & 431.

54. 1. Cognĭto Caesăris *adventu*, Ariovistus legātos ad eum mittit. 2. Ite, [9] *deis* [10] bene *juvantĭbus*. 3. Pythagŏras, *Tarquinio Superbo regnante*, in Italiam venit. 4. *Virtūte exceptā*, nihil amicitiā [11] praestabilius est. 5. Germāni pellĭbus [12] utuntur, magnā corpŏris *parte nudā*. 6. Natus est Augustus, *Cicerōne et Antonio consulĭbus*.

---

[1] 163, 3.	[4] 414, 5.	[9] 295.
[2] 363.	[6] 378.	[10] 51, 6.
[3] 428, 1, 2).	[7] 191, II.; 391.	[11] 417.
[4] 362.	[8] 163, 3.	[12] 419.

7. Rŏmāni, *Scipiōne duce, ponte facto*, superavērunt Ticīnum flumen.

> RULE XXXII.—*Cases with Prepositions.*—432–435.

55. I. ACCUSATIVE.—1. Sophŏcles ad summam *senec-tūtem* tragoedias fecit. 2. Adulescentes senum praeceptis ad virtūtum' *studia* ducuntur. 3. Piĕtas est justitia ad-versus *deos*. 4. Ante *lucem* galli canunt. 5. Epaminon-das Lacedaemonios vicit apud *Mantinēam*. 6. Legiōnes Etruscōrum cis *Padum* fusae sunt. 7. Utilitātis dere-lictio contra *natūram* est. 8. Justitia erga *deos* religio' dicĭtur, erga *parentes*, piĕtas. 9. Ratio conciliat inter *se*' homĭnes. 10. Amicitia est propter *se* expetenda.' 11. Anĭmus per *somnum* curis' vacuus est. 12. Post *me* erat Aegīna. 13. Secundum *flumen* paucae statiōnes videbantur. 14. Germāni trans *Rhenum* incŏlunt.

II. ABLATIVE.—1. A primā' *aetāte* me philosophia delectāvit. 2. Cantābit vacuus coram *latrōne* viātor. 3. Sex menses' cum *Antiŏcho* philosŏpho fui. 4. Scipio ob egregiam victoriam de *Hannĭbăle* appellātus est Afri-cānus. 5. Virtus ex *viro* appellāta est. 6. Cato prae *cetĕris* floruit. 7. Caesar legiōnes pro *castris* constituit. 8. Vita nihil sine magno *labōre* dedit mortalĭbus.' 9. Aqua erat *pectorĭbus* tenus.'

III. ACCUSATIVE OR ABLATIVE.—1. In *amnem* ruunt. 2. Gallia est divīsa in *partes* tres. 3. Homo doctus in *se* semper divitias habet. 4. Sub ipsa *moenia* progressi sunt. 5. Saepe est etiam sub *pallio* sordĭdo sapientia. 6. Virtus omnia subter *se* habet.

---

[1] 396, II.   [4] 232.   [7] 378.
[2] 362.   [5] 419, III.   [8] 384, II.
[3] 448, 1.   [6] 441, 6; 166.   [9] 434, 4.

SYNTAX OF ADJECTIVES.

RULE XXXIII.—*Agreement of Adjectives.*—438, 439.

56. 1. *Vera* amicitia *sempiterna* est. 2. *Verae* amicitiae *sempiternae* sunt. 3. Venit hiems *glaciālis.* 4. Fugit *irreparabĭle* tempus. 5. Nihil est ab *omni* parte *beātum.* 6. *Atra* nubes condĭdit lunam. 7. Hora *quota* est? 8. *Qualis* est *tua* mens? 9. Nemo nascĭtur *dives.* 10. Stultitia et temerĭtas *fugienda* [1] sunt. 11. Labor voluptasque, *dissimillĭmă* [2] natūrā, [3] inter se sunt *juncta.* 12. Non terret *sapientem* [4] mors. 13. *Fortes* [4] fortūna adjŭvat. 14. *Primā* [4] luce *summus* mons a Labiēno tenebātur. [5] 15. Feriunt *summos* fulgŭra montes. 16. Roscius *assiduus* [7] ruri [6] vixit. 17. Philosophiae [8] nos *totos* tradĭmus. 18. Themistŏcles *absens* proditiōnis [10] est *accusātus.* 19. Triumphus *clarior* quam *gratior* [11] fuit.

SYNTAX OF PRONOUNS.

RULE XXXIV.—*Agreement of Pronouns.*—445.

57. 1. Omne anĭmal *se ipsum* [12] dilĭgit. 2. Ad *quas* res aptissĭmi erĭmus, in *iis* elaborabĭmus. 3. Nihil expĕdit, *quod* non decet. 4. Non est vir [13] fortis, *qui* [14] labōrem fugit.

58. PERSONAL AND POSSESSIVE.—446–449.—1. Omnia

---

[1] 460; 439, 3.	[6] 468.	[11] 444, 2.
[2] 163, 2; 439, 3.	[7] 443.	[12] 452.
[3] 414.	[8] 424, 2; 421, II.	[13] 362.
[4] 441.	[9] 384, II.	[14] 445, 6.
[5] 441, 6.	[10] 410, II.	

animalia *se* dilĭgunt. 2. *Te* [1] *tua,* [2] *me* delectant *mea.*
3. Ad amīcum de amicitiā scripsi. 4. *Ego* beātus sum.
5. In philosophiae studio aetātem consumpsi. 6. Aristīdes non effūgit civium *suōrum* invidiam.

59. DEMONSTRATIVE.—450–452.—1. *Haec* est tyran·
nōrum vita. 2. *Noc ipsi* [3] consolāmur. 3. *Ille* est vir.
4. Ab *ipso* Graccho *eădem haec* audīmus. 5. Homo habet memoriam et *eam* [4] infinītam. ·

60. RELATIVE.—453.—1. In mundo Deus est, *qui*
regit, *qui* gubernat, *qui* cursus astrōrum, mutatiōnce
tempŏrum, rērum vicissitudĭnes conservat. 2. Riden-
tur, [5] mala *qui* compōnunt carmĭna. 3. *Eădem* est utilitātis, *quae* [6] honestātis, regŭla. 4. Servi morĭbus [7] iisdem
erant, *quibus* [7] domĭnus. 5. Anĭmal hoc provĭdum,
sagax, acūtum, memor, plenum ratiōnis, [8] *quem* [9] vocā-
mus homĭnem, generātum est a Deo. 6. Perutĭles
Xenophontis libri sunt; *quos* [10] legĭte studiōsc.

61. INTERROGATIVE.—454.—1. O dii [11] immortāles, [12]
quam rem publĭcam habēmus, in *quā* urbe vivĭmus ? 2.
Quae in me est facultas ?

62. INDEFINITE.—455–459.—1. Exspectābam [13] *alĭ-
quem* meōrum. [14] 2. Veni Athēnas, [15] neque me *quisquam*
ibi agnōvit. 3. Aut *nemo,* aut, si *quisquam,* Cato sapiens fuit. 4. *Quidam* consŭlem laudant. 5. Optĭmum [16]
quidque [17] rarissĭmum est. 6. Consŭlum *alter* [18] exercĭtum
perdĭdit, *alter* vendĭdit.

---

[1] 371.	[7] 428.	[13] 468.
[2] 441, 1.	[8] 399, 2, 2).	[14] 441, 1.
[3] 452, 1.	[9] 445, 4.	[15] 379.
[4] 451, 2.	[10] 453.	[16] 165 ; 441, 2.
[5] 453, 2.	[11] 51, 5.	[17] 458, 1.
[6] 451, 3.	[12] 369.	[18] 151.

SYNTAX OF VERBS.

AGREEMENT.

RULE XXXV.—*Verb with Subject.*—460–463.

63. 1. Homĭnes, dum *docent,*[1] *discunt.* 2. Tantum *scimus,*[2] quantum memoriā *tenēmus.* 3. Ego libertātem *pepĕri ;* ego patriam *līberāvi.*[3] 4. *Crescit* amor nummi, quantum[3] ipsa pecunia *crescit.* 5. Pars perexigua Romam inermes[4] *delāti sunt.* 6. Uterque[5] eōrum exercĭtum ex castris *edūcunt.*[6] 7. Corinthus, totīus Graeciae lumen, *exstinctum*[7] *est.* 8. Ratio et oratio *conciliat*[8] inter se homĭnes. 9. Castor et Pollux ex equis *pugnavērunt.*[9]

INDICATIVE—TENSES AND USE.

RULE XXXVI.—*Use of Indicative.*—474.

64. PRESENT.—466, 467.—1. Virtus ab omnĭbus *laudātur.* 2. Nulla *habēmus* arma contra mortem. 3. In proelio cita mors *venit,* aut victoria laeta.

65. IMPERFECT.—468, 469.—1. Laelius oratiōnem suam *exornābat.* 2. *Exspectābam* adventum Menandri. 3. Lycurgi leges *vigēbant.* 4. Ut Romae[10] consŭles, sic Carthagĭne quotannis bini reges *creabantur.*

66. FUTURE AND FUTURE PERFECT.—470, 473.—1. Ro-

---

mam[1] quum *venĕro*, quae[2] *perspexĕro*, *scribam* ad tc.
2. Ut sementem *fecĕris*, ita *metes*. 3. Si te[3] *rogavĕro*
alĭquid,[4] non *respondēbis ?*

67. PERFECT AND PLUPERFECT.—471, 472.—1. Hostes, ubi primum nostros equĭtes *conspexērunt*,[4] celerĭter
nostros *perturbavērunt*. 2. Ipse semper cum Graecis
Latīna *conjunxi*.] 3. Civĭtas haec semper a me *defensa
est*. 4. Lacedaemoniōrum gens fortis *fuit*, dum Lycurgi
leges vigēbant. 5. Summā curā[5] exspectābam adventum
Menandri, quem[6] ad te *misĕram*. 6. Hannĭbal tres modios aureōrum annulōrum Carthagĭnem *misit*, quos
manĭbus[7] equĭtum Romanōrum[8] *detraxĕrat*.

SUBJUNCTIVE.—TENSES AND USE.

RULE XXXVII.—*Sequence of Tenses.*—480, 481.

68. 1. Ego vos hortor, ut amicitiam omnĭbus rebus[9]
humānis *anteponātis*.[10] 2. Philosophia nos docuit, ut
nosmet[11] ipsos *noscerēmus*.[12] 3. Dubĭtant nonnulli de
mundo, casūne[13] ipse *sit effectus*,[14] an mente divīnā. 4.
Epaminondas quaesīvit, salvusne[15] *esset* clipeus. 5. Epaminondas rogāvit, *essentne fusi* hostes. 6. Ego in causis
publĭcis ita sum versātus, ut *defendĕrim* multos.

RULE XXXVIII.—*Potential Subjunctive.*—485, 486.

69. 1. *Quaerat* quispiam, cujusnam[16] causā[17] mun
dus factus sit.[14] 2. *Videas* rebus[12] injustis justos[18]

---

[1] 379.	[7] 434, 1.	[13] 526, II. 1.
[2] 445, 6.	[8] 438.	[14] 525.
[3] 374.	[9] 386.	[15] 526, I.
[4] 460, 2.	[10] 489, 490.	[16] 188, 3.
[5] 414, 3.	[11] 184, 6.	[17] 414.
[6] 445.	[12] 492, 2; 374, 4.	[18] 441, 545.

maxĭme ¹ dolēre.² 3. Equĭdem *vellem*,³ ut redīres. 4. Forsĭtan *quaeras* qui iste terror sit. 5. Hoc sine ullā⁴ dubitatiōne *confirmavĕrim*. 6. Quid *faciātis ?*⁵ 7. Quis haec *faciat ?* 8. Quid *videātur* Deo⁶ magnum in rebus humānis?

RULE XXXIX.—*Subjunctive of Desire.*—487; 488.

70. 1. *Imitēmur* majōres nostros. 2. *Valeant* cives mei; *sint* incolŭmes, *sint* beāti; *stet* haec urbs praeclāra. 3. Religio et fides *anteponātur*⁷ amicitiae.⁸ 4. Orātor *imitētur* Demosthĕnem. 5. Is qui impĕrat aliis⁹ *serviat* ipse nulli ¹⁰ cupiditāti. 6. In rebus prospĕris superbiam arrogantiamque*fugiāmus*. 7. Ne quis, tanquam parva, *fastidiat* grammaticae elementa.

RULE XL.—*Subjunctive of Purpose or Result.*—489.

71. UT AND NE.—490–493.—1. Romāni ab arātro abduxērunt Cincinnātum, ut dictātor *esset*.¹¹ 2. Phaëthon optāvit, ut in currum ¹² patris ¹³ *tollerētur*.¹⁴ 3. Caesar ad Lamiam scripsit, ut ad ludos omnia *parāret*.¹⁴ 4. Timoleon orāvit omnes, ne id *facĕrent*.¹⁴ 5. Decrēvit senātus, ut consul *vidēret*,¹⁴ ne quid res publĭca detrimenti ¹⁵ *capĕret*.¹⁴ 6. Discipŭlos id unum ¹⁷ moneo, ut praeceptōres ¹⁸ non minus, quam ipsa studia *ament*.¹⁴

72. UT AND UT NON.—494–496.—1. Tanta vis probĭtātis est, ut eam in hoste etiam *diligāmus*. 2. Dives est, cui ¹⁹ tanta possessio est, ut nihil *optet* amplius. 3. Epaminondas adeo fuit veritātis ²⁰ dilĭgens, ut ne joco ²¹ qui-

---

¹ 305, 2 ; 105.	⁸ 386.	¹⁵ 374, 4.
² 550.	⁹ 385.	¹⁶ 396, III.
³ 293.	¹⁰ 151.	¹⁷ 374, 5
⁴ 151.	¹¹ 480.	¹⁸ 371.
⁵ 486, II.	¹² 435.	¹⁹ 387.
⁶ 384.	¹³ 77, II. 1.	²⁰ 399.
⁷ 463, 1	¹⁴ 492.	²¹ 414, 2.

dem[1] *mentirētur.* 4. Quis est tam miser, ut non Dei munificentiam *sensĕrit ?* 5. Alcibiădes erat eā sagacităte,[2] ut decĭpi[3] non *posset.*[4]

73. Quo, Quin, Quominus.—497–499.—1. Lex brevis est, quo facilius ab imperītis *teneātur.* 2. Nunquam accēdo ad te, quin abs te *abeam*[5] doctior. 3. Quis dubĭtet,[6] quin in virtute divitiae *sint ?* 4. Quid obstat, quominus Deus *sit* beātus?

74. Relative.—500, 501.—1. Caesar equitātum, qui *sustinēret* hostium impĕtum, misit. 2. Non tu is es, quem nihil *delectet.* 3. Ego is sum, qui nihil unquam meā, potius quam meōrum civium causā,[7] *fecĕrim.*[8] 4. Nihil est quod Deus efficĕre[9] non *possit.* 5. Nullum est anĭmal praeter homĭnem, quod *habeat* notitiam alĭquam Dei. 6. Inventi sunt multi,[10] qui non modo pecuniam,[11] sed vitam etiam profundĕre[12] pro patriā parāti[13] *essent.*

Rule XLI.—*Subjunctive of Condition.*—503–513.

75. Dum, Modo, Dummodo.—505.—1. Odĕrint,[14] dum *metuant.* 2. Multi omnia recta[15] neglĭgunt, dummŏdo potentiam *consequantur.* 3. Omnia postposui, dummŏdo praeceptis[16] patris *parērem.*

76. Ac si, Ut si, Quasi, etc.—506.—1. Regem laudavērunt ac si hostes *vicisset.* 2. Patres metus cepit,[16] velut si jam ad portas hostis *esset.* 3. Quid[17] testĭbus[18] utor, quasi res dubia *sit.*

77. Si, Nisi, etc. : Qui=Si is, etc.—507–513.—1.
Anĭmum rege, qui, nisi *paret, impĕrat.*[1] 2. Si beātam
vitam *volŭmus*[2] adipisci,[3] virtūti opĕra *danda est.* 3.
Thucydĭdis oratiōnes ego laudo ; imitāri neque *possim,*[4]
si *velim,*[5] nec *velim* fortasse, si *possim.* 4. Non *possem*[6]
vivĕre, nisi in litteris *vivĕrem.*[7] 5. Consilium, ratio, sententia nisi *essent*[8] in senĭbus,[7] non summum[6] consilium[6]
majōres nostri *appellassent*[10] senūtum.

Rule XLII.—*Subjunctive of Concession.*—515, 516.

78. Licet, Quamvis, etc.—1. Licet ipsa vitium[11] *sit*
ambitio, frequenter tamen causa virtūtum est.[12] 2. Non
est magnus pumilio, licet in monte *constitĕrit.* 3. Quamvis se[13] ipso contentus *sit* sapiens,[14] amīcis[15] illi opus est.
4. Ego, qui sero Graecas littĕras *attigissem,* tamen complūres Athēnis[16] dies[17] sum commorātus.

79. Etsi, Tametsi, Etiamsi.—1. Eloquentiae[18] stu-
dendum est, etsi eā[19] quidam perverse *abutuntur.* 2.
Hoc, etiamsi nobilitātum non *sit,*[20] tamen honestum est ;
etiamsi a nullo[21] *laudētur,* est laudabĭle.

Rule XLIII.—*Subjunctive of Cause.*—517–520.

80. Quum, Qui.—518, 519.—1. Quum vita sine ami-
cis metus[22] plena *sit,* ratio ipsa monet amicitias compa-
rāre. 2. Quum *sint* in nobis consilium, ratio, prudentia,

---

[1] 508.

[2] 293.

[3] 552.

[4] 509, 289.

[5] 510.

[6] 510; 463, II.

[7] 66.

[8] 163. 3.

[9] 373.

[10] 510, 1 ; 234.

[11] 362.

[12] 460, 2.

[13] 419, IV.

[14] 441.

[15] 419, 3.

[16] 421.

[17] 378.

[18] 384.

[19] 419.

[20] 460, 2.

[21] 151.

[22] 399, 2, 2).

necesse est, Deum ' haec ipsa habēre ' majōra. 3. Quum *venissem* ' Athēnas,' sex menses ' cum Antiŏcho, nobilissĭmo ' philosŏpho,' fui. 4. Caninius. fuit mirificā vigilantiā,' qui suo toto consulātu ' somnum non *vidĕrit*.''

81. QUOD, QUIA, ETC.—520.—1. Plato escam '' malōrum appellat voluptātem, quod eā '² homĭnes *capiantur*, velut hamo pisces.] 2. Nemo unquam est oratōrem, quod Latīne *loqueretur*, admirātus. 3. Mater irata est, quia non *rediĕrim*.

RULE XLIV.—*Subjunctive of Time with Cause.*—521–523.

82. 1. Dum relĭquae naves *convenīrent*, ad horam nonam exspectāvit. 2. Quievēre '' milĭtes, dum praefectus arma '' *inspicĕret*. 3. Tragoedi quotidie, antĕquam *pronuntient*, vocem sensim excĭtant. 4. Ante '' vidēmus fulguratiōnem, quam sonum *audiāmus*. 5. Caesar ad Pompeii castra '' pervēnit, priusquam Pompeius *sentīret*.''

RULE XLV.—*Subjunctive in Indirect Questions.*—525.

83. 1. Nescis, quantas vires virtus *habeat*.'' 2. Nomen tantum virtūtis usurpas; quid '' ipsa *valeat*, ignōras. 3. Lepĭdus declarāvit quantum *habēret* odium servitūtis.'' 4. Caesar equitātum omnem praemittit, qui '' videant,'' quas in partes iter *faciant*.] 5. Non intellĭgunt homĭnes, quam magnum vectīgal '' *sit* parsimonia.'' 6. In orato-

---

545; 45, 6.	⁹ 426.	¹⁷ 523, 2.
² 549.	¹⁰ 519.	¹⁸ 525, 2; 480.
³ 518, II. 1.	¹¹ 373.	¹⁹ 380, 2.
⁴ 379.	¹² 414.	²⁰ 396, II.
⁵ 378.	¹³ 235.	²¹ 445, 5.
⁶ 162.	¹⁴ 131, 1, 4).	²² 500.
⁷ 362.	¹⁵ 523, 3, 2).	²³ 362.
⁸ 428.	¹⁶ 132; 379, 4.	²⁴ 367.

rĭbus Graecis, admirabĭle est, quantum inter omnes unus *excellat.* 7. Mihi non minōri ¹ curae ² est, qualis res publĭca post mortem meam *futūra sit,* quam qualis hodie *sit.*

RULE XLVI.—*Subjunctive by Attraction.*—527.

84. 1. Me admŏnes, ut me intĕgrum, quoad *possim,* servem.³ 2. Quid est, cur non orātor de rebus iis eloquentissĭme dicat,⁴ quas *cognōrit.* 3. Jussit ut, quae *venissent,* naves Euboeam petĕrent.⁵⌐ 4. In Hortensio memoria fuit tanta, ut, quae secum *commentātus esset,* ea verbis ⁶ iisdem ⁶ reddĕret,⁷ quibus *cogitavisset.* 5. Recordatiōne ⁸ nostrae amicitiae sic fruor, ut beāte vixisse ⁹ videar,⁷ quia cum Scipiōne *vixĕrim.*¹⁰

RULE XLVII.—*Subjunctive in Indirect Discourse.*—529.

85. 1. Socrătes dicēbat,¹¹ omnes ¹² in eo, quod *scīrent,* satis ¹³ esse ¹⁴ eloquentes. 2. Apud Hypănim ¹⁵ fluvium, Aristotĕles ait,¹⁶ bestiŏlas quasdem nasci, quae unum diem *vivant.* 3. Ariovistus Caesări ¹⁷ respondit: quid sibi *vellet ?* ¹⁸ cur in suas possessiōnes *venīret ?* jus esse belli, ut, qui *vicissent,* iis,¹⁹ quos *vicissent,* quemadmŏdum *vellent, imperārent.*⌐4. Legatiōni Ariovistus respondit: si quid ipsi ²⁰ a Caesăre opus *esset,*²¹ sese ad eum ventūrum fuisse ;²² si quid ille a se *velit,* illum ad se venīre ²² oportēre. 5. Divĭco ita cum Caesăre egit: si pacem popŭlus Romănus cum Helvetiis *facĕret,*²³ in eam

---

¹ 165.
² 390.
³ 489.
⁴ 525.
⁵ 414.
⁶ 186.
⁷ 489, 494.
⁸ 419

⁹ 549, 4, 1).
¹⁰ 481, I. 2.
¹¹ 469, II.
¹² 545.
¹³ 582.
¹⁴ 530, I.
¹⁵ 85, III. 1.
¹⁶ 297, II. 1.

¹⁷ 384.
¹⁸ 298.
¹⁹ 385.
²⁰ 452, 5.
²¹ 532, 2.
²² 549, 2.
²³ 533, 3.

partem itūros ' Helvetios,' ubi eos Caesar esse *voluisset ;'* sin bello persĕqui ' *perseverāret, reminisceretur* pristĭnae vĭrtūtis ' Helvetiōrum.

IMPERATIVE—TENSES AND USE.

RULE XLVIII.—*Imperative.*—535.

86. 1. *Sperne* voluptātes. 2. *Consŭlĭte* vobis,' Patres ' conscripti, *prospicĭte* patriae, *conservāte* vos,' conjŭges, libĕros, fortunasque vestras ; popŭli Romāni nomen salutemque *defendĭte*. 3. *Vive* memor leti ;' fugit hora. 4. Valetudĭnem tuam *cura* diligenter. 5. Virtūtes *excĭta,* si forte dormiunt. 6. Poëmăta dulcia *sunto*.'° 7. Impius '' ne '² *audēto* '³ placāre donis iram deōrum. 8. Consŭles militiae summum jus *habento,* nemĭni *parento.* 9. *Noli* '⁴ te oblivisci '⁵ Cicerōnem esse. 10. *Cura* ut quam primum '⁵ venias.'⁶.

INFINITIVE—TENSES AND USE.

Tenses of Infinitive.—540-544.

RULE XLIX.—*Subject of Infinitive.*—545.

Predicate after Infinitive.—546, 547.

Infinitive as Subject.—549.

87. 1. *Virum bonum esse,* semper est utile.'⁷ 2. Omnĭbus bonis '⁸ expĕdit, *salvam esse rem publĭcam.* 3. A Deo. *mundum* necesse '⁷ est *regi.* 4. Concedendum est '⁹

' 530, I. ; 545, 3 ; 295.	⁸ 448.	'⁴ 538, 2.
² 545.	⁹ 399, 2, 2).	'⁵ 305, 6.
³ 532, 4.	'° 537, II.	'⁶ 535, 1, 1).
⁴ 552.	¹¹ 441.	'⁷ 438, 3.
⁵ 406, II.	'² 538, 1.	'⁸ 441, 384.
⁶ 384.	'³ 271, 3.	'⁹ 301, 2.
⁷ 369.		

C

in virtūte solā *posĭtam esse beātam vitam.* 5. *Laelium doctum fuisse* tradĭtum est. 6. *Lectitavisse*[1] Platōnem studiōso Demosthĕnes dicĭtur.[1] 7. Non *esse*[2] *cupĭdum* pecunia[3] est. 8. Non *esse emācem* vectīgal est. 9. *Contentum* suis rebus[4] *esse* maxĭmae[5] sunt divitiae. 10. *Dilĭgĕre* parentes[6] prima[7] naturae lex[8] est. 11. Lycurgi temporĭbus[9] Homērus *fuisse* dicĭtur. 12. *Imperāre* sibi maxĭmum est imperium. 13. Parentes suos non *amāre*[10] impĭĕtas est. 14. Constat ad salūtem civium *inventas esse leges.* 15. Pecuniam *praeferre*[9] amicitiae[10] sordĭdum est. 16. Nihil est tam angusti anĭmi,[11] quam *amāre* divitias. 17. Ex malis *elĭgĕre* minĭma oportet.

Infinitive as Object.—550, 551.

88. 1. *Ferre* labōrem consuetūdo docet. 2. *Vincĕre* scis, Hannĭbal,[12] victoriā[13] *uti* nescis. 3. Magister tuus te magnā mercēde[14] nihil[15] *sapĕre*[16] docuit. 4. Num sum vel Graece *loqui,* vel Latīne docendus? 5. Non omnes sciunt *referre*[17] beneficium. 6. A Graecis[18] Galli urbes moenĭbus[19] *cingĕre* didicērunt. 7. Non *utĭlem* arbĭtror *esse* futurārum rerum *scientiam.* 8. Concēde *nihil esse bonum,* nisi quod honestum sit.[20] 9. Nonne poĕtae post mortem *nobilitāri* volunt? 10. *Syracūsas maxĭmam esse Graecārum urbium*[21] *omnium* audivistis. 11. Socrātes parens[22] philosophiae jure[23] *dici* potest.[24] 12. Nunquam putāvi *fore,*[25] ut supplex ad te venīrem.[26] 13. Cato *esse* quam *vidēri* bonus[27] malēbat.[28]

---

[1] 549, 4, 1).
[2] 545, 2, 2).
[3] 362.
[4] 419, IV.
[5] 165.
[6] 371.
[7] 166.
[8] 426.
[9] 292, 2.

[10] 386, 1.
[11] 401.
[12] 369.
[13] 419.
[14] 416.
[15] 371, 3.
[16] 374, 4.
[17] 292, 2.
[18] 425.

[19] 414.
[20] 531.
[21] 396, 2, 3).
[22] 547, I.
[23] 414.
[24] 290.
[25] 544.
[26] 293.

Infinitive in Special Constructions.—553.

89. 1. Consilium erat *continuāre*[1] bellum. 2. Bene et beāte vivĕre est honeste et recte *vivĕre.* 3. Postumio negotium dabātur *vidĕre,*[2] ne quid[3] res publĭca detrimenti[4] capĕret.[5] 4. Fuit fama Themistŏclem venēnum suā sponte[6] *sumpsisse.* 5. Consilium fuit in Graeciam *redīre.* 6. Fama est Romŭlum Romam *condidisse.* 7. Fama est Homērum caecum *fuisse.*

Subject and Object Clauses.—554–558.

90. Subject Clauses.—555, 556.—1. Quaerĭtur, quid faciendum sit.[7] 2. Verum[8] est amicitiam inter bonos esse. 3. Relĭquum est, ut certēmus[9] officiis[10] inter nos. 4. Accēdit quod[11] patrem[12] amo.

91. Object Clauses.—557, 558.—1. Non dubĭto, tu quid responsūrus sis.[7] 2. Rogāvi pervenissentne[13] Agrigentum. 3. Sentīmus nivem esse albam; dulce, mel. 4. Democrĭtus dicit innumerabĭles esse mundos. 5. Memĭni gloriātum esse Hortensium,[14] quod nunquam bello[15] civīli interfuisset.[16]

Gerunds and Gerundives.—559–566.

92. Genitive.—563.—1. Sapientia ars[17] *vivendi* putanda est. 2. Caesar *loquendi* finem facit. 3. Mihi[18] *discendi,* tibi *docendi* facultātem otium praebet. 4. *Legendi* semper occasio est, *audiendi,* non semper. 5. Epa-

---

[1] 553, I.
[2] 553, II.
[3] 190, 1.
[4] 396, 2, 3).
[5] 492.
[6] 414, 2.

[7] 525.
[8] 438, 3.
[9] 495, 2.
[10] 414.
[11] 554, IV.
[12] 447.

[13] 526, L
[14] 545.
[15] 386.
[16] 529.
[17] 362.
[18] 384, II.

8

minondas studiōsus erat *audiendi*.[1]   6. Maxĭme[2] sum
cupĭdus te[3] *audiendi*.   7. Demosthĕnes *Platōnis* studiōsus *audiendi* fuit.   8. Multi propter gloriae cupiditātem
cupĭdi sunt *bellōrum gerendōrum*.   9. *Exercendae memoriae* gratiā,[4] quid quoque die[5] audiĕrim,[6] commemŏro
vespĕre.

93. Dative.—564.—1. Crassus *disserendo*[7] par non
erat.   2. *Solvendo*[8] civitātes non erant.   3. Nuina *sacerdotĭbus*[9] *creandis* anĭmum adjēcit.   4. Mons *pecŏri* bonus
alendo erat.   5. Consul *placandis diis* dat opĕram.   6.
Sunt nonnulli *acuendis* puerōrum *ingeniis* non inutĭles
lusus.

94. Accusative.—565.—1. Homo ad *intelligendum*[10]
et ad *agendum* est natus.   2. Breve tempus aetātis satis
longum est ad bene[11] *vivendum*.   3. Bene sentīre rectē-
que facĕre[12] satis est ad bene beatēque *vivendum*.   4.
Pythagŏras Lacedaemŏna[13] ad *cognoscendas* Lycurgī
leges contendit.   5. Ubii navium magnam copiam ad
transportandum exercĭtum pollicebantur.   6. Catilīna,
nobilissĭmi genĕris[14] vir, sed ingenii pravissĭmi, ad *delen-
dam patriam* conjurāvit cum audacissĭmis viris.

95. Ablative.—566.—1. Nihil[15] *agendo*[16] homĭnes
male agĕre[17] discunt.   2. Lycurgi leges laborĭbus erudi-
unt juventūtem, *venando, currendo, algendo, aestuando*.
3. Omnis loquendi elegantia augētur *legendis oratorĭbus*[18]
et *poētis*.   4. Virtūtes cernuntur in *agendo*.   5. Multa[18]
de bene beatēque *vivendo* a Platōne disputāta sunt.

---

[1] 399, 2, 2).	[7] 391, 1.	[13] 379 ; 68.
[2] 305, 2 ; 165.	[8] 384.	[14] 396, IV.
[3] 371.	[9] 384, II.	[15] 371.
[4] 414, 2.	[10] 433.	[16] 414.
[5] 426.	[11] 559.	[17] 550.
[6] 525 ; 234.	[12] 549.	[18] 441, 1.

SUPINE.—567–570.

RULE L.—*Supine in* UM.—569.

Supine in U.—570.

96. 1. Lacedaemonii Agesilāum *bellātum* misērunt in Asiam. 2. Themistŏcles Argos ¹ *habitātum* concessit. 3. Hannĭbal patriam ² *defensum* revocātus est. 4. Veientes pacem *petītum* oratōres Romam mittunt. 5. Quod optĭmum ³ *factu* ⁴ videbĭtur, facies. 6. Quid est taın jucundum *cognĭtu* atque *audītu*, quam sapientĭbus sententiis ⁵ ornāta oratio ? 7. Plerăque *dictu*, quam re ⁶ sunt faciliōra.⁷

PARTICIPLES.—571–581.

97. 1. Alexander *moriens* ⁸ annŭlum dedit Perdiccae. 2. Hippias in Marathonia pugnā cecĭdit, arma contra patriam *ferens*.⁹ 3. Apelles pinxit Alexandrum Magnum fulmen *tenentem* in templo Ephesiae Diānae. 4. Sol *occĭdens* ¹⁰ noctem confĭcit. 5. Terra *mutāta* ¹¹ non mutat mores. 6. Dionysius tyrannus, Syracūsis ¹² *expulsus*, Corinthi ¹³ puĕros docēbat. 7. Hannĭbal imperātor ¹⁴ *factus* omnes gentes Hispaniae bello subēgit. 8. Sacerdos *vincta* in custodiam datur. 9. Regĭbus *exactis*, consŭles creāti sunt. 10. *Perdĭtis* ¹⁵ rebus omnĭbus, tamen ipsa ¹⁶ virtus se sustentāre ¹⁷ potest. 11. Athenienses, non *exspectāto* ¹⁸ auxilio, in proelium egrediuntur.¹⁹ 12. Sperne

¹ 379.	⁸ 578, I.	¹⁴ 362, 3.
² 371.	⁹ 292.	¹⁵ 578, IV.
³ 165.	¹⁰ 578, II.	¹⁶ 452.
⁴ 570, 429.	¹¹ 580.	¹⁷ 552, 1.
⁵ 414.	¹² 425.	¹⁸ 581.
⁶ 429.	¹³ 421, II.	¹⁹ 223.
⁷ 163, 2.		

voluptātes ; nocet *empta* dolōre [1] voluptas. 13. Dilapsi sunt in oppĭda, moenĭbus [2] se *defensūri*.[3] 14. Puĕris sententias *ediscendas* [4] damus. 15. Lentŭlus attribuit urbem *inflammandam* Cassio,[5] totam Italiam *vastandam* Catilīnae.

SYNTAX OF PARTICLES.

RULE LI.—*Use of Adverbs.*—582–585.

CONJUNCTIONS, 587, 588.

98. ADVERBS.—1. Sapientis [6] anĭmus *semper* vacat vitio,[7] *nunquam* turgescit ; *nunquam* sapiens irascĭtur. 2. *Semper* in proelio iis [8] maxĭmum [9] est pericŭlum qui [9] *maxĭme* timent. 3. *Ut* secunda [10] *moderāte* tulĭmus,[11] *sic* adversam fortūnam *fortĭter* ferre debēmus.

99. CONJUNCTIONS.—1. Horae cedunt *et* dies *et* menses *et* anni. 2. *Neque* pecuniae *neque* tecta magnifĭca [12] *neque* opes [13] *neque* imperia *neque* voluptātes in bonis rebus numerandae sunt. 3. Attĭcus *neque* mendacium dicēbat *neque* pati potĕrat. 4. Virtus *nec* erĭpi *nec* surrĭpi potest unquam ; *neque* naufragio [14] *neque* incendio amittĭtur. 5. *Aut* labōres *aut* sumptus suscipĕre nolunt.[15] 6. Est philosŏphi [16] habēre [17] non vagam, *sed* certam sententiam. 7. Jus suā sponte [18] est expetendum ; *etĕnim* omnes viri boni jus ipsum amant.

---

[1] 416.	[7] 387.	[13] 133, 1.
[2] 414.	[8] 165.	[14] 414, 4.
[3] 578, V.	[9] 445.	[15] 293.
[4] 384, II.	[10] 441, 1.	[16] 401.
[5] 441.	[11] 292.	[17] 549.
[6] 419, III.	[12] 164.	[18] 414, 2.

PART SECOND

LATIN SELECTIONS.

FABLES.

Note.—It is recommended that, in reading the Fables and Anecdotes, special attention should be given to *Gender* and to the *Declension of Nouns, Adjectives and Pronouns.*

The Kid and the Wolf.

100. Hoedus, stans [1] in tecto domus,[2] lupo [3] praetereunti maledixit. Cui lupus, "*Non tu,*" inquit,[4] "*sed tectum mihi maledīcit.*"

Saepe locus [5] et tempus homĭnes [6] timĭdos audāces [7] reddit.[8]

The Oxen.

101. In eōdem prato pascebantur [9] tres [10] boves [11] in maxĭmā concordiā, et sic ab omni ferārum incursiōne [12] tuti erant. Sed dissidio [13] inter illos orto, singŭli a feris [14] petīti et laniāti sunt.

Fabŭla docet, quantum boni sit [15] in concordiā.

---

[1] 438, 1.	[6] 72, 2.	[11] 66.
[2] 119, 1.	[7] 373, 3.	[12] 100, 3.
[3] 384.	[8] 463, I.	[13] 431.
[4] 297, II. 2.	[9] 468.	[14] 414, 5.
[5] 141.	[10] 175.	[15] 525.

The Woman and the Hen.

102. Mulier quaedam habēbat gallīnam, quae ei[1] quotidie ovum pariēbat aureum. Hinc suspicāri[2] coepit,[3] illam auri massam intus celāre, et gallīnam occīdit. Sed nihil in eā repĕrit, nisi quod[4] in aliis gallīnis reperīri solet.[5] Ităque dum majorĭbus[6] divitiis[7] inhiābat, etiam minōres perdĭdit.

The Peasant and the Mouse.

103. Mus[8] a rustĭco deprehensus tam acri morsu ejus digĭtos vulnerāvit, ut ille eum dimittĕret,[9] dicens: "*Nihil, mehercŭle, tam pusillum est, quod de salūte*[10] *desperāre debeat,*[11] *modo se defendĕre velit.*"[12]

The Fox and the Grapes.

104. Vulpes[13] uvam in vite conspicāta ad illam subsiliit omnium virium[14] suārum contentiōne,[15] si eam forte attingĕre posset. Tandem defatigāta ināni labōre discēdens dixit: "*At nunc etiam acerbae sunt, nec eas in viā repertas*[16] *tollĕrem.*"[17]

Haec fabŭla docet, multos ea contemnĕre, quae se assĕqui posse despērent.[18]

The Wolf and the Crane.

105. In faucĭbus lupi os inhaesĕrat. Mercēde[19] igĭtur condūcit gruem,[20] qui illud extrăhat.[21] Hoc grus longitudĭne[22] colli facĭle effēcit. Quum autem mercēdem

---

[1] 384, II.	[8] 115, 1.	[15] 414; 100, 3.
[2] 552.	[9] 489; 494.	[16] 578, III.
[3] 297; 460, 2.	[10] 73, E. 2; 115, 2.	[17] 503; 503, 2.
[4] 445, 6.	[11] 500.	[18] 501, I.
[5] 271, 3.	[12] 505.	[19] 416; 104, 1.
[6] 165.	[13] 43, 3.	[20] 66, 2.
[7] 386.	[14] 66.	[21] 100, 1.

postulāret,[1] subrīdens lupus et dentĭbus[2] infrendens, " *Num tibi*," inquit, " *parva merces*[3] *vidētur, quod caput incolŭme ex lupi faucĭbus extraxisti ?* "

The Trumpeter.

106. Tubĭcen[4] ab hostĭbus captus, " *Ne*[5] *me*," inquit, " *interficĭte ; nam inermis sum, neque*[6] *quidquam habeo praeter hanc tubam.*" At hostes, " *Propter hoc ipsum*," inquiunt, " *te interimēmus, quod, quum ipse pugnandi*[7] *sis*[8] *imperītus, alios ad pugnam incitāre soles.*"

Fabŭla docet, non solum maleficos[9] esse puniendos, sed etiam eos, qui alios ad male faciendum [10] irrītent.[11]

The Husbandman and his Sons.

107. Agricŏla senex, quum mortem [12] sibi [13] appropinquāre sentīret,[14] filios convocāvit, quos,[15] ut fiĕri [16] solet, interdum discordāre novĕrat,[17] et fascem virgulārum afferri [18] jubet. Quibus allātis, filios hortātur, ut hunc fascem frangĕrent. Quod [19] quum facĕre non possent, distribuit singŭlas virgas, iisque celerĭter fractis, docuit illos, quam firma res [20] esset[21] concordia, quamque imbecillis discordia.

The Mice.

108. Mures aliquando habuērunt consilium, quomŏdo sibi [22] a fele cavērent. Multis aliis [23] positis,

---

[1] 518, II.	[9] 441 ; 545.	[17] 278, 3.
[2] 110, 1.	[10] 559, 565.	[18] 292, 2 ; 551.
[3] 362.	[11] 501, I.	[19] 453.
[4] 76, 1.	[12] 110 ; 105.	[20] 362.
[5] 538, 1.	[13] 386.	[21] 525.
[6] 587, I. 2.	[14] 518, II.	[22] 385, 3.
[7] 563 ; 399.	[15] 545.	[23] 431.
[8] 518, I.	[16] 294.	

omnĭbus placuit, ut ei [1] tintinnabŭlum annecterētur; [2] sic
enim ipsos [3] sonĭtu admonĭtos eam fugĕre posse. Sed
quum jam inter mures quaererētur,[4] qui feli tintinnabŭlum annectĕret,[5] nemo repertus est.

Fabŭla docet, in suadendo [6] plurĭmos [7] esse audāces,
sed in ipso pericŭlo timĭdos.

The Enemies.

109. In eādem navi [8] vehebantur duo,[9] qui inter se
capitalia odia exercēbant. Unus [9] eōrum in prorā, alter [10]
in puppi [11] residēbat. Ortā tempestāte ingenti, quum
omnes de vitā desperārent, interrŏgat is, qui in puppi
sedēbat, gubernatōrem, *utram* [10] *partem navis prius submersum iri existimāret.* Cui gubernātor, "*Proram,*"
respondit. Tum ille, "*Jam mors mihi non molesta est,
quum inimīci mei mortem adspectūrus sim.*" [12]

The Tortoise and the Eagle.

110. Testūdo aquĭlam magnopĕre orābat, ut sese
volāre docēret.[13] Aquĭla ei ostendēbat quidem, eam [14]
rem [15] petĕre natūrae [16] suae contrariam; sed illa nihĭlo [17]
minus instābat, et obsecrābat aquĭlam, ut se volŭcrem
facĕre vellet.[18] Ităque ungŭlis arreptam aquĭla sustŭlit
in sublīme, et demīsit illam, ut per aërem ferrētur.[19] Tum
in saxa incĭdens comminūta interiit.[19]

Haec fabŭla docet, multos cupiditatĭbus suis occaecā-
tos consilia prudentiōrum respuĕre, et in exitium ruĕre
stultitiā [20] suā.

---

[1] 386.	[8] 62, III.	[15] 371.
[2] 495, 2.	[9] 441; 175.	[16] 391.
[3] 545.	[10] 151.	[17] 418.
[4] 518, II.	[11] 62, III.	[18] 293.
[5] 525.	[12] 517.	[19] 295, 3.
[6] 566, II.	[13] 489.	[20] 414, 2.
[7] 165; 441.	[14] 545.	

The Lion.

111. Societātem junxĕrant[1] leo, juvenca, capra, ovis. Praedā autem, quam cepĕrant, in quattuor partes aequāles divīsā,[2] leo, " *Prima*," ait,[3] " *mea est ; debētur enim haec praestantiae meae.* · *Tollam et secundam, quam merētur[4] robur[5] meum. Tertiam vindĭcat sibi[6] egregius labor meus. Quartam qui sibi arrogāre voluĕrit,[7] is[8] sciat,[9] se habitūrum me inimīcum sibi.*"[10] Quid facĕrent[11] imbecilles bestiae, aut quae sibi leōnem infestum habēre vellet ?[12]

ANECDOTES.

Anaxagoras.

112. Anaxagŏram ferunt,[13] nuntiātā[14] morte filii, dixisse : " *Sciēbam me genuisse mortālem.*"[15]

Thales.

113. Thales interrogātus, quid esset[16] Deus, " *Quod,*" inquit, " *initio*[16] *et fine caret.*"

114. Thales interrogātus, quid esset difficĭle,[16] " *Se ipsum,*" inquit, "*nosse.*"[17] Interrogātus, quid esset facĭle : " *Altĕrum,*" inquit, "*admonēre.*"

115. Thales rogātus, quid maxĭme commūne esset hominĭbus,[18] " *Spes,*" respondit, " *hanc enim et illi habent, qui aliud nihil.*"

116. Quum Thales interrogarētur,[19] quid esset omnium vetustissĭmum, respondit : " *Deus, quod nunquam esse coepit.*"[20]

---

[1] 463, II.	[8] 451.	[15] 419, III.
[2] 431, 2, (1).	[9] 487.	[16] 163, 2.
[3] 297, II.	[10] 391.	[17] 234, 2.
[4] 225.	[11] 485 ; 486, II.	[18] 391.
[5] 77, IV.	[12] 292.	[19] 518, II.
[6] 384, II. ; 449, I.	[13] 357, I.	[20] 297.
[7] 485.	[14] 525.	

Socrates.

117. Socrătes, in pompā quum magna vis auri argentīque ferrētur,[1] " *Quam multa non desidĕro,*" inquit.

118. Sapientissĭmus Socrătes dicēbat,[2] *scire se*[3] *nihil, praeter hoc ipsum, quod nihil sciret:*[4] *relĭquos hoc etiam nescīre.*

Scipio Africanus.

119. Scipio Africānus nunquam ad negotia publĭca accedēbat, antĕquam in templo Jovis[5] precātus esset.[6]

120. Scipio Africānus Ennii poëtae imagĭnem[7] in sepulcro gentis Corneliae collocāri jussit,[8] quod Scipiōnum ıs gestas carminĭbus suis illustravĕrat.[9]

Antigonus and the Cynic.

121. Ab Antigŏno Cynĭcus quidam petiit [10] talentum. Respondit,[11] *plus*[12] *esse, quam quod*[13] *Cynĭcus petĕre debēret.*[4] Repulsus petiit denarium. Respondit rex, *minus*[13] *esse quam quod*[13] *regem decēret dare.*[14]

Cicero.

122. Cicĕro Dolabellae [15] dicenti, se [16] triginta annos habēre,[17] " *Verum est,*" inquit, " *nam hoc jam ante viginti annos audīvi.*"

The Lacedaemonians.

123. Lacedaemonii, Philippo minitante [18] per littĕras, se omnia quae conarentur [19] prohibitūrum,[20] quaesivērunt, *num se esset*[21] *etiam mori prohibitūrus.*

---

[1] 518, II.	[6] 471, II.	[26] 384.
[2] 469, II.	[9] 472.	[16] 545.
[3] 545.	[10] 234.	[17] 551, L
[4] 531.	[11] 460, 2.	[18] 431, 2, (1).
[5] 66, 3.	[23] 165.	[20] 531.
[6] 523, II. 2.	[13] 371 ; 445, 6.	[20] 545, 3.
[7] 72, 3.	[14] 549.	[21] 525.

124. Leonĭdas, Lacedaemoniōrum rex, quum Xerxes scripsisset,[1] " *Mitte arma ;* " respondit, " *Veni et cape.*"

125. Quum ad Leonĭdam quidam milĭtum[2] dixisset,[1] " *Hostes sunt prope nos ;* " " *Et nos,*"[3] inquit, "*prope illos.*"

126. E Lacedaemoniis[4] unus, quum Perses hostis in colloquio dixisset[1] glorians, " Solem[5] prae jaculōrum multitudĭne[6] et sagittārum non vidēbĭtis," " *In umbrā igĭtur,*" inquit, "*pugnabĭmus.*"

127. Lacedaemonius quidam quum riderētur,[1] quod claudus in pugnam iret,[7] " *At mihi,*" inquit, "*pugnāre,*[8] non fugĕre est propositum.*"

Solon.

128. Solon quum interrogarētur,[1] cur nullum supplicium constituisset[9] in eum, qui parentem necasset,[10] respondit, *se id nemĭnem factūrum*[11] *putasse.*[12]

Theophrastus, the Philosopher.

129. Theophrastus ad quendam, qui in convivio prorsus silēbat ; " *Si stultus es,*" inquit, " *rem facis sapientem ; si sapiens, stultam.*"

Theocrĭtus, the Poet.

130. Miser poëta praelegĕrat Theocrĭto[13] versus suos. Tum interrogābat,[14] quosnam maxĭme approbāret,[8] " *Quos*[15] *omisisti,*" respondit.

---

[1] 518, II.	[6] 72, 2.	[11] 545, 3.
[2] 396, III.	[7] 520, II.	[12] 234.
[3] 367, 3.	[8] 549.	[13] 386, 1.
[4] 398, 4, 2).	[9] 525 ; 481, II.	[14] 460, 2.
[5] 112 ; 75.	[10] 500, 2 ; 234.	[15] 445, 6.

Cornelia.

131. Cornelia, Gracchōrum mater, quum Campāna matrōna, apud illam hospĭta,' ornamenta sua pulcherrĭma,' ipsi ostendĕret,' traxit eam sermōne,' donec e scholā redīrent ' libĕri. Tum, " *Et haec*," inquit, " *mea sunt ornamenta.*"

Themistocles.

132. Memoriam in Themistŏcle fuisse singulārem ferunt. Ităque quum ei Simonĭdes artem memoriae pollicerētur,' " *Obliviōnis*," ' inquit, " *mallem ;* ' nam memĭni etiam, quae' nolo ; oblivisci non possum, quae volo.*"

133. Themistŏcles quum consulerētur,' utrum bono viro paupĕri, an minus probāto divĭti filiam collocāret,' " *Ego vero*," inquit, " *malo virum, qui pecuniā* " *egeat*," *quam pecuniam, quae viro.*"

134. Themistŏcles interroganti," utrum Achilles " esse mallet," an Homērus, respondit : " *Tu vero mallesne* " *te in Olympĭco certamĭne victōrem* " *renuntiāri, an praeco* " *esse, qui victōrum nomĭna* " *proclāmat.*"

Diogenes, the Cynic.

135. Diogĕnes Cynĭcus Myndum " profectus, quum vidēret ' magnifĭcas " portas et urbem exiguam, Myndios monuit, ut portas claudĕrent," ne urbs egrederētur."

363.
' 163, 1.
' 518, II.
' 414, 4.
' 295, 3 ; 522, II.
' 397, 1, (3).
' 485, 486, 3.

' 445, 6.
' 525 : 526, II. 1.
" 419, III.
" 501, I.
" 575 ; 384.
" 547, 1.
" 525.

" 346, II. 1, 1) ; 485.
" 546.
" 76, 1.
" 379.
" 164.
" 489.

Thrasybulus.

136. Quum quidam Thrasybūlo, qui civitātem Athenlensium a tyrannōrum dominatiōne liberāvit, dixisset: [1] *" Quantas tibi gratias Athēnae debent!"* ille respondit: *" Dii faciant, ut quantas ipse patriae debeo gratias, tantas ei videar* retulisse."*

Xerxes.

137. Xerxes refertus donis [1] fortūnae, non equitātu, [2] non pedestribus copiis, non navium multitudĭne, non infinīto pondĕre [3] auri contentus, praemium ei proposuit, qui invenisset [4] novam voluptātem.

Metellus Pius.

138. Metellus Pius, in Hispaniā bellum gerens [5] interrogātus, quid postĕro die [6] factūrus esset? [7] *" Tunĭcam meam,"* inquit, *" si id [8] elŏqui posset, comburĕrem."* [9]

Publius Rutilius Rufus.

139. Publius Rutilius Rufus quum amīci cujusdam injustae rogatiōni [10] resistĕret, [11] atque is per summam [12] indignatiōnem dixisset, "Quid ergo mihi [13] opus est amicitiā [14] tuā, si, quod [15] rogo, non facis?" *" Immo,"* inquit, *" quid mihi tuā, si propter te alĭquid injuste factūrus sum?"*

Philip.

140. Mulier quaedam a Philippo, quum a convivio

---

[1] 518, II.	[7] 500, 2.	[12] 510, 1.
[2] 487.	[8] 578, I.	[13] 385.
[3] 492, 1 ; 549, 4.	[9] 426.	[14] 163, 3.
[4] 419, III.	[10] 545.	[15] 419, 3.
[5] 419, IV.	[11] 371.	[16] 445, 6.
[6] 84, 1.		

temulentus recedĕret,[1] damnāta, "*A Philippo*," inquit, "*temulento ad Philippum sobrium provŏco.*"

Titus.

141. Titus amor et deliciae genĕris humāni appellā-tus est. Recordātus quondam super coenam, quod nihil cuiquam toto[2] die[3] praestitisset,[4] memorabĭlem illam meritōque laudātam vocem edĭdit: "*Amīci, diem perdĭdi.*"

Xenophon.

142. Xenŏphon, quum solemne sacrum facĕret,[5] filium apud Mantineam in proelio cecidisse[6] cognōvit. Corōnam deposuit, sed, ut audīvit fortissĭme pugnantem interiisse,[7] corōnam capĭti[8] reposuit, numĭna testātus, se[9] majōrem ex virtūte filii voluptātem, quam ex morte dolōrem sentīre.

Diagoras, the Rhodian.

143. Diagŏras Rhodius, quum tres ejus filii in ludis Olympĭcis victōres renuntiāti essent,[1] tanto affectus est gaudio,[2] ut in ipso stadio, inspectante popŭlo,[10] in filiōrum manĭbus[11] anĭmam reddĕret.[12]

Euripides, the Tragic Poet.

144. Athenienses quondam ab Euripĭde postulābant, ut ex tragoediā sententiam quandam tollĕret.[13] Ille autem in scenam progressus dixit, se fabŭlas componĕre solēre,[14] ut popŭlum docēret,[15] non ut a popŭlo discĕret.

---

[1] 518, II.	[6] 295, 3.	[11] 118, 1, (1).
[2] 151.	[7] 384, II.	[12] 494.
[3] 426.	[8] 545.	[13] 492, 3.
[4] 554, IV.	[9] 414, 4.	[14] 272, 3.
[5] 551, I.	[10] 431; 431, 2, (1).	[15] 491.

Tiberius, the Roman Emperor.

145. Tiberius praesidĭbus¹ onerandas tribūto² provincias³ suadentĭbus⁴ rescripsit : " *Boni pastōris*⁵ *est, tondēre*⁶ *pecus, non deglubĕre.*"

146. Tiberius, Iliensium legātis⁷ paulo⁸ serius⁹ de morte filii Drusi consolantĭbus, irrīdens, *se quoque*, respondit, *vicem*¹⁰ *eōrum dolēre, quod egregĭum civem Hectŏrem*¹¹ *amisissent.*¹² Effluxĕrant autem tum plus quam mille¹³ anni a morte Hectŏris.

Simonides.

147. Quum de Simonĭde¹⁴ quaesivisset¹⁵ tyrannus Hiĕro, quid esset¹⁶ Deus; deliberandi¹⁷ sibi unum diem postulāvit. Quum idem¹⁸ ex eo postridie quaerĕret,¹⁹ biduum petīvit. Quum saepius duplicāret numĕrum diērum, admiransque Hiĕro requirĕret, cur ita facĕret¹⁶ ; " *Quia*," inquit, " *quanto*¹⁹ *diutius considĕro, tanto mihi res vidētur obscurior.*"

¹ 384 ; 81, 2.	⁸ 418.	¹⁴ 374, 3, 4).
² 419, 2, 1).	⁹ 444, 1 & 4.	¹⁵ 518, II.
³ 545.	¹⁰ 133, 1 ; 371, 3, 1).	¹⁶ 525.
⁴ 577.	¹¹ 363.	¹⁷ 563.
⁵ 401.	¹² 531.	¹⁸ 371.
⁶ 549.	¹³ 178.	¹⁹ 418.
⁷ 431, 2, (1).		

ROMAN HISTORY.

Note.—It is recommended that, in reading the Roman History, special attention should be given to the *Synopsis of Conjugation* and to the *Formation of the Parts of the Verb.*—213-288.

Period I.—Italian and Roman Kings.

FROM THE EARLIEST TIMES TO THE BANISHMENT OF TARQUIN, 510 B. C.

Early Italian Kings.—Aeneas in Italy.

148. Antiquissĭmis[1] temporĭbus[2] Saturnus in Italiam venisse dicĭtur.[3] Ibi haud procul a Janicŭlo arcem condĭdit, eamque Saturniam[4] appellāvit. Hic Itălos primus[5] agricultūram[6] docuit.[7]

149. Postea Latīnus in illis regionĭbus imperāvit. Sub hoc rege Troja in Asiā eversa est. Hinc Aenēas, Anchīsae filius, cum multis Trojānis, quibus[8] ferrum Graecōrum pepercĕrat,[9] aufūgit,[10] et in Italiam pervēnit.[11] Ibi Latīnus rex ei[11] benigne recepto filiam Laviniam in matrimonium dedit.[9] Aenēas urbem condĭdit, quam in honōrem conjŭgis[12] Lavinium appellāvit.

Ascanius and the Kings of Alba.

150. Post Aenēae mortem Ascanius, Aenēae filius, regnum accēpit. Hic sedem regni in alium locum

---

[1] 444, 1.	[5] 442, 1.	[9] 273, I. 2.
[2] 426.	[6] 374.	[10] 273, II. 1.
[3] 549, 4.	[7] 213, II.	[11] 384, II.
[4] 373.	[8] 385.	[12] 96, 3.

transtŭlit,[1] urbemque condĭdit in monte [2] Albāno, eamque Albam Longam nuncupāvit. Eum secūtus est [3]
Silvius, qui post Aenēae mortem a Laviniā genĭtus erat.
Ejus postĕri omnes, usque ad Romam condĭtam,[4] Albae [5]
regnavērunt.

151. Silvius Procas, rex Albanōrum, duos filios relīquit,[6] Numitōrem et Amulium. Horum minor [7] natu,[8]
Amulius, fratri optiōnem dedit, utrum regnum habēre
vellet,[9] an bona,[10] quae pater reliquisset.[11] Numĭtor pa-
terna bona praetŭlit ;[1] Amulius regnum obtinuit.

Birth of Romulus and Remus.

152. Amulius, ut regnum firmissĭme possidēret,[12]
Numitōris filium per insidias interēmit,[13] et filiam fra-
tris, Rheam Silviam, Vestālem virgĭnem fecit.[13] Nam
his Vestae sacerdotĭbus non licet viro [14] nubĕre. Sed
haec a Marte gemĭnos filios, Romŭlum et Remum, pepĕ-
rit.[15] Hoc quum Amulius comperisset,[16] matrem in
vincŭla conjēcit, puĕros autem in Tibĕrim [17] abjĭci
jussit.[18]

153. Forte Tibĕris aqua ultra ripam se effudĕrat,[6]
et, quum puĕri in vado essent posĭti,[19] aqua refluens [20] eos
in sicco relīquit. Ad eōrum vagītum lupa accurrit,[21]
eosque uberĭbus suis aluit. Quod [22] videns Faustŭlus
quidam, pastor illīus regiōnis, puĕros sustŭlit,[1] et uxōri
Accae Laurentiae nutriendos [23] dedit.

---

[1] 292, 2.	[9] 525.	[17] 62, II. 2.
[2] 110, 1.	[10] 441, 1.	[18] 269.
[3] 283.	[11] 527.	[19] 518, I.
[4] 580.	[12] 491.	[20] 578, II.
[5] 421, II.	[13] 214, I.	[21] 255, I. 4.
[6] 273, II. 1.	[14] 385, 2.	[22] 453.
[7] 165.	[15] 273, I. 1.	[23] 578, V.
[8] 429	[16] 518, II.	

Rome founded, 753 B.C.

154. Sic Romŭlus et Remus pueritiam inter pastōres transegērunt.[1] Quum adolevissent,[2] et forte comperissent, quis ipsōrum avus, quae mater fuisset,[3] Amulium interfecērunt, et Numitōri avo regnum restituērunt. Tum urbem condidērunt in monte Aventīno, quam Romŭlus a suo nomĭne Romam vocāvit. Haec quum moenĭbus[4] circumdarētur,[5] Remus occīsus est, dum fratrem irrīdens moenia transiliēbat.

Seizure of the Sabine Women.

155. Romŭlus, ut civium numĕrum augēret,[6] asȳlum patefēcit,[6] ad quod multi ex civitatĭbus suis pulsi accurrērunt. Sed novae urbis civĭbus[7] conjŭges deērant. Ităque festum Neptūni et ludos instituit. Ad hos quum multi[8] ex finitĭmis popŭlis cum mulierĭbus et liberis venissent,[9] Romāni inter ipsos ludos spectantes[9] virgĭnes rapuērunt.

156. Popŭli illi, quorum virgĭnes raptae erant, bellum adversus raptōres suscepērunt. Quum Romae[10] appropinquārent,[2] forte in Tarpēiam virgĭnem incidērunt, quae in arce sacra procurābat. Hanc rogābant, ut viam in arcem monstrāret,[11] eīque permisērunt, ut munus sibi poscĕret.[12] Illa petiit, ut sibi darent,[13] quod[13] in sinistris manĭbus[14] gerĕrent,[15] annŭlos aureos et armillas signifĭcans. At hostes in arcem ab eā perducti scutis Tarpēiam obruērunt; nam et ea in sinistris manĭbus gerēbant.

---

[1] 255, II.	[6] 273, II. 1.	[11] 492, 2.
[2] 518, II.	[7] 386, 2.	[12] 273, I. 2.
[3] 525.	[8] 441, 1.	[13] 445, 6.
[4] 131, 1; 414.	[9] 578, I.	[14] 118, 1.
[5] 269; 491.	[10] 386.	[15] 527.

The Sabines are received into the City.—Death of Romulus.

157. Tum Romŭlus cum hoste, qui montem Tarpē-
ium tenēbat, pugnam conseruit in eo loco, ubi nunc
forum Romānum est.   In mediā[1] caede raptae[2] processē-
runt, et hinc patres, hinc conjŭges et socĕros complecte-
bantur, et rogābant, ut caedis finem facĕrent.[3]   Utrīque
his precĭbus commōti sunt.   Romŭlus foedus icit, et Sabīnos in urbem recēpit.

158. Postea civitātem descripsit.[4]   Centum senatōres legit,[5] eosque quum ob aetātem, tum ob reverentiam
iis debĭtam, Patres appellāvit.   Plebem in triginta curias
distribuit, easque raptārum nominĭbus nuncupāvit.   Anno regni tricesĭmo septĭmo, quum exercĭtum lustrāret,[6]
inter tempestātem ortam[7] repente ocŭlis[8] homĭnum sub-
ductus est.   Hinc alii[9] eum a senatorĭbus interfectum,
alii ad deos sublātum[10] esse existimavērunt.

Numa Pompilius.

159. Post Romŭli mortem unīus anni interregnum
fuit.   Quo elapso,[11] Numa Pompilius Curĭbus,[12] urbe in
agro Sabinōrum, natus rex creātus est.   Hic vir bellum
quidem nullum gessit ; nec minus tamen civitāti[13] profuit.
Nam et leges dedit, et sacra plurĭma instituit, ut popŭli
barbări et bellicōsi mores mollīret.[13]   Omnia autem,
quae faciēbat, se nymphae Egeriae, conjŭgis suae, mo-
nĭtu facĕre dicēbat.   Morbo decessit,[14] quadragesĭmo
tertio imperii anno.

---

[1] 441, 6.   [6] 518, II.   [11] 431, 2.
[2] 575.   [7] 577.   [12] 421, II.
[3] 492, 2.   [8] 386.   [13] 491.
[4] 258, I. 3.   [9] 459.   [14] 258, I. 2.
[5] 255, II.   [10] 292, 2.

Tullus Hostilius.

160. Numae[1] successit Tullus Hostilius, cujus avus se in bello adversus Sabīnos fortem et strenuum virum praestitĕrat.[2] Rex[3] creātus bellum Albānis indixit, idque trigeminōrum, Horatiōrum et Curiatiōrum, certamĭne finīvit. Albam propter perfidiam Metii Suffetii diruit. Quum triginta duōbus annis[4] regnasset,[5] fulmĭne ictus cum domo suā arsit.[6]

Ancus Marcius.

161. Post hunc Ancus Marcius, Numae ex filiā nepos, suscēpit imperium. Hic vir aequitāte et religiōne avo[7] simĭlis, Latīnos bello domuit,[8] urbem ampliāvit, et nova ei[9] moenia circumdĕdit. Carcĕrem primus[10] aedificāvit. Ad Tibĕris ostia urbem condĭdit, Ostiamque vocāvit. Vicesĭmo quarto anno imperii morbo obiit.[11]

Lucius Tarquinius Priscus.

162. Deinde regnum Lucius Tarquinius Priscus accēpit, Demarāti filius, qui tyrannos patriae Corinthi fugiens in Etruriam venĕrat. Ipse Tarquinius, qui nomen ab urbe Tarquiniis accēpit, aliquando Romam[12] profectus[13] erat.

163. Quum Romae[14] commorarētur,[15] Anci regis familiaritātem consecūtus est, qui eum filiōrum suōrum tutōrem[16] relīquit. Sed is pupillis[17] regnum intercēpit. Senatorĭbus, quos Romŭlus creavĕrat, centum alios ad-

---

[1] 386.	[6] 269.	[11] 295, 3.
[2] 261, 2.	[7] 391.	[12] 379.
[3] 362, 3.	[8] 260.	[13] 283.
[4] 378, 1.	[9] 384, II. 1.	[14] 421, II.
[5] 518, II.	[10] 442, 1.	[15] 373.

dĭdit, qui minōrum gentium sunt appellāti. Plura bella felicĭter gessit, nec paucos agros, hostĭbus[1] ademptos, urbis territorio adjunxit. Primus[2] triumphans urbem intrāvit. Cloācas fecit;[3] Capitolium inchoāvit. Tricesĭmo octāvo imperii anno per Anci filios,[4] quibus[5] regnum eripuĕrat, occīsus est.

Servius Tullius.

164. Post hunc Servius Tullius suscēpit imperium, genĭtus ex nobĭli femĭnā, captīvā tamen et famŭlā. Quum adolevisset,[6] rex ei filiam in matrimonium dedit.

165. Quum Priscus Tarquinius occīsus esset, Tanăquil de superiōre[7] parte domus popŭlum allocūta est, dicens: *regem grave quidem, sed non letāle vulnus accepisse; eum petēre, ut popŭlus, dum convaluisset,[8] Servio Tullio obedīret.*[9] Sic Servius regnāre coepit, sed bene imperium administrāvit. Montes tres urbi adjunxit.[10] Primus omnium censum ordināvit. Sub eo Roma habuit octoginta tria millia civium cum his, qui iu agris erant.

166. Hic rex interfectus est scelĕre filiae Tulliae et Tarquinii Superbi, filii ejus regis, cui[11] Servius successĕrat. Nam ab ipso Tarquinio interfectus est. Tullia in forum properāvit, et prima conjŭgem regem salutāvit. Quum domum[12] redīret, aurīgam super patris corpus, iu viā jacens,[13] carpentum agĕre jussit.

Banishment of Tarquinius Superbus, 510 B. C.

167. Tarquinius Superbus cognōmen morĭbus[13] merŭit. Bello[14] tamen strenuus plures finitimōrum popu-

---

[1] 386.
[2] 442, 1.
[3] 255, II.
[4] 414, 5, 1).
[5] 386, 2.
[6] 518, II.
[7] 163, 3.
[8] 533, 4.
[9] 492, 2.
[10] 258, I. 1.
[11] 379, 3.
[12] 577.
[13] 414, 4.
[14] 429.

lōrum vicit.' Templum Jovis in Capitolio aedificāvit.
Postea, dum Ardeam oppugnābat,' urbem Latii, imperium perdĭdit.

168. Lucius Brutus, Collatīnus, aliĭque nonnulli in
exitium regis conjurārunt,' populōque persuasērunt,' ut
ei portas urbis claudĕret.' Exercĭtus quoque, qui civitātem Ardeam cum rege oppugnābat, eum relīquit. Fugit
ităque cum uxōre et libĕris suis. Ita Romae septem reges regnavērunt annos ducentos quadraginta quattuor.

PERIOD II.—ROMAN STRUGGLES AND CONQUESTS.

FROM THE ESTABLISHMENT OF THE COMMONWEALTH TO THE FIRST PUNIC WAR,
264 B. C.

Consuls at Rome, 509 B. C.—War with Tarquin.

169. Tarquinio expulso,' consŭles coepēre ' pro uno
rege duo creāri, ut, si unus malus esset,' alter eum coër-
cēret.' Annuum iis imperium tribūtum est, ne per
diuturnitātem potestātis insolentiōres redderentur.' Fuērunt igĭtur anno primo, expulsis regĭbus, consŭles Lucius
Junius Brutus, acerrĭmus ¹⁰ libertātis vindex, et Tarquinius Collatīnus. Sed Collatīno ¹¹ paulo post dignĭtas
sublāta est.¹² Placuĕrat enim, ne quis ex Tarquiniōrum
familiā Romae manēret.¹³ Ergo cum omni patrimonio
suo ex urbe migrāvit, et in ejus locum Valerius Publicŏla consul factus est.¹⁴

---

¹ 251, 1.	⁶ 431, 2.	¹¹ 386.
² 468.	⁷ 235, 297.	¹² 292, 2.
³ 234.	⁸ 509.	¹³ 492.
⁴ 269, I.	⁹ 491.	¹⁴ 294.
⁵ 492, 2.	¹⁰ 163, 1.	

170. Commōvit[1] bellum urbi rex Tarquinius. In
primā pugnā Brutus consul, et Aruns, Tarquinii filius,
sese invĭcem occidērunt. Romāni tamen ex eā pugnā
victōres recessērunt.[2] Brutum Romānae matrōnae, quasi
commūnem patrem, per annum luxērunt.[3] Valerius
Publicŏla Spurium Lucretium, collēgam[3] sibi[4] fecit;
quum morbo exstinctus esset,[5] Publicŏla Horatium Pul-
villum sibi collēgam sumpsit.[6] Ita primus annus quinque consŭles habuit.

War with Porsena, 508 *B. C.*

171. Secundo quoque anno itĕrum Tarquinius bellum Romānis intŭlit,[7] Porsĕnā, rege Etruscōrum, auxilium ei ferente.[8] In illo bellŏ Horatius Cocles solus
pontem ligneum defendit, et hostes cohibuit, donec pons[9]
a tergo ruptus esset.[10] Tum se cum armis in Tibĕrim[11]
conjēcit, et ad suos transnāvit.

172. Dum Porsĕna urbem obsidēbat, Quintus Mucius Scaevŏla, juvĕnis fortis anĭmi, in castra hostium se
contŭlit eo consilio,[12] ut regem occidĕret.[13] At ibi scribam regis pro ipso rege interfēcit. Tum a regiis satel-
litĭbus comprehensus et ad regem deductus, quum
Porsĕna eum ignĭbus allātis[14] terrēret,[15] dextram arae
accensae imposuit, donec flammis consumpta esset.[16]
Hoc facĭnus rex mirātus juvĕnem dimīsit[16] incolŭmem.
Tum hic, quasi beneficium refĕrens, ait,[17] *trecentos alios
juvĕnes in eum conjurasse.*[18] Hac re terrĭtus Porsĕna

---

[1] 270, II. 1.
[2] 258, I. 2.
[3] 373.
[4] 384.
[5] 518, II.; 273, II. 1.
[6] 258, I. 4.

[7] 292, 2.
[8] 431, 2.
[9] 110, 1.
[10] 522, II.
[11] 62, II. 2.
[12] 414, 2.

[13] 492.
[14] 580.
[15] 518, II.
[16] 258, I. 2.
[17] 297, II.
[18] 234.

D

pacem cum Romānis fecit, Tarquinius autem Tuscŭlum[1] se contŭlit, ĭbīque privātus consenuit.[2]

Secession to the Mons Sacer, 494 *B. C.*

173. Sexto decĭmo anno post reges exactos,[3] popŭlus Romae seditiōnem fecit, quæstus quod tribūtis et militiā a senātu exhaurirētur.[4] Magna pars plebis urbem relīquit, et in montem trans Aniēnem[5] amnem[6] secessit. Tum patres turbāti Menenium Agrippam misērunt ad plebem, qui eam senatui conciliāret.[7] Hic iis inter alia fabŭlam narrāvit de ventre et membris humāni corpŏris; quā popŭlus commōtus est, ut in urbem redīret.[8] Tum primum tribūni plebis creāti sunt, qui plebem adversum nobĭlitātis superbiam defendĕrent.[7]

Banishment of Coriolanus, 491 *B. C.*

174. Undevicesĭmo anno post exactos reges, Caius Marcius, Coriolānus dictus ab urbe Volscōrum Coriŏlis, quam bello cepĕrat, plebi invīsus[9] fĭĕri coepit. Quare urbe[10] expulsus ad Volscos, acerrĭmos Romanōrum hostes, contendit, et ab iis dux[11] exercĭtus factus Romānos saepe vicit. Jam usque ad quintum milliarium urbis accessĕrat, nec ullis civium suōrum legationĭbus flecti potĕrat, ut patriae[12] parcĕret.[8] Denĭque Veturia mater et Volumnia uxor ex urbe ad eum venērunt;[13] quarum fletu et precĭbus commōtus est, ut exercĭtum removēret.[8] Quo facto[14] a Volscis ut prodĭtor occīsus[9] esse dicĭtur.

---

[1] 379.	[6] 107, 1.	[11] 362, 3.
[2] 282, I. 1.	[7] 500.	[12] 385.
[3] 580.	[8] 494.	[13] 463, II.
[4] 520, II.	[9] 547, 1.	[14] 431, 2, (3).
[5] 72, 4.	[10] 425.	

The Fabii cut off at the Cremĕra, 477 B. C.

175. Romāni quum adversum Veientes bellum gerĕrent,[1] familia Fabiōrum sola[2] hoc bellum suscēpit.
Profecti[3] sunt trecenti sex nobilissĭmi homĭues, duce[4]
Fabio consŭle.[5] Quum saepe hostes vicissent,[6] apud
Cremĕram fluvium castra posuĕrunt. Ibi, quum Veientes dolo[7] usi eos in insidias pellexissent, in proelio exorto[8]
omnes periērunt. Unus superfuit ex tantā familiā, qui
propter aetātem puerīlem duci non potuĕrat ad pugnam.
Hic genus propagāvit ad Quintum Fabium Maxĭmum
illum, qui Hannibălem prudenti cunctatiōne debilitāvit.

Rome taken by the Gauls, 390 B. C.

176. Galli Senŏnes ad urbem venērunt, Romānos
apud flumen Alliam vicērunt, et urbem etiam occupā-
runt. Jam nihil praeter Capitolium defendi potuit. Et
jam praesidium fame[9] laborābat, et in eo erant, ut pacem a Gallis auro[10] emĕrent,[11] quum Camillus cum manu
milĭtum superveniens hostes magno proelio superāvit.

Valor of Titus Manlius Torquatus, 361 B. C.

177. Anno trecentesĭmo nonagesĭmo tertio post urbem condĭtam Galli itĕrum ad urbem accessĕrant, et
quarto milliario[11] trans Aniēnem fluvium consedĕrant.
Contra eos missus est Titus Quinctius. Ibi Gallus quidam eximiā corpŏris magnitudĭne[12] fortissĭmum Romanōrum ad certāmen singulāre provocāvit. Titus Manlius,

---

[1] 518, II.   [5] 363.   [9] 416.
[2] 151.   [6] 419, I.   [10] 494.
[3] 283.   [7] 577.   [11] 422, 1, 2).
[4] 430, 431.   [8] 414, 2.   [12] 428.

4

nobilissĭmus juvĕnis, provocatiōnem accepit, Gallum
occīdit, eumque torque[1] aureo spoliāvit, quo ornātus
erat. Hinc et ipse et postĕri ejus *Torquāti* appellāti
sunt. Galli fugam capessivērunt.[2]

Beginning of Samnite Wars, 343 *B. C.*

178. Postea Romāni bellum gessērunt[3] cum Samni-
tĭbŭs, ad quod Lucius Papirius Cursor cum honōre dictatōris profectus est.⟩ Qui[4] quum negotii cujusdam causā
Romam redīret,[5] praecēpit Quinto Fabio Rulliāno, magistro equĭtum, quem apud exercĭtum relīquit, ne pugnam cum hoste committĕret.[6] Sed ille occasiōnem
nactus[7] felicissĭme dimicāvit, Samnītes delēvit. Ob
hanc rem a dictatōre capĭtis[8] damnātus est. At ille in
urbem confūgit,[9] et ingenti favōre[10] milĭtum et popŭli
liberātus est; in Papirium autem tanta exorta[11] est
seditio, ut paene ipse interficerētur.[12]

The Roman Army is made to pass under the yoke, 321 *B. C.—The
Samnites are conquered*, 290 *B. C.*

179. Duōbus annis[13] post Titus Veturius et Spurius
Postumius consŭles bellum adversum Samnītes gerēbant.
Hi a Pontio Thelesīno, duce hostium, in insidias inducti
sunt.⟋ Nam ad Furcŭlas Caudīnas Romānos pellexit[14] in
angustias, unde sese expedīre non potĕrant. Ibi Pontius
patrem suum Herennium rogāvit, quid faciendum[15] pu-
tāret.[16] Ille respondit, *aut omnes occidendos esse, ut*

---

[1] 419, 2, 1).	[7] 283.	[12] 494.
[2] 332, I. 2).	[8] 410, 2.	[13] 418.
[3] 272, I.	[9] 273, II.	[14] 272, I. 2.
[4] 453.	[10] 414, 4.	[15] 545, 3.
[5] 518, II.	[11] 283, 2.	[16] 374, 4; 525.
[6] 492, 2.		

Romanōrum vires frangerentur,[1] *aut omnes dimittendos, ut beneficio obligarentur.* Pontius utrumque[2] consilium improbāvit, omnesque sub jugum misit. Samnītes denīque post bellum undequinquaginta annōrum superāti sunt.

War with Pyrrhus, 281 B. C.

180. Devictis Samnitĭbus,[3] Tarentīnis bellum indictum est, quia legātis Romanōrum injuriam fecissent.[4] Hi Pyrrhum, Epīri regem, contra Romānos auxilium poposcērunt.[5] Is mox in Italiam venit, tumque primum Romāni cum transmarīno hoste pugnavērunt. Missus est contra eum consul Publius Valerius Laevīnus. Hic, quum exploratōres Pyrrhi cepisset,[6] jussit eos per castra duci, tumque dimitti, ut renuntiārent[7] Pyrrho, quaecunque[7] a Romānis agerentur.[8]

181. Pugnā commissā,[9] Pyrrhus auxilio elephantōrum vicit. Nox proelio finem dedit. Laevīnus tamen per noctem fugit. Pyrrhus Romānos mille octingentos cepit, eosque summo[9] honōre[10] tractāvit. Quum eos, qui in proelio interfecti erant, omnes adversis vulnerĭbus et truci vultu etiam mortuos jacēre vidēret,[8] tulisse ad coelum manus dicĭtur cum hac voce: *"Ego cum talĭbus viris*[11] *brevi orbem*[12] *terrārum subigĕrem."*[11]

182. Postea Pyrrhus Romam perrexit; omnia ferro ignēque vastāvit; Campaniam depopulātus est, atque ad Praeneste[13] venit, milliario[14] ab urbe octāvo decĭmo. Mox terrōre exercĭtus,[15] qui cum consŭle sequebātur, in Campaniam se recēpit. Legāti ad Pyrrhum de captīvis

---

[1] 491.	[6] 518, II.	[11] 503, 2, 2); 510.
[2] 151, 4.	[7] 445, 6.	[12] 107, 2
[3] 431, 2, (1).	[8] 527.	[13] 379, 1.
[4] 520, II.	[9] 163, 3.	[14] 422, 1.
[5] 273, I. 2.	[10] 414, 3.	[15] 396, II.

redimendis¹ missi² honorifĭce ab eo suscepti sunt ; captīvos sine pretio reddĭdit. Unum ex legātis, Fabricium,
sic admirātus est, ut ei quartam partem regni sui pro-
mittĕret,³ si ad se transīret ;⁴ sed a Fabricio contemptus⁵
est.

183. Quum jam Pyrrhus ingenti Romanōrum admi-
ratiōne tenerētur,⁶ legātum misit Cineam, praestantissĭ-
mum virum, qui pacem petĕret⁷ eā conditiōne, ut
Pyrrhus eam partem Italiae, quam armis occupavĕrat,
retinēret.⁸ Romāni respondērunt, eum cum Romānis
pacem habēre non posse, nisi ex Italiā recessisset.⁹ Cineas
quum rediisset, Pyrrho eum interroganti, qualis ipsi
Roma visa esset, ¹⁰ respondit, *se regum patriam vidisse.*¹¹

184. In altĕro proelio Pyrrhus vulnerātus est, ele-
phanti interfecti, viginti millia hostium caesa sunt.
Pyrrhus Tarentum fugit. Interjecto anno, Fabricius
contra eum missus est. Ad hunc medĭcus Pyrrhi nocte
venit promittens, se Pyrrhum venēno occisūrum,¹² si
munus sibi darētur.⁴ Hunc Fabricius vinctum redūci
jussit ad domĭnum. Tunc rex admirātus illum dixisse
fertur : "*Ille est Fabricius, qui difficilius ab honestāte,
quam sol a cursu suo averti potest.*" Paulo post Pyrrhus, tertio etiam proelio fusus,¹³ a Tarento recessit.

---

¹ 566, II. ; 580.	⁶ 518, II.	¹⁰ 525.
² 577.	⁷ 500, 1.	¹¹ 542, 1.
³ 494.	⁸ 495, 3.	¹² 545, 3.
⁴ 509.	⁹ 533, 4.	¹³ 273, II. 2.
⁵ 281.		

PERIOD III.—ROMAN TRIUMPHS.

FROM THE FIRST PUNIC WAR TO THE CONQUEST OF GREECE, 146 B. C.

First Punic War, 264 *B. C.*

185. Anno quadringentesĭmo nonagesĭmo post urbem condĭtam Romanōrum exercĭtus primum in Siciliam trajecērunt,[1] regemque Syracusārum Hierōnem, Poenosque, qui multas civitātes in eā insŭlā occupavĕrant, superavērunt. Quinto anno hujus belli, quod contra Poenos gerebātur, primum Romāni, Caio Duillio, Cnaeo Cornelio Asĭnā consulĭbus,[2] mari[3] dimicavērunt. Duillius Carthaginienses vicit,[4] triginta naves occupāvit, quattuordĕcim mersit,[5] septem millia hostium cepit, tria millia occīdit. Nulla victoria Romānis gratior fuit.

First Punic War, continued.—Invasion of Africa, 256 *B. C.*

186. Paucis annis interjectis, bellum in Afrĭcam est translātum. Hamilcar, Carthaginiensium dux, pugnā navāli superātus est ; nam, perdĭtis sexaginta quattuor navĭbus, se recēpit ; Romāni viginti duas amisērunt. Quum in Afrĭcam venissent,[6] Poenos in plurĭbus[7] proeliis vicērunt, magnam vim[8] homĭnum cepērunt, septuaginta quattuor civitātes in fidem accepērunt. Tum victi Carthaginienses pacem a Romānis petiērunt.[9] Quam[10] quum Marcus Atilius Regŭlus, Romanōrum dux, dare nollet[11] nisi durissĭmis conditionĭbus, Carthaginienses auxilium petiērunt a Lacedaemoniis. Hi Xanthippum

---

[1] 461, 1 ; 200, 2, 1).   [5] 258, I. 1.   [9] 234.

[2] 431.   [6] 518, II.   [10] 453.

[3] 422, 1.   [7] 165, 1.   [11] 518.

[4] 273, II.   [8] 66.

misērunt, qui Romānum exercĭtum magno proelio vicit. Regŭlus ipse captus et in vincŭla conjectus est.

187. Non tamen ubīque fortūna Carthaginiensĭbus favit.[1] Quum alĭquot proeliis victi essent,[2] Regŭlum rogavērunt, ùt Romam proficiscerētur,[3] et pacem captivorumque permutatiōuem a Romānis impetrāret. Ille quum Romam venisset, inductus in senātum dixit, *se desiisse*[4] *Romānum esse ex illā die, quā*[5] *in potestātem Poenōrum venisset.*[6] Tum Romānis suasit,[7] ne pacem cum Carthaginiensĭbus facĕrent: *illos enim tot casĭbus fractos spem nullam nisi in pāce habēre:*[8] *tanti*[10] *non esse, ut tot millia captivōrum propter se unum et paucos, qui ex Romānis capti essent,*[9] *redderentur.*[11] Haec sententia obtinuit. Regressus igĭtur in Afrĭcam crudelissĭmis suppliciis exstinctus est.[12]

End of the First Punic War, 241 B. C.

188. Tandem, Caio Luꞔatio Catŭlo, Aulo Postumio consulĭbus, anno belli Punĭci vicesĭmo tertio magnum proelium navāle commissum est contra Lilybaeum, promontorium Siciliae. In eo proelio septuaginta tres Carthaginiensium naves captae, centum viginti quinque demersae,[13] triginta duo millia hostium capta, tredĕcim millia occīsa sunt. Statim Carthaginienses pacem petiĕrunt, eisque pax tribūta[14] est. Captīvi Romanōrum, qui tenebantur a Carthaginiensĭbus, reddĭti sunt. Poeni Siciliā,[15] Sardiniā, et cetĕris insŭlis, quae inter Italium Africamque jacent, decessērunt, omnemque Hispaniam, quae citra Ibērum est, Romānis permisērunt.

---

[1] 270.
[2] 518, II.
[3] 492, 2; 374, 4.
[4] 234.
[5] 426.
[6] 531.
[7] 269.
[8] 492, 2.
[9] 530, 1.
[10] 402, 1.
[11] 495, 2.
[12] 272, I.
[13] 272, II.
[14] 279.
[15] 434, 1.

Siege of Saguntum.—The Second Punic War, 218 *B. C.*

189. Paulo¹ post Punĭcum bellum renovātum est per Hannibălem, Carthaginiensium ducem, quem pater² Hamilcar novem annos³ natum aris⁴ admovĕrat, ut odium perenne in Romānos jurūret.⁵ Hic annum agens vicesĭmum aetātis Saguntum, Hispaniae civitātem, Romānis⁶ amīcam, oppugnāre aggressus est.⁷ Huic Romāni per legātos denuntiavērunt, ut bello⁸ abstinēret.⁹ Qui quum legātos admittĕre nollet,¹⁰ Romāni Carthagĭnem misērunt, ut mandarētur⁴ Hannibăli, ne bellum contra socios popŭli Romāni gerĕret.¹¹ Dura responsa a Carthaginiensĭbus reddĭta. Saguntīnis interea fame victis, Romāni Carthaginiensĭbus bellum indixērunt.

Hannibal crosses the Alps, 218 *B. C.—Battles of the Ticĭnus, Trebia, and Lake Trasimēnus.—Battle of Cannae,* 216 *B. C.*

190. Hannĭbal, fratre Hasdrubăle in Hispaniā relicto,¹² Pyrenaeum et Alpes transiit. Tradĭtur in Italiam octoginta millia pedĭtum, et viginti millia equĭtum, septem et triginta elephantos abduxisse. Interea multi Ligŭres et Galli Hannibăli se conjunxērunt. Primus¹³ ei occurrit Publius Cornelius Scipio, qui, proelio ad Ticīnum commisso, superātus est, et, vulnĕre accepto,¹³ in castra rediit. Tum Sempronius Gracchus conflixit ad Trebiam amnem. Is quoque vincĭtur.¹⁴ Multi popŭli se Hannibăli dedidērunt. Inde in Etrūriam progressus Flaminium consulem ad Trasimēnum lacum supĕrat.¹⁴

---

¹ 418.
² 447.
³ 378.
⁴ 386.
⁵ 491.

⁶ 391.
⁷ 283.
⁸ 425, 2.
⁹ 492, 2.
¹⁰ 518.

¹¹ 492.
¹² 431, 2, (3).
¹³ 442, 1.
¹⁴ 467, III.

Ipse Flaminius interemptus, Romanōrum viginti quinque millia caesa sunt.

191. Quingentesĭmo duodequadragesĭmo anno post urbem condĭtam Lucius Aemilius Paulus et Caius Terentius Varro contra Hannibălem mittuntur. ⁊ Quamquam intellectum erat, Hannibălem non alĭter vinci posse quam morā, Varro tamen, morae¹ impatiens, apud vicum, qui Cannae appellātur, in Apuliā pugnāvit; ambo consŭles victi, Paulus interemptus est. In eā pugnā consulāres aut praetorii viginti, senatōres triginta capti aut occīsi;² milĭtum quadraginta millia, equĭtum tria millia et quingenti periērunt. In his tantis malis nemo tamen pacis mentiōnem facĕre dignātus est. Servi, quod³ nunquam ante factum,³ manumissi et milĭtes facti sunt.

192. Post eam pugnam multae Italiae civitātes, quae Romānis⁴ paruĕrant, se ad Hannibălem transtulērunt.⁵ Hannĭbal Romānis obtŭlit, ut captīvos redimĕrent;⁶ responsumque est a senātu, *eos cives non esse necessarios, qui armāti capi potuissent.*⁷ Hos omnes ille postea variis suppliciis interfēcit, et trēs modios aureōrum annulōrum Carthagĭnem misit, quos manĭbus⁸ equĭtum Romanōrum et senatōrum detraxĕrat.⁹ Interea in Hispaniā frater Hannibălis, Hasdrŭbal, qui ibi remansĕrat¹⁰ cum magno exercĭtu, a duōbus Scipionĭbus vincĭtur,¹¹ perditque in pugnā triginta quinque millia homĭnum.

193. In Siciliā res prospĕre gesta est.¹² Marcellus magnam hujus insŭlae partem cepit, quam Poeni occu-

---

¹ 399, 2.	⁵ 292, 2.	⁹ 258, I. 1.
² 460, 8.	⁶ 492.	¹⁰ 269.
³ 445, 7.	⁷ 500, 2.	¹¹ 467, III.
⁴ 385.	⁸ 386, 2.	¹² 272, I.

pavĕrant ; Syracūsas, nobilissĭmam urbem, expugnāvit, et ingentem inde praedam Romam [1] misit. Laevīnus in Macedoniā cum Philippo et multis Graeciae popŭlis amicitiam fecit ; et in Siciliam profectus [2] Hannōnem, Poenōrum ducem, apud Agrigentum cepit ; quadraginta civitātes in deditiōnem accēpit, viginti sex expugnāvit. Ita omni Siciliā receptā,[3] cum ingenti gloriā Romam regressus est.

194. Interea in Hispaniam, ubi duo Scipiōnes ab Hasdrubăle interfecti erant, missus est Publius Cornelius Scipio, vir Romanōrum omnium fere primus.[4] Hic, puer duodeviginti annōrum, in pugnā ad Ticīnum, patrem singulāri virtūte servāvit. Deinde post cladem Cannensem multos nobilissimōrum juvĕnum Italiam deserĕre cupientium,[5] auctoritāte suā ab hoc consilio deterruit. Viginti quattuor annos natus in Hispaniam missus, die,[6] quā venit, Carthagĭnem Novam cepit, in quā omne aurum et argentum et belli apparātum Poeni habēbant, nobilissĭmos quoque obsĭdes,[7] quos ab Hispānis accepĕrant. Hos obsĭdes parentĭbus reddĭdit. Quare omnes fere Hispaniae civitātes ad eum uno anĭmo [8] transiērunt.

195. Anno quarto decĭmo postquam in Italiam Hannĭbal venĕrat, Scipio consul creātus, et in Afrĭcam missus est. Ibi contra Hannōnem, ducem Carthaginiensium, prospĕre pugnat, totumque ejus exercĭtum delet.[9] Secundo proclio undĕcim millia homĭnum occīdit, et castra cepit cum quattuor millĭbus et quingentis militĭbus. Quā [10] re audītā,[9] omnis fere Italia Hannibălem desĕrit. Ipse a Carthaginiensĭbus in Afrĭcam redīre jubētur. Ita Italia liberāta est.

---

[1] 379.	[5] 577.	[8] 414, 3.
[2] 283.	[6] 426.	[9] 264.
[3] 431, 2, (3).	[7] 81, 2.	[10] 453.
[4] 166.		

Battle of Zama, 202 B. C.

196. Post plures pugnas et pacem plus semel frustra tentātam, pugna ad Zamam committĭtur, in quā peritissĭmi duces copias suas ad bellum educēbant. Scipio victor recēdit; Hannĭbal cum paucis equitĭbus evādit. Post hoc proelium pax cum Carthaginiensĭbus facta est. Scipio, quum Romam rediisset,[1] ingenti gloriā triumphāvit, atque Africānus appellātus est. Sic finem accēpit secundum Punĭcum bellum post annum undevicesĭmum quam[2] coepĕrat.

War with Philip.—Cynoscephalae, 197 B. C.

197. Finīto Punĭco bello, secūtum est Macedonĭcum contra Philippum regem. Superātus est rex a Tito Quinctio Flaminio apud Cynoscephălas, paxque ei data est.

War with Perseus.—Pydna, 168 B. C.

198. Philippo, rege Macedoniae, mortuo, filius ejus Perseus rebellāvit, ingentĭbus copiis parātis. Dux Romanōrum, Publius Licinius consul, contra eum missus, gravi proelio a rege victus est. Rex tamen pacem petēbat. Cui[3] Romāni eam praestāre noluērunt,-nisi his conditionĭbus, ut se et suos Romānis dedĕret.[4] Mox Aemilius Paulus consul regem ad Pydnam superāvit, et viginti millia pedĭtum ejus occīdit. Equitātus cum rege fugit. Urbes Macedoniae omnes, quas rex tenuĕrat, Romānis se dedidērunt. Ipse Perseus ab amīcis desertus in Pauli potestātem venit. Hic, multis etiam aliis rebus gestis,[5] cum ingenti pompā Romam rediit in nave Persei, inusitātae magnitudĭnis;[6] nam sedĕcim remōrum ordĭnes

---

[1] 518, II.
[2] 427, 3.
[3] 453.
[4] 495, 3.
[5] 431, 2, (3).
[6] 396, IV.

habuisse dicĭtur. Triumphāvit magnificentissĭme¹ in curru aureo, duōbus filiis utrōque latĕre² adstantibus. Ante currum inter captīvos duo regis filii et ipse Perseus ducti sunt.

Third Punic War, 149 B. C.

199. Tertium deinde bellum contra Carthagĭnem susceptum est. Lucius Marcius Censorīnus et Manius Manlius consŭles in Afrĭcam trajecĕrunt, et oppugnavē-runt Carthagĭnem. Multa ibi praeclāre gesta sunt per Scipiōnem,³ Scipiōnis Africāni nepōtem, qui tribūuus⁴ in Afrĭcā militābat.

200. Quum jam magnum esset⁵ Scipiōnis nomen, tertio anno postquam Romāni in Afrĭcam trajecĕrant, consul est creātus, et contra Carthagĭnem missus. Is hanc urbem a civĭbus acerrĭme⁶ defensam⁷ cepit ac diruit. Ingens ibi praeda facta, plurimăque inventa sunt, quae multārum civitātum excidiis Carthāgo collegĕrat. Haec omnia Scipio civitatĭbus Italiae, Siciliae, Afrĭcae reddĭ-dit, quae sua recognoscēbant. Ita Carthāgo septingente-sĭmo anno, postquam condĭta erat, delēta est. Scipio nomen Africāni juniōris⁸ accēpit.

---

¹ 305; 164. ⁴ 363. ⁷ 578, IV.
² 422, 1. ⁵ 518, II. ⁸ 168, 3.
³ 414, 5, 1). ⁶ 305; 168, 1.

PERIOD IV.—CIVIL DISSENSIONS.

FROM THE CONQUEST OF GREECE TO THE DISSOLUTION OF THE ROMAN COMMON-WEALTH, 31 B. C.

Numantia taken, 133 *B. C.*

201. Deinde bellum exortum est cum Numantīnis, civitūte Hispaniae. Victus[1] ab his Quintus Pompēius, et post eum Caius Hostilius Mancīnus consul, qui pacem cum iis fecit infāmem, quam popŭlus et senātus jussit[2] infringi, atque ipsum Mancīnum hostĭbus tradi. Tum Publius Scipio Africānus in Hispaniam missus est. Is primum milĭtem ignāvum et corruptum correxit;[3] tum multas Hispaniae civitātes partim bello cepit, partim in deditiōnem accēpit. Postrēmo ipsam Numantiam fame ad deditiōnem coēgit, urbemque evertit; relĭquam[4] provinciam in fidem accēpit.

Mithridatic War.—First Civil War.—Marius, Sulla, 88 *B. C.*

202. Anno urbis condĭtae sexcentesĭmo sexagesĭmo sexto primum Romae bellum civīle exortum est; eōdem anno etiam Mithridatĭcum. Causam bello civīli Caius Marius dedit. Nam quum Sullae bellum adversus Mithridātem, regem Ponti, decrētum esset,[5] Marius ei[6] hunc honōrem eripĕre conātus est. Sed Sulla, qui adhuc cum legionĭbus suis in Italiā morabātur,[7] cum exercĭtu Romam venit, et adversarios quum[8] interfēcit, tum fugāvit. Tum rebus Romae utcunque composĭtis, in Asiam profectus est, pluribusque proeliis Mithridātem coēgit, ut pacem a

---

[1] 460, 3.	[4] 441, 6.	[7] 468.
[2] 463, 3.	[5] 518, II.	[8] 587, I. 5.
[3] 214, I.	[6] 386, 2.	

Romānis petĕret,[1] et Asiā, quam invasĕrat, relictā, regni sui finĭbus[2] contentus esset.

Civil War, continued.

203. Sed dum Sulla in Graeciā et Asiā Mithridātem vincit,[3] Marius, qui fugātus fuĕrat, et Cornelius Cinna, unus ex consulĭbus,[4] bellum in Italiā reparārunt,[5] et ingressi Romam nobilissĭmos ex senatu et consulāres viros interfecērunt; multos proscripsērunt; ipsīus Sullae domo eversā, filios et uxōrem ad fugam compulērunt.[6] Universus relīquus senātus ex urbe fugiens ad Sullam in Graeciam venit, orans ut patriae subvenīret.[7] Sulla in Italiam trajēcit, hostium exercĭtus vicit,[8] mox etiam urbem ingressus est, quam caede[9] et sanguĭne civium replēvit. Quattuor millia inermium,[10] qui se dedidĕrant, interfĭci jussit; duo millia equĭtum et senatōrum proscripsit.[10] Tum de Mithridāte triumphāvit. Duo haec bella funestissĭma, Italĭcum, quod et sociāle dictum est, et civīle, ultra centum et quinquaginta millia homĭnum, viros consulāres viginti quattuor, praetorios septem, aedilitios sexaginta, senatōres fere ducentos consumpsērunt.[11]

War of the Gladiators.—Spartacus, 73 B. C.

204. Anno urbis sexcentesĭmo octogesĭmo primo novum in Italiā bellum commōtum[12] est. Septuaginta enim quattuor gladiatōres, ducĭbus[13] Spartăco, Crixo, et Oenomao, e ludo gladiatorio, qui Capuae[14] erat, effugērunt, et per Italiam vagantes paene non levius bellum,

---

[1] 492, 2.
[2] 419, IV.
[3] 467, 4.
[4] 398, 4.
[5] 234.
[6] 273, I. 2.
[7] 273, II.
[8] 419, 2, 1).
[9] 441.
[10] 258, I. 3.
[11] 258, I. 4.
[12] 270, II.
[13] 430, 431.
[14] 421, II.

quam Hannĭbal, movērunt.' Nam contraxērunt' exercĭtum fere sexaginta millium armatōrum, multosque
duces et duos Romānos consŭles vicērunt. Ipsi victi
sunt in Apuliā a Marco Licinio Crasso proconsŭle, et,
post multas calamitātes Italiae, tertiŭ anno' huic bello
finis est imposĭtus.

Pompey puts down the Pirates, 67 *B. C.*—*Is appointed successor to
Lucullus.—Death of Mithridates*, 63 *B. C.*

205. Per illa tempŏra pirātae omnia maria infestā-
bant ita, ut Romānis,' toto orbe' terrārum victorĭbus,
sola navigatio tuta non esset.' Quare id bellum Cnaeo
Pompēio decrētum est, quod intra paucos menses incre-
dibĭli felicitāte et celeritāte confēcit. Mox ei delātum'
bellum contra regem Mithridātem et Tigrānem. Quo'
suscepto, Mithridātem in Armeniā Minōre nocturno
proelio vicit, castra diripuit, et quadraginta millĭbus ejus
occīsis, viginti tantum de exercĭtu suo perdĭdit et duos
centuriōnes. Mithridātes fugit' cum uxōre et duōbus
comitĭbus," neque" multo post, Pharnăcis filii sui sedi-
tiōne coactus," venēnum hausit." Hunc vitae finem
habuit Mithridātes, vir ingentis industriae atque consilii.
Regnāvit annis" sexaginta, vixit septuaginta duōbus:
contra Romānos bellum habuit annis quadraginta.

Victories of Pompey over Tigranes : he takes Jerusalem, 63 *B. C.*

206. Tigrăni deinde Pompēius bellum intŭlit. Ille
se ei dedĭdit, et in castra Pompēii venit, ac diadēma

' 270.	' 494.	" 587, I. 2.
' 272.	' 292, 2 ; 460, 3.	" 273, II.
' 426.	' 453 ; 431, 2, (3).	" 286, I.
' 391.	' 273, II.	" 378, 1.
' 422, 1, 1).	" 81.	

suum in ejus manĭbus collocāvit, quod ci Pompēius reposuit. Parte¹ regni eum multāvit et grandi pecuniā. Tum alios etiam reges et popŭlos superāvit. Armeniam Minōrem Deiotăro,² Galatiae regi, donāvit, quia auxilium contra Mithridātem tulĕrat. Seleuciam, vicīnam Antiochīae³ civitātem, libertāte⁴ donāvit, quod regem Tigrānem non recepisset.⁴ Inde in Judaeam transgressus, Hierosolȳmam, caput gentis, tertio mense cepit, duodĕcim millĭbus Judaeōrum occīsis, cetĕris in fidem receptis. His⁵ gestis finem antiquissĭmo bello imposuit. Ante triumphantis currum ducti sunt filii Mĭthridātis, filius Tigrānis, et Aristobūlus, rex Judaeōrum. Praelāta ingens pecunia, auri atque argenti infinītum pondus. Hoc tempŏre nullum per orbem terrārum grave bellum erat.

Catiline's Conspiracy, 63 B. C.

207. Marco Tullio Cicerōne⁶ oratūre et Caio Antonio consulĭbus, anno ab urbe condĭtā⁷ sexcentesĭmo nonagesĭmo primo Lucius Sergius Catilīna, nobilissĭmi genĕris vir, sed ingenii pravissĭmi, ad delendam⁸ patriam conjurāvit cum quibusdam claris quidem, sed audacĭbus viris. A Cicerōne urbe⁹ expulsus est, socii ejus deprehensi et in carcĕre strangulāti sunt. Ab Antonio, altĕro consŭle, Catilīna ipse proelio victus est et interfectus.

Caesar Consul, 59 B. C.: in Gaul, 58 B. C.

208. Anno urbis condĭtae sexcentesĭmo nonagesĭmo quinto Caius Julius Caesar cum Lucio Bibŭlo consul est factus. Quum ei Gallia decrēta esset,¹⁰ semper vincendo¹¹

---

¹ 425, 2, 2).	⁵ 414.	⁹ 425.
² 384, 1.	⁶ 430, 431.	¹⁰ 518, II.
³ 391.	⁷ 580.	¹¹ 566, L
⁴ 520, II.	⁸ 565, 1.	

usque ad Oceănum Britannĭcum procĕssit.[1] Domuit[2]
autem annis novem fere omnem Galliam, quae inter
Alpes, flumen Rhodănum, Rhenum et Oceănum est.
Britannis mox bellum intŭlit,[3] quibus[4] ante eum ne
nomeu quidem Romanōrum cognĭtum[5] erat; Germā-
nos quoque trans Rhenum aggressus, ingentĭbus proeliis
vicit.

Civil War of Pompey and Caesar, 49 B. C.

209. Bellum civīle successit,[1] quo Romāni nomĭnis
fortūna mutāta est. Caesar enim victor e Galliā rediens,
absens coepit poscĕre altĕrum consulātum; quem[6] quum
multi sine dubitatiōne deferrent,[7] contradictum est a
Pompēio et aliis, jussusque est, dimissis exercitĭbus, in
urbem redīre. Propter hanc injuriam ab Arimĭno, ubi
milĭtes congregātos[8] habēbat, infesto exercĭtu[9] Romam
contendit. Consŭles cum Pompēio, senatusque omnis
atque universa nobilĭtas ex urbe fugit,[10] et in Graeciam
transiit; et, dum senātus bellum contra Caesărem parā-
bat, hic vacuam urbem ingressus dictatōrem se fecit.

*Defeat of Pompey's party in Spain.—Battle of Pharsalia, 48 B. C.
—Death of Pompey.*

210. Inde Hispanias petiit,[11] ibīque Pompēii legiōnes
superāvit; tum in Graeciā adversum Pompēium ipsum
dimicāvit. Primo proelio victus est et fugātus; evāsit[12]
tamen, quia, nocte interveniente, Pompēius sequi no-
luit;[13] dixitque Caesar, nec Pompēium scire vincĕre, et
illo tantum die se potuisse superāri. Deinde in Thessaliā apud Pharsālum ingentĭbus utrimque copiis[14] com-

[1] 258, I. 2.	[6] 453.	[11] 234.
[2] 260.	[7] 518.	[12] 272, II.
[3] 292, 2.	[8] 388, 1, 2).	[13] 293.
[4] 391.	[9] 414, 7.	[14] 414.
[5] 575.	[10] 463, I.	

missis dimicavērunt. Nunquam adhuc Romānae copiae
majōres neque meliorĭbus ducĭbus¹ convenĕrant. Pug-
nātum est² ingenti contentiōne,³ victusque ad postrēmum
Pompēius, et castra ejus direpta sunt. Ipse fugātus
Alexandrīam petiit, ut a rege Aegypti, cui tutor⁴ a senātu datus fuĕrat, accipĕret⁵ auxilia. At hic fortūnam
magis quam amicitiam secūtus,⁶ occīdit Pompēium, caput
ejus et annŭlum Caesări misit. Quo⁷ conspecto, Caesar
lacrĭmas fudisse⁸ dicĭtur, tanti viri intuens caput, et genĕri quondam⁹ sui.

Caesar assassinated in the Senate-House, 44 B. C.

211. Quum ad Alexandrīam venisset Caesar, Ptolemaeus ei insidias parāre voluit, quā de causā regi bellum
illātum¹⁰ est. Rex victus in Nīlo periit, inventumque
est corpus ejus cum lorīcā aureā. Caesar, Alexandrīā¹¹
potītus, regnum Cleopātrae dedit.¹² Tum inde profec-
tus⁹ Pompeiānārum partium reliquias est persecūtus,
bellisque¹³ civilĭbus toto terrārum orbe¹⁴ composĭtis, Romam rediit. Ubi quum insolentius¹⁵ agĕre coepisset,¹⁶
conjurātum est in eum a sexaginta vel amplius senatorĭbus, equitibusque Romānis. Praecipui fuĕrunt inter
conjurātos¹⁷ Bruti duo ex genĕre illīus Bruti, qui, regĭbus expulsis, primus Romae consul fuĕrat. Ergo Caesar,
quum in curiam venisset, viginti tribus vulnerĭbus confossus est.

---

¹ 414, 7.	⁷ 453; 431, 2, (3).	¹³ 431, 2, (3).
² 301, 1	⁸ 273, II. 2.	¹⁴ 422, 1, 1).
³ 414, 3.	⁹ 583,2.	¹⁵ 444, 1 & 4.
⁴ 362.	¹⁰ 292, 2.	¹⁶ 297.
⁵ 491.	¹¹ 419.	¹⁷ 575.
⁶ 283.	¹² 261.	

The Second Triumvirate, Octavius, Antony, and Lepidus, 43 B. C.—
Death of Cicero.

212. Interfecto Caesăre, anno urbis septingentesĭmo
decĭmo bella civilia reparāta sunt. Senātus favēbat
Caesăris percussorĭbus,[1] Antonius consul a Caesăris par-
tĭbus stabat. Ergo turbātā re publĭcā, Antonius, multis
scelerĭbus commissis, a senātu hostis[2] judicātus est.
Fusus fugatusque Antonius, amisso exercĭtu, confūgit ad
Lepĭdum, qui Caesări[3] magister equĭtum fuĕrat, et tum
grandes copias milĭtum habēbat; a quo susceptus est.
Mox Octaviānus cum Antonio pacem fecit, et quasi vin-
dicatūrus patris sui mortem, a quo per testamentum
fuĕrat adoptātus, Romam cum exercĭtu profectus extorsit,[4] ut sibi, juvĕni vigĭnti annōrum, consulātus darētur.[5]
Tum junctus cum Antonio et Lepĭdo rem publĭcam armis tenēre coepit, senatumque proscripsit. Per hos etiam
Cicĕro orātor occīsus est, multīque alii nobĭles.[6]

Battle of Philippi, 42 B. C.

213. Interea Brutus et Cassius, interfectōres Caesăris, ingens bellum movērunt.[7] Profecti[8] contra eos
Caesar Octaviānus, qui postea Augustus est appellātus,
et Marcus Antonius, apud Philippos, Macedoniae urbem,
contra eos pugnavērunt.[9] Primo proelio victi sunt Antonius et Caesar; periit[10] tamen dux nobilitātis Cassius;
secundo Brutum et infinītam nobilitātem, quae cum illis
bellum suscepĕrat, victam[11] interfecērunt. Tum victōres rem publĭcam ita inter se divisērunt,[12] ut Octaviā-

---

[1] 385.
[2] 302.
[3] 390, 2.
[4] 269, II.
[5] 492, 1.
[6] 460, 3.
[7] 270.
[8] 439.
[9] 463, II.
[10] 295, 3.
[11] 579.
[12] 272, II.

nus Caesar Hispanias, Gallias, Italiam teneret :[1] Antonius Orientem, Lepidus Africam acciperet.

Battle of Actium, 81 B. C.

214. Paulo[2] post Antonius, repudiātā sorōre Caesăris Octaviāni, Cleopātram, regīnam Aegypti, uxōrem duxit. Ab hac incitātus ingens bellum commōvit, dum Cleopātra cupiditāte muliĕbri optat Romae regnāre. Victus est ab Augusto navāli pugnā clarā et illustri apud Actium, qui[3] locus in Epīro est. Hinc fugit iu Aegyptum, et, desperātis rebus, quum omnes ad Augustum transīrent,[4] se ipse interēmit.[5] Cleopātra quoque aspĭdem sibi admīsit, et venēno ejus exstincta[6] est. Ita bellis toto orbe[7] confectis, Octaviānus Augustus Romam rediit anno duodecĭmo postquam consul fuĕrat. Ex eo inde tempŏre rem publĭcam per quadraginta et quattuor annos solus obtinuit. Ante enim duodĕcim annis[8] cum Antonio et Lepĭdo tenuĕrat. Ita ab initio principātus ejus usque ad finem quinquaginta sex anni fuĕre.

---

[1] 494.
[2] 418.
[3] 445, 8.

[4] 518.
[5] 278, II.
[6] 281.

[7] 422, 1, 1).
[8] 378, 1.

NOTE.—It is recommended that, in reading the Grecian History, special attention should be given to *Irregular, Defective,* and *Impersonal ,Verbs.*— 289-301.

PERIOD I.—GRECIAN TRIUMPHS.

FROM THE PERSIAN INVASION, 490 B. C., TO THE PELOPONNESIAN WAR, 431 B. C.

Darius invades Scythia: prepares to invade Greece.

215. Multis in Asiā felicĭter gestis, Darīus Scythis bellum intŭlit,[1] et armātis septingentis millĭbus[2] homĭnum Scythiam[3] ingressus, quum hostes ei pugnae potestātem non facĕrent,[4] metuens, ne, interrupto ponte Istri, redītus sibi intercluderētur,[5] amissis octoginta millĭbus homĭnum, trepĭdus refūgit. Inde Macedoniam domuit: et quum ex Eurōpā in Asiam rediisset,[6] hortantĭbus amīcis ut Graeciam redigĕret[7] in suam potestātem, classem quingentārum navium comparāvit, eīque Datim[8] praefēcit et Artaphernen;[9] hisque ducenta pedĭtum millia, et decem equĭtum dedit.

Battle of Marathon, 490 B. C.

216. Praefecti regii, classe ad Euboeam appulsā, celerĭter Eretriam cepērunt. Inde ad Attĭcam accessērunt, ac suas copias in Campum Marathōna deduxērunt.

---

[1] 292, 2.	[4] 518, II.	[7] 492, 2.
[2] 414, 7.	[5] 492, 4.	[8] 62, II. 2.
[3] 371, 4.	[6] 295, 3.	[9] 68.

Is abest ab oppĭdo circĭter millia passuum decem. Hoc
in tempŏre nulla civĭtas Atheniensĭbus[1] auxilio fuit,
praeter Plataeenses; ea mille[2] misit milĭtum. Ităque
horum adventu decem millia armatōrum complēta sunt:
quae[3] manus mirabĭli flagrābat pugnandi cupiditāte.
Athenienses copias ex urbe eduxērunt, locōque[4] idoneo
castra fecērunt; deinde postĕro die, sub montis radicĭbus
proelium commisērunt.   Datis etsi non aequum locum
vidēbat suis, tāmen, fretus numĕro[5] copiārum suārum,
confligĕre cupiēbat.   Ităque in aciem pedĭtum centum,
equĭtum decem millia produxit, proeliumque commīsit.
In quo tanto[6] plus virtūte valuērunt Athenienses, ut de-
cemplĭcem numĕrum hostium profligārint;[7] adeōque
perterruērunt, ut Persae non castra, sed naves petiĕrint.
Quā pugnā nihil est nobilius; nulla enim unquam tam
exigua manus tantas opes prostrāvit.

Xerxes invades Greece, 480 *B. C.*

217. Quum Darīus, bellum instauratūrus, in ipso
apparātu decessisset,[8] filius ejus Xerxes Eurōpam[9] cum
tantis copiis invāsit, quantas neque antea neque postea
habuit quisquam: hujus enim classis mille et ducentārum navium[10] longārum fuit, quam duo millia onerariā-
rum sequebantur: terrestres autem exercĭtus septingen-
tōrum millium pedĭtum, equĭtum quadringentōrum
millium fuērunt.   Cujus[11] de adventu quum fama in
Graeciam esset perlāta, et maxĭme Athenienses peti
dicerentur,[12] propter pugnam Marathoniam, misērunt
Delphos consultum,[13] quidnam facĕrent[14] de rebus suis.

---

[1] 390.	[6] 418.	[11] 453.
[2] 178.	[7] 234; 182, 2.	[12] 549, 4.
[3] 445, 8.	[8] 518.	[13] 569.
[4] 422, 1, 2).	[9] 371, 4.	[14] 525.
[5] 419, IV.	[10] 401.	

Deliberantĭbus Pythia respondit, ut moenĭbus ligneis se munīrent.[1] Id responsum quo valēret, quum intelligĕret nemo, Themistŏcles persuāsit, consilium esse Apollĭnis, ut in naves se suăque conferrent :[2] eum enim a deo significāri murum ligneum. Tali consilio probāto, addunt ad superiōres totĭdem naves trirēmes : suăque omnia, quae movēri potĕrant, partim Salamīna,[3] partim Troezēna, deportant ; arcem sacerdotĭbus paucisque majorĭbus natu,[4] ac sacra procuranda[5] tradunt ; reliquum oppĭdum relinquunt.

Actions at Thermopylae and Artemisium, 480 *B. C.*

218. Hujus consilium plerisque civitătibus displicē-bat, et in terrā dimicāri[6] magis placēbat. Ităque missi sunt delecti[7] cum Leonĭdā, Lacedaemoniōrum rege, qui Thermopỹlas occupārent,[8] longiusque barbăros progrĕdi non paterentur. Hi vim[9] hostium non sustinuērunt, eoque loco omnes interiērunt.[10] At classis commūnis Graeciae trecentārum navium,[11] in quā ducentae erant Atheniensium, primum apud Artemisium, inter Euboeam continentemque terram, cum classiariis regiis conflixit :[12] angustias enim Themistŏcles quaerēbat, ne multitudĭne circumirētur.[13] Hinc etsi pari proelio[14] discessĕrant, tamen eōdem loco non sunt ausi[15] manēre, quod erat pericŭlum, ne, si pars navium adversariōrum Euboeam superasset,[16] ancipĭti premerentur[17] pericŭlo. Quo factum est, ut ab Artemisio discedĕrent,[18] et exadversum Athēnas, apud Salamīna, classem suam constituĕrent.

[1] 492, 2.	[7] 575.	[13] 491.
[2] 495, 3.	[8] 500, 1.	[14] 414, 3.
[3] 68.	[9] 66.	[15] 271, 3.
[4] 429.	[10] 295, 3.	[16] 509.
[5] 578, V.	[11] 397, 2.	[17] 492, 4.
[6] 549.	[12] 258, I. 1	[18] 495, 2.

Battle of Salamis, 480 *B. C.*

219. At Xerxes, Thermopȳlis expugnātis, protĭnus accessit astu,[1] idque, nullis defendentĭbus, interfectis sacerdotĭbus, quos in arce invenĕrat, incendio delēvit. Cujus famā perterrĭti classiarii quum manēre non audērent, et plurĭmi[2] hortarentur, ut domos suas quisque discedĕrent,[3] moenĭbusque se defendĕrent; Themistŏcles unus restĭtit, et, universos pares hostĭbus esse posse[4] aiēbat,[5] dispersos testabātur peritūros, idque Eurybiădi, regi Lacedaemoniōrum, qui tum summae[6] imperii praeĕrat, fore[7] affirmābat. Quem quum minus, quam vellet,[8] movēret,[9] noctu de servis suis, quem habuit fidelissĭmum,[10] ad regem misit, ut ei nuntiāret suis verbis : *adversarios ejus in fugā esse, qui[11] si discessissent,[12] majōre cum labōre, et longinquiōre tempŏre bellum confectūrum,[13] quum singŭlos consectāri cogerētur ; quos si statim aggrederētur, brevi universos oppressūrum.* Hoc eo valēbat, ut ingratiis ad depugnandum omnes cogerentur.[14] Hac re audītā, barbărus, nihil doli subesse credens, postridie alienissĭmo sibi[15] loco, contra opportunissĭmo hostĭbus, adeo angusto mari[16] conflixit, ut ejus multitūdo navium explicāri non potuĕrit.[17] Victus ergo est magis consilio Themistŏclis, quam armis Graeciae.

Xerxes flies back into Asia.

220. Hic etsi male rem gessĕrat, tamen tantas habēbat reliquias copiārum, ut etiamtum his[18] opprimĕre

---

[1] 128; 371, 4.	[7] 297, III. 2.	[13] 545, 3.
[2] 165, 441.	[8] 527.	[14] 495.
[3] 492, 2; 461, 3.	[9] 518.	[15] 391.
[4] 290.	[10] 453, 5.	[16] 422, 1, 1).
[5] 297, II. 1.	[11] 453.	[17] 482, 2.
[6] 386.	[12] 509.	[18] 414, 4.

H

posset hostes.   Itĕrum ab eōdem gradu depulsus est.
Nam Themistŏcles, verens ne bellāre perseverāret,[1] certiōrem eum fecit, id agi,[2] ut pons,[3] quem ille in Hellesponto fecĕrat, dissolverētur,[4] ac redĭtu in Asiam exclu-
derētur.   Ităque in Asiam reversus est, seque a Themistŏcle non superātum,[5] sed conservātum judicāvit.   Sic
unīus viri prudentiā Graecia liberāta est.

Battles of Plataea and Mycale, 479 B. C.

221. Postĕro anno quam Xerxes in Asiam refugĕrat,
Graeci, duce Pausaniā, Mardonium, regis genĕrum, apud
Plataeas fudērunt :[6] quo proelio ipse dux cecĭdit,[7] Bar-
barorumque exercĭtus interfectus est.   Eōdem forte die
in Asiā, ad montem Mycălen, Persae a Graecis navāli
proelio superāti sunt.   Jamque omnĭbus pacātis, Athenienses belli damna reparāre coepērunt.[8]

PERIOD II.—CIVIL WARS IN GREECE.

FROM THE PELOPONNESIAN WAR TO THE ACCESSION OF PHILIP OF MACEDON,
860 B. C.

The Peloponnesian War, 431 B. C.—Pericles.

222. Hoc bellum, quo[9] nullum aliud florentes Graeciae res gravius afflixit, saepe susceptum et deposĭtum
est.   Initio Spartāni fines Attĭcae populabantur, hostes-
que ad proelium provocābant.   Sed Athenienses, Perĭclis
consilio,[10] ultiōnis tempus exspectantes intra moenia se

---

[1] 492, 4.	[5] 545, 3.	[8] 297.
[2] 551, 3.	[6] 273, II.	[9] 417.
[3] 110, 1.	[7] 273, I.	[10] 414, 2.
[4] 495, 3.		

continēbant. Deinde, paucis diēbus interjectis, naves conscendunt, et, nihil sentientĭbus Lacedaemoniis, totam Laconiam depraedantur. Clara quidem haec Perĭclis expeditio est habĭta; sed multo clarĭor privāti patrimonii contemptus fuit. Nam in populatiōne ceterōrum agrōrum, Perĭclis agros hostes intactos reliquērant, ut aut invidiam ei apud cives concitārent,[1] aut in proditiōnis suspiciōnem adducĕrent. Quod intellĭgens, Perĭcles agros rei publĭcae dono dedit. Post haec alĭquot diēbus interjectis, navāli proelio dimicātum est.[2] Victi Lacedaemonii fugērunt. Post plures[3] annos, fessi malis, pacem in annos quinquaginta fecēre, quam sex annos[4] servavērunt.

Expedition of the Athenians against Sicily, 415 B. C.

223. Bello inter Catinienses et Syracusānos exorto,[5] Athenienses Catiniensĭbus opem ferunt.[6] Classis ingens decernĭtur; creantur duces Nicias, Alcibiădes et Lamăchus; tantaeque vires in Siciliam effūsae sunt, ut iis ipsis terrōri[7] essent, quibus auxilio venērant. Nicias et Lamăchus duo proelia pedestria secundo Marte[8] pugnant; munitionibusque urbi Syracusārum[9] circumdătis, incōlas etiam marīnis commeatĭbus[10] interclūdunt. Quibus rebus fracti[11] Syracusāni, auxilium a Lacedaemoniis petivērunt.[12] Ab his mittĭtur Gylippus, qui auxiliis partim in Graeciā, partim in Siciliā contractis, opportūna bello loca[13] occŭpat. Duōbus deinde proeliis vic-

---

[1] 491.
[2] 301, 1.
[3] 165, 1.
[4] 378.
[5] 288, 2.
[6] 292; 467, III.
[7] 390.
[8] 414, 3; 705, II.
[9] 396, V.
[10] 386, 1.
[11] 273, II.
[12] 278, 2.
[13] 141.

tus, tertio hostes in fugam conjēcit, sociosque obsidiōne'
liberāvit. In eo proelio Lamăchus fortĭter pugnans occīsus est.

Successes of Alcibiades against the Lacedaemonians.

224. Alcibiădes summā curā ' classem instruit, atque
in bellum adversus Lacedaemonios perrexit. Hac expe-
ditiōne tanta subĭto rerum commutatio facta est,' ut Lacedaemonii, qui paulo ante victōres viguĕrant, perterrĭti
pacem petĕrent ;' victi enim erant quinque terrestrĭbus
proeliis, tribus navalĭbus, in quibus trecentas trirēmes
amisĕrant, quae captae in hostium venĕrant potestātem.
Alcibiădes simul cum collēgis recepĕrat Ioniam, Helles-
pontum, multas praeterea urbes Graecas, quae in orā
sitae sunt Asiae : quarum expugnavĕrant quam plurĭmas,
in his Byzantium ; neque minus multas consilio ad amicitiam adjunxĕrant, quod in captos clementiā ' fuĕrant
usi. Inde praedā ' onusti, locupletāto exercĭtu, maxĭmis
rebus gestis, Athēnas venērunt.

Cyrus favors Lysander and the Lacedaemonians, 407 *B. C.*

225. Dum haec geruntur, a Lacedaemoniis Lysander classi bellōque praeficĭtur ; et Darīus, rex Persārum,
filium suum, Cyrum, Ioniae Lydiaeque praeposuit, qui
Lacedaemonios auxiliis opibusque ad spem fortūnae
priōris ' erexit. Aucti ' igĭtur virĭbus ' Alcibiădem cum
centum navĭbus in Asiam profectum,'' dum agros populātur, repentīno adventu oppressēre.'' Magnae et in-
opinātae cladis nuntius quum Athēnas venisset, tanta

---

¹ 425, 3.	⁵ 419, I.	⁹ 429.
² 414, 3.	⁶ 419, III.	¹⁰ 283.
³ 294.	⁷ 166.	¹¹ 235.
⁴ 494.	⁸ 269.	

Atheniensium desperatio fuit, ut statim Conōnem in Alcibiădis locum mittĕrent, ducis se fraude magis quam belli fortūnā victos¹ arbitrantes.

Fatal defeat of the Athenians at Aegospotamos, 405 *B. C.*

226. Ităque Conon classem maxĭmā industriā adornat; sed navĭbus⁹ exercĭtus deĕrat. Nam, ut numĕrus milĭtum explerētur, senes et puĕri arma capĕre coacti sunt. Plurĭbus ităque proeliis adverso Marte pugnātis, tandem Lysander, Spartanōrum dux, Atheniensium exercĭtum, qui, navĭbus relictis, in terram praedātum¹ exiĕrat,⁴ ad Aegos flumen oppressit, eōque impĕtu totum bellum finīvit. Hac enim clade res Atheniensium penĭtus inclināta est.

Athens surrenders to Lysander, 404 *B. C.—The Thirty Tyrants.*

227. Lysander Athēnas navigāvit, miseramque civĭtātem, obsidiōne circumdătam, fame⁵ urget. Athenienses, multis fame et ferro amissis, pacem petivēre. Quum nonnulli nomen Atheniensium delendum,¹ urbemque incendio consumendam censērent,⁹ Spartāni negārunt, se passūros, ut ex duōbus Graeciae ocŭlis alter eruerētur;⁷ pacemque Atheniensĭbus sunt pollicĭti, si longi muri brachia dejicĕrent,⁸ navesque tradĕrent; denĭque si res publĭca triginta rectōres, ex civĭbus deligendos, accipĕret. His legĭbus acceptis, tota civĭtas subĭto mutāri coepit. Triginta rectōres rei publĭcae constituuntur, Lacedaemoniis⁹ et Lysandro dedĭti, qui brevi tyrannĭdem in cives exercēre coepērunt.

---

¹ 545, 3.	⁴ 295, 3.	⁷ 495, 1.
² 386, 2.	⁵ 414, 4.	⁸ 509.
³ 569.	⁶ 518, II.	⁹ 384.

Thrasybulus occupies Phyle, 404 *B. C.*

228. Quum triginta tyranni, praeposĭti a Lacedaemoniis, servitūte oppressas tenērent Athēnas, Thrasybūlus Phylen [1] confūgit, quod [2] est castellum in Attĭcā
munitissĭmum, quum non plus secum habēret, [3] quam
triginta de suis.   Hinc, virĭbus paulātim auctis, in Pirae-
um transiit, [4] Munychiamque munīvit.   Hanc bis tyranni
oppugnāre sunt adorti, ab eāque turpĭter repulsi protĭnus
in urbem, armis impedimentisque amissis, refugērunt.
In secundo proelio cecĭdit [5] Critias, triginta tyrannōrum
acerrĭmus. [6]

Epaminondas.—Battle of Leuctra, 371 *B. C.: of Mantinèa*, 362 *B. C.*

229. Epaminondas, dux Thebānus, apud Leuctra
superāvit Lacedaemonios.   Idem imperātor apud Mantinēam gravĭter vulnerātus concĭdit. [7]   Hujus casu aliquantum [8] retardāti sunt Boeotii, neque tamen prius
pugnā [9] excessērunt, quam [10] hostes profligārunt. [11]   At
Epaminondas quum animadvertĕret, mortifĕrum se vulnus accepisse, simulque, si ferrum, quod ex hastīli [12] in
corpŏre remansĕrat, extraxisset, [13] anĭmam statim emissū-
rum, usque eo retinuit, quoad renuntiātum est, vicisse [14]
Boeotios.   Id postquam audīvit, " *Satis*," inquit, " *vixi ;
invictus enim morior.*"   Tum, ferro extracto, confestim
exanimātus est.

---

[1] 50, 379.	[6] 163, 1.	[11] 234.
[2] 445, 4.	[7] 255, I. 4.	[12] 63.
[3] 518, II.	[8] 335, 4.	[13] 533, 8.
[4] 295, 3.	[9] 434, 1.	[14] 549.
[5] 273, I.	[10] 523, 2, 2).	

PERIOD III.—GRAECO-MACEDONIAN EMPIRE.

FROM THE ACCESSION OF PHILIP TO THE DEATH OF ALEXANDER, 323 B. C.

Decline of the Grecian States.—Rise of the Macedonian Power.

230. Post Leuctrĭcam pugnam Lacedaemonii se
nunquam refecērunt; et Thebae, quod,' quamdiu Epa•
minondas praefuit rei publĭcae' caput fuit totīus Graeciae, post ejus interĭtum perpetuo aliēno paruērunt imperio. Athenienses, non ut olim in classem et exercĭtum,
sed in dies festos apparatusque ludōrum redĭtus publĭcos
effundēbant, frequentiusque in theātris quam in castris
versabantur. Quibus rebus effectum est, ut obscūrum
antea Macedŏnum nomen emergĕret;' et Philippus, obses
triennio' Thebis habĭtus in Epaminondae domo, hujus
praestantissĭmi viri et Pelopĭdae virtutĭbus erudītus,
Graeciae servitūtis jugum imponĕret.

Extension of Philip's power.

231. Philippus, quum magnam gloriam apud omnes
natiōnes adeptus esset,' Olynthios aggredĭtur. Hanc urbem antīquam et nobĭlem exscindit, et praedā' ingenti
fruĭtur. Inde auraria in Thessaliā, argenti metalla in
Thraciā occŭpat. His ita gestis, forte evēnit, ut eum
fratres duo, reges Thraciae, disceptatiōnum suārum judĭ-
cem' eligĕrent.' Sed Philippus ad judicium, velut ad
bellum, instructo exercĭtu' supervēnit, et regno' utrumque spoliāvit.

Battle of Chæronea, 338 B. C.

232. Quum, in Scythiam praedandi[1] causa profeotus,[2] Scythas dolo vicisset, diu dissimulātum bellum Atheniensībus infert,[3] quorum causae Thebāni se junxērunt. Proelio ad Chaeronēam commisso, quum Athenienses longe majōre milĭtum numĕro praestārent,[4] tamen assiduis bellis[5] indurātā Macedŏnum virtūte vincuntur. Non tamen immemŏres pristĭnae virtūtis[6] cecidērunt; quippe adversis vulnerĭbus[7] omnes loca, quae tuenda[8] a ducĭbus accepĕrant, morientes corporĭbus texērunt. Hic dies universae Graeciae et[9] gloriam dominatiōnis et vetustissĭmam libertātem finīvit.

Philip prepares to invade Persia.

233. Hujus victoriae callĭde dissimulāta laetitia est. Non solĭta[10] sacra Philippus illā die fecit; non in convivio risit;[11] non corōnas aut unguenta sumpsit; et, quantum in illo fuit, ita vicit, ut victōrem nemo sentīret.[12] Atheniensĭbus et captīvos gratis remīsit, et bello consumptōrum[13] corpŏra sepultūrae reddĭdit. Composĭtis in Graeciā rebus, omnium civitātum legātos ad formandum rerum praesentium statum[14] evocāri Corinthum[15] jubet. Ibi pacis leges universae Graeciae pro merĭtis singulārum civitātum statuit, conciliumque omnium, velŭti unum senātum,[16] ex omnĭbus legit. Auxilia deinde singulārum civitātum describuntur; nec dubium erat, eum Persārum imperium et suis et Graeciae virĭbus impugnatūrum esse.

---

[1] 563.

[2] 283.

[3] 292, 2.

[4] 518, I.

[5] 414, 4.

[6] 399, 2, 2).

[7] 428.

[8] 578, V.

[9] 587, I. 5.

[10] 575.

[11] 269.

[12] 494.

[13] 565, 1.

[14] 379.

[15] 363.

Death of Philip, 336 *B. C.*

234. Interea dum auxilia e Graeciā coeunt,[1] nuptias Cleopātrae filiae, et Alexandri, quem regem Epīri fecĕrat, magno apparātu[2] celĕbrat. Ubi quum Philippus ad ludos spectandos, medius inter duos Alexandros, filium et genĕrum, contendĕret,[3] Pausanias, nobĭlis ex Macedonĭbus adolescens, occupātis angustiis, Philippum in transĭtu obtruncat. Hic ab Attălo indīguo modo tractātus, quum saepe querēlam ad Philippum frustra detulisset,[4] et honorātum insŭper adversarium vidēret, iram in ipsum Philippum vertit, ultionemque, quam ab adversario non potĕrat, ab inīquo judĭce exēgit.

Alexander the Great succeeds to the Macedonian Throne, 336 *B.C.*

235. Philippo[5] Alexander filius successit, et virtūte[6] et vitiis patre major. Vincendi ratio utrīque[7] diversa. Hic[8] apertā vi, ille artĭbus bella tractābat. Deceptis[9] ille gaudēre[10] hostĭbus,[11] hic palam fusis. Prudentior ille consilio, hic animo magnificentior.[12] Iram pater dissimulāre, plerumque etiam vincĕre; hic ubi exarsisset,[13] nec dilatio ultiōnis, nec modus erat. Vini[14] uterque nimis avĭdus; sed ebrietātis diversa ratio. Pater de convivio in hostem procurrĕre, manum conserĕre, perĭculis se temĕre offerre; Alexander non in hostem, sed in suos saevīre. Regnāre ille cum amīcis volēbat; hic in amīcos regna exercēbat. Amāri pater malle, hic metui. Litterārum cultus utrīque simĭlis. Sollertiae[15] pater majōris, hic fidei. Verbis atque oratiōne Philippus, hic

---

[1] 295, 3.	[6] 429.	[11] 414, 2.
[2] 414, 8.	[7] 387.	[12] 164.
[3] 518, II.	[8] 450, 2, 1).	[13] 486, 5.
[4] 292, 2.	[9] 580.	[14] 399, 2, 2).
[5] 386.	[10] 545, 1.	[15] 401, 403.

rebus moderatior. Parcendi victis[1] filio anĭmus promp-
tior; ille nec sociis[2] abstinēbat. Frugalitāti pater, lux-
uriae filius magis dedĭtus erat. Quibus[3] artibus orbis
imperii fundamenta pater jecit, opĕris totīus gloriam
filius consummāvit.

Beginning of Alexander's Reign.

236. Imperio suscepto, prima Alexandro cura pater-
nārum exsequiārum fuit; in quibus ante omnia caedis[4]
conscios ad tumŭlum patris occīdi jussit. Inter initia
regni multas gentes rebellantes compescuit;[5] orientes
nonnullas seditiōnes exstinxit. Deinde ad Persĭcum
bellum proficiscens, patrimonium omne suum, quod in
Macedoniā et Eurōpā habēbat, amīcis divīsit; *sibi*[6]
Asiam sufficĕre praefātus.[7] Nec exercitui[8] alius quam
regi anĭmus fuit. Quippe omnes oblīti conjŭgum[9] libe-
rorumque, et longinquae a domo militiae, nihil cogi-
tābant nisi Orientis opes. Quum delāti[10] in Asiam
essent, primus[11] Alexander jacŭlum velut in hostīlem
terram jecit; armatusque de navi[12] tripudianti[13] simīlis
prosiluit,[14] atque ita hostias caedit, precātus, ne se regem
illae terrae invītae[15] accipiant.[16] In Ilio quoque ad tu-
mŭlos herōum,[17] qui Trojāno bello cecidĕrant, parentāvit.

Battle of the Granĭcus, 334 B. C.

237. Inde hostem petens milītes a populatiōne Asiae
prohibuit, *parcendum*[18] *suis rebus* praefātus, *nec per-*

---

[1] 385, 575.	[7] 297, II. 3.	[13] 575, 391, 1.
[2] 425, 2.	[8] 387.	[14] 285.
[3] 453.	[9] 406.	[15] 443, 1.
[4] 399, 2, 2).	[10] 292, 2.	[16] 492, 3.
[5] 275, I.	[11] 442, 1.	[17] 68.
[6] 386.	[12] 62, III.	[18] 545, 3.

denda ea, quae possessūri [1] *venĕrint.* In exercĭtu ejus
fuēre pedĭtum triginta duo millia, equĭtum quattuor
millia quingenti, naves centum octoginta duae. Hac
tam parvā manu universum terrārum orbem [2] vincĕre
est aggressus. Quum ad tam periculōsum bellum exercĭtum legĕret, [3] non juvĕnes robustos, sed veterānos, qui
cum patre patruisque militavĕrant, elēgit : ut non tam
milĭtes, quam magistros militiae electos putāres. [4] Prima
cum hoste congressio in campis Adrastīae fuit. In acie
Persārum sexcenta millia milĭtum fuērunt, quae non
minus arte Alexandri quam virtūte Macedŏnum super-
āta, terga vertērunt. Ităque magna caedes Persāruin
fuit. De exercĭtu Alexandri novem pedĭtes, centum
viginti equĭtes cecidēre ; quos rex magnifĭce humātos
statuis equestrĭbus donāvit ; cognātis eōrum autem im-
munitātes dedit. Post victoriam major [5] pars Asiae ad
eum defēcit. Habuit et plura [6] proelia cum praefectis
Darīi, quos jam non tam armis, quam terrōre nomĭnis
sui vicit.

Battle of Issus, 333 *B. C.*

238. Interea Darīus cum quadringentis millĭbus
pedĭtum ac centum millĭbus equĭtum in aciem procēdit.
Commisso proelio, Alexander non ducis magis quam
milĭtis munia [7] exsequebātur. Macedŏnes cum rege
ipso in equĭtum agmen irrumpunt. Tum vero simĭlis
ruīnae strages erat. Circa currum Darīi jacēbant nobilissĭmi duces, ante ocŭlos regis egregiā morte [8] defuncti.
Jamque qui Darīum vehēbant equi, confossi hastis et
dolōre efferāti, jugum quatĕre et regem curru [9] excutĕre

---

[1] 578, V.	[4] 486, 4.	[7] 131, 4.)
[2] 107, 2.	[5] 165.	[8] 419, I.
[3] 518, II.	[6] 165, 1.	[9] 434, 1.

coepĕrant : quum ille, verĭtus ne vivus venīret ' in hostium potestātem, desĭlit,' et in equum, qui ad hoc ipsum sequebātur, imponĭtur.   Tum vero cetĕri dissipantur metu.   Inter captīvos castrōrum mater et uxor et filiae duae Darīi fuēre : in quas Alexander ita se gessit,' ut omnes ante eum reges et continentiā' et clementiā vincĕret.'

Alexander in Egypt, 332 *B. C.—He visits the Temple of Jupiter Ammon.*

239. Aegyptii, olim Persārum opĭbus infensi, Alexandrum laeti' recepērunt.   A Memphi' rex in interiōra' penĕtrat ; compositisque rebus ita, ut nihil ex patrio Aegyptiōrum more mutāret, adīre Jovis Ammōnis oracŭlum' statuit.   Quatriduo per vastas solitudĭnes absumpto, tandem ad sedem consecrātam deo'' ventum est,'' undĭque ambientĭbus ramis contectam.   Regem propius adeuntem maxĭmus natu'' e sacerdotĭbus FILIUM appellat, *hoc nomen illi parentem Jovem reddĕre* affirmans. Ille se vero et accipĕre ait '' et agnoscĕre, humānae sortis'' oblītus.   Consŭlit deinde, an totīus orbis imperium sibi destināret '' PATER.   Aeque in adulatiōnem composĭtus, terrārum omnium rectōrem fore ostendit.   Post haec instĭtit quaerĕre, an omnes parentis sui interfectōres poenas dedissent.   Sacerdos PARENTEM ejus negat ullīus scelĕre posse violāri, PHILIPPI autem omnes luisse supplicia.   Sacrificio deinde facto, dona et sacerdotĭbus et deo data,'' permissumque amīcis, ut ipsi quoque consulĕrent '' Jovem.   Nihil amplius quaesivērunt, quam an

---

' 492, 4.	' 62, II. 2.	'' 297, II. 1.
' 467, III.	' 441, 1.	'' 406, II.
' 272, I.	' 371, 4.	'' 525.
' 429.	'' 384.	'' 460, 3.
' 494.	'' 301, 1.	'' 492.
' 413, 1.	'' 168, 3.	

auctor esset sibi divīnis honorĭbus colendi suum regem.
Hoc quoque acceptum fore Jovi² vates respondit. Rex
ex Ammōne rediens³ elēgit urbi locum, ubi nunc est
Alexandrīa, appellatiōnem trahens ex nomĭne auctōris.

Darius makes his last proposals of Peace.

240. Jam Darīus pervenĕrat Arbēla⁴ vicum, nobĭlem suā clade factūrus. Raro in ullo proelio tantum
sanguĭnis⁵ fusum est. Tandem Darīi aurīga, qui ante
ipsum sedens equos regēbat, hastā transfixus est; nec
aut Persae aut Macedŏnes dubitavēre, quin ipse rex esset
occīsus.⁶ Cedĕre⁷ Persae, et laxāre ordĭnes; jamque non
pugna, sed caedes erat, quum Darīus quoque currum
suum in fugam vertit; victōri Alexandro Asiae imperium obtĭgit.⁸

Disturbances in Greece.

241. Dum haec in Asiā gerebantur, Graecia fere
omnis, spe recuperandae libertātis,¹ ad arma concurrĕrat,
auctoritātem Lacedaemoniōrum secūta. Dux hujus belli
Agis, rex Lacedaemoniōrum, fuit. Quem⁹ motum Anti-
păter, dux¹⁰ ab Alexandro in Macedoniā relictus, in ipso
ortu oppressit. Magna tamen utrimque caedes fuit.
Agis rex, quum suos terga dantes vidēret, dimissis satel-
litĭbus¹¹ ut Alexandro felicitāte, non virtūte inferior
viderētur,¹² tantam stragem hostium edĭdit,¹³ ut agmĭna
interdum fugāret. Ad postrēmum, etsi a multitudĭne
victus, gloriā tamen omnes vicit.

---

¹ 563. ⁶ 498. ¹⁰ 362, 3.
² 391. ⁷ 545, 1. ¹¹ 81.
³ 295, 3. ⁸ 273, I. ¹² 491.
⁴ 379. ⁹ 453. ¹³ 273, I.
⁵ 396, III.

Alexander invades India.

242. Post haec Indiam petit, ut Oceăno finīret imperium. Cui gloriae ut etiam exercĭtus ornamenta convenīrent, phalĕras equōrum et arma milĭtum argento indūcit. Quum ad Nysam urbem venisset, oppidānis[1] non repugnantĭbus parci jussīt.

Alexander returns to Babylon, 324 B. C.

243. Ab ultĭmis[2] oris Oceăni Babyloniam reversus, convivium solemnĭter instituit. Ibi quum totus[3] in laetitiam effūsus esset, recedentem jam e convivio Medius Thessălus, instaurātā comissatiōne invītat. Accepto pocŭlo, inter bibendum[4] velŭti telo confixus ingemuit, elatusque e convivio semianĭmis, tanto dolōre cruciātus est, ut ferrum in remedia poscĕret.[5] Venēnum accepisse credĭtur.

Death of Alexander, 323 B. C.

244. Quartī die Alexander indubitātam mortem sentiens, *agnoscĕre se fatum domus majōrum suōrum,* ait, *nam plerosque Aeacidārum intra tricesĭmum annum defunctos.* Tumultuantes deinde milĭtes, insidiis periisse[6] regem suspicantes, ipse sedāvit, eosque omnes ad conspectum suum admīsit, osculandamque[7] dextram porrexit.[8] Quum lacrimārent[9] omnes, ipse non sine lacrĭmis tantum, verum etiam sine ullo tristiōris mentis argumento fuit. Ad postrēmum corpus suum in Ammōnis templo condi jubet. Quum deficĕre eum amīci vidērent, quaerunt, quem imperii faciat herēdem;[10] respondit,

---

[1] 385.	[5] 494.	[8] 214, I. 1.
[2] 166.	[6] 295, 3.	[9] 518, L
[3] 443.	[7] 578, V.	[10] 373.
[4] 565, 1.		

Dignissĭmum. Hac voce omnes amīcos suos ad aemŭlam regni cupiditātem accendit. Sextā die, praeclūsā voce, exemptum digĭto¹ annŭlum Perdiccae tradĭdit, quae res gliscentem amicōrum discordiam sedāvit. Nam etsi non voce nuncupātus heres,² judicio tamen electus³ esse videbātur.

Remarks on the character of Alexander.

245. Decessit Alexander mensem unum tres et triginta annos⁴ natus, vir supra humānum modum vi⁵ anĭmi praedĭtus. Omĭna quaedam magnitudĭnem ejus in ipso ortu portendisso existimabantur. Quo die natus est, pater ejus nuntium duārum victoriārum accēpit; alterius, belli Illyrĭci, alterius, certamĭnis Olympiāci, in quod quadrīgas misĕrat. Puer acerrĭmis litterārum studiis erudītus fuit. Exactā pueritiā, per quinquennium Aristotĕle, philosŏpho praestantissĭmo, usus est magistro. Accepto tandem imperio tantam militĭbus suis fiduciam fecit, ut, illo praesente, nullīus hostis arma timērent.⁶ Ităque cum nullo hoste unquam congressus est, quem non vicĕrit;⁷ nullam urbem obsēdit, quam non expugnavĕrit. Victus denĭque est non virtūte hostīli, sed insidiis suīrum et fraude.

---

¹ 434, 1.   ⁴ 378.   ⁶ 494.
² 362, 3.   ⁵ 419, III.   ⁷ 501, 1.
³ 547.

SUGGESTIONS TO THE LEARNER.

———•———

I. The preparation of a Reading Lesson in Latin involves

1. A knowledge of the Meaning of the Latin.
2. A knowledge of the Structure of the Latin Sentences.
3. A translation into English.

MEANING OF THE LATIN.

II. Remember that almost every inflected word in a Latin sentence requires the use of both the Dictionary and the Grammar to ascertain its meaning.

The Dictionary gives the meaning of the word without reference to its Grammatical properties of *case, number, mood, tense,* etc., and the Grammar, the meaning of the endings which mark those properties. The Dictionary will give the meaning of *mensa,* a table, but not of *mensarum,* of tables; the Grammar alone will give the force of the ending *arum.*

III. Make yourself so familiar with all the endings of inflection, with their exact form and force, whether in declension or conjugation, that you will not only readily distinguish the different parts of speech from each other, but also the different forms of the same word with their exact and distinctive force.

IV. In taking up a Latin sentence,

1. Notice carefully the endings of the several words, and thus determine which words are *nouns,* which *verbs,* etc.

2. Observe the force of each ending, and thus determine *case, number, voice, mood, tense,* etc.

This will be found to be a very important step toward the mastery of the sentence. By this means you will discover not only the relation of the words to each other, but also an important part of their meaning, that which they derive from their endings.

V. The key to the meaning of any simple sentence (345, I.) will be found in the simple subject and predicate, i. e., in the Nominative and its Verb. Hence in looking out the sentence, observe the following order. Take

1. The Subject, or Nominative.

The ending will in most instances enable you to distinguish this from all other words, except the adjectives which agree with it. These may be looked out at the same time with the subject.

Sometimes the subject is not expressed, but only implied, in the ending of the verb. It may then be readily supplied, as it is always a pronoun of such person and number as the verb indicates; as, *audio*, I hear, the ending *io* showing that the subject is *ego;* *auditis*, you hear, the ending *itis* showing that the subject is *vos.*

2. The Verb, with Predicate Noun or Adjective, if any.

This will be readily known by the ending. Now combining this with the Subject, you will have an outline of the sentence. All the other words must now be associated with these two parts.

3. The Modifiers of the Subject, i. e., adjectives agreeing with it, nominatives in apposition with it, genitives dependent upon it, etc.

But perhaps some of these have already been looked out in the attempt to ascertain the subject.

In looking out these words, bear in mind the meaning of the subject to which they belong. This will greatly aid you in selecting from the dictionary the true meaning in the passage before you.

4. The Modifiers of the Verb, i. e., (1) Oblique cases, Accusatives, Datives, etc., dependent upon it, and (2) Adverbs qualifying it.

Bear in mind all the while the force of the case and the meaning of the verb, that you may be able to select for each word the true meaning in the passage before you.

VI. In complex and compound sentences (345, II., III.), discover first the connectives which unite the several members, and then proceed with each member as with a simple sentence.

VII. In the use of Dictionary and Vocabulary, remember that you are not to look for the particular form which occurs in the sentence, but for the Nom. Sing. of nouns, adjectives, and pronouns, and for the First Pers. Sing. Pres. Indic. Act. of Verbs. Therefore,

1. In Pronouns, make yourself so familiar with their declension, that any oblique case will at once suggest the Nom. Sing.

If *vobis* occurs, you must remember that the Nom. Sing. is *tu.*

2. In Nouns and Adjectives, make yourself so familiar with the case-endings, that you will be able to drop that of the given case, and substitute for it that of the Nom. Sing.

Thus, mens*ibus:* stem *mensi*, Nom. Sing. *mensis*, which you will find in the Vocabulary. So duc*em, duc, ducs, dux.*

3. In Verbs, change the ending of the given form into that of the First Pers. Sing. of the Pres. Indic. Act.

Thus, amābat; stem ama, First Pers. Sing. Pres. Indic. Act. amo, which you will find in the Vocabulary. So amaverunt; First Pers. Perf. amavi, Perf. stem amae, Verb stem ama; amo.

To illustrate the steps recommended in the preceding suggestions, we add the following

Model.

VIII. Themistŏcles imperātor servitūte totam Graeciam liberāvit.

1. Without knowing the meaning of the words, you will discover from their *forms*,

1) That *Themistŏcles* and *imperātor* are probably nouns in the Nom. Sing.

2) That *servitūte* is a noun in the Abl. Sing.

3) That *totam* and *Graeciam* are either nouns or adjectives in the Accus. Sing.

4) That *liberāvit* is a verb in the Act. voice, Indic. mood, Perf. tense, Third Person, Singular number.

2. Now, turning to the Vocabulary for the meaning of the words, you will learn,

1) That *Themistŏcles* is the name of an eminent Athenian general: THEMISTOCLES.

2) That *libĕro*, for which you must look, not for *liberāvit*, means *to liberate;* LIBERATED.

Themistocles liberated.

3) That *imperātor* means *commander;* THE COMMANDER.

Themistocles, the commander, liberated.

4) That *Graeciam* is the name of a country: GREECE.

Themistocles the commander liberated Greece.

5) That *totus* means *the whole, all:* ALL.

Themistocles the commander liberated all Greece.

6) That *servitus* means *servitude:* FROM SERVITUDE.

Themistocles the commander liberated all Greece from servitude.

STRUCTURE OF THE LATIN SENTENCE.

IX. The structure of a sentence is best shown by *analyzing* it and *parsing* the words which compose it.

Analysis.

X. Tell whether the sentence is simple, complex, or compound.

XI. In analyzing a Simple sentence (345, I.), name,

1. The Subject and Predicate, (1) in the simple form, and (2) in the complex form (347, 350).

2. The Modifiers of the Subject, (1) in the simple form, and (2) in the complex form (352).

8. The Modifiers of the Predicate, (1) in the simple form, and (2) in the complex form (354–356).

If the Modifiers are complex, the analysis may be continued till all complex elements are explained.

Model.

XII. In his castris Cluilius, Albānus rex, morĭtur. *Cluilius, the Alban king, dies in this camp.*

1. This is a simple sentence.
2. *Cluilius* is the simple subject, and *morĭtur*, the simple predicate. *Cluilius Albānus rex,* is the complex subject, and *in his castris morĭtur* is the complex predicate.
8. *Rex* is the simple modifier of the subject *Cluilius,* and *Albānus rex,* the complex modifier, as *rex* is modified by *Albānus.*
4. *In castris* is the simple modifier of the predicate *morĭtur,* showing *where* he dies, and *in his castris* is the complex modifier, as *castris* is modified by *his.*

XIII. In analyzing a Complex sentence (845, II.),

1. Name the sentence, or clause,[1] used as an element in it with its connective (357).
2. Analyze the sentence as a whole, like a simple sentence.
8. Analyze the subordinate clause (845, 2).

Model.

XIV. Donec eris felix, multos numerābis amīcos. *So long as you are prosperous, you will number many friends.*

1. This is a complex sentence.
2. *Donec eris felix,* is a clause introduced as a modifier of *numerābis,* showing *when* you will number.
8. *Tu,* implied in *numerābis,* is the subject; *numerābis* is the simple predicate, *donec eris felix, multos numerābis amīcos* is the complex predicate.
4. *Amicos* is the simple object of the predicate *numerābis,* and *multos amicos* the complex object. *Donec eris felix* is the adverbial modifier of the predicate.
5. *Donec eris felix* is a simple sentence, with the connective *donec. Tu,* implied in *eris,* is the subject, and *eris felix,* the predicate, *eris* being the copula (353) and *felix* the predicate adjective.

---

[1] If the sentence is abridged, show wherein (858, 859).

XV. In analyzing a Compound sentence (845, III.),

1. Separate it into its members and name the connectives.[1]
2. Analyze each member as a separate sentence.

Model.

XVI. Sol ruit et montes umbrantur.
The sun descends and the mountains are shaded.

1. This is a compound sentence (845, III.).
2. The members are *sol ruit* and *montes umbrantur*, connected by the conjunction *et*.
3. The members are simple sentences, and are analyzed accordingly.

Parsing.

XVII. In parsing a word,

1. Name the Part of Speech to which it belongs.
2. Inflect[2] it, if capable of inflection.
3. Give its gender, number, case, voice, mood, tense, person, etc.[3]
4. Give its Syntax and the Rule for it.[4]

Model.

XVIII. Romāni ab arātro abduxērunt Cincinnātum, ut dictātor esset, *The Romans took Cincinnatus from the plough, that he might be dictator.*

1. *Romāni* is an adjective : *Romānus, a, um,* STEM, *Romano ;* decline. It is in the *Nom. Plur. Masc.*, is used substantively (441), and is the *subject* of *abduxērunt.* Give Rule III.
2. *Abduxērunt* is an active verb : *ab-dūco, ab-ducĕre, ab-duxi, ab-ductum,* compounded of *ab* and *duco* (313, II.); STEM, *ab-duc,* PERFECT STEM, *ab-dux.* Give *synopsis* of the *mood* (219, I.). Inflect the *tense,* i. e., the Indicative Perf. Act. (209). It is in the *Active* voice, *Indic.* mood, *Perf.* tense, *Third* person, *Plur.* number, and agrees with *Romāni.* Give Rule XXXV.
3. *Cincinnātum* is a Proper noun (39, 1), of the Second Decl.; STEM

---

[1] If the sentence is abridged, name the compound elements.
[2] Inflect, i. e., decline, compare or conjugate.
[3] That is, such of these properties as it possesses.
[4] No special Rule is deemed necessary for Prepositions, Conjunctions, or Interjections. Prepositions are provided for by the rule for *Cases with Prepositions.* Conjunctions are mere connectives, and are quite fully explained under *Moods.* Interjections are only expressions of emotion, or mere marks of address, explained under *Cases.*

Cincinnato; decline, used only in the singular (130, 1). It is in the *Accus. Sing. Masc.*, and is the *direct object* of *abduxĕrunt.* Give Rule V.

4. *Ab* is a preposition used with the Abl. *Arātro.*

5. *Arātro* is a noun of the Second Decl.; sᴛᴇᴍ *aratro;* decline. It is in the *Abl. Sing. Neut.*, and is used with the Prep. *ab.* Give Rule XXXII.

6. *Ut* is a conjunction of purpose (491), connecting *abduxĕrunt* and *esset.*

7. *Esset* is an intransitive verb: *sum, esse, fui* (204). Give *synopsis* of the *mood,* and inflect the *tense,* i. e., Subj. Imperf. It is in the *Subj.* mood, *Imperf.* tense, *Third* person, *Sing.* number, and agrees with the pronoun *is,* he, implied in the ending (460, 2). Give Rule XXXV.

8. *Dictātŏr* is a noun of the Third Decl.; sᴛᴇᴍ *dictātŏr;* decline (60). It is in the *Nom. Sing. Masc.*, and agrees, as Predicate noun, with the omitted subject of *esset.* Give Rule I.

TRANSLATION.

XIX. In translating, render as literally as possible without doing violence to the English.

In many important idioms of the Latin, a literal translation would not only fail to do justice to the original, but would also be a gross perversion of the mother-tongue. The following suggestions are intended to aid the pupil in disposing of such cases; but even in these, it is earnestly recommended that he should first construe literally, in order that he may be made to feel the force of the Latin construction before attempting a translation.

Participles.

XX. These are much more extensively used in Latin than in English; hence the frequent necessity, in translating them, of deviating from the Latin construction. They may generally be rendered in some one of the following ways [1] (571–581):

1. Literally:

Pyrrhus proelio fusus a Tarento recessit, *Pyrrhus having been defeated in battle withdrew from Tarentum.*

2. By a Relative Clause:

Omnes aliud agentes, aliud simulantes imprŏbi sunt, *All who do one thing and pretend another are dishonest.*

3. By a Clause with a Conjunction:

---

[1] The pupil must early learn to determine from the context the appropriate rendering in each instance.

1). With a Conjunction of Time,—*while, when, after,* etc.

Uva maturāta dulcescit, *The grape, when it has ripened* (having ripened), *becomes sweet.*

2). With a Conjunction of Cause, Reason, Manner,—*as, for, since,* etc.

Milĭtes perfĭdiam verĭti revertērunt, *The soldiers returned, because they feared perfidy.*

3). With a Conjunction of Condition,—*if.*

Accusātus damnabĭtur, *If he is accused, he will be condemned.*

4). With a Conjunction of Concession,—*though, although.*

Urbem acerrĭme defensam cepit, *He took the city, though it was valiantly defended,* or *though valiantly defended.*

4. By a Verbal Noun:

Ad Romam condĭtam, *to the founding of Rome,* lit. *to Rome founded.* Ab urbe condĭtā, *from the founding of the city.* Post reges exactos, *after the expulsion of the kings.*

5. By a Verb:

Rex ei benigne recepto filiam dedit, *The king received him kindly and gave him his daughter,* lit. *gave his daughter to him kindly received.*

XXI. Participles with *non* or *nihil* are sometimes best rendered by *Participial* nouns dependent upon *without :*

Non ridens, *without laughing.*

XXII. Future Participles are sometimes best rendered by *Infinitives,* or by *Participial Nouns* with *for the purpose of :*

Rediit belli casum tentatūrus, *He returned to try* (about to try) *the fortune of war.*

XXIII. The Ablative Absolute is sometimes best rendered (1) by a *Clause* with,—*when, while, after, for, since, if, though,* etc., (2) by a *Noun* with a *Preposition,—in, during, after, by, from, through,* etc., or (3) by an *Active Participle* with its *Object :*

Servio regnante, *while Servius reigned,* or *in the reign of Servius* (lit. *Servius reigning*). Duce Fabio, *under the command of Fabius* (lit. *Fabius being commander*).

Sometimes, as in the last example, a word denoting the *doer* of an action can be best rendered by the word which denotes the *thing done.* Thus, instead of *commander, consul, king,* we have command, consulship, reign.

Subjunctive.

XXIV. This may be rendered as follows:

1. With the *Potential* signs, *may, can, might, could, would, should* (485):

Forsĭtan quaerātis, *Perhaps you may inquire.* Hoc nemo dixĕrit, *No one would say this.*

2. By the English Indicative. This is generally the best rendering

1) In clauses denoting Cause, or Time and Cause (517, 521):

Quum vita metus plena sit, *since life is full of fear.* Quum Romam venisset, *when he had come to Rome.*

2) In Indirect Questions (525):

Quaerĭtur, cur dissentiant, *It is asked why they disagree.*

3) In the Subjunctive by Attraction (527):

Vereor, ne, dum minuĕre velim labōrem, augeam, *I fear I shall increase the labor, while I wish to diminish it.*

4) In the Subordinate Clauses of Indirect Discourse (531):

Hippias gloriātus est, annŭlum quem habēret se suā manu confecisse, *Hippias boasted that he had made with his own hand the ring which he wore* (had).

5) In Relative Clauses defining indefinite antecedents, and sometimes in clauses denoting *result* (501, 494, 495):

Sunt qui putent, *there are some who think.* Ita vixit ut Atheniensĭbus esset carissĭmus, *He so lived, that he was very dear to the Athenians.*

6) Sometimes in Conditional and Concessive clauses, and in clauses with *Quin* and *Quomĭnus* (510, 515, 498, 499):

Dum metuant, *if only* (provided) *they fear.* Si voluisset, dimicasset, *If he had wished, he would have fought.* Ut desint vires, tamen est laudanda voluntas, *Though the strength fails, still the will should be approved.* Adest nemo, quin videat, *There is no one present who does not see.*

3. By the Infinitive. This is often the best rendering

1) In Relative Clauses denoting Result: hence after *dignus, indignus, idoneus, aptus,* etc. (501):

Non is sum qui his utar, *I am not such a one as to use* (he who may use) *these things.* Fabŭlae dignae sunt, quae legantur, *The fables are worthy to be read* (which, *or* that they, should be read).

2) Sometimes in Relative Clauses denoting Purpose, and other clauses denoting Result (500, 494):

Decemvĭri creāti sunt qui leges scribĕrent, *Decemvirs were appointed to prepare the laws* (who should prepare).

Infinitive.

XXV. The Infinitive has a much more extensive use in Latin than in English. The following points require notice (539 ff.).

· 1. The Infinitive with a Subject is rendered by a *Finite* verb with *that:*

Dixit se regem vidisse, *He said that he had seen the king.*

2. The Historical Infinitive (545, 1) is rendered by the Imperfect Indicative:

Iram pater dissimulāre, *The father concealed his anger.*

3. The Infinitive is sometimes best rendered by a *Participial noun* with *of, with,* etc.

Insimulātur mysteria violasse, *He is accused of having violated the mysteries.*

Miscellaneous Idioms.

XXVI. The following Miscellaneous Idioms are added:

1. *Certiōrem facĕre* should be rendered, *to inform,* and *certior fiĕri, to be informed:*

Caesar certior factus est, *Caesar was informed.*

2. *Inter se,* lit. *between themselves,* is often best rendered, *from each other, to each other, together.*

Omnes inter se diffērunt, *They all differ from each other.*

3. *Ne—quidem,* with one or more words between the parts, should be rendered, *not even;* or *even—not:*

Ne nomen quidem, *not even the name.*

4. When two or more verbs stand together in the same compound tense, the copula (*sum*) is generally expressed only with the last, but in rendering, the copula should be expressed only with the first:

Captus et in vincŭla conjectus est, *He was taken and thrown into chains.*

5. *Quanto—tanto,* lit. *by as much as—by so much,* is often best rendered before comparatives, *the—the:*

F

Quanto diutius considĕro, tanto res vidētur obscurior, *the longer* (by as much as the longer) *I consider the subject, the more obscure* (by so much the more obscure) *does it appear.*

6. A Clause with *quomĭnus*, by which, or that, the less, may generally be rendered by a *Clause* with *that*, by the *Infinitive*, or by a *Participial noun* with *from*.

Per eum stetit quomĭnus dimicarētur, *It was owing to him* (stood through him) *that the engagement was not made.* Non recusāvit quomĭnus poenam subiret, *He did not refuse to submit to punishment.* Regem impediit quomĭnus pugnāret, *He prevented the king from fighting.*

NOTES.

GRAMMATICAL EXERCISES.

For Explanation of References, see page ix.

1. Ala. As the Latin has no article, a noun may, according to the **1** connection in which it is used, be translated (1) without the article; as, *ala*, wing; (2) with the indefinite article *a*, or *an* ; as, *ala*, a wing; (3) with the definite article *the* ; as, *ala*, the wing.

4, 23. Post Romuli mortem. For the position of the preposition, **3** see 602, II. 3.

7. Servus bonus. In Latin the adjective generally follows its noun, as in this example, though sometimes it precedes it, as in English. When emphatic the adjective is placed before its noun; as, *vera amicitia* (7, 25). See Grammar, 598; 598, 2.

11, 18. Leges . . . sunto, *let the laws be*, etc. The third person of **5** the Future Imperative is often best rendered by *let*, instead of *shall*.

13, 28. Omnium. This agrees with *militum*.

19, 2. Consul. See note on " *Consules* " (169).——4. **Vini deus.** **9** The ancient Romans recognized a great number of gods and goddesses. Almost every object in nature was under the special care of some one of these fabulous deities. Bacchus presided over the cultivation of the vine, and was the god of festivity.——6. **Testis temporum,** *the witness of times*, i. e. competent to testify in regard to them. Tempŏra, *times*, involves events.——**Habetur,** *is regarded.*——9. **Evaserat;** from *evādo.*

20, 1. Expulsus est; from *expello.*——2. **Regis pater.** *Regis* refers to Tarquinius Priscus, the fifth king of Rome.——6. **Didicit;** from *disco.*——7. **Dictator.** See note on " *Cum honŏre dictatŏris* " (178). ——**Voverat;** from *voveo.*——8. **Interfecerunt;** from *interficio.*

21, 5. Malorum. This depends upon *mater.* **10**

22, 6. Perdidi; from *perdo.*

23, 6. Fecit, lit, *made ;* render *composed,* or *wrote.*——8. **Condidit;** from *condo.*——12. **Vixerunt;** from *vivo.*——16. **Luxerunt;** from

6

11 *lugeo.*——20. **Sum praetervectus;** from *praetervĕho.*——21. **Transierunt;** from *transeo.* See 295, 3.

24, 5. **Nutricem ... Siciliam.** The ancient Romans annually received large supplies of grain from Sicily. Hence the epithets here applied to it.

25, 3. **Belli;** construe with *artem,* the art of war.——9. **Edoctus fuerat;** from *edoceo.*——10. **Petierunt;** from *peto:* See 234, 278, 2.

12 ——13. **Iberum traduxit.** This was at the beginning of the second Punic war, 218 B. C. The Ebro was the boundary between the Roman and the Carthaginian possessions in Spain.——**Traduxit;** from *tradūco.*——14. **Transducti sunt;** from *transdūco.*

26, 3. **Bestiolae.** This refers to the insect known as the *ephemeran.* ——4. **Natus;** from *nascor.*——6. **Exstruxerunt;** from *exstruo.*—— 7. **Longos quaterna cubita,** *each four cubits long.* Quaterna is a *distributive.* See 174, 2, 1).

27, 2. **Rediit;** from *redeo,* 295, 3.——3. **Concessit;** from *concēdo.* ——4. **Numerum,** *quantity.* The word generally means *number.*—— **Misit;** from *mitto.*——8. **Ibo;** from *eo,* 295.

13 28, 2. **Nigrantes terga,** literally, *black as to their backs.*——3. **Ictus;** from *ico.*——**Cecidit;** from *cado.*——4. **Incensus est;** from *incendo.*

29, 3. **Videt,** *sees it.* The object is the pronoun understood, referring to *conjurationem.*

30, 9. **Non dat,** *does not allow;* lit. *give.*——10. **Omnes.** This agrees with *nos* implied in *damus.*

14 31, 6. **Persuasit;** from *persuadeo.*——8. **Pepercerunt;** from *parco.*

32, 1. **Affuit;** from *adsum.* For the assimilation of *d* before *f,* see 338, 2, *ad.*——2. **Adjunxit;** from *adjungo.*——3. **Singulorum,** *of individuals;* it depends upon *saluti.*——5. **Terrorem injecit,** *he struck terror into,* i. e. inspired with terror; lit. *threw terror into.*——**Injecit;** from *injicio.*——6. **Pugnae .... Salaminem.** This was the famous victory gained, 480 B. C., by the Greeks over the Persians.

34, 1. **Caesari erant agenda,** lit. *were to Caesar to be done.*

15 36, 10. **Delegerunt;** from *delĭgo.*

37, 2. **Tuae litterae,** *your letter.* This is the common meaning of the plural of this word.——5. **Notus;** Participle from *nosco,* used adjectively, 575.

38, 1. **Esto,** *let there be.*

16 39, 4. **Erat,** *it was.*——I. 2. **Sustinuerunt;** from *sustineo.*——4. **Ventorum pater.** Aeŏlus is meant: he was the god of the winds, and ruled them at pleasure.——5. **Singulorum facultates,** *the resources of individuals.* See 441, 1.——IV. 1. **Tarquinius.** Tarquinius Superbus,

17 the last king of Rome, is meant.——3. **Dederunt;** from *do.*——V. 2.

PAGE

Senat, lit. *sounds ;* here *expresses, means.*——**Vox voluptatis,** *the word* **17**
pleasure ; lit. *the word of pleasure.*——5. **Exhorruit ;** from *exhorresco.*

40, 3. **Famae mendacia,** *the falsehoods of report,* i. e. the falsehoods
circulated by report.——8. **Nescium fingit.** Socrates, one of the most
eminent philosophers of antiquity, had such a contempt for all pedantry
and conceit of knowledge, that he claimed to know only one thing ;
viz., *that he knew nothing.*

41, 1. **Poena ;** supply *est,* 460, 2.——3. **Fuit,** *was,* i. e. consisted of.
——4. **Erat somni ;** supply *man* in rendering.——6. **Senescentis ;** sup- **18**
ply *aetatis* from the preceding clause.——12. **Ceteri ;** supply *vendunt.*

42, 7. **Suorum,** *his own,* i. e. faults (*vitiōrum*).

43, 9. **Hujus ;** belongs to *gloriae.* **19**

44, I. 1. **Cato ;** supply *magnus habebātur* from preceding clause.
——II. 1. **Res . . . constituit,** *managed the affairs,* etc. He was governor of the Chersonesus.——III. 7. **Pisces ;** supply *capiuntur.*—— **20**
IV. 3. **Sacra,** *sacred rites.* King Numa was the reputed founder of the
early religious institutions of Rome.

45, 3. **Viginti talentis,** *twenty talents,* more than $20,000, a high
price for an oration, but the purchaser was a wealthy king, and the author one of the most finished of the Attic orators.——**Vendidit ;** from
vendo.

46, 1. **Aurum ;** supply *vilius est* from the preceding clause.——10.
Adversam ; supply *fortūnam.*——11. **Virtutis,** *that of virtue.* It de- **21**
pends upon *sitis* understood.

47, 2. **Major ;** lit. *greater ;* render *older.*——3. **Caesaris ;** supply
castris.

48, I. 5. **Functus sum ;** from *fungor.*——III. 9. **Hectora . . . .** **22**
Achilles. These were the two most eminent warriors in the Trojan war ;
the former a Trojan, the latter a Greek.

49, 2. **Gesta sunt ;** from *gero.*——3. **Vixit ;** from *vivo.*——5. **Tra-
jecit ;** from *trajicio.*——6. **Fabricius, Aristides.** They were both distinguished for rare integrity and uprightness. The latter was surnamed
the Just. With *Fabricius* supply *fuit.*——7. **Mortuus est ;** from *morior.*
——12. **Timotheus ;** supply *vixit.*

50, 7. **Destiterunt ;** from *desisto.*——11. **Expulsus est ;** from *ex-* **23**
pello.——13. **Bello Persico,** *in the Persian war,* i. e. the war with Persia. Themistocles gained the celebrated victory of Salamis, 480 B. C.

51, 4. **Qua nocte—eadem**=*eādem nocte, quā, on the same night in
which.* The antecedent *nocte* is incorporated into the relative clause
according to 445, 9.——**Dianae . . . . templum.** This temple of Diana
at Ephesus in Ionia was celebrated for its beauty and magnificence.——
9. **Condita erat ;** from *condo.*

52, 2. **Conjunxit ;** from *conjungo.* **24**

PAGE

24 53, 1. **Quidam,** *some,* i. e. some persons.——**Non re,** *not in reality.*——5. **Par;** agrees with *Ancus.*

54, 1. **Cognito;** from *cognosco.*——4. **Excepta;** from *excipio.*——6. **Natus est;** from *nascor.*——**Cicerone . . . . consulibus;** XXIII. See also notes on "*Consules*" (169) and "*Duillio*" (185).

25 55, I. 1. **Ad summam senectutem,** *till extreme old age.*——5. **Vicit;** from *vinco.*——6. **Fusae sunt;** from *fundo.*——8. **Erga parentes, pietas**=*justitia erga parentes pietas dicitur.*——II. 4. **Africanus;** so called because of his great victory at Zama in Africa.——5. **Ex viro,** i. e. from the word *vir,* man.——6. **Floruit;** from *floresco,* 282, I.——8. **Dedit;** from *do.*——III. 2. **Divisa est;** from *divido.*——4. **Progressi sunt;** from *progredior.*——5. **Est,** *there is.*——**Sub pallio sordido,** *under a soiled coat,* i. e. in the poor man, among the poor.

26 56, 5. **Ab omni parte;** lit. *from every part;* render, *in all respects.*——6. **Condidit;** from *condo.*——9. **Dives.** This is a predicate adjective: *is born rich.*——11. **Dissimillima natura,** *very dissimilar* (things) *by nature.*

57, 2. **Ad quas res, in iis**=*in iis rebus, ad quas, in those things for which.* See note on "*Qua nocte, eadem*" (51, 4).

27 58, 2. **Tua;** supply *delectant.*——3. **Amicum,** *a friend,* i. e. my friend; possessive omitted according to 447.——5. **Consumpsi;** from *consumo.*

60, 1. **Deus est,** *there is a God.*——**Temporum,** *of the seasons.*——**Rerum,** *of events.*——2. **Mala;** construe with *carmina.*——3. **Honestatis;** depends upon *regula* understood, 397, 1, (3).——4. **Dominus;** supply *erat.*

62, 1. **Meorum,** *of my friends,* lit. *of my,* or *mine.*——2. **Agnovit;** from *agnosco.*——3. **Si quisquam;** supply *sapiens fuit.*——5. **Optimum quidque,** lit. *every best thing;* render, *all the best things, whatever is best,* or *the best thing ever,* 458, 1.——6. **Perdidit;** from *perdo.*

28 63, 3. **Peperi;** from *pario,* 280.——5. **Delati sunt;** from *defero,* 292, 2.——6. **Exercitum,** *his army.* Observe the omission of the possessive, 447.——7. **Exstinctum est;** from *exstinguo,* to put out, extinguish, applicable to a light. The language is figurative; the beautiful city of Corinth is represented as a light, *lumen.*

64, 3. **Victoria;** supply *venit.*

65, 4. **Consules;** supply *bini creabantur* from the next clause.——**Bini,** *two by two,* i. e. *two each year,* distributive, 174, 2.

29 66, 1. **Perspexero;** from *perspicio.*

67, 1. **Ubi primum,** *when first,* i. e. as soon as.——2. **Cum Graecis Latina,** lit. *Latin things with Greek things;* render, *Latin studies with Greek studies.*——**Conjunxi;** from *conjungo.*——4. **Lycurgi leges.** Lycurgus was the great Spartan law-giver. His laws contributed much

to the prosperity and greatness of Sparta.——6. **Aureorum annulorum. 29**
The wearing of gold rings was one of the special privileges of senators
and knights.——**Detraxerat ;** from *detrăho.*

68, 3. **Nonnulli,** *not none,* i. e. some, 585, 1.——**Casune ;** *casu* with
the interrogative enclitic *ne* appended.——**Sit effectus ;** from *efficio.*——
4. **Quaesivit ;** from *quaero.*——**Salvusne . . . clipeus.** This was his
question when mortally wounded at Mantinēa. Ancient warriors took
special pride in preserving their shields.——5. **Essent fusi ;** from
fundo.——6. **In causis,** *in suits at law.*

69, 3. **Redires ;** from *redeo.*   **30**

70, 7. **Tanquam parva,** *as small,* i. e. unimportant.

71, 1. **Abduxerant ;** from *abdūco.*——**Cincinnatum.** Cincinnatus,
who was thus summoned from the plough to the dictatorship in an hour
of great national peril, acted with such remarkable promptness and
energy, that in a few days he conquered the enemy, entered Rome in
triumph, and was rewarded with a golden crown. He then quietly re-
signed his dictatorship and returned to his farm.——**Dictator.** See note
on "*Cum honore dictatōris*" (178).——2. **Patris,** *of his father,* i. e.
the Sun. The story is, that he asked his father, the sun, for the use of
his chariot for a day, but that he found himself unable to manage the
fiery steeds.——5. **Decrevit ;** from *decerno.*——**Ut consul . . . . ne
. . . . caperet.** This was the usual formula by which a Roman citizen
might be clothed with the power of dictator.

72, 1. **Ut . . . diligamus ;** XXIV. 2, 5).——4. **Senserit ;** from **31**
sentio.

73, 2. **Quin . . . . abeam ;** XXIV. 2, 6).——4. **Quominus sit ;**
lit. *by which,* or *that, the less God should be ;* render, *that God should
be,* or *God from being,* XXVI. 6.

74, 1. **Qui sustineret,** lit. *who should sustain ;* render, *to sustain,*
XXIV. 3.——4. **Quod . . . possit ;** XXIV. 2, 5).——6. **Inventi sunt ;**
from *invenio.*

75, 1. **Dum metuant ;** XXIV. 2, 6).

77, 4. **Nisi in litteris,** *if not in letters,* i. e. in literary pursuits, stu- **32**
dies.——5. **Non . . . senatum.** Senatus, *senate,* is derived from *senex,*
and meant originally an assembly of *old men.*

78, 2. **Constiterit ;** from *consisto.*——4. **Qui . . . attigissem,** *though
I had commenced* (touched) *Greek studies* (letters); XXIV. 2, 6).——
Attigissem ; from *attingo.*

80, 1. **Quum . . . sit ;** XXIV. 2, 1).——2. **Necesse est.** The subject is the clause, *Deum . . . . majŏra.* Hence *necesse* is neuter, **33**
438, 3 ; 42, III. 2.——**Deum . . . . habere ;** XXV. 1.——**Haec habere
majora,** lit. *to have these greater,* i. e. in a higher degree.——4. **Suo
toto . . . non viderit.** As the term of the consular office was a year,

33 this seems a very remarkable statement. But the truth \s, Caninius was appointed only to fill.a vacancy of a few hours at the very end of the consular year. Hence the remark is only a playful one.

81, 1. **Malorum,** *of evils ;* from *malum.*——**Quod .... capiantur ;** XXIV. 2, 1). The Subjunctive implies that the reason is assigned on Plato's authority.——**Pisces ;** supply *capiantur.*——2. **Latine,** *in Latin.*——3. **Redierim ;** from *redeo,* 295, 3.

82, 1. **Dum .... convenirent ;** XXIV. 2, 1).——**Ad horam nonam,** *till the ninth hour,* i. e. till 3 P. M. For the divisions of the Roman day, see 711.——2. **Quievere ;** from *quiesco.*——3. **Vocem ... excitant.** The immense audiences before which the ancient tragedians acted, rendered this precaution quite indispensible.

83, 1. **Quantas .... habeat ;** XXIV. 2, 2).——2. **Tantum,** *only.* ——4. **Qui .... videant ;** XXIV. 3, 2).——**Quas in partes,** lit. *into what parts ;* render, *in what direction.*——6. **Unus,** *one,* viz. Demos-
34 thenes.——7. **Est.** The subject is the clause, *qualis res ... sit,* 555.

84, 1. **Ut ... servem,** *that I should keep myself neutral,* i. e., in respect to the civil wars.——2. **Quas cognorit.** XXIV. 2, 3).——**Cognorit ;** for *cognovĕrit,* 234, 2.——3. **Jussit ;** from *jubeo,* 269.——**Quae ;** refers to *naves,* as its antecedent.——5. **Ut—videar ;** XXIV. 2, 5).—— **Vixisse ;** from *vivo.*

85, 1. **Quod scirent ;** XXIV. 2, 4).——2. **Bestiolas.** Reference is here made to the insect known as the *ephemeran.*——3. **Respondit ;** from *respondeo.*——**Sibi, suas.** Here *sibi* refers to Caesar, the subject of the subordinate clause, while *suas* refers to Ariovistus, the subject of the principal clause. See 449, II.——**Vicissent ;** from *vinco.*——4. **Si ... esset .... fuisse.** In the *direct* discourse, this would have the Imperfect Subjunctive in both clauses, the third form of the conditional sentence (510). For changes in the *conclusion,* see 533, 2, 2).—— **Ille,** *he,* i. e. Caesar.——**A se,** *from himself,* i. e. Ariovistus.——5. **Egit ;**
35 from *ago, treated, argued.*——**Reminisceretur.** In the *direct* discourse, this would have been in the Imperative : hence the Subjunctive here according to 530, II.

86, 2. **Patres conscripti,** *conscript fathers,* often used in addressing the Roman senate.——5. **Dormiant ;** supply pronoun referring to *virtutes,* they.——6. **Sunto,** *let them be.*——8. **Militiae summum jus,** *the supreme control of military affairs.*——**Parento ;** supply pronoun, referring to *consules.*——9. **Te ;** subject of *esse.*——10. **Quam primum,** *as soon as possible,* 444, 3.

36 87, 4. **Positam esse ;** from *pono.*——5. **Traditum est ;** from *trado.* ——7. **Cupidum ;** Acc. Masc. Sing. agreeing with *aliquem,* any one, the omitted subject of *esse.*——9. **Suis rebus ;** *with one's own things. Suis* refers to the omitted subject of *esse.*——**Sunt ;** agrees by attraction with

Pred. Nom. *divitiae*, instead of the subject clause, 462.——11. **Lycurgi 36 temporibus.** This was in the ninth century B. C.——14. **Inventas esse;** from *invenio*.——16. **Amare;** supply *est*.——17. **Minima;** *the smallest*, i. e. the smallest evils (*mala*).

88, 4. **Graece loqui,** *to speak in Greek*.——**Latine;** supply *loqui*. ——6. **Didicerunt;** from *disco*.——13. **Esse;** supply *bonus*.

89, 3. **Videre .... caperet.** This was the duty, or business, *ne-* **37** *gotium*, assigned to Postumius. The language is the usual form of decree by which the Dictator was clothed with extraordinary power, in order to save the state. See note on " *Cum honōre dictatōris* " (178). Postumius was Dictator.——4. **Themistoclem.** This is the subject of the infinitive *sumpsisse*, while the whole clause, *Themistoclem .... sumpsisse*, is in apposition with *fama*.——**Sumpsisse;** from *sumo*.

90, 3. **Inter nos;** lit. *between ourselves ;* render, *with each other*.—— 4. **Accedit quod;** lit. *it is added that*, i. e. there is the additional fact that.

91, 1. **Tu;** subject of *responsūrus sis*.——2. **Pervenissentne;** *pervenissent* and *ne*.——3. **Mel;** subject of *esse* understood.——5. **Interfuisset;** from *intersum*.

92, 3. **Discendi;** supply *facultātem*, 397, 1, (3).——4. **Audiendi;** supply *occasio*.——7. **Platonis audiendi,** *of hearing Plato ;* lit. *of Plato* **38** *to be heard*. *Platōnis* depends upon *studiōsus*, while the gerundive *audiendi* agrees with it, 562.——9. **Quid audierim,** *what I have heard.*

93, 3. **Sacerdotibus creandis;** lit. *to priests to be appointed ;* render, *to the appointment of priests*, 580.——**Adjecit;** from *adjicio*.——6. **Nonnulli,** *some*, 585, 1.

94, 1. **Ad intelligendum;** lit. *to understanding ;* render, *to understand*.——**Est natus;** from *nascor*, lit. *has been born ;* render, *is born*, 471, 3.——4. **Ad cognoscendas .... leges;** lit. *to the laws to be learned ;* render, *to learn*, or *study the laws*, etc.——**Lycurgi leges.** The laws of Lycurgus, the great law-giver of Sparta, were very famous in antiquity.——6. **Catilina .... conjuravit.** This iniquitous conspiracy was formed during the consulship of the orator Cicero, 63 B. C., by whom it was fortunately discovered and defeated.

95, 1. **Nihil agendo,** *by doing nothing.*

96, 2. **Concessit;** from *concēdo*.——3. **Defensum;** from *defendo*. **39** ——5. **Facies;** the object is *id*, the omitted antecedent of *quod*.——6. **Cognita;** from *cognosco*.——**Oratio;** supply *jucunda est* from the preceding clause.

97, 2. **Hippias.** He had once been tyrant of Athens, but having been driven from the throne, he repaired to the Persian court and espoused the Persian cause.——**Cecidit;** from *cado*.——8. **Pinxit;** from *pingo*.——**Temple .... Dianae.** See note on the same, (51, 4).

PAGE

39 ——5. **Terra mutata ;** lit. *earth,* or *land, having been changed;* render, *change of country,* 580.——6. **Expulsus ;** from *expello.*——7. **Factus ;** from *facio,* Pass. *fio.*——**Subegit ;** from *subigo.*——8. **Vincta ;** from *vincio.*——9. **Regibus exactis ;** lit. *the kings having been expelled ;* render, *when,* or *after, the kings were expelled,* 431, 2, (1). This refers to the overthrow of the regal form of government at Rome by the banishment of Tarquin, 510 B. C. See below (167, 168).——

40 12. **Empta ;** from *emo.*——13. **Dilapsi sunt ;** from *dilābor.*

98, 3. **Secunda ;** *prosperous things,* i. e. prosperity.

99, 2. **In bonis rebus ;** lit. *in good things ;* render, *among good things,* i. e. as blessings.——4. **Eripi, surripi.** *Eripio* means *to tear away forcibly ; surripio, to take away stealthily.*

FABLES.

41　　100. **Praetereunti ;** Dative Sing. Part. of *praetereo,* 295, 3.——**Inquit ;** the object is the clause, or sentence, "*Non . . . . maledixit,*" 357, I.

101. **Orto ;** from *orior.*——**Quantum boni,** lit. *how much of a good thing ;* render, *how much good,* 396, 2, 3). Both adjectives are here used *substantively,* 441, 2.

42　　102. **Coepit,** *she* (the woman) *began.*——**Illam,** *that she,* i. e. the hen.——**Minores ;** supply *divitias.*——**Perdidit ;** from *perdo.*

103. **Deprehensus ;** from *deprehendo.*——**Mehercule ;** lit. *by Hercules ;* render, *indeed,* 589, 590.

104. **Subsilit ;** from *subsilio.*——**Si . . . . posset ;** *if perchance she might be able,* i. e. to ascertain whether she might, a dependent question, 525, 1.——**Acerbae sunt ;** *they are sour,* agreeing with *uvae* understood. ——**Repertas ;** from *reperio.*——**Quae ;** depends upon *assĕqui.*——**Quae . . . . desperent ;** XXIV. 2, 5).

105. **Inhaeserat ;** from *inhaereo.*——**Qui extrahat ;** lit. *who may remove it ;* render, *that he may remove it,* or *to remove it,* XXIV. 3, 2). ——**Hoc,** *this,* i. e. the removal of the bone.——**Quam . . . . postularet ;**

43 XXIV. 2, 1).——**Videtur ;** the subject is the clause, *quod . . . . extraxisti.*——**Extraxisti ;** from *extrăho.*

106. **Propter hoc ipsum,** *on account of this very thing,* or *for this very reason.*——**Quum,** *though.*——**Eos ;** supply *esse puniendos.*

107. **Quum . . . . sentiret ;** XXIV. 2, 1).——**Ut fieri solet,** *as is wont to happen. Solet* is used impersonally.——**Quibus allatis,** *which*

PAGE

having been brought, i. e. when these were brought, 431, 2.——**Quibus ;** **43**
see 453.——**Allatis ;** from *affèro*, 292, 2.——**Quod ;** *which*, or *this*, i. e.
the breaking of the bundle of rods ; it refers to the clause, *ut . . . . frangèrent.*——**Imbecillis ;** supply *res esset* from the preceding clause.

108. **Quemodo,** *how*, i. e. to determine *how*.——**Propositis ;** from
propòno.——**Posse ;** depends upon a verb of saying understood ; *for* **44**
thus, they said, *they would be able*, etc., 530, 1.——**Nemo repertus est,**
no one was found, i. e. who would do it.——**Repertus est ;** from *reperio*.

109. **Unus ;** supply *residēbat.*——**Orta ;** from *orior*.——**Quum . . . .**
desperarent, *while all despaired*, etc., 518, II.——**Interrogat.** The two
objects are *gubernatōrem*, and the clause, *utram . . . . existimāret*, 374, 4.
——**Submersum iri ;** Fut. Pass. Infin. of *submergo*, *would be submerged*,
would go down.——**Proram.** The full form would be : *Proram prius
submersum iri existimo.*——**Ille ;** supply *dixit*, 367, 3.——**Quum . . . .**
sim ; XXIV. 2, 1).——**Adspectarus sim ;** from *adspicio*.

110. **Illa,** *she*, i. e. the tortoise.——**Se volucrem facere,** *to make her
winged*, i. e. to teach her to fly.——**Arreptam ;** from *arripio*, agrees
with *illam : the eagle carried her, seized in his talons*=seized her in his
talons and carried her ; XX. 5 ; 579.——**Sustulit ;** from *tollo*.——**In
sublime,** *on high*.

111. **Junxerant ;** from *jungo*.——**Ovis ;** supply *et* before this word. **45**
Prima ; supply *pars*.——**Quartam ;** supply *partem*, the object of *arrogāre.*——**Habiturum ;** supply *esse*, 545, 3.

ANECDOTES.

112. **Sciebam . . . . mortalem ;** object of *dixisse*, 857, L.——**Genuisse ;** from *gigno*.——**Mortalem ;** agrees with *eum* understood.

113. **Quod,** *that which.* The full form would be, *Deus est id
quod*, etc.

114. **Se ipsum nosse ;** supply *difficile est.*——**Nosse ;** for *novisse*.

115. **Spes ;** supply *communis est*, etc.——**Qui ;** supply *habent*.

116. **Deus ;** supply *est*, etc.

117. **In pompa.** In the sacred processions, so common at the reli- **46**
gious festivals at Athens, the consecrated vessels of gold and silver
were often displayed.

118. **Scire . . . . nihil.** See note on " *Nescium fingit* " (40, 8).

119. **Scipio Africanus.** This is the celebrated Roman general who
conquered Hannibal at Zama. See below (196) and note on " *Africanus* " (196).——**Antequam . . . . precatus esset ;** XXIV. 2, 1).

46   120. **Gentis Corneliae.** This was the *gens* to which Scipio belonged.
——**Jussit ;** from *jubeo*.——**Res gestas,** lit. *things done,* i. e. deeds,
achievements.   *Gestas,* participle from *gero*.

121. **Plus esse,** *that it,* i. e. the talent, *was more.*——**Quod,** *that
which ;* supply *id*.

122. **Se .... habere,** *that he had thirty years,* i. e. was thirty
years old.

123. **Quae conarentur ;**   XXIV. 2, 4).——**Quaesiverant ;** from
quaero.

47   124. **Scripsisset ;** from *scribo*.——**Cape ;** supply *ea,* them, i. e.
arms (*arma*).

125. **Quum .... dixisset ;** XXIV. 2, 1).——**Nos ;** supply *sumus*.

126. **Prae .... multitudine,** *because of the multitude*.

127. **Est propositum ;** from *propŏno*.

128. **Solon ;** the great law-giver of Athens.——**Cur .... constituisset ;** XXIV. 2, 2).

129. **Sapientem ;** this agrees with *rem,* and *stultam,* with *rem* understood.——**Sapiens ;** supply *es*.

130. **Quos ;** *those which ;* supply *eos*.

48   131. **Ipsi ;** refers to Cornelia.——**Traxit ;** from *traho ; detained.*
——**Donec .... redirent ;** XXIV. 2, 1).——**Haec,** *these,* i. e. the children.   It is attracted from *hi* to *haec,* to agree with the Pred. Noun,
ornamenta, 445, 4.

132. **Ferunt,** *they report, say.*   For the omission of the subject, see
460, 2.——**Oblivionis ;** supply *artem*.——**Quae,** *those things which ;*
supply *ea*.

133. **Bono viro pauperi,** lit. *to a good poor man ;* render, *to a good
man who was poor,* 442.——**Minus probato diviti ;** *to one less upright,
who was rich.*——**Filiam ;** *a daughter,* not *his* daughter.——**Virum.**
Vir means *man* in the noblest sense of the word, *the true man.*——
Quae ; supply *egeat*.

134. **Achilles, Homerus.**   The former is the hero of the *Iliad,* the
latter, its author.——**Olympico certamine,** *the Olympic contest.*   The
Olympic Games were celebrated once in four years at Olympia in Elis,
and were the most famous games in Greece.   To be crowned victor at
these games was a coveted honor, while the herald had but an humble
office.

135. **Profectus ;** from *proficiscor.*——**Quum videret ;** XXIV. 2, 1).
——**Egrederetur ;** from *egredior*.

49   136. **Tyrannorum dominatione.**   This refers to the oppressive rule
of the *Thirty Tyrants* appointed over Athens by the Spartans.   See
below (228).   The city was liberated from them by the heroism of
Thrasybulus.——**Quantas gratias, tantas**=*tantas gratias, quantas*.

137. **Proposuit ;** from *propŏno.*——**Qui invenisset,** *who should* **49** *discover.* The Pluperfect is explained by the fact that the discovery must *precede* the giving of the reward.

138. **Id,** *that,* i. e. what he intended to do.

139. **Is,** *he,* i. e. the friend.——**Per ... indignationem,** *with* (lit. *through*) *the greatest indignation.*——**Quid mihi tua ;** supply *opus est amicitiā* from the preceding question. *Tuā* agrees with *amicitiā* to be thus supplied.

140. **Philippe.** This is Philip, king of Macedonia.

141. **Titus amor ... humani.** Titus was the most beloved of the **50** Roman Emperors.——**Quod nihil praestitisset,** *that he had rendered no service.* The Subjunctive implies that this fact was the reason which the writer would give *on the authority of Titus* for the exclamation, *Amici .... perdĭdi.* See 520, II.——**Praestitisset ;** from *praesto.*—— **Edidit ;** from *edo.*

142. **Cecidisse ;** from *cado.*——**Cognovit ;** from *cognosco.*——**Coronam.** Crowns, or wreaths, were often worn by the ancient Romans on sacred and festive occasions.——**Deposuit ;** from *depŏno.*——**Voluptatem ;** depends upon *sentīre.*

143. **In lud. Ol. Victores.** See note on "*Olympĭco certamĭne*" (134).——**Affectus est ;** from *afficio.*——**Stadio,** *race-course.* Races formed a prominent feature in the Olympic contests.

144. **Progressus ;** from *progredior.*——**Fabulas,** *fables ;* here *tragedies.*——**Ut ... doceret.** This implies that he aimed to *instruct,* rather than to *please* the people.

145. **Praesidibus,** *the presidents,* or *governors,* i. e. of the provinces. **51** *Praesidĭbus* depends upon *rescripsit.*——**Onerandas ;** supply *esse.*

146. **Vicem eorum,** *their fate.*——**Hectorem,** *Hector,* the most famous Trojan warrior.——**Effluxerant ;** this agrees with *anni.*——**Plus quam mille,** *more than a thousand years.* *Plus,* when thus introduced, has no effect upon the construction ; otherwise we might expect the verb *effluxĕrant* to be put in the singular. See 417, 3.

147. **Quaesivisset ;** from *quaero.*——**Idem,** *the same thing,* i. e. the same question.——**Petivit,** *he,* i. e. Simonides, *asked. Duplicāret* below has the same subject.——**Quanto diutius—tanto obscurior,** *the longer—the more obscure.* Quanto—tanta, lit. *by as much as—by so much,* is often best rendered before comparatives, *the—the,* XXVI. 5.

ROMAN HISTORY.

52   148. **In Italiam.** What construction would be used with the name of a town? 379.——**Janiculo:** a hill on the west side of the Tiber, not one of the *seven* hills of Rome, though included within the wall built by Aurelian in the third century.

149. **Troja . . . eversa est.** This refers to the famous Trojan war, said to have taken place in the twelfth century B. C.——**Eversa est;** from *everto.*——**Hinc,** *hence,* i. e. from Troy.——**Pepercerat;** from *parco.*——**Ei benigne recepto . . . dedit,** lit. *gave to him kindly received:* render, *received him kindly and gave,* 579.——**Laviniam;** a town in Latium a few miles south of Rome.

53   150. **Monte Albano.** Mount Albanus is about 16 miles southeast of Rome.——**Eum,** *him,* i. e. Ascanius.——**Genitus erat;** from *gigno.*—— **Ejus.** For whom does this pronoun stand?

151. **Minor natu;** lit. *smaller in respect to birth,* or *age:* render, *younger.*——**Bona,** lit. *good things=goods, property.*

152. **Vestalem virginem.** The *Vestal Virgins* were the priestesses of the goddess Vesta: they ministered in her temple, and, by turns, watched the perpetual fire upon her altars night and day. They were bound by an oath of chastity, whose violation was punished by death. ——**Viro;** indirect object after *nubĕre,* to marry=*to veil one's self for,* in allusion to the custom of the bride's wearing the veil at the marriage ceremony.——**Peperit;** from *pario.*——**Hoc,** *this,* i. e. the fact spoken of in the preceding sentence.——**Quum . . . . comperisset.** XXIV. 2, 1).——**Comperisset;** from *comperio.*

153. **Effuderat;** from *effundo.*——**Quum . . . . essent positi;** XXIV. 2, 1).——**Essent positi;** from *pono.*——**Siceo;** supply *loco.*

54   154. **Sic,** *thus,* i. e. as explained above.——**Transegerunt;** from *transigo.*——**Quum adolevissent . . . comperissent;** XXIV. 2, 1).—— **Adolevissent;** from *adolesco.*——**Quis;** subject of *fuisset* understood. ——**Quae . . . fuisset;** XXIV. 2, 2).——**Aventino;** one of the seven hills of Rome. According to the best authority, Romulus founded his city not on the *Aventine* as here stated, but on the *Palatine,* which stands a little to the north of it.——**Quum . . . . circumdaretur,** XXIV. 2, 1).

155. **Asylum.** This was a place of refuge where exiles and even criminals might obtain shelter and protection.——**Quum . . . . venissent;** XXIV. 2, 1).——**Inter ipsos ludos,** *in the midst of the very games.*

156. Quum ... appropinquarent ; XXIV. 2, 1).——In Tarpeiam **54**
... inciderunt. *They fell in with,* or *met Tarpeia,* etc.——**Annales**
.... armillas. Rings and bracelets were often awarded to soldiers
who had distinguished themselves in battle.

157. Tarpeium. This was one of the seven hills of Rome: it was **55**
also called *Capitolinus.* The Capitol was built upon it.——**Forum**
Romanum. This was an open space in the form of an irregular quad-
rangle between the Palatine and Capitoline Hills. In this were held
the great public meetings of the Roman people.——**In media caede,** *in*
the midst of the slaughter, 441, 6.——**Raptae ;** supply *mulieres.*——
Hinc .... hinc, *on the one side .... on the other.*——**Foedus icit,** *made*
a compact. **Ico,** lit. *to strike,* has reference to striking and slaying the
victim in ratification of treaties, compacts, etc.——**In urbem recepit,**
lit. *received into the city:* the meaning is, *he received them into full citi-*
zenship.

158. Descripsit ; from *describo.*——**Quum .... tum,** *not only*
.... but also.——**Quum .... lustraret ;** XXIV. 2, 1). *Lustraret,*
reviewed, lit. *purified,* as there were certain ceremonies appointed for
the review of a Roman army.——**Ortam ;** from *orior.*——**Interfectum ;**
from *interficio.* Supply *esse.*

159. Interregnum. This was the interval between the death of
one king and the accession of his successor to the throne. In this instance the government was administered by the senate.——**Elapso ;**
from *elabor.*——**Natus ;** from *nascor.*——**Gessit ;** from *gero.*——**Ege-**
riae monitu ... dicebat. This was the device of Numa to give sanc-
tity to his institutions, as Egeria was a goddess.——**Morbo decessit,** lit.
died from disease, i. e. died a natural death.

160. Successit ; from *succedo.*——**Praestiterat ;** from *praesto.*—— **56**
Horatiorum et Curiatiorum. After the necessary preparations for hos-
tilities had been made both by the Albans and the Romans, and the
two armies were already drawn up face to face, it was agreed to decide
the question of supremacy by a combat between the three brothers, the
Horatii, on the part of the Romans, and the three Curiatii, also brothers, on the part of the Albans. The Curiatii were all slain ; one of
the Horatii survived ; his victory therefore decided the question in
favor of Rome. See *Schmitz's Hist. Rome.*——**Perfidiam Metii Suffetii.**
Metius Suffetius, dictator of the Albans, having been summoned by the
Romans to aid them against the Veientines, drew off his forces at the
very moment of battle, and awaited the issue of the engagement. For
this perfidy he was put to death, and Alba was razed to the ground.
See *Schmitz's Hist. Rome.*——**Annis.** What is the common construction for duration of time ? 378.

161. Nova et moenia circumdedit. The same thought may be ex-

PAGE

56 pressed thus: *Novis eam moenĭbus circumdĕdit;* in which *eam* is the *direct object*, and *moenĭbus*, the ablative of *means*. 884, II. 1.——**Morbe obiit.** Compare *morbo decessit* (159).

162. **Qui .... Tarquinĭis accepit.** He was called *Tarquinius* from the city *Tarquinii* in Etruria, where he lived many years.

57 163. **Minorum gentium,** supply *patres,* or *senatōres.*——**Nec paucæ,** lit. *nor a few;* render, *and not a few.*——**Ademptos,** from *adĭmo.*——**Triumphans,** *triumphing=in triumph.* The honor of entering Rome with an imposing triumphal procession was, in later times, often award-ed to victorious generals.——**Capitolium.** The term Capitol was some-times applied to the temple of Jupiter, and sometimes to the whole Capitoline Hill, including both the temple and the citadel.——**Per Anci filios.** What is the usual construction for the agent after passive verbs? 414, 5.

164. **Genitus;** from *gigno.*——**Adolevisset;** from *adolesco.*

165. **Tanaquil ... dicens, regem ... obediret.** This was the de-vice which Tanaquil, the widow of the murdered Tarquin, employed to place her son-in-law, Servius Tullius, upon the throne. Her success was complete.——**Dicens.** What is the direct object of this transitive par-ticiple? 550.——**Convaluisset;** from *convalesco.*——**Montes tres.** The *Viminal, Esquiline,* and *Coelian* Hills are undoubtedly meant, though the *Coelian* was probably added under the reign of Ancus Marcius. The other *four* of the *seven* hills, the *Palatine, Capitoline, Quirinal,* and *Aventine,* were already occupied.——**Censum.** The *census* was taken every five years for the purpose of ascertaining the number of citizens, the amount of property, etc.——**In agris,** *in the fields,* i. e. in the coun-try, or territory about Rome.

166. **Interfectus est;** from *interficio.*——**Quum ... rediret;** XXIV. 2, 1).

167. **Cognomen .. meruit;** he was called *Superbus,* because his character deserved the title.——**Moribus;** observe the difference of meaning between the singular and the plural, 132.

58 168. **In exitium,** lit. *into the destruction;* render, *for the destruc-tion.* What cases does *in* admit, and with what significations? 435, 1. **Ei,** *against him,* indirect object.

169. **Consules.** The consuls were joint presidents of the Roman Commonwealth, with all the power and most of the insignia of office which the kings had assumed.——**Annuum,** *for one year.*——**Placuerat,** lit. *it had pleased, seemed good;* render, *it had been determined.*——**Tarquiniorum familia.** Collatinus belonged to this family. He was accordingly deprived of his office and went into exile.——**In ejus locum,** lit. *into his place:* here, by a difference of idiom, it must be rendered, *in his place.*

170. **Sese invicem,** lit. *themselves in turn ;* render, *each other.*—— **59**
Luxerant; from *lugeo.*——**Quinque consules.** One consul had been
deprived of his office during the year, one had been slain in battle, and
another had died.

171. **Horatius . . . . esset.** This achievement of Horatius Cocles,
and that of Mucius Scaevola, mentioned below (172), became famous in
the annals of Rome. They have been celebrated in prose and verse.
See Macaulay's Lays of Ancient Rome.——**Donee . . . raptus esset,**
XXIV. 2, 1).——**Ad suos,** *to his friends, companions.*

172. **Castra;** observe difference of meaning between the singular and the plural. 132.——**Scribam pro rege.** He mistook the secre-
tary for the king.——**Terreret,** *endeavored to terrify.* 469, 1.——
Donee . . . . consumpta esset. XXIV. 2, 1).——**Consenuit;** from **60**
consenesco.

173. **Exactos;** from *exigo.*——**Questus;** from *queror.*——**Quod**
. . . . **exhauriretur;** XXIV. 2, 1).——**Secessit;** from *secedo.*——**Patres,** *senators,* see above (158).——**Qui . . . . conciliaret;** XXIV. 3, 2).
——**Tribuni plebis.** The tribunes were at first two in number, then
five, and finally ten. Their persons were sacred and they were clothed
with great power. They might at any time, by their power of *veto,* arrest the action of the magistrates, or even of the senate.

174. **Milliarium urbis,** lit. *milestone of the city ;* render, *milestone
from the city.* The Roman roads were furnished with milestones mark-
ing the distance from the city.

175. **Duce Fabio consule,** lit. *Fabius the consul* (being) *leader ;* **61**
render, *under the command of Fabius the consul.*——**Quum . . . . vicissent,** XXIV. 2, 1).——**Pellexisset;** from *pellicio.*——**Exorto;** from
exorior.——**Perierant;** from *pereo.*——**Potuerat;** from *possum.*——
Prudenti cunctatione, *by prudent delay.* Fabius, in the second Punic
war, deliberately adopted the policy of weakening Hannibal by *delay,* i. e.
by not allowing him an engagement. His policy was entirely successful.

176. **In eo erant, ut . . . . emerent,** *they were in this,* i. e. in such
a condition, *that they would purchase ;* the meaning is, *they were on the
point of purchasing.*

177. **Magnitudine.** What other case might have been used ? 896, IV.
——**Provocavit,** *challenged.*——**Hinc,** *hence,* i. e. from the fact of taking **62**
the *torquis* and adorning himself with it. *Torquati* is derived from
torquis.

178. **Cum honore dictatoris,** *with the rank of dictator.* The dictator
was appointed only in times of great danger, and was invested with almost unlimited power for a period of six months.——**Magistro equitum.**
This is the title of an officer always appointed in connection with the
dictator, or by him.——**Occasionem nactus,** *taking advantage of a fa-*

62 *vorable opportunity.*——**Nactus;** from *nanciscor.*——**Capitis,** lit. *of the head ;* render, *to death.*

179. **Post,** *afterwards.*——**Quid . . . . putaret;** XXIV. 2, 2).——

63 **Respondit.** What is the direct object? 550.——**Dimittendos;** supply *esse.*——**Sub jugum.** The yoke was thus used as the symbol of submission and servitude ; it consisted of a spear supported horizontally by two others placed in an upright position.

180. **Quia . . . . fecissent.** If this reason had been given on the authority of the narrator, the indicative would have been used. The subjunctive implies that this was the reason then alleged for waging the war. See 520, II.——**Primum . . . transmarino hoste.** Their previous wars had been waged with various nations in Italy and Gaul.—— **Quum . . . . cepisset;** XXIV. 2, 1).——**Quaecunque . . . . agerentur;** XXIV. 2, 3).

181. **Auxilio elephantorum.** The Romans had never before met elephants in battle, and indeed were unacquainted with the animal. The battle was fought in Lucania ; accordingly the Romans called the elephants Lucanian oxen, *boves Lucae.*——**Per noctem,** *during the night.* ——**Adversis vulneribus,** *with wounds in front :* it was a disgrace to receive a wound in the back.——**Etiam mortuos,** *even in death.*——**Ego . . . . subigerem ;** in apposition with *voce.*

182. **Perrexit ;** from *pergo.*——**Octavo decimo.** What other form **64** of this numeral is common? 174.——**De captivis redimendis ;** lit. *concerning captives to be ransomed :* the meaning is, *to treat concerning the ransoming of captives.*——**Fabricium.** Fabricius was celebrated for his integrity. See note on *" Fabricius "* above (49, 6).——**Ut . . . . promitteret ;** XXIV. 2, 5).——**Contemptus est ;** from *contemno.*

183. **Quum . . . . teneretur ;** XXIV. 2, 1).——**Qui . . . preteret,** lit. *who should seek :* render, *that he might ask,* or *to ask ;* XXIV. 3, 2).——**Ut Pyrrhus . . . . obtineret.** This clause expresses the *condition* on which Cineas was to ask peace, and may accordingly be regarded as in apposition with *conditiōne.* 495, 3.——**Ex Italia.** What construction would be used, if the name of a *town* should be substituted here ? 421, II.——**Rediisset ;** from *redeo,* 295, 3.——**Pyrrho ;** indirect object of *respondit ;* the *direct* object is the clause, *se regum patriɔm vidisse.* 550.——**Qualis . . . . visa esset.** XXIV. 2, 2).

184. **Altero,** *second.*——**Interfecti ;** supply *sunt.*——**Vinctum ;** from *vincio,* bound, or *in chains.*——**" Ille . . . ab honestate . . . potest."** This entire sentence, as a direct quotation, is the object of *dixisse,* 357, I. ——**Ille est Fabricius qui.** *Fabricius is that one who,* i. e. the man, who.——**Honestate ;** supply *averti potest.*——**A Tarente.** What is the common construction ? 423, I. ; 423, 1.——**Recessit ;** from *recēdo.*

65 185. **Post urbem conditam,** lit. *after the city built ;* render, *after the* *building of the city*, 580. Rome, the city here spoken of, is said to **65** have been founded 753 B. C.——**Primam . . . dimicaverunt.** This was the first naval engagement of the Romans. Their previous wars had been waged only on land.——**Duillio . . . consulibus.** The date of an event was generally denoted by the names of the two *consuls* for that year; *in the consulship of Duillius and Asina*, lit. *Duillius, Asina, consuls*, or *being consuls*. These names are thus put in the *Ablative Absolute*, generally without the connective *et*.——**Mersit;** from *mergo*.

186. **Paucis . . . interjectis**, lit. *a few years having been thrown between;* render, *after a few years had intervened*, or *after an interval of a few years*, 431, 2.——**Est translatum;** from *transfero*.——**Sexaginta quattuor.** May *quattuor* stand before *sexaginta?* If so, would *et* be expressed, or omitted? 174, foot-note.——**Viginti duas;** supply *naves*.——**Amiserunt;** from *amitto*.——**Quum . . . venissent;** XXIV. 2, 1).——**In fidem acceperunt**, *received under their protection*, though as subject states.——**Captus;** supply *est* from next clause. See also **66** XXVI. 4.——**Conjectus est;** from *conjicio*.

187. **Favit.** How is the Perfect of this verb formed? 270. How is the Perfect regularly formed in the second conjugation? 213, II.—— **Quum victi essent;** XXIV. 2, 1).——**Ut . . . proficisceretur . . . et impetraret.** Verbs of *asking* take two Accusatives, or Objects: these clauses may accordingly be treated as one of the objects of *rogaverunt*, while at the same time they express the *purpose* of the request. 492, 2; 874, 4.——**Dixit.** Give the direct object of this verb, 550.——**Desiisse;** from *desino*.——**Illa die.** What is the usual gender of *dies?* 121.—— **Illos**, *that they*, i. e. the Carthaginians.——**Illos . . . . habere.** This infinitive-clause does not strictly depend upon *suasit*, but upon a verb, or participle, signifying *to say*, involved in it. 530, 1.——**Fractos;** from *frango*.——**Tanti non esse**, *that it was not of so much importance= worth the while*.

188. **Punici**, *Punic*, i. e. Carthaginian. The word is derived from *Poeni*.——**Captae, demersae, capta;** supply *sunt* from *occisa sunt*.—— **Demersae;** from *demergo*.——**Citra Iberum**, *on this side of the Ebro*, i. e. on the side toward Rome, the northern side.——**Decesserunt;** from *decedo*.

189. **Novem annos natum**, lit. *having been born nine years:* render, **67** *when he was nine years old;* XX. 3.——**Hic . . . aetatis**, *he living*, or *passing the twentieth year of his age;* render, *he when in his twentieth year;* XX. 3.——**Qui quum**, *when he*, i. e. Hannibal, 453.——**Miserunt.** The object is *legatos* understood, though it is scarcely necessary to supply it in translating.——**Socios**, *the allies*, meaning the citizens of Saguntum.——**Reddita;** supply *sunt*.

190. **Fratre . . . relicto.** Hannibal left his brother in Spain to

67 take care of that province in his absence.——**Transiit;** from *transeo,* 295, 3.——**Traditur,** *he,* i. e. Hannibal, *is said.*——**Se conjunxerunt.** Why is *se* here used, rather than *eos* or *illos?* 449, I.——**Dediderunt** ;

68 from *dedo.*——**Progressus** ; from *progredior.*——**Interemptus;** from *interimo ;* supply *est.*

191. **Quingentesimo duodequadragesimo.** For combination of numerals, see 174.——**Intellectum erat;** from *intelligo.* The infinitive-clause, *Hannibalem . . . posse,* is the subject.——**Mora.** The Roman general, Fabius, had adopted with great success the policy of weakening Hannibal by *delay,* i. e. by not allowing him an engagement. See above (175).——**Victi, capti, occisi;** supply *sunt* with each participle.—— **Perierunt;** from *pereo.*——**Quod.** This relative does not relate to any particular word as its antecedent, but to the leading proposition, or the fact mentioned in it; the relative is accordingly neuter, as clauses used substantively uniformly take that gender, 42, III. 2.——**Factum;** supply *erat.*

192. **Obtulit;** from *offero.* Here *obtulit* takes *Romanis* as its *indirect* object, while the *direct* object appears in the form of a clause, viz. *ut captivos redimerent.* This is plainly the *offer* made to the Romans; but this clause also states the *purpose* of the offer, viz. *that they might ransom the prisoners.* Hence the subjunctive *redimerent.* 492. ——**Qui . . . potuissent,** *who had been able ;* XXIV. 2, 5).——**Armati.** The senate regarded it as a disgrace, that any should be captured so long as they had arms to defend themselves.——**Aureorum annulorum.** See note on the same (67, 6).——**Hos omnes.** Observe position at the beginning of the sentence to mark emphasis. 594, I.——**Detraxerat;** from *detraho.* How is the Perfect formed? 258, I. 1.——**Hasdrubal . . . . exercitu.** See above (190, line 1).——**Remanserat;** from *remaneo.*——**Duobus Scipionibus.** These were Cnaeus Cornelius Scipio and Publius Cornelius Scipio, the latter the father of Publius Cornelius Scipio Africanus, who defeated Hannibal at Zama. See below (196).

193. **Res prospere gesta est,** *a successful battle was fought.* In a military sense, *rem gero* frequently has this meaning.——**Magnam hujus**

69 **insulae partem.** For arrangement of words, see 598, 3.——**Inde,** *thence,* i. e. from Syracuse.——**In Macedonia.** What construction would have been used, if this had been the name of a *town* instead of that of a country? 421, II.——**In deditionem accepit,** lit. *received into surrender ;* the meaning is, *accepted the terms of a surrender.*——**Regressus est;** from *regredior.*

194. **Duo Scipiones.** See *duobus Scipionibus* (192) and note on the same. They were both slain in battle within a month of each other, in the year 212 B. C.——**Hic, puer duodeviginti annorum,** *he when a boy eighteen years of age,* 363, 3.——**Post cladem Cannensem,** *after the*

defeat at Cannae (191).——**Viginti quattuor** . . . . **natus,** lit. *having* **69** *been born twenty-four years ;* render, *when twenty-four years of age.* ——**Carthaginem Novam,** *New Carthage,* a city in Spain, founded soon after the first Punic war by Hasdrubal, brother-in-law of Hannibal. It was named after Carthage in Africa ; its present name is *Carthagena.* ——**Parentibus,** *to their parents.*——**Transierunt ;** from *transeo.*

195. **Creatus ;** supply *est.*——**Millibus . . . militibus.** When is *millia* followed by the Genitive and when by its own case ? 178.—— **Qua re audita,** lit. *which thing having been heard ;* render, *having heard this,* or *on hearing this,* 431, 2, 3).

196. **Plus semel**=*plus quam semel, more than once.*——**Ad Zamam,** **70** *near Zama.*——**Peritissimi duces,** Hannibal and Scipio are meant.—— **Scipio victor recedit,** lit. *withdrew victor ;* render, *left the field as victor,* or simply *was victorious.*——**Ingenti gloria triumphavit.** Compare *cum ingenti gloria . . . regressus est* (193).——**Africanus.** This title was conferred upon Scipio in commemoration of his victories in *Africa.* See also *nomen Africani junioris* (200).

197. **Finito Punico bello.** Which Punic war is meant ? (185 and 189).——**Macedonicum ;** supply *bellum.*——**Contra Philippum.** This limits *bellum* understood, *the war against Philip,* 352, II.——**Regem.** Philip was king of Macedonia.

198. **Rebellavit,** *rebelled,* i. e. renewed the war against Rome.—— **Rex.** What king ?——**Dederet, dediderunt ;** from *dedo.*——**Remorum ordines,** *banks of oars.* These were arranged, one above another, so that the oars belonging to the highest *ordo,* or *bank,* were much longer than those belonging to the lowest. War-vessels generally had three banks, and were accordingly called *triremes* (*tres, remi*), but it was no uncommon thing to see vessels with four or five banks, and some are said to have had thirty or forty.——**Ante currum,** *before the chariot,* **71** i. e. of the conqueror. In the triumphal procession, the captives and spoils preceded the chariot of the victor, while the victorious army followed it.

199. **Susceptum est ;** from *suscipio.*——**Ibi,** *there,* i. e. in Africa.—— **Per Scipionem.** What is the common construction for the *Agent* of passive verbs ? 414, 5.——**Tribunus,** *tribune,* an officer in the army commanding a part of a legion. The number of tribunes to each legion was at first three or four, afterward six.——**Nepotem,** *grandson,* but only by adoption. He was the son of Aemilius Paulus, the celebrated general, who conquered Macedonia. See above (198).

200. **Quum . . . esset . . . nomen,** *when now the name of Scipio was* (or, *had become*) *great ;* XXIV. 2, 1).——**Missus ;** supply *est.*—— **Acerrime defensam,** lit. *most valiantly defended ;* render, *though* (it was) *most valiantly defended.*——**Facta ;** supply *est.*——**Plurima,** *very many*

71 *things,* referring especially to the works of art, statues and votive offerings, which the Carthaginians had taken from the temples of the conquered cities in Sicily.

72 201. **Exortum est;** from *exorior.*——**Civitate.** Logically this is in apposition with *Numantia* implied in *Numantinis.*——**Victus;** supply *est.*——**Pacem infamem.** The terms were that Numantia should remain free and independent.——**Tradi;** depends upon *jussit* in the line above.——**Militem;** lit. *soldier,* the individual representing the class; render, *soldiery.*——**Correxit;** from *corrigo.*——**Partim—partim;** lit. *partly—partly;* render, *either—or.* These words may, however, be often best rendered by *some—others,* followed by *of.* Thus, *he captured some of the many cities of Spain and accepted others,* etc.—— **In deditionem accepit.** See note on the same (193).

202. **Anno urbis conditae . . . sexto,** *in the six hundred and sixty-sixth year from,* or *after* (lit. *of*) *the founding of the city.* *Urbis conditae* is here equivalent to *post urbem conditam* (185), or *ab urbe condita* (207).——**Romae.** What case would have been used, if this had been a noun of the third declension? 421, II.——**Mithridaticum;** supply *bellum.*——**Marius, Sullae.** These generals were the leaders of rival political parties. Marius was supported by the common people and Sulla by the nobles.——**Adversus Mithridatem.** This limits *bellum,* 398, 4.——**Quum . . . decretum esset;** the meaning is: *when the management of the war had been entrusted to him by a decree of the Senate.* The Subjunctive is here rendered according to XXIV. 2, 1). ——**Decretum esset;** from *decerno.*——**Ei,** i. e. *Sullae.*——**Quum—tum.** Usual meaning, *not only—but also;* *both—and,* etc.; render here *either —or.*——**Compositis;** from *compono.*——**Profectus est;** from *proficiscor.*

73 ——**Asia, quam invaserat.** Not all Asia, but that portion of it which he had invaded, referring especially to those portions of Asia Minor west of his own dominions.

203. **In Graecia et Asia.** Mithridates, emboldened by his success in Asia Minor, had sent an army into Greece. Athens and Thebes were at this time in his possession.——**Fugatus fuerat.** Marius had been for some time in concealment.——**Unus ex,** *one of;* lit. *one from.* ——**Ingressi;** from *ingredior.*——**Multos proscripserunt,** *proscribed many.* In the civil wars, Sulla caused lists of the names of those persons whom he wished to have killed to be exposed to public inspection. Those whose names were on these lists were outlawed or proscribed, and any one might slay them and claim a reward; their property was confiscated, and their descendants were excluded from all offices of honor and trust. See *Smith's Dict. of G. and R. Antiquities;* also *Schmitz's Hist. of Rome.*——**Compulerunt;** from *compello.*——**Sanguine.** Gender? **Civium.** Genitive plural, how formed? 65, 3, 1).

——**De**, lit. *concerning ;* render in this instance, *over.*——**Italicum, 73 civile ;** supply *bellum.*——**Sociale dictum est ;** this is the predicate of the relative clause.——**Viros consulares,** *men who had been consuls,* i. e. men of consular rank or dignity=*ex-consuls.* The consuls, it will be remembered, were two in number, were elected for one year, and had all the powers of king. See note on " *Consules* " (169).——**Praetorios,** *those who had been praetors.* When the office of praetor was first insti- tuted, only one was appointed, who was to act as a kind of third consul with the leading part in the administration of justice ; about a century later a second was added, called *praetor peregrinus,* to administer jus- tice among foreigners and strangers resident at Rome. The number of praetors was increased from time to time, until at the beginning of the civil wars of Sulla and Marius, it was six ; and in the dictatorship of Sulla it was raised to eight. See *Smith's Dict. of G. and R. Antiqui- ties,* and *Schmitz's Hist. Rome.*——**Aedilitios,** *those who had been aediles.* The *aediles* (from *aedes*) were Roman magistrates who had charge of the public buildings, highways, etc., and acted as city police. They were at first two in number, afterwards more. See *Smith's Dict.*—— **Senatores.** The Roman senate (from *senex*) was regarded as a body of *elders* or *fathers* (patres). The number was at first 100 (see 158), then 200 (see 163), and finally 300, which continued to be the number until the time of the civil wars between Sulla and Marius. The number was then increased to 500 or 600 by the election of a large body of Roman knights. See *Smith's Dict.*

204. **Commotum est ;** from *commoveo.*——**Gladiatores.** Gladiators were men who fought for the amusement of the Roman people. They consisted mostly of prisoners, slaves, and malefactors ; they were trained in the skilful use of weapons at schools established for the pur- pose (*ludo gladiatorio*).——**Capuae,** *at Capua.*——**Hannibal ;** subject **74** of *movit* understood.——**Contraxerunt ;** from *contraho :* explain for- mation of the Perfect ; 258, I. 1.——**Vicerunt ;** from *vinco.*——**Pro- consule.** The *proconsul,* as the name implies, was one who acted with the power of a consul. Those who had been consuls (*viri consulares*) were often allowed to assume the government of provinces, and to ex- ercise in these provinces all the powers of a consul ; they were then called *proconsuls.*——**Italiae.** Is this genitive *objective,* or *subjective?* 396, II.

205. **Per illa tempora.** How could *tempora* be governed without the preposition ? 378. *Per* makes the idea of duration more promi- nent, *throughout those times.*——**Maria.** What is the ending of the stem ? 63.——**Id bellum,** *this war,* i. e. that against the pirates.——**De- cretum est ;** from *decerno.* For the meaning see note on "*Quum* . . . . *decretum esset* " (202).——**Menses ;** give gender, 107, 2.——**Contra**

74 regem. This limits *bellum.*——**Quo suscepto,** lit. *which having been undertaken ;* render, *having undertaken this ;* 431, 2, (3).——**Tantum,** *only.*——**Coactus ;** from *cogo.*——**Hausit ;** from *haurio.*——**Hunc vitae finem.** For the order of these words, see 598, 3, and for their position at the beginning of the sentence, see 594, I.

206. **Ille se ei.** What nouns are represented by these pronouns ?

75 ——**Dedidit ;** from *dedo.*——**Grandi pecunia,** *a large sum of money,* according to Plutarch, 6,000 talents, more than $6,000,000.——**Seleuciam libertate donavit.** What two constructions occur ? 384, 1.——**Quia ... tulerat ; quod ... recepisset.** These are both causal clauses. The first, with the *Indicative,* states the reason as a *fact,* while the second, with the *Subjunctive,* implies that the reason was assigned *by Pompey.* 520.——**Occisis ;** from *occido.*——**His gestis,** lit. *by means of these things done,* i. e. *by these achievements,* Abl. of Means, 414, 4.——**Antiquissimo bello.** This war continued nearly thirty years.——**Ante triumphantis currum,** lit. *before the chariot of* (him) *triumphing ;* render, *before his chariot, as he triumphed,* referring to the triumphal procession.——**Filii Mithridatis.** They were five in number.——**Infinitum pondus.** According to Plutarch, this amounted to 20,000 talents, more than $20,000,000.——**Orbem terrarum,** strictly *the world,* but sometimes used by the Romans with special reference to the *Roman Empire.*

207. **Cicerone et Antonio consulibus,** lit. *Cicero and Antony* (being) *consuls :* render, *when Cicero and Antony were consuls,* or, *in the consulship of Cicero,* etc.——**Deprehensi ;** from *deprehendo.* Supply *sunt* from the next clause.

208. **Quum .... decreta esset,** *when Gaul had been assigned to him by decree,* i. e. as a military province ; XXIV, 2, 1).——**Vincendo processit,**

76 *proceeded by conquering,* i. e. advanced victoriously.——**Oceanum Britannicum,** *British Ocean,* i. e. the English Channel.——**Omnem Galliam quae,** etc. Not all Gaul, but that portion which is bounded as described.——**Ne nomen quidem,** *not even the name ;* 602, III. 2.——**Cognitum ;** from *cognosco.*

209. **Absens.** It was unlawful for a general, while in command of an army, to offer himself as a candidate for the consulship, and indeed for any one to do so while absent from Rome. Caesar was both absent from Rome and in command of an army.——**Quem quum ... deferrent, contradictum est,** etc., *when many would confer this,* etc., *opposition* (or, objection) *was made.*——**Dimissis ;** from *dimitto.*——**Transiit ;** from *transeo.*——**Dictatorem.** See note on "*Dictatoris*" (178).

210. **Inde,** *thence,* i. e. from Rome.——**Hispanias,** *Spain.* The plural is often used, as the country was divided into two parts, viz. *ulterior,* on this side of the Ebro, i. e. on the side toward Rome, and

ulterior, beyond the Ebro.——**Nec . . . . superari.** This entire clause **76** is the object of *dixit.* **550.**——**Nec**, *and not,* 587, I. 2.——**Vincere.** This is the object of *scire ;* Caesar said that Pompey did not know (what ?) *to conquer,* or *how to conquer.*——**Ingentibus . . . . commissis,** *with great forces engaged on both sides.*——**Pugnatum est,** *the battle was* **77** *fought.*——**Direpta sunt ;** from *diripio.*——**A rege Aegypti.** This king was the last of the Ptolemies and the brother of Cleopatra.——**Occidit ;** *slew,* though not with his own hands. He employed men to do it.—— **Generi.** Pompey had married Julia, the daughter of Caesar ; while she lived, she was, of course, a strong bond of union between the two, but she had died six years before the battle of Pharsalia.

211. **Qua de causa,** *for which cause.* For the order of words, see 602, II. 1.——**Pompeianarum . . . . reliquias,** *the remnant of Pompey's party.*——**Insolentius agere.** He allowed himself to be proclaimed consul for ten years, imperator and dictator for life. This was a virtual overthrow of the Roman Republic.——**Conjuratum est ;** *a conspiracy was formed.*——**Sexaginta vel amplius,** *sixty or more.*——**Inter conjuratos ;** lit. *among the having conspired,* i. e. among the conspirators. ——**Bruti duo ;** viz. *Marcus* and *Decimus.*——**Illius Bruti.** See above (169).——**Regibus expulsis,** lit. *the kings having been banished ;* render, *after the banishment of the kings.*——**Quum . . . venisset ;** XXIV. 2, 1).——**Confossus est ;** from *confodio.*

212. **Interfecto ;** from *interficio.*——**A Caesaris partibus stabat,** **78** *favored the party of* Caesar (stood by the party, etc.).——**Magister equitum.** See note on *"Magistro equitum"* (178).——**Susceptus est ;** from *suscipio.*——**Octavianus.** He was the son of Octavius, but was adopted by Julius Caesar, with the name *Octavianus Caesar.*——**Patris sui,** i. e. his father by adoption, *Julius Caesar.*——**Extorsit ;** from *extorqueo.*——**Ut . . . daretur.** This clause expresses both the *direct object* of *extorsit* and the *purpose* of the action : *Caesar extorted* (what ?) *that the consulship should be given,* and (for what purpose ?) *in order that it might be given.* See 492, 1.——**Viginti annorum.** The age required by law was forty-three.——**Junctus ;** from *jungo.*——**Proscripsit.** See note on *"Proscripserunt"* (203).——**Per hos.** By whom ?

213. **Profecti.** This is in the plural to agree with *Octavianus et Antonius.*——**Secundo ;** supply *proelio.*——**Infinitam nobilitatem, quae,** lit. *the infinite nobility, which ;* render, *the countless nobles, who.*—— **Victam interfecerunt,** lit. *they slew* (them) *being conquered ;* render, *they conquered and slew.* See 579.——**Hispanias.** See note on this word (210).——**Gallias.** The plural is used because the Romans divided **79** the country into two parts, viz. *Gallia ulterior* or *Transalpina,* or *Gaul beyond the Alps ;* and *Gallia citerior* or *Cisalpina,* or *Gaul on this side of the Alps ;* i. e. on the side toward Rome.

79   214. **Repudiata sorore.** Antony had married Octavia, the sister of Octavianus.——**Uxorem duxit,** *married,* lit. *lead as wife.* The language is explained by the fact that the bride was usually conducted to her new home by her husband and friends. See note on "*Nubĕre*" (152). ——**Qui locus.** The relative here has only the force of an adjective. ——**Desperatis rebus,** lit. *things having been despaired of ;* render, as *his cause was desperate* (or *hopeless*).——**Interemit ;** from *interimo.*—— **Ex eo inde tempore,** *from this time,* or *from this time forth. Inde* need not be translated.——**Ante ;** Adverb, *before,* or *previously.*

GRECIAN HISTORY.

80   215. **Pugnae .... facerent,** *did not give him an opportunity of coming to an engagement.* XXIV. 2, 1).——**Ponte Istri,** *the bridge over the Ister,* i. e. the Danube ; lit. *the bridge of the Ister.*——**Quum redilsset ;** XXIV. 2, 1); 518, II.——**Eique.** *Ei* refers to the fleet.

216. **Praefecti regii,** *the royal commanders,* i. e. Datis and Artaphernes.——**Appulsa ;** from *appello.*——**In Campum Marathona,** *into* **81** *the plain of Marathon.* For ending *a*, see 68, 1.——**Ab oppido,** *from the city,* i. e. from Athens.——**Circiter .... decem.** The distance by any suitable road was somewhat greater than this.——**Ea,** *this,* i. e. this state ; supply *civitas.*——**Decem .... completa sunt,** *the number of ten thousand armed men was completed,* or *filled up.* Thus there were 9000 Athenians and 1000 Plataeans.——**Sub montis radicibus,** *at the base of the mountain.*——**Commiserunt ;** from *committo.*——**Suis,** *for his men,* 441, 1.——**Tanto plus,** *so much more.*

217. **Quum Darius decessisset,** *when Darius had died ;* XXIV. 2, 1).——**Decessisset ;** from *decēdo.*——**In ipso apparatu,** *in the midst of his very preparations,* i. e. while actually engaged in preparing for a second invasion.——**Hujus classis,** *the fleet of this one,* i. e. Xerxes ; render *his fleet.*——**Navium longarum,** *ships of war,* called *longae,* because they were built much longer than the ships of burden (*onerariarum*).——**Navium .... fuit,** *was of .... ships,* i. e. *consisted of,* etc. ——**De adventu.** This is an attributive modifier of *fama,*—the report *of his approach.*——**Peti,** *to be aimed at.*——**Miserunt Delphos,** *they sent to Delphi ;* object omitted, *sent messengers.* The Delphic oracle was the most famous in Greece.——**De rebus suis,** lit. *concerning their* **82** *things,* i. e. *for their safety.*——**Id .... valeret,** *what this answer meant.*——**Ut .... conferrent.** This clause is the predicate after *esse,*

as it states what the design was.——**Eum—ligneum,** *for that that* **82** *wooden wall was meant,* etc., i. e. that that was the wooden wall meant, etc.——**Triremes.** See note on " *Remorum ordines* " (108).——**Majoribus nata,** *old or aged men, elders.*

218. **Hujus consilium,** *the plan of this one,* i. e. Themistocles.—— **Delecti,** *picked men.*——**Qui . . . . accuparent ;** XXIV. 3, 2.——**Thermopylas.** Thermopylae is a narrow pass between Locris and Thessaly, immortalized as the scene of one of the most remarkable instances of heroic daring and self-sacrifice recorded in history, that of Leonidas and his three hundred Spartans, here mentioned.——**Barbaros,** Barbarians, i. e. the Persians. The term was applied to all who were not Greeks. ——**Non sustinuerunt.** They were unable to resist the overwhelming force brought against them, but they performed prodigies of valor unsurpassed in the annals of war.——**Classis . . . . navium,** *the common fleet of Greece* (i. e. the fleet of all Greece), *consisting of,* etc.——**Angustias.** The narrow channel, *Euripus,* between Boeotia and Euboea, is here meant.——**Ancipiti periculo,** *by a double danger,* i. e. by being confined in the channel with one foe in front and another in the rear. ——**Exadversum Athenas,** *over against Athens.* *Exadversum,* like *adversum,* admits the Accus., 433.

219. **Thermopylis ;** see above (218).——**Astu,** *the city,* i. e. Athens. **83** The word is often thus applied.——**Idque,** *and this,* i. e. the city of Athens.——**Cujus,** *of this,* i. e. of the burning of the city.——**Themistocles unus restitit,** *Themistocles alone stood firm, objected.*——**Universos,** *all together, united.*——**Idque . . . . affirmabat,** lit. *he affirmed to Eurybiades that this would be,* etc., i. e. he assured him that this would be the result.——**Summae,** dative depending upon *praeërat.* 386.—— **De servis suis, quem,** etc., *one of his servants, whom,* etc.——**Suis verbis,** *in his words,* i. e. *in his name, from him.*——**Nuntiaret.** This verb has *ei* as its *indirect* object, and all the rest of the sentence after *verbis* as its *direct* object. 550.——**Confecturum ;** supply *eum,* referring to the king.——**Oppressurum ;** from *opprimo.*——**Hoc eo valebat,** *the object of this was.*——**Barbarus,** *barbarian,* meaning Xerxes.—— **Contra,** *on the contrary, on the other hand.*——**Explicari,** *to be unfolded,* i. e. to be brought into successful action.

220. **Hic etsi . . . . gesserat,** *although he* (Xerxes) *had fought an unsuccessful battle ;* 516, III.——**Ut . . . . posset hostes ;** XXIV. 2, 5).——**Ab eodem,** *by the same one,* i. e. Themistocles : *eödem,* it **84** must be observed, does not belong to *gradu.*——**Gradu,** *from his position.*——**Certiorem fecit ;** XXVI. 1.——**Id agi,** lit. *that it was doing ;* render, *was in contemplation.*——**In Hellesponto,** *over the Hellespont.* ——**Reversus est ;** from *reverto, revertor,* Dep. in certain forms. See 273, III. *verto.*——**Unius viri,** *of one man,* i. e. Themistocles.

PAGE

84   221. **Quam**—*postquam ;* 427, 3.——**Interfectus est,** *destroyed, cut in pieces.*

222. **Periclis.** Pericles, a distinguished orator and statesman of Athens, directed the counsels of state for many years. The period in which he lived is famous in Grecian history as the "*Age of Pericles.*"

85 ——**Interjectis ;** from *interjicio.*——**Clara ;** observe its position ; 594, I.——**Patrimonii contemptus,** *disregard of patrimony,* referring to the fact that he gave his ancestral estates to the republic, as explained below.——**Hostes ;** subject of *reliquĕrant.*——**In suspicionem adducerent ;** supply *eum ; that they might bring him into suspicion of treachery.*——**Navali . . . . dimicatum est,** lit. *it was fought,* etc. ; render, *a naval battle was fought.*——**In annos quinquaginta,** lit. *into fifty years ;* render, *for fifty years.*

223. **Decernitur,** *is decreed,* or *authorized.*——**Effusae sunt ;** from *effundo.*——**Ut . . . essent ;** XXIV. 2, 5).——**Iis, quibus ;** i. e. to the Catinienses.——**Secundo Marte pugnant,** lit. *they fight, Mars being propitious ;* render, *they fight a successful battle,* or *successfully.*——**Ab his,** *by these,* i. e. the Lacedaemonians.——**Contractis ;** from *contrăho.*

86   224. **Triremes.** See note on "*Remōrum ordĭnes*" (198).——**In hostium potestatem,** *into the power of the enemy. In* is construed with *potestatem.* Observe separation, 602, II. 3.——**Simul cum,** *at the same time with,* or simply *with.*——**Sitae sunt ;** from *sino.*——**Quam plurimas.** *Quam* before a superlative is intensive, and is often best rendered by *possible ;* as, *quam plurimas, the greatest possible number, as many as possible,* or sometimes *very many.*——**Neque minus multas,** lit. *nor less many=and not less many=and as many more.*

225. **Darius.** This was *Darius the Second,* and not the one spoken **87** of above (215).——**Ut . . . . mitterent ;** XXIV. 2, 5).——**In . . . . locum,** lit. *into the place of ;* render, *to take the place of, to succeed.*

226. **Ut numerus . . . . expleretur,** *that the number . . . . might be filled,* i. e. to raise the required number of soldiers.——**Coacti sunt ;** from *cogo.*——**Proeliis adverso Marte pugnatis,** lit. *battles fought, Mars being adverse ;* render, *having lost battles,* or *having fought unsuccessfully.*——**Res . . . . inclinata est.** The power of the Athenians was utterly overthrown by this defeat. The figure involved in the verb *inclĭno,* to incline, fall, is that of a building leaning and ready to fall.

227. **Nomen Atheniensium,** *the Athenian name=the Athenian state* or *nation.*——**Negarunt . . . . passuros,** lit. *denied that they would permit ;* render, *said that they would not permit.*——**Passuros.** What is the object ? 554, III.——**Duobus oculis,** *the two eyes ,* these were *Athens* and *Sparta.*——**Longi muri brachia.** Reference is here made to the long walls which connected Athens with its ports.——**Triginta**

rectores. These are known in history as " *The Thirty Tyrants.*"—— **87**
Dediti, *devoted to,* i. e. to the interests of.

228. **Thrasybulus.** See note on " *Thrasybûlo* " (136).——**Quod.** **88**
This relative, it will be observed, does not agree with its antecedent
Phylen, but with the Predicate noun *castellum ;* 445, 4.——**Triginta**
de suis, lit. *thirty from* (of) *his ;* render, *thirty of his associates,* or
thirty associates.

229. **Idem imperator,** *the same,* i. e. Epaminondas, *when commander,*
3C3, 3.——**Boeotii,** *the Boeotians.* They were the inhabitants of Boeotia, north of Attica, of which Thebes was the chief city.——**Ex hastili,**
from the spear. The iron point, separated from the shaft, had re-
mained in the flesh.——**Extraxisset ;** from *extrăho.*——**Vicisse Boeo-**
tios, *that the Boeotians* (his own men) *had conquered.*

230. **Leuctricam pugnam,** *the battle of Leuctra.* This battle des- **89**
troyed the power of Sparta and made Thebes the leading state in
Greece, but Thebes speedily lost the supremacy after the death of Epaminondas.——**Athenienses, non ut olim.** Formerly Athens had been
eminent in war and had been for many years the leading state in
Greece, but of late the sterner virtues had disappeared from the Athenian character, and the love of ease, luxury, and festivity had taken
their places. Thus Athens, Sparta, and Thebes, each of which had
been in turn the leading state in Greece, had now become weak and
degenerate. This state of things enabled Macedonia to rise to power,
as mentioned in the next sentence.——**Obses . . . . Thebis.** In the
year 369 B. C., when the power of Thebes was supreme in Greece,
Amyntas, king of Macedonia, had been obliged to send his son Philip
as a hostage to that powerful capital.

231. **Auraria ;** supply *metalla* from the next clause.——**Argenti**
. . . . Thracia. There were also *gold* mines in Thrace near Philippi.

232. **Diu dissimulatum.** He had long intended to make war upon **90**
Athens, but had from policy concealed that intention.——**Quorum**
causae . . . . junxerunt, *to whose cause the Thebans had joined them-*
selves, i. e. with whom they had allied themselves.——**Quum,** *though ;*
516, II.——**Assiduis bellis indurata,** *hardened,* or *strengthened by con-*
tinual wars. Philip had a well-disciplined army of veterans, long accustomed to severe and constant service.——**Adversis vulneribus.** See
note on the same (181).——**Hic dies . . . . finivit.** The battle of
Chaeronea reduced Greece to a Macedonian province.

233. **Hujus victoriae . . . . laetitia,** lit. *joy of this victory ;* render, *joy on account of this victory.*——**Coronas, unguenta.** The Greeks
often made use of *crowns, garlands, ointments,* and *perfumes* on joyous
and festive occasions.——**Quantum . . . . fuit,** lit. *as much as was in*
him ; render, *as far as was in his power.*——**Ut . . . . victorem**

90 .... **sentiret,** *that no one would recognize the victor,* i. e. the fact that he was such.——**Bello consumptorum,** *of those slain in war,* or *battle. Consumptōrum* is used substantively ; 575.——**Ad formandum** .... **statum,** lit. *to form the state of present things ;* the meaning is, *to adjust* or *settle the posture of affairs.*——**Auxilia,** *the quotas,* i. e. the quotas which the several states were to furnish.——**Erat ;** the subject is the clause, *eum .... esse ;* 549.——**Suis ;** supply *viribus.*

91   234. **Medius inter duos,** *in the middle between the two,* or simply, *between the two. Medius* is explained by *inter duos.*——**Occupatis angustiis.** He had deliberately placed himself in a narrow passage with the determination to slay the king as he passed.——**Ab Attalo,** *by Attalus,* one of Philip's generals.——**Adversarium,** *his adversary,* meaning Attalus.——**Non poterat ;** supply *exigĕre.*——**Ab iniquo judice,** *from the unjust judge,* meaning Philip.

     235. **Deceptis hostibus,** lit. *in the deceived enemy ;* render, *in deceiving the enemy.* 580.——**Gaudere,** *rejoiced,* Historical Infinitive, of which several other examples occur in this paragraph.——**Hic ;** supply *gaudĕre.*——**Fusis ;** supply *hostĭbus.*——**Hic .... exercebat,** *the latter was wont to exercise his royal power upon,* or *against, his friends.*——**Amari ;** depends upon *malle.*——**Metui ;** supply *malle.*——**Sollertiae pater ;** supply *erat.*——**Ille .... abstinebat,** *he did not abstain from* (i. e. from oppressing or annoying) *even his allies.*——**Nec=et non,** is here rendered *not even.*——**Quibus artibus,** *by these arts,* referring to the enumeration just given of the characteristics of the father and son, Philip and Alexander.

     236. **Caedis conscios .... occidi jussit.** It was a common custom in antiquity thus to slay murderers and assassins upon the graves of their victims, to appease the shades, or spirits, of the dead. In the same way, in war, prisoners were often slain over the graves of fallen heroes.——**Sibi .... praefatus.** There is no little ostentation in this statement. It was of course made for *effect.*——**Opes.** Object of *cogitabant* understood ; construed literally, the passage would read thus : *they thought of nothing if not the riches,* i. e. *if they did not think of the riches,* etc. ; render, *they thought of nothing except the,* etc.—— **In Illo,** *in Ilium,* i. e. in the *district,* not in the *city ;* hence the Ablative with *in,* not the Genitive, as in the names of towns.——**Tumulos heroum.** In the vicinity of Troy, mounds are still pointed out as the burial places of heroes, who three thousand years since fell in the Trojan war.

     237. **Parcendum suis rebus.** Alexander thus inspires his soldiers with courage and confidence. He speaks of the country as already

93 *his* and *theirs.*——**In exercitu .... duae.** Observe that the *copulative connectives* are omitted between the several subjects.——**Veteranes,**

veterans, used substantively, 441.——**Electos ;** supply *esse.*——**In cam- 93**
pis Adrastiae, *in the plains of Adrastia,* in the vicinity of the river
Granicus, from which the battle took its name : *battle of the Granicus.*

238. **Defuncti ;** from *defungor.*——**Confossi ;** from *confodio.*——
Ad hoc ipsum, *for this very purpose.*——**Omnes ante eam reges,** lit. *all* **94**
before him kings, i. e. all the kings before him, or before his time.

239. **Nihil ex .... Aegyptiorum more.** Alexander was careful not
to give offence by disregarding the customs of the country.——**Jovis
Ammonis oraculum.** The oracle of Jupiter Ammon was one of the
most celebrated in the world.——**Sedem consecratam deo.** This was
situated in a beautiful oasis of the Libyan desert.——**Parentem Jovem,**
parent or *father Jupiter,* i. e. *his* father Jupiter. Thus the priest, per-
ceiving his ambitious vanity, flattered him with the title—*son of Jupiter.*——**Parentem ejus,** *his parent,* i. e. Jupiter. The priest still
continues his flattery.——**An auctor .... colendi .... regem,** lit. *whe-* **95**
ther he, i. e. Jupiter, *would be to them the author of worshipping the
king with divine honors,* i. e. whether he would authorize them to worship their king with divine honors.

240. **Nobilem,** *famous.*——**Quin .... esset occisus,** *that the king
himself was slain ;* XXVI. 6.

241. **Spe .... libertatis.** Greece, it will be remembered, lost its
independence by the battle of Chaeronea. See above (232).

242. **Cui gloriae,** *this glory,* i. e. that of conquest and empire. **96**

243. **Recedentem ;** supply *eum.*——**Invitat,** *invites,* i. e. invites
him to drink with him.——**Ut .... posceret ;** XXIV. 2, 5).——**Inter
bibendum,** *while drinking.*

244. **Aeacidarum.** Alexander was, by his mother, a lineal descendant of Aeacus, the grandfather of Achilles.——**Sine ullo .... argumento,** *without any mark of a more sad mind,* i. e. without any indication of unusual sadness.——**Dignissimum.** Adjective used substan- **97**
tively ; object of *facere* understood.——**Judicio,** *by a tacit decision,*
opposed to *voce.*

245. **Quo die**=*die, quo, the day, on which.* Here the relative must
not be rendered according to 453.——**Alterius—alterius,** *the one—the
other.*——**Belli Illyrici,** *that of the Illyrian war,* i. e. the victory gained
in it.——**Certaminis Olympiaci.** See note on " *Olympico certamine* "
(134).——**Puer,** *when a boy ;* 363, 8.——**Quadrigas.** Chariots and
horses were often sent to the Olympic games to contend for the
prizes.——**Aristotele .... magistro.** Philip placed the youthful Alexander under the special instruction of Aristotle, the celebrated philosopher of Athens. Both teacher and pupil have left names famous in
the annals of the world.——**Tantam .... fiduciam fecit,** *he inspired
his soldiers with such confidence.*

LATIN-ENGLISH VOCABULARY.

For Explanation of References and Abbreviations, see page ix.

A

A. An abbreviation of *Aulus.*

A, ab, abs, prep. with abl. From, by.

Ab-dūco, ĕre, duxi, ductum. To lead away, take away, remove.

Ab-eo, ĭre, ĭvi, or *ii, ĭtum.* To go away, depart, withdraw from. 295.

Ab-hinc, adv. Henceforth, from this time, before, ago, since.

Abjicio, ĕre, jēci, jectum, (ab, jacio). To throw away, throw, reject; prostrate, humble.

Abripio, ĕre, ripui, reptum, (ab, rapio). To take away, carry off.

Ab-rumpo, ĕre, rūpi, ruptum. To break off *or* away, rend, sever.

Absens, entis, part. (absum). Absent.

Abstineo, ĕre, tinui, tentum, (abs, teneo). To keep *or* hold back, abstain from.

Ab-sum, esse, fui. To be absent *or* away, to be distant from. 204, 290.

Ab-sūmo, ĕre, sumpsi, sumptum. To take from *or* away; destroy, consume.

Ab-undo, āre, āvi, ātum. To abound, abound in, superabound, have an abundance.

Ab-ūtor, ūti, ūsus sum, dep. To use up, consume, abuse.

Ac, a shortened form of *atque.* And. *Ac si,* as if.

Acca, ae, f. Acca, a Roman name.

Acca Laurentia, ae, f. Acca Laurentia, the wife of Faustulus, and nurse of Romulus and Remus, (153).

Accēdo, ĕre, cessi, cessum, (ad, cedo). To approach, come to, accede to; be added to. *Accēdit,* impers., it is added, there is the additional fact that.

Accendo, ĕre, cendi, censum, (ad, candeo). To set on fire, kindle; to excite, inflame.

Acceptus, a, um, part. (accipio). Accepted; acceptable, pleasing.

Accipio, ĕre, cēpi, ceptum, (ad, capio). To accept, receive.

Accurro, ĕre, curri, (*cucurri* rare), *cursum,* (ad, curro). To run to, hasten to.

Accūso, āre, āvi, ātum, (ad, causa). To call to account, to accuse.

Acer, acris, acre. Sharp; powerful, valiant; diligent, intense, severe. 163, 1.

Acerbus, a, um, (acer). Sour, unripe, morose, disagreeable.

Achaia, ae, f. Achaia, an important

province in the northern part of the Peloponnesus.

Achilles, is, m. Achilles, the most celebrated Grecian hero in the Trojan war, son of Peleus and Thetis, (134).

Acies, ii, f. The order of battle, battle array; line of soldiers; army in battle array.

Acquiesco, ĕre, quiĕvi, quiĕtum (ad, quiesco). To become quiet, to repose; to acquiesce in.

Acriter, acrius, acerrime, adv. (acer). Vehemently, valiantly. 305.

Actium, ii, n. Actium, a promontory and town at the entrance of the Ambracian Gulf on the western coast of Greece, celebrated for the victory of Augustus over Antony and Cleopatra, (214).

Acuo, ĕre, ui, ūtum. To sharpen, quicken; stimulate.

Acūtus, a, um, part. (acuo). Sharpened, pointed, sharp, acute, intelligent, clear-sighted.

Ad, prep. with acc. To, towards; until; at, near.

Ad-do, ĕre, dĭdi, dĭtum. To add, carry to, appoint to.

Ad-dūco, ĕre, duxi, ductum. To lead to, conduct, bring, induce.

Ad-eo, adv. So, to such an extent.

Ad-eo, ĭre, ĭvi or *ii, ĭtum.* To go to, approach, visit; encounter. 295.

Ad-huc, adv. Thus far, as yet, even yet; still.

Adĭmo, ĕre, ĕmi, emptum, (ad, emo). To take from, deprive of.

Adipiscor, ci, adeptus sum, dep. (ad, apiscor). To cbtain, get possession of.

Adjicio, ĕre, jēci, jectum, (ad, jacio). To throw or cast to or against, add to; *anĭmum adjicĕre,* to direct or give attention to.

Ad-jungo, ĕre, junxi, junctum. To join to, unite with.

Adjūtor, ōris, m. (adjŭvo). Aid, helper, assistant.

Ad-jŭvo, āre, jūvi, jūtum. To help, assist, support.

Ad-ministro, āre, āvi, ātum. To administer, manage.

Ad-mirabĭlis, e. Admirable, wonderful.

Ad-mirātio, ōnis, f. (admīror). Admiration, respect.

Admīror, āri, ātus sum, dep. (ad, mīror). To admire, wonder at.

Ad-mitto, ĕre, mīsi, missum. To send to or forward, to admit, receive.

Admŏdum, adv. (ad, modus). Very, exceedingly.

Ad-moneo, ĕre, ui, ĭtum. To admonish, warn.

Admonĭtus, us, m. (admoneo). Warning, advice; instigation.

Ad-moveo, ĕre, mōvi, mōtum. To move to, apply to, bring to.

Adolescens, entis, adj. and subs., m. and f. (adolesco). Young, growing; a young man, a youth.

Adolescentia, ae, f. (adolescens). Youth.

Ad-olesco, ĕre, olĕvi, ultum. To grow, grow up, increase.

Ad-opto, āre, āvi, ātum. To choose, adopt; take for a son, daughter, etc.

Ad-orior, īri, ortus sum, dep. To attack, attempt, strive; begin. 288, 2.

Ad-orno, āre, āvi, ātum. To adorn, furnish, equip.

Adrastia, ae, f. Adrastia, a district and city of Mysia, (237).

Adspicio, ĕre, spexi, spectum, (ad, specio). To see, look at, behold.

Ad-sto, āre, stĭti, stătum. To stand near, stand by.

Ad-sum, esse, fui. To be present *or* at hand, assist, stand by. 204, 290.

Adulatio, ōnis, f. Adulation, flattery.

Advectus, a, um, part. (advĕho). Brought, carried to.

Ad-vĕho, ĕre, vexi, vectum. To conduct, convey, import.

Ad-venio, ĭre, vcni, ventum. To come to, arrive.

Adventus, us, m. (advenio). Arrival, approach.

Adversarius, a, um. adj. (adversus). Opposite, opposing.

Adversarius, ii, m. subs. (adversus). Adversary, opponent, antagonist.

Adversus, a, um, part. (adverto). Opposite, over against, adverse, hostile; fronting, in front.

Adversus, or *adversum,* adv., and prep. with acc. (adverto). Against, towards, opposite to.

Aeacĭdes, ae, m. A patronymic denoting a descendant of Aeacus, who was the grandfather of Achilles. The name is often applied to Achilles; Alexander the Great also claimed it for himself, (244).

Aedes, or *aedis, is, f.* Temple *in the sing.; but in the plur.* dwelling, habitation, house. 132.

Aedifico, āre, āvi, ātum, (aedes, facio). To build.

Aedilĭtius, or *aedilicius, a, um,* (aedes). Pertaining to the aediles.

Aedilĭtius, i, m., one who has been aedile. The aediles were Roman magistrates who had charge of the public buildings, highways, &c., and acted as city police.

Aegina, ae, f. Aegina, an island near Attica, (55).

Aegos flumen. Aegospotamos, a river and town in the Thracian Chersonesus, noted for the defeat of the Athenians by Lysander, (226).

Aegrōtus, a, um. Sick, ill, diseased.

Aegyptus, i, f. Egypt, (210).

Aegyptius, a, um, Egyptian; subs. *Aegyptius, i,* m., an Egyptian, (239).

Aemilius, ii, m. The family name of several distinguished Romans. *Lucius Aemilius,* surnamed *Paulus,* fell in the battle of Cannae, (191). Another of the same name conquered Perseus and reduced Macedonia to a Roman province, (198).

Aemŭlus, a, um. Emulous; *often used substantively, as,* rival, competitor.

Aenēas, ae, m. Aeneas, a Trojan prince who after the destruction of Troy is said to have fled into Italy and formed a settlement, (149).

Aequalis, e. Equal, like.

Aeque, aequius, aequissĭme, adv. (aequus). Equally, similarly.

Aequipăro, āre, āvi, ātum. To equal, make equal.

Aequĭtas, ātis, f. (aequus). Equality, equity, justice.

Aequus, a, um. Equal, similar; just, fair; favorable, propitious.

Aër, aëris, m.   The air, atmosphere.

Aestǐmo, āre, āvi, ātum.   To value, estimate. *Parvi aestimāre*, to think little of, esteem lightly.

Aestuo, āre, āvi, ātum.   To be in agitation; to be warm, endure heat.

'Aetas, ātis, f. Age, time of life, life.

Affěro, ferre, attǔli, allātum, (ad, fero).   To bring, carry to, report.

Afficio, ěre, fěci, · fectum (ad, facio).   To affect, influence.

Affīgo, ěre, fixi, fixum, (ad, fīgo).   To affix, fasten to.

Affirmo, āre, āvi, ātum, (ad, firmo).   To affirm, confirm, ratify.

Afflictus, a, um, part. (afflīgo).   Afflicted, troubled, prostrated.

Afflīgo, ěre, flixi, flictum, (ad, flīgo).   To afflict, trouble, overthrow.

Affluo, ěre, fluxi, fluxum, (ad, fluo).   To flow toward ; overflow, abound in.

Afrǐca, ae, f. Africa, (200).

Africānus, a, um, (Afrǐca). African. Also the surname given to the two most distinguished Scipios for their achievements in Africa during the Punic wars, (196, 200).

Ager, agri, m.   Field, land, territory.

Agesilāus, i, m. Agesilaus, a Spartan king, (96).

Agger, ěris, m. Mound, rampart, wall.

Aggredior, i, gressus sum, dep. (ad, gradior).   To approach, attack, attempt.

Agis, ǐdis, m. Agis, king of the Lacedaemonians in the time of Alexander the Great, (241).

Agitātus, a, um, part. (agǐto).   Agitated, troubled.

Agǐto, āre, āvi, ātum.   To harass, trouble, think of.

Agmen, ǐnis, n. (ago).   An army, *generally on the march,* band of soldiers, troop.

Agnosco, ěre, nōvi, nǐtum, (ad, (g)nosco).   To recognize.

Ago, ěre, ēgi, actum.   To conduct, drive, do, act, execute, treat, argue ; *annum vicesǐmum agěre,* to be in his (or her) twentieth year.

Agricǒla, ae, m. (ager, colo).   Husbandman, farmer.

Agricultūra, ae, f. Agriculture.

Agrigentum, i, n. Agrigentum, a large and wealthy town in Sicily.

Agrippa, ae, m. A family name among the Romans.   *Menenius Agrippa* induced the people who had revolted at Rome and taken up their quarters upon *Mons Sacer* to return into the city, (173).

Aio, ais, ait, etc., defect. To say, affirm. 297, II. 1.

Ala, ae, f. Wing.

Alǎcer, cris, cre. Active, prompt, joyful.

Alba, ae, f. ; or *Alba Longa, ae,* f. A city of Latium founded by Ascanius, (150).

Albānus, a, um. Alban. *Mons Albānus,* a rocky mountain sixteen miles southeast of Rome, (150).

Albānus, i, m. An Alban, a citizen of Alba, (151).

Albus, a, um. White.

Alcibiādes, is, m. Alcibiades, an Athenian general in the Peloponnesian war, (223–225).

Alexander, dri, m. Alexander. The

most distinguished of this name
was the son and successor of
Philip, king of Macedonia, (235–
245). A second of the same name
was king of Epirus and son-in-law
of Philip, (234).

Alexandria, ae, f.   Alexandria, a
celebrated city of Egypt, built by
Alexander the Great; (239).

Algeo, ĕre, alsi.   To be cold, to feel
cold, endure cold.

Alias.   Otherwise, at another time;
non alias, on no other occasion.

Aliĕnus, a, um, (alius).   Belonging
to another, foreign; unfavorable.

Aliquando.   At some time, once,
formerly, finally, now at last.

Aliquantum, adv.   Somewhat, in
some degree.

Aliquis, qua, quod, and *quid,* (alius,
quis).   Some one, some.

Aliquot, indecl. pl. adj.   Several,
some.

Aliter, adv. (alius).   Otherwise.

Alius, a, ud, (gen. alius, etc.) Other,
another; *alius — alius,* one — another: *alii—alii,* some—others,
(151).

Allia, ae, f.   The river Allia, a few
miles north of Rome, (176).

Allŏquor, lŏqui, cūtus sum, dep.
(ad, loquor).   To speak to, address.

Alo, ĕre, alui, alĭtum or *altum.*   To
support, keep, nourish, strengthen,
feed.

Alpes, ium, f.   The Alps, a high
range of mountains north of
Italy.

Alte, ius, issĭme, adv. (altus).   On
high, high.

Alter, ĕra, ĕrum, (gen. alterius). One

of two, the other; *alter—alter,*
the one — the other; *alter* as
numeral = *second.* 151, 2.

Altus, a, um.   High, noble, great;
deep, profound; *altum* substantively, the sea, the deep.

Amabĭlis, e, (amo).   Lovely, amia-
ble.

Ambio, īre, īvi or *ii, ītum,* (amb, or
ambi, eo).   To surround, encompass. 295, 3.

Ambitio, ōnis, f. (ambio).   Can-
vassing, flattery, ambition.

Ambo, ae, o.   Both. 175, 2.

Amentia, ae, f. (amens).   Folly,
want of reason.

Amicitia, ae, f. (amicus).   Friendship.

Amicus, i, m.   Friend.

Amicus, a, um.   Friendly, kind.

A-mitto, ĕre, mīsi, missum.   To send
away, to lose.

Ammon, or *Hammon, ōnis,* m.   An
appellation of Jupiter as worship-
ped in Africa, (239).

Amnis, is, m.   River.

Amo, āre, āvi, ātum.   To love.

Amor, ōris, m. (amo).   Love, affection, desire; a loved object, darling.

Amphitheātrum, i, n.   Amphithe-
atre, *in Rome* a circular or oval
building used for public specta-
cles.

Ample, ius, issĭme, adv. (amplus).
Abundantly, amply.

Amplio, āre, āvi, ātum, (amplus).
To enlarge.

Amplĭus, adv. (comp. of *ample*).
More, further.

Amplus, a, um.   Ample, spacious,
large.

Amulius, ii, m. Amulius, son of Procas king of Alba; he was the brother of Numitor, (152).

An, interrog. particle. Or, whether. 346, II, 2.

Anaxagŏras, ae, m. Anaxagoras, a distinguished Greek philosopher of Clazomenae, (112).

Anaxarchus, i, m. Anaxarchus, a philosopher of Abdera, who accompanied Alexander into Asia.

Anceps, ancipitis. Twofold, double.

Anchīses, ae, m. Anchises, the father of Aeneas. 50.

Ancus, i, m.; or *Ancus Martius, ii,* m. The fourth king of Rome, (161).

Angor, ŏris, m. Anxiety, care, anguish.

Angustia, ae, f. (angustus), used mostly in pl. Narrow pass, difficulty; straits, channel.

Angustus, a, um. Narrow, confined, contracted, small.

Anĭma, ae, f. Breath, life.

Animadverto, ĕre, verti, versum (animus, adverto). To notice, observe, perceive.

Anĭmal, ālis, n. Animal.

Anĭmus, i, m. Mind, soul, courage.

Anio, Aniēnis, m. The Anio, a small river of Italy, a tributary of the Tiber, (173).

Annecto, ĕre, nexui, nexum, (ad, necto). To tie to, annex, fasten to.

Annŭlus, or *anŭlus, i,* m. Ring.

Annus, i, m. Year.

Annuus, a, um, (annus). Lasting a year, for a year, annual.

Ante, adv., and prep. with acc. Before, *in respect to place or time;* formerly.

Antea, adv. (ante, ea). Formerly, hitherto.

Ante-pōno, ĕre, posui, posĭtum. To place before; to prefer.

Antĕ-quam, adv. Before, before that.

Antigŏnus, i, m. Antigonus, king of Macedonia, (121).

Antiochīa, ae, f. Antioch, the chief city of Syria, founded by Seleucus, and named by him in honor of his father Antiochus, (206).

Antiŏchus, i, m. 1. Antiochus the Great, king of Syria. 2. Antiochus, the Academic philosopher and teacher of Cicero, (80).

Antipāter, tri, m. Antipater, one of Alexander's generals; after the death of Alexander he received the government of Greece and Macedonia, (241).

Antīquus, a, um. Ancient, early.

Antistes, ĭtis, m. and f. President; priest, priestess.

Antonius, ii, m. Antony; *Marcus Antonius* formed a triumvirate with Octavianus and Lepidus, (212). *Caius Antonius* was the colleague of Cicero in the consulship, (207).

Anxiĕtas, ātis, f. Anxiety, solicitude.

Apelles, is, m. Apelles, a distinguished Greek painter in the time of Alexander the Great, (97).

Aperte, ius, issĭme, adv. (apertus). Openly, publicly.

Apertus, a, um, part. (aperio). Opened; open, free, clear, manifest.

Apollo, ĭnis, m. Apollo, the god of divination.

Apparātus, us, m. Preparation, equipment.

Apparātus, a, um, part. (apparo). Prepared, ready, equipped.

Appellatio, ōnis, f. (appello). Name, title.

Appello, āre, āvi, ātum, (ad, pello). To call, name.

Appello, ĕre, pŭli, pulsum, (ad, pello). To drive to, bring to, induce.

Appĕto, ĕre, petīvi, petii, petītum, (ad, peto). To long for, strive after; assail: *appĕtens, entis*, desiring, desirous of.

Appius, ii, m. Appius, a Roman name. *Appius Claudius, ii*, m., one of the Decemviri, (20).

Apprŏbo, āre, āvi, ātum, (ad, probo). To approve, favor.

Appropinquo, āre, āvi, ātum, (ad, propinquo). To approach, come near.

Aptus, a, um. Fitted, adapted, suited, proper.

Apud, prep. with acc. At, near, among, at the house of, in the works of (*applied to authors*).

Apulia, ae, f. Apulia, a province in southern Italy, (204).

Aqua, ae, f. Water.

Aquĭla, ae, f. Eagle.

Ara, ae, f. Altar.

Arabs, ăbis. Arabian; *subs.* an Arabian, inhabitant of Arabia in Asia, (26).

Arātrum, i, n. Plough.

Arbēla, ōrum, n. Arbela, a town in Assyria, famous for the victory of Alexander over Darius, (240).

Arbĭtror, āri, ātus sum, dep. To think, judge, regard.

Arcĕo, arcēre, arcui. To inclose, restrain, keep from.

Ardea, ae, f. Ardea, a city of La-

tium, a few miles south of Rome, (167).

Ardeo, ēre, arsi, arsum. To be on fire, burn.

Ardesco, ĕre, arsi. To take fire, kindle.

Aresco, ĕre, arui. To become dry, to dry.

Arethūsa, ae, f. Arethusa, a celebrated fountain in Sicily, near Syracuse.

Argentĕus, a, um, (argentum). Made of silver, of silver.

Argentum, i, n. Silver.

Argos, n. (only in nom. and acc.), or *Argi, ōrum*, m. pl. Argos, the capital of the province of Argolis in the Peloponnesus; the name was often applied to the province itself and poetically to all Greece, (96).

Argumentum, i, n. Argument, sign, mark.

Ariminum, i, n. Ariminum, a town in Umbria on the Adriatic, (209).

Ariovistus, i, m. Ariovistus, king of a German tribe in the time of Caesar, (47).

Aristīdes, is, m. Aristides, an Athenian general and statesman, renowned for his integrity, (49).

Aristobūlus, i, m. A king of Judea, who was taken by Pompey and carried as prisoner to Rome, (206).

Aristotĕles, is, m. A distinguished philosopher, and the teacher of Alexander the Great, (85, 245).

Arma, ōrum, n. pl. Arms, force of arms.

Armātus, a, um, part. (armo). Armed.

Armenia, ae, f. Armenia, a country of Asia, divided by the river Euphrates into two unequal parts, viz. : the eastern, called *Armenia Major*, and the western, called *Armenia Minor*, (205).

Armilla, ae, f. Bracelet.

Armo, āre, āvi, ātum, (arma). To arm.

Arripio, ĕre, ripui, reptum, (ad, rapio). To seize upon, seize.

Arrŏgans, antis, part. (arrŏgo). Proud, arrogant.

Arrŏgantia, ae, f. (arrŏgans). Arrogance, pride.

Arrŏgo, āre, āvi, ātum, (ad, rogo). To claim, arrogate.

Ars, artis, f. Art, skill.

Artaphernes, is, m. Artaphernes, nephew of Darius, (215).

Artemisium, ii, n. Artemisium, a promontory and town on the island of Euboea, (218).

Artus, us, m. ; sing. rare. Joint, limb.

Aruns, Aruntis, m. 1. Aruns, the brother of Tarquin the Proud, (39, iv.). 2. Aruns, the son of Tarquin, (170).

Arx, arcis, f. Citadel.

Ascanius, ii, m. Ascanius, the son of Aeneas, (150).

Asia, ae, f. Asia, (16).

Asĭna, ae, m. Asina, a surname of Cnaeus Cornelius, who was the colleague of Duillius in the consulship in the early part of the first Punic war, (185).

Aspis, ĭdis, f. Asp.

Asporto, āre, āvi, ātum, (abs, porto). To bear or carry away.

Assĕquor, sĕqui, sĕcūtus sum, dep. (ad, sequor). To overtake, obtain.

Asseveratio, ōnis, f. Declaration, assertion.

Assiduus, a, um. Assiduous ; frequent ; continual, incessant, constant.

Assigno, āre, āvi, ātum, (ad, signo). Assign, bestow.

Asto, for *ad-sto*.

Astrum, i, n. Star, constellation.

Astu, n, indec. City, *generally applied to* Athens.

Asylum, i, n. Asylum, place of refuge.

At, conj. But, yet.

Ater, tra, trum. Dark, black, gloomy.

Athēnae, ārum, f. pl. Athens, the capital of Attica, (227).

Atheniensis, e, adj. (Athēnae). Athenian ; subs. *Atheniensis, is*, m., an Athenian, (216).

Atilius, ii, m. Atilius, a Roman name. See *Regŭlus*.

Atque, conj. And, and also, and besides; *atque—atque*, both—and.

Attălus, i, m. Attalus, one of Philip's generals, (234).

Attĭca, ae, f. An important state in Greece, (216).

Attĭcus, a, um, (Attĭca). Attic, Athenian ; subs. *Attĭcus, i*, m. An inhabitant or citizen of Attica, (36).

Attĭcus, i, m. Atticus, a surname of the Roman, Titus Pomponius, (99).

Attingo, ĕre, tĭgi, tactum, (ad, tango). To attain, touch, enter upon, undertake, commence.

Attius, ii, m. Attius, a Roman name, (89).

Attribuo, ĕre, tribui, tribūtum, (ad, tribuo). To attribute to, ascribe to, to bestow, to assign, or impute to.

Auctor, ōris, m. (augeo). Author, founder, approver, adviser, authority.

Auctorītas, ātis, f. (auctor). Authority, influence.

Audacia,.ae, f. (audax). Boldness, insolence, audacity.

Audax, audācis, (audeo). Bold, audacious, desperate.

Audeo, ēre, ausus sum. To dare, attempt. 271, 3.

Audio, īre, īvi or *ii, ītum.* To hear, listen to.

Aufugio, ēre, fūgi, fugītum, (ab, fugio). To flee from; run away from. 338, 1, *ab.*

Augeo, ēre, auxi, auctum. To enlarge, increase.

Augŭror, āri, ātus sum, dep. To augur, predict, foretell.

Augustus, i, m. Augustus, surname of Octavius Caesar, the first of the Roman Emperors. This surname was also often applied to the Emperors generally, (213).

Aulus, i, m. Aulus, a Roman praenomen.

Aurarius, a, um, (aurum). Pertaining to gold; *auraria metalla,* gold mines.

Aureus, a, um, (aurum). Made of gold, golden.   [driver.

Aurīga, ae, m. and f. Charioteer,

Auris, is, f. Ear.

Aurum, i, n. Gold.

Aut, conj. Or; *aut—aut,* either—or, partly—partly.

Autem, conj. But, moreover.

Auxilium, ii, n. (augeo.) Aid; *plur.* auxiliaries.

Avaritia, ae, f. (avārus). Avarice.

Avārus, a, um. Avaricious.

Aventīnus, i, m. The Aventine, one of the seven hills of Rome, (154).

Averto, ēre, verti, versum, (ab, verto). To avert, turn from, remove.

Avīdus, a, um. Desirous, eager.

Avis, is, f. Bird.

Avus, i, m. Grandfather.

B.

Babylonia, ae, f. Babylonia, a province of Syria: also Babylon, the capital of Babylonia, (243).

Bacchantes, ium, pl. (bacchor). Votaries of Bacchus.

Bacchor, āri, ātus sum, dep. (Bacchus). To celebrate the festival of Bacchus, to revel. *Bacchans, antis,* part. revelling.

Bacchus, i, m. The god of wine, (19).

Barba, ae, f. Beard.

Barbărus, a, um. Foreign, barbarous, rude.

Barbărus, i, m. Foreigner, barbarian.

Beāte, ius, issime, adv. (beātus). Happily.

Beātus, a, um. Happy.

Belgae, ārum. The Belgians, a warlike people in the north of Gaul, (25).

Bellicōsus, a, um, (bellum). Warlike.

Bello, āre, āvi, ātum, (bellum). To carry on war.

Bellum, i, n. War.

Bene, melius, optime, adv. Well 305, 2.

Beneficium, ii, n. (benefīcus, *from* bene, facio). Benefit, favor, kindness.

Benevolentia, ae, f. (benevŏlens,

from bene, volo). Kindness, benevolence.

Benigne, ius, issime, adv. (benignus). Kindly.

Benignus, a, um. Kind, good, benignant.

Bestia, ae, f. A beast.

Bestiŏla, ae, f. (bestia). A small animal, insect.

Bibo, ĕre, bibi, bibĭtum. To drink.

Bibŭlus, i, m. Bibulus, a Roman name; *Lucius Bibŭlus* was Cæsar's colleague in the consulship, (208).

Biduum, i, n. (biduus). A period of two days.

Biduus, a, um, (bis, dies). Continuing two days.

Biennium, ii, n. (bis, annus). A period of two years, two years.

Biformis, e, (bis, forma). Having two forms, biformed.

Bini, ae, a, distribute. Two by two, two and two. 174, 2.

Bis, adv. Twice.

Boeotius, ii, m. (Boeotia). A Boeotian, inhabitant of Boeotia in central Greece, (229).

Bolētus, i, m. Mushroom.

Bonĭtas, ātis, f. (bonus). Goodness, excellence.

Bonum, i, n. (bonus). Blessing, prosperity, any good; pl. *bona,* goods, property.

Bonus, a, um; melior, optĭmus. Good, noble, brave. 165.

Bos, Bovis, m. and f. Ox, cow. 43, 2; 66.

Brachium, ii, n. Arm, fore-arm.

Brevis, e. Short, brief; *brevi* (tempŏre), in a short time, shortly.

Britannĭcus, a, um, (Britannia,

Great Britain). British, English, (208).

Britannus, i, m. (Britannia). A Briton, (208).

Brutus, i, m. Brutus, a Roman name. *Lucius Junius Brutus* was one of the first consuls of Rome, (168). *Marcus Junius Brutus* and *Decĭmus Junius Brutus* acted prominent parts in the assassination of Caesar, (211).

Byzantium, ii, n. Byzantium, a city on the Bosphorus, now Constantinople.

C.

C. An abbreviation of *Caius; Cn.* of *Cnaeus.*

Cado, ĕre, cecĭdi, casum. To fall, fall in battle, perish.

Caecus, a, um. Blind.

Caedes, is, f. (caedo). Slaughter, bloodshed.

Caedo, ĕre, cecidi, caesum. To cut, kill, slay.

Caesar, ăris, m. Caesar, a surname of the Julian family; *Caius Julius Caesar,* a distinguished general and statesman. The title, or surname, *Caesar,* was also applied generally to denote the Roman emperors, (208).

Caius, ii, m. Caius, a Roman name. See *Caesar.*

Calamĭtas, ātis, f. Loss, calamity, disaster.

Callĭde, ius, issĭme, adv. (callĭdus). Shrewdly, skilfully.

Camillus, i, m. Camillus, a distinguished Roman general, (176).

Campania, ae, f. Campania, a province in Central Italy, (182).

Campānus, a, um, (Campania). Campanian, of Campania. *Subs.* a Campanian, (44, 131).

Campus, i, m. A plain, field of battle.

Candīdus, a, um. White, clear, bright, light.

Canīnīus, ii, m. Caninius, a Roman consul, (80).

Cannae, ārum, f. plur. Cannae, a village in Apulia, famous for the great victory of Hannibal over the Romans, (191).

Cannensis, e, adj. (Cannae). Belonging to Cannae, of Cannae, (194).

Cano, ĕre, cecĭni, cantum. To sing, sound, crow.

Canto, āre, āvi, ātum, (cano). To sing, play.

Cantus, us, m. (cano). Singing, song, melody.

Capax, ācis, (capio). Capacious, large, comprehensive, able.

Capesso, ĕre, ivi, ītum, (capio). To take, seize; *fugam capessĕre,* to resort to flight, betake one's self to flight. 332, 4.

Capillus, i, m. Hair.

Capio, ĕre, cēpi, captum. To take, take possession of, hold, receive.

Capitālis, e, (caput). Deadly, mortal, *capitāle crimen,* a capital crime or offence.

Capitolium, ii, n. Capitol. This term is applied sometimes to the temple of Jupiter, and sometimes to the whole Capitoline Hill, including both the temple and the citadel of Rome.

Capra, ae, f. A she-goat.

Captivītās, ātis, f. (captīvus.) Captivity, bondage.

Captīvus, a, um, (capio). Captive, enslaved; *substantively,* a prisoner, a captive.

Captus, a, um, part. (capio). Captured, taken.

Capua, ae, f. Capua, the chief city of Campania, (204).

Caput, ĭtis, n. Head, capital; *capĭtis damnāre,* to condemn to death.

Carcer, ĕris, m. Prison.

Careo, ēre, carui, carĭtum. To be destitute, be free from, be without.

Carmen, ĭnis, n. A song, poem; poetry.

Caro, carnis, f. Flesh.

Carpentum, i, n. Chariot, carriage.

Carthāgo, ĭnis, f. Carthage, an ancient city in Northern Africa, (189). *Carthāgo Nova.* New Carthage, a town in Spain; now *Carthagena,* (194).

Carthaginiensis, e, adj. (Carthāgo). Carthaginian; subs. *Carthaginiensis, is,* m. a Carthaginian, (185).

Carus, a, um. Dear.

Cassius, ii, m. Cassius, a Roman name. *Lucius Cassius,* one of the accomplices of Catilina, (97, 15). *Caius Cassius,* one of the conspirators against Caesar, (213).

Caste, ius, issĭme, adv. (castus). Virtuously, chastely.

Castus, a, um. Chaste, pure.

Castellum, i, n. dimin. (castrum). Castle, fortress. 315, 3.

Castor, ŏris, m. Castor, son of Tyndarus and brother of Pollux, (63, 9).

Castra, ōrum, n. (pl. of *castrum,* a castle). Camp. 132.

Casus, us, m. (cado). Fall, misfortune, chance, accident.

Catilīna, ae, m. Catiline. *Lucius Sergius Catilīna,* the notorious conspirator against the Roman government, (207).

Catinensis or *Catiniensis, is,* m. A Catinean, a citizen of Catina, a city in Sicily, (223).

Cato, ōnis, m. Cato, the name of several distinguished Romans. The most celebrated was *Marcus Porcius Cato,* the *Censor,* (88, 13).

Catūlus, i, m. Catulus, surname of *Caius Lutatius,* a Roman consul at the close of the first Punic war, (188).

Caudīnus, a, um. Caudine; *Furcūlae Caudīnae,* the Caudine Forks, a narrow defile near Caudium, in Italy, (179).

Causa, ae, f. Cause, purpose, business, suit at law.

Causidīcus, i, m. (causa, dico). Pleader, advocate; speaker.

Cautes, is, f. A crag, cliff, rock.

Caveo, ēre, cāvi, cautum. To shun, avoid, guard against; *sibi ab aliquo cavēre,* to protect one's self from any one.

Cedo, ēre, cessi, cessum. To give place to, yield to, withdraw, depart.

Celĕber, bris, bre. Renowned, celebrated.

Celĕbro, āre, āvi, ātum, (celĕber). To celebrate, solemnize.

Celer, celĕris. Swift. 163, 1.

Celerĭtas, ātis, f. (celer). Celerity, swiftness.

Celerĭter, ius, rĭme, adv. (celer). Swiftly, quickly. 305, 2.

Cella, ae, f. Store-room, storehouse; *cella penaria,* granary.

Celo, āre, āvi, ātum. To hide, conceal.

Censeo, ēre, censui, censum. To think, judge, decree.

Censorīnus, i, m. Censorinus, surname of *Lucius Marcius,* a Roman consul in the third Punic war, (199).

Censua, us, m. Census.

Centum, indec. Hundred.

Centurio, ōnis, m. (centum). Centurion.

Cerno, ēre, crēvi, crētum. To perceive, see, discern.

Certāmen, ĭnis, n. (certo). Contest, game, engagement.

Certātim, adv. (certātus, *from* certo). Earnestly, eagerly.

Certo, āre, āvi, ātum. To fight, struggle, contend, endeavor.

Certus, a, um. Sure, certain; *certiōrem facĕre,* to inform.

Cesso, āre, āvi, ātum, (cedo). To cease, pause.

Cetĕrus, a, um, nom. sing. m. not used. The other, the rest.

Chaeronēa, ae, f. Chaeronea, a town in Boeotia, the birth-place of Plutarch, (232).

Chersonēsus, i, f. The Chersonesus, a peninsula in Thracia, west of the Hellespont.

Christiānus, a, um. Christian, *often used substantively.*

Cicātrix, īcis, f. Scar.

Cicĕro, ōnis, m. Cicero, the celebrated Roman orator, (207).

Cincinnātus, i, m. Cincinnatus, a

renowned Roman citizen and dictator, (71).

Cineas, ae, m. A friend and favorite minister of Pyrrhus.

Cingo, ĕre, cinxi, cinctum. To surround, encompass ; crown ; invest.

Cinna, ae, m. Cinna, a surname among the Romans. *Lucius Cornelius Cinna*, confederate of Marius in the civil war, (203).

Circa, prep. with acc. About, around, among.

Circĭter, prep. with acc. About, near.

Circum = circa.

Circum-do, dăre, dĕdi, dătum. To place around, surround, invest.

Circum-eo, ĭre, ĭvi or *ii, ĭtum.* To go around, surround, encompass, 295.

Circumspicio, ĕre, spexi, spectum. (circum, specio). To look round, look for, seek.

Circum-venio, ĭre, vēni, ventum. Tu come around, encompass, surround, circumvent, deceive.

Cis, prep. with acc. On this side of, within.

Cito, āre, āvi, ātum. To excite, urge, hasten ; *cităto equo*, at full gallop *or* speed.

Cito, citius, citissĭme, adv. (citus). Soon, quickly.

Citra, adv., and prep. with acc. On this side.

Citus, a, um. Quick, swift, rapid.

Civĭlis, e, (civis). Civil, domestic.

Civilĭtas, ătis, f. (civĭlis). Civility, politeness.

Civis, is, m. and f. Citizen.

Civĭtas, ătis, f. (civis). City, state, citizenship.

Clades, is, f. Loss, slaughter, destruction, defeat.

Clam, adv., and prep. with acc. or abl. Secretly, without the knowledge of.

Clarus, a, um. Splendid, renowned, illustrious, clear.

Classiarius, ii, m. (classis). A marine, *pl.* naval forces.

Classis, is, f. A fleet.

Claudius, ii, m. The fourth Roman emperor, (41). *Appius Claudius*, one of the decemviri, (26).

Claudo, claudĕre, clausi, clausum. To close, shut.

Claudus, a, um. Lame.

Clemens, entis. Mild, gentle, clement.

Clementia, ae, f. (clemens). Mildness, clemency.

Cleopātra, ae, f. Cleopatra, queen of Egypt, (211). Another of the same name was the daughter of Philip of Macedon, (234).

Clipeus, or *clypeus, i*, m. Shield.

Cloāca, ae, f. Sewer, drain.

Cnaeus, or *Cneus, i*, m. Cnaeus, a Roman name ; as *Cnaeus Pompeius*.

Coarguo, ĕre, coargui, (cum, arguo). To arraign, accuse, indict ; convict. ·

Cocles, ĭtis, m. Cocles, a Roman surname. *Horatius Cocles*, a Roman, distinguished in the war with Porsĕna, (171).

Coelum, i, n. The heavens, sky, weather.

Coena, ae, f. Principal meal of the Romans, supper, dinner.

Coeo, ĭre, ĭvi or *ii, ĭtum*, (cum, eo) To collect, assemble. 295.

Coepi, isti, it, def. To begin. 297.

Coerceo, ercēre, crcui, ercītum, (cum, arceo). To check, confine, restrain.

Cogĭto, āre, āvi, ātum. To think, ponder.

Cognātus, a, um. Related, subs. a relative.

Cognĭtus, a, um, part. (cognosco). Ascertained, known.

Cognōmen, ĭnis, n. (cum, nomen or gnomen). Surname.

Cognomĭno, āre, āvi, ātum, (cognōmen). To surname, call, name.

Cognosco, ĕre, nōvi, nĭtum, (cum, nosco or gnosco). To ascertain, learn, recognize.

Cogo, ĕre, coēgi, coactum. To collect, force, compel.

Cohibeo, ĕre, ui, ĭtum, (cum, habeo). To hold, check, confine.

Cohors, cohortis, f. Cohort, tenth part of a legion.

Collatīnus, i, m. Collatinus, surname of Tarquinius, the colleague of Brutus in the consulship, (169).

Collēga, ae, m. Colleague.

Collĭgo, ĕre, lēgi, lectum, (cum, lego). To collect, bring together.

Collŏco, āre, āvi, ātum, (cum, loco). To place, set, erect; to give in marriage.

Colloquium, ii, n. (collŏquor). Conversation, interview.

Collŏquor, lŏqui, locūtus sum, dep. (cum, loquor). To converse, talk with.

Collum, i, n. Neck.

Colo, ĕre, colui, cultum. To cultivate; honor, worship.

Color, ōris, m. Color, complexion.

Combūro, ĕre, bussi, bustum, (cum, buro = uro, to burn). To burn, consume.

Comes, ĭtis, m. and f. Companion.

Comissatio, ōnis, f. Revelling.

Commeātus, us, m. Supplies.

Commemŏro, āre, āvi, ātum, (cum, memŏro). To recall, remember, commemorate, mention.

Commentor, āri, ātus sum, dep. To meditate, muse upon, consider, think, devise, invent.

Commĭgro, āre, āvi, ātum, (cum, migro). To migrate.

Comminuo, ĕre, minui, minūtum, (cum, minuo). To dash in pieces, crush; lessen; weaken.

Committo, ĕre, misi, missum, (cum, mitto). To bring together, unite, intrust, commit; pugnam committĕre, to engage in battle.

Commŏdum, i, n. Advantage, benefit.

Commŏdus, a, um, (cum, modus). Suitable, fit, proper, convenient.

Commonĕfacio, ĕre, fēci, factum, (cum, moneo, facio). To put in mind, remind, impress earnestly.

Commŏror, āri, ātus sum, (cum, moror). To tarry, delay.

Commoveo, ĕre, mōvi, mōtum, (cum, moveo). To move, excite.

Commūnis, e. Common.

Communĭter, adv. (commūnis). In common, conjointly.

Commutatio, ōnis, f. Change.

Compăro, āre, āvi, ātum, (cum, paro). To prepare, make, procure, compare.

Compello, āre, āvi, ātum, (cum, pello). To address, call.

Compello, ĕre, pŭli, pulsum, (cum.

pello). To thrust together, to force, compel, impel.

Compensatio, ōnis, f. Compensation, exchange, barter.

Comperio, īre, pĕri, pertum. To find, find out.

Compes, ĕdis, f. (cum, pes). Fetter, chain.

Compesco, ĕre, cui. To confine, check.

Complector, ti, plexus sum, (cum, plector). To embrace, encompass.

Compleo, ēre, ēvi, ētum, (cum, pleo). To fill, complete.

Complūres, a. More than one; several, very many.

Compōno, ĕre, posui, posĭtum, (cum, pono). To settle, adjust, adapt, compose.

Comporto, āre, āvi, ātum, (cum, porto). To carry, bear, collect.

Compos, ŏtis, (cum, potis). Having the mastery or control over anything; sharing in, partaking of.

Comprehendo, ĕre, di, sum, (cum, prehendo). To seize, arrest, comprehend.

Concēdo, ĕre, cessi, cessum, (cum, cedo). To concede, grant; to depart, withdraw; *pass. impers.,* it is conceded.

Concĭdo, ĕre, cĭdi, (cum, cado). To fall, perish.

Concilio, āre, āvi, ātum, (concilium). To unite, conciliate, procure, win.

Concilium, ii, n. Council, meeting.

Concio, ōnis, f. Public assembly.

Concĭto, āre, āvi, ātum, (cum, cito). To raise; excite, excite rebellion.

Concordia, ae, f. (concors, *harmonious*). Concord, harmony.

Concurro, ĕre, curri (*cucurri*), cur-

sum, (cum, curro). To meet, assemble; engage, fight; rush to.

Conditio, ōnis, f. (condo). Condition, terms.

Condo, ĕre, dĭdi, dĭtum, (cum, do). To found; conceal, hide; place, bury.

Condūco, ĕre, duxi, ductum, (cum, duco). To conduct, collect; hire, contract for.

Confĕro, conferre, contŭli, collātum, (cum, fero). To collect, confer, compare; engage battle; *se conferre,* to betake one's self.

Confestim, adv. Immediately.

Conficio, ĕre, fēci, fectum, (cum, facio). To finish, accomplish, make, produce, wear out.

Confĭdo, ĕre, fisus sum, (cum, fido). To trust, confide in.

Confĭgo, ĕre, fixi, fixum, (cum, figo.) To transfix, fasten together.

Confingo, ĕre, finxi, fictum, (cum, fingo). To form, feign, pretend.

Confirmo, āre, āvi, ātum, (cum, firmo). To make firm, strengthen; encourage; corroborate.

Confĭsus, a, um, part. (confĭdo). Trusting, relying upon.

Conflĭgo, ĕre, flixi, flictum, (cum, fligo). To engage, fight.

Confodio, ĕre, fōdi, fossum, (cum, fodio). To pierce, wound.

Confugio, ĕre, fūgi, fugĭtum, (cum, fugio). To flee for refuge.

Congredior, grĕdi, gressus sum, dep. (cum, gradior). To encounter, fight.

Congrĕgo, āre, āvi, ātum, (cum, grego). To collect, congregate.

Congressio, ōnis, f. (congredior). Engagement, battle.

Conjicio, ĕre, jēci, jectum, (cum, jacio). To discharge, hurl, throw, drive.

Conjungo, ĕre, junxi, junctum, (cum, jungo). To join, combine.

Conjuratio, ōnis, f. (conjūro). Conspiracy.

Conjurātus, a, um, part. (conjūro). Having conspired.

Conjūro, āre, āvi, ātum, (cum, juro). To conspire.

Conjux, ūgis, m. and f. (conjungo). Husband, wife.

Conon, ōnis, m. Conon, a celebrated Athenian general, (39, 111).

Conor, āri, ātus sum, dep. To endeavor, attempt.

Conscendo, ĕre, scendi, scensum, (cum, scando). To ascend, embark.

Conscius, a, um. Privy to; conscious of; subs. accomplice, confidant.

Conscrībo, ĕre, scripsi, scriptum (cum, scribo). To summon; to enrol, arrange, order; compose.

Conscriptus, a, um, part. (conscrībo). Enrolled, assembled. Patres conscripti, conscript fathers, i. e. senators.

Consĕcro, āre, āvi, ātum (cum, sacro). To consecrate.

Consector, āri, ātus sum, dep. (cum, sector). To follow, pursue.

Consenesco, ĕre, senui (cum, senesco). To grow old.

Consĕquor, sĕqui, secūtus sum, (cum, sequor). To succeed, follow, pursue; secure, obtain.

Consĕro, ĕre, ui, tum, (cum, sero). To join together; manum or pug-

nam conserĕre, to join battle, engage in battle.

Conservo, āre, āvi, ātum, (cum, servo). To preserve, watch over, rescue.

Considĕro, āre, āvi, ātum. To inspect, examine.

Consīdo, ĕre, sēdi, sessum, (cum, sido). To encamp, settle.

Consilium, ii, n. Counsel, advice, wisdom, intention, design, council.

Consisto, ĕre, stĭti, stĭtum, (cum, sisto). To place or station one's self, to stand.

Consōlor, āri, ātus sum, dep. (cum, solor). To comfort, console.

Conspectus, us, m. (conspicio). Sight, presence.

Conspicio, ĕre, spexi, spectum, (cum, specio). To see, observe.

Conspĭcor, āri, ātus sum, dep. (conspicio). To behold, see.

Conspiratio, ōnis, f. (conspīro). Union, conspiracy.

Constanter, ius, issĭme, adv. (consto). Consistently.

Constantia, ae, f. (consto). Constancy, firmness.

Constat, impers.,(consto). It is known, is an admitted fact.

Constituo, ĕre, ui, ūtum, (cum, statuo). To constitute; build, erect; station, place; appoint, arrange, manage.

Consto, āre, stĭti, stātum, (cum, sto). To stand together, halt.

Consuesco, ĕre, ēvi, ētum, (cum, suesco). To be accustomed.

Consuetūdo, ĭnis, f. (consuesco). Custom, usage, habit.

Consul, ŭlis, m. (consŭlo). Consul, Roman chief magistrate.

Consulāris, e.   Consular; *subs.* one who has been consul, one of consular rank.

Consulātus, us, m. (consul). Consulship.

Consŭlo, ĕre, su.ui, sultum. To consult, consider; *with dat.* to consult for one's good.

Consummo, āre, āvi, ātum. To finish, accomplish, complete.

Consŭmo, ĕre, sumpsi, sumptum, (cum, sumo). To consume, wear out, waste, use, employ.

Contĕgo, ĕre, texi, tectum, (cum, tego). To cover.

Contemno, ĕre, tempsi, temptum, (cum, temno). To contemn, despise, disregard.

Contemptus, us, m. (contemno). Contempt, scorn, disregard.

Contendo, ĕre, tendi, tentum, (cum, tendo). To contend, strive, attempt, labor; betake one's self, go.

Contentio, ōnis, f. (contendo). Effort, contest, struggle, exertion.

Contentus, a, um. Content, contented.

Contĭnens, entis, (contineo). Adjoining, continuous; *subs.* f. continent.

Continentia, ae, f. (contineo). Forbearance, self-control.

Contineo, ĕre, tinui, tentum, (cum, teneo). To hold, keep, check.

Continuo, āre, āvi, ātum, (continuus). To connect, unite, continue.

Contra, adv., and prep. with acc. Against, opposite to, contrary to; on the contrary.

Contra-dīco, ĕre, dixi, dictum. To contradict, object to.

H

Contrăho, ĕre, traxi, tractum, (cum, traho). To collect, incur, contract.

Contrarius, a, um. (contra). Contrary to, opposite.

Contrucīdo, āre, āvi, ātum, (cum, trucido). To slay, kill, mangle.

Contueor, tuĕri, tuĭtus sum, dep. (cum, tueor). To survey, look upon, behold; consider, ponder.

Convalesco, ĕre, lui, (cum, valesco). To gain strength, recover.

Conveniens, entis, (convenio). Becoming, fit, proper.

Convenien'er, ius, issīme, adv. (convenio). Fitly, suitably, agreeably, consistently.

Convenio, īre, vīni, ventum, (cum, venio). To convene, assemble, meet, agree, harmonize, befit.

Converto, ĕre, verti, versum, (cum, verto). To turn, change, alter, convert.

Convinco, ĕre, vici, victum, (cum, vinco). To conquer, convict.

Convivium, ii, n. Feast, banquet.

Convŏco, āre, āvi, ātum, (cum, voco). To assemble, call together.

Copia, ae, f. Abundance, supply, ability, power; *pl.* forces, stores, supplies.

Coram, adv., and prep. with abl. In the presence of, before.

Corinthus, i, f. Corinth, a city of Achaia, (162).

Corinthius, a, um, (Corinthus). Corinthian, subs. *Corinthius, ii,* m. a Corinthian, (45).

Coriolānus, i, m. Coriolanus, a surname given to *Caius Marcius,* derived from *Coriōli,* the name of a town which he had taken in war, (174).

Coriŏli, ōrum, m. pl. Coriŏii, a
town in Latium, (174).

Cornelia, ae, f. Cornelia, the mother of the Gracchi, (131).

Cornelius, ii, m. Cornelius, the name
of a distinguished Roman gens,
including the Scipios; as, Publius
Cornelius Scipio, (190, 194).

Cornelius, a, um. Belonging to the
Cornelian family, (120).

Cornu, us, n. Horn, wing of an
army.

Corōna, ae, f. Garland, crown.

Corpus, ŏris, n. Body, community.

Corrĭgo, ĕre, rexi, rectum, (cum,
rego). To reform, correct.

Corripio, ĕre, ripui, reptum, (cum,
rapio). To seize, lay hold of.

Corrumpo, ĕre, rūpi, ruptum, (cum,
rumpo). To corrupt, bribe, seduce.

Crassus, i, m. Crassus, a Roman
name, (93). Marcus Licinius
Crassus, a Roman general, (204).

Creber, bra, brum. Frequent, nu-
merous.

Credo, ĕre, credĭdi, credĭtum. To
trust, believe.

Cremĕra, ae, f. The Cremera, a
river of Etruria, in Italy, (175).

Creo, āre, āvi, ātum. To appoint,
elect, make.

Cresco, ĕre, crēvi, crētum. To grow,
increase.

Crimen, ĭnis, n. Crime, accusation.

Crimĭnor, āri, ātus sum, dep. (crimen). To accuse.

Crinis, is, m. Hair.

Critias, ae, m. Critias, one of the
thirty tyrants at Athens, (228).

Crixus, i, m. Crixus, a leader in
the war of the gladiators, (204).

Crucio, āre, āvi, ātum, (crux). To
pain, afflict, torture.

Crudēlis, e. Cruel.

Crudelĭtas, ātis, f. (crudēlis). Cruelty.

Crudelĭter, ius, issĭme, adv. (crudēlis). Cruelly.

Cubĭtum, i, n. The elbow, a cubit.

Culpa, ae, f. Fault, blame.

Cultūra, ae, f. (colo). Agriculture,
cultivation.

Cultus, us, m. Culture, necessaries,
as food, clothing, etc.

Cum, prep. with abl. With.

Cum, conj. = quum.

Cumae, ārum, f. Cumae, an ancient
city and colony in Campania, on
the sea-coast, renowned for its
Sibyl, (49, 7).

Cunctatio, ōnis, f. (cunctor). Delay.

Cunctor, āri, ātus sum. To delay,
hesitate.

Cunctus, a, um. All, all together,
entire.

Cupĭde, ius, issĭme, adv. (cupĭdus).
Eagerly.

Cupidĭtas, ātis, f. (cupĭdus). Desire,
wish.

Cupĭdus, a, um, (cupio). Desirous,
having desires, avaricious, covet-
ous, fond of.

Cupio, ĕre, īvi or ii, ītum. To desire.

Cur, adv. Why, wherefore.

Cura, ae, f. Care, management,
anxiety.

Cures, ium, f. pl. Cures, the ancient capital of the Sabines,
(159).

Curia, ae, f. Senate-house; ward.

Curiatii, ōrum, m. pl. The Curiatii,

three brothers who were selected from the Alban army to engage in combat with the three Horatii, also brothers, from the Romans, (160). See note on "*Horatiorum et Curiatiorum,*" (160).

Curius, ii, m. Curius, a Roman name, (27).

Curo, are, avi, atum. To care for, take care of.

Curro, ere, cucurri, cursum. To run.

Currus, us, m. (curro). Chariot.

Cursor, oris, m. Cursor, surname of *Lucius Papirius,* dictator in the Samnite war, (178).

Cursus, us, m. (curro). Course.

Custodia, ae, f. Care, charge of, custody, confinement.

Custodio, ire, ivi or *ii, itum,* (custos). To guard, preserve, watch.

Custos, odis, m. and f. Guard, keeper.

Cynicus, i, m. A Cynic philosopher, a Cynic.

Cynoscephalae, arum, f. pl. Cynoscephalae, "Dogs' Heads," two hills in Thessaly, (197).

Cyprus, i, f. Cyprus, an island in the Mediterranean sea, near Asia Minor, (27, 11).

Cyrus, i, m. The name of two eminent Persian princes; *Cyrus, the Great,* the founder of the Persian empire, (13), and *Cyrus, the son of Darius,* (225).

D.

Damnatio, onis, f. Condemnation.

Damno, are, avi, atum, (damnum). To condemn; *capitis damnare,* to condemn to death.

Damnum, i, n. Loss, damage.

Darius, ii, m. Darius, a celebrated king of Persia, (215).

Datis, is, m. Datis, one of the generals of Darius, (215).

De, prep. with abl. From, of, concerning, on the subject of, over.

Debeo, ere, ui, itum. To owe, ought.

Debeor, eri, debitus sum, dep. To be due, belong.

Debilito, are, avi, atum. To weaken, disable.

De-cedo, ere, cessi, cessum. To depart, withdraw, die.

Decem, indecl. Ten.

Decemplex, icis, (decem, plico, *to fold*). Tenfold.

Decem-vir, viri, m. A decemvir.

De-cerno, ere, crevi, cretum. To decide; contend, fight; decree, intrust by decree.

Decet, decuit, impers. It is seemly, becoming, becomes.

Decido, ere, cidi, cisum, (de, caedo). To cut off; decide, determine.

Decimus, a, um, (decem). Tenth.

Decipio, ere, cepi, ceptum, (de, capio). To deceive.

De-claro, are, avi, atum. To make clear, manifest; declare, pronounce.

Decretum, i, n. (decerno). Decree.

Decus, oris, n. Ornament, honor.

De-decus, oris, n. Disgrace.

Dedicatio, onis, f. (dedico). Dedication.

Dedico, are, avi, atum, (de, dico). To dedicate.

Deditio, onis, f. (dedo). Surrender.

De-do, ere, didi, ditum. To surren-

8

der; devote one's self to, give one's self up to.

De-dūco, ĕre, duxi, ductum. To bring down, conduct; remove; lead.

De-fatigo, āre, āvi, ātum. To weary, fatigue.

Defectio, ōnis, f. (deficio). Failure, eclipse, defection.

De-fendo, ĕre, fendi, fensum. To defend, ward off.

De-fĕro, ferre, tŭli, lātum. To offer, exhibit, bestow, present: carry *or* bear away.

Deficio, ĕre, fēci, fectum, (de, facio). To fail, spend itself; be eclipsed; desert, revolt.

De-flāgro, are, āvi, ātum. To burn, burn down, consume, destroy.

Deformis, e, (de, forma). Deformed, ugly.

De-fungor, gi, functus sum. To discharge, execute; die.

De-glūbo, ĕre, —, gluptum. To flay, to skin.

Dein or *deinde,* adv. Then, afterwards.

Deiotārus, i, m. Deiotarus, a king of Galatia, (206).

Dejicio, ĕre, jēci, jectum, (de, jacio) To throw down, overthrow, slay.

De-lecto, āre, āvi, ātum. To allure; to delight, please.

Delectus, a, um, (delĭgo). Chosen.

Deleo, ĕre, ēvi, ĕtum. To destroy, efface, put an end to.

De-lĭbĕro, are, āvi, ātum. To deliberate.

Deliciae, ārum, f. pl. Delights, pleasures; delight, darling, beloved.

Delĭgo, ĕre, legi, lectum, (de, lego). To choose, select; love.

Delirium, ii, n. Madness, dotage, instances of it.

Delos or *Delus, i, f.* Delos, a small island in the Aegean sea, (27, 10).

Delphi, ōrum, m. pl. Delphi, a town of Phocis, celebrated for the temple and oracle of Apollo (217).

Demarātus, i, m. Demaratus, the father of Tarquinius Priscus, (162).

De-mergo, ĕre, mersi, mersum. To plunge in, bury in, sink.

De-mitto, ĕre, mĭsi, missum. To let down, drop, send away, send.

Democrĭtus, i, m. Democritus, a celebrated Grecian philosopher, (91).

Demorior, mŏri, mortuus sum, (de, morior). To die.

Demosthĕnes, is, m. Demosthenes, the most celebrated of the Grecian orators, (92, 7).

Demum, adv. At length, finally.

Denarius, ii, m. Denarius, a Roman silver coin, worth about sixteen cents.

Deni, ae, a. Ten by ten, ten at a time.

Denĭque, adv. Finally.

Dens, dentis, m. A tooth.

De-nūdo, āre, āvi, ātum. To make naked, strip.

Denuntiatio, ōnis, f. (denuntio). Denunciation, warning.

De-nuntio, āre, āvi, ātum. To declare, denounce.

Denuo, adv. Again, afresh.

De-pello, ĕre, pŭli, pulsum. To drive away, expel.

De-pōno, ĕre, posui, posĭtum. To

lay down or aside, deposit, depose.

De-popŭlor, ari, ātus sum. To pillage, depopulate.

De-porto, āre, āvi, ātum. To carry off or away.

Depraedor, āri, ātus sam, (de, praedor). To ravage, plunder.

Deprehendo, ĕre, di, sum, (de, prehendo). To seize, catch, detect, surprise.

De-pugno, āre, āvi, ātum. To fight.

Derelictio, ōnis, f. (de, relinquo). Neglect, disregard.

De-scribo, ĕre, scripsi, scriptum. To describe; impose; assess; designate; divide.

Desĕro, ĕre, serui, sertum, (de, sero). To abandon, desert.

De-sidĕro, āre, āvi, ātum. To long for, wish, desire earnestly.

Desilio, īre, silui, sultum, (de, salio). To alight, dismount.

Desino, ĕre, sivi or sii, situm, (de, sino). To cease, desist.

Desipio, ĕre, (de, sapio). To be void of understanding, be foolish, be delirious.

De-sisto, ĕre, stiti, stitum. To desist, leave off.

Desperatio, ōnis, f. (despēro). Despair, desperation.

De-spēro, āre, āvi, ātum. To despair.

Despicio, ĕre, spexi, spectum, (de, specio). To despise, disregard.

Destino, āre, āvi, ātum. To destine, appoint, design.

De-sum, esse, fui. To fail, be wanting.

De-terreo, ēre, ui, itum. To deter.

Detineo, ēre, tenui, tentum, (de, teneo). To de'ain, hinder.

Detrăho, ĕre, traxi, tractum, (de, traho). To draw or take away or from, detract.

Detrimentum, i, n. Loss, damage, detriment, harm.

Deus, i, m. God, deity. See 51, 5.

De-vasto, āre, —, ātum. To devastate, pillage.

De-venio, īre, vēni, tentum. To come down, arrive, reach.

De-vinco, ĕre, vici, victum. To conquer.

Dexter, tra, trum. Right, on the right hand.

Dextra, ae, f. The right hand.

Di. See Dis.

Diadēma, ātis, n. Diadem.

Diagŏras, ae, m. Diagoras, a Rhodian athlete, who distinguished himself in the Olympic games, (143).

Diāna, ae, f. The goddess Diana, the daughter of Jupiter and Latona, and sister of Apollo, (97).

Dico, ĕre, dixi, dictum. To say, call.

Dictātor, ōris, m. (dico). Dictator, an officer appointed by the Romans in times of great danger.

Dido, us, or ōnis, f. Dido, the foundress of Carthage, daughter of Belus, (44, III.)

Dies, ēi, m. and f. Day.

Difficĭle, ius, līme, adv. (difficĭlis). With difficulty.

Difficĭlis, e, (dis, facĭlis). Difficult. 163, 2.

Digĭtus, i, m. Finger.

Dignĭtas, ātis, f. (dignus). Dignity, rank, office.

Dignor, āri, ātus sum, (dignus). To deem worthy, deign.

Dignus, a um. Worthy.

Di-lăbor, tābi, lapsus sum, dep. To fall asunder, go to pieces; flee; scatter, disperse.

Dilātio, ōnis, f. Delay, delaying.

Dilĭgens, entis, (dilīgo). Fond of, mindful, diligent, observant.

Diligenter, ius, issĭme, adv. (dilīgens). Carefully, diligently, earnestly.

Diligentia, ae, f. (dilīgens). Diligence.

Dilīgo, ĕre, lexi, lectum, (dis, lego). To choose, love.

Dimĭco, āre, āvi, ātum, (dis, di, mico). To encounter, fight.

Di-mitto, ĕre, misi, missum. To dismiss, let go.

Diogĕnes, is, m. Diogenes, the noted Cynic philosopher of Greece, (135).

Dion, ōnis, m. Dion, brother-in-law of the tyrant Dionysius of Syracuse, (31).

Dionysius, ii, m. Dionysius, tyrant of Syracuse, (26).

Diripio, ĕre, ripui, reptum, (dis, di, rapio). To lay waste, pillage.

Diruo, ĕre, dirui, dirŭtum, (dis, di, ruo). To destroy, demolish.

Dis, or *di,* insep. prep. Asunder, not.

Dis-cēdo, ĕre, cessi, cessum. To depart, retire from.

Disceptatio, ōnis, f. Debate, quarrel.

Disciplīna, ae, f. Discipline, instruction.

Discipŭlus, i, m. (disco). A learner, scholar, disciple.

Disco, ĕre, didĭci. To learn.

Discordia, ae, f. Strife, discord.

Discordo, āre, āvi, ātum, (discors, discordant). To differ, be at variance, disagree.

Discrīmen, ĭnis, n. Danger, crisis.

Dis-curro, ĕre, curri, cursum. To run different ways, run about, separate.

Dispergo, ĕre, spersi, spersum, (dis, di, spargo). To scatter, disperse.

Displiceo, ēre, plicui, plicĭtum, (dis, placeo). To displease.

Dis-pŭto, āre, āvi, ātum. To compute, estimate; examine, investigate, discuss.

Dis-sĕro, ĕre, serŭi, sertum. To examine, argue, discuss.

Dissidium, ii, n. Dissension.

Dis-simĭlis, e. Unlike, dissimilar.

Dissimŭlo, āre, āvi, ātum. To dissemble, conceal, omit.

Dis-sĭpo, āre, āvi, ātum. To dissipate, scatter.

Dis-solvo, ĕre, solvi, solūtum. To destroy, abolish, dissolve.

Dis-tribuo, ĕre, tribui, tribūtum. To distribute.

Districtus, a, um, (distringo). Busy, occupied with.

Distringo, ĕre, strinxi, strictum, (di, stringo). To occupy, engage attention.

Ditio, ōnis, f. Rule, sway.

Diu, diutius, diutissĭme, adv. Long, for a long time.

Diutĭnus, a, um, (diu). Of long duration, lasting.

Diuturnĭtas, ātis, f. (diuturnus). Long time.

Diversus, a, um. Diverse, unlike, opposite.

Dives, ĭtis. Rich.

Divĭco, ōnis, m. Divico, a distinguished Helvetian general, (85, 5).

Divĭdo, ĕre, divīsi, divīsum. To divide, allot.

Divīnus, a, um. Divine.

Divitiae, ārum, f. (dives). Riches, wealth.

Divus, a, um. Divine; *subs.* god, goddess.

Do, dāre, dedi, datum. To give, grant, impute, allow.

Doceo, ēre, ui, tum. To teach.

Doctrīna, ae, f. Instruction, learn-) ing, erudition, doctrine.

Doctus, a, um, (doceo). Learned, skilled.

Documentum, i, n. Lesson, proof, specimen, mark.

Dolabella, ae, m. Dolabella, a Roman name. *Publius Cornelius Dolabella,* son-in-law of Cicero, (122).

Doleo, ēre, ui, ītum. To grieve.

Dolor, ōris, m. (doleo). Pain, grief.

Dolus, i, m. Artifice, deceit.

Domestīcus, a, um, (domus). Domestic, private, personal.

Domicīlium, ii, n. (domus). Habitation, abode.

Dominātio, ōnis. Rule, tyranny.

Dominātus, us, m. Rule, sovereignty.

Domīnus, i, m. Master, owner.

Domo, āre, ui, ītum. To subdue.

Domus, us or *i,* f. House, home; *domi,* at home.

Donec, conj. Until.

Dono, āre, āvi, ātum, (donum). To give, present with.

Donum, i, n. (do). Present, gift.

Dormio, īre, īvi or *ii, ītum.* To sleep, slumber, rest.

Dos, dotis, f. Gift, dowry.

Drusus, i, m. Drusus, son of the Emperor Tiberius, (146).

Dubitatio, ōnis, f. (dubīto). Doubt, hesitation.

Dubīto, āre, āvi, ātum. To doubt, hesitate.

Dubius, a, um. Doubtful; *neut. of ten subs.* doubt.

Ducenti, ae, a. Two hundred.

Duco, ēre, duxi, ductum. To lead, conduct; *with uxōrem,* to marry.

Duillius, ii, m. Duillius, a Roman name. *Caius Duillius,* a Roman commander and consul in the first Punic war, (185).

Dulcis, e. Sweet, pleasant, agreeable.

Dum, conj. While, until, provided.

Dum-mŏdo, conj. So long as, provided that.

Duo, ae, o. Two, both. 175.

Duodĕcim, indec. (duo, decem). Twelve.

Duodecĭmus, a, um, (duodĕcim). Twelfth.

Duodequadragesĭmus, a, um. Thirty-eighth.

Duo-de-viginti, indec. Eighteen.

Duplex, ĭcis. Double.

Duplĭco, āre, āvi, ātum, (duplex). To double, increase.

Dūritia, ae, f. (durus). Hardiness, austerity, rigid temperance, hardship.

Durus, a, um. Hard, harsh, rude.

Dux, ducis, m. and f. (duco). Leader, guide, general.

E

E or *ex,* prep. with abl. From, out of, of.

Ebrĭĕtas, ātis, f. Drunkenness.

E-disco, ēre, dĭdĭci. To learn by heart, commit to memory.

E-do, edĕre, edĭdi, edĭtum. To set forth, publish; do, perform, make, utter.

E-doceo, ĕre, docui, doctum. To teach one thoroughly, inform, instruct.

E-dūco, ĕre, duxi, ductum. To lead out or forth.

Effĕro, āre, āvi, ātum. To enrage, madden, render unmanageable.

Effĕro, ferre, extūli, elātum, (ex, fero). To bring forth, carry forth or out; elate.

Efficio, ĕre, fēci, fectum, (ex, facio). To effect, occasion, accomplish, make, render.

Effluo, ĕre, fluxi, fluxum, (ex, fluo). To flow out, pass away, disappear.

Effugio, ĕre, fūgi, fugītum, (ex, fugio). To flee, escape from, escape.

Effundo, ĕre, fūdi, fūsum, (ex, fundo). To pour out, pour; indulge in; squander, waste.

Egeo, egēre, egui. To need, to want, require, to be without.

Ege·a, ae, f. Egeria, a prophetic nymph from whom Numa professed to receive instructions, (159).

Ego, mei, I. Egomet, I myself. 184, 6.

Egredior, egrĕdi, egressus sum, dep. (e, gradior). To go or come out, to go forth, to go, to run away.

Egregie, adv. (egregius). Excellently, remarkably.

Egregius, a, um. Excellent, distinguished.

Ejicio, ĕre, ejēci, ejectum, (e, jacio). To throw or drive out, expel; reject.

E-lābor, elābi, elapsus sum, dep. To slip away, get off, escape.

E-labōro, āre, āvi, ātum. To labor, exert one's self.

Elegantia, ae, f. Elegance, taste, propriety.

Elementa, ōrum, n. pl. The first principles, rudiments, elements.

Elephantus, i, m. Elephant.

Elīgo, ĕre, elēgi, electum, (e, lego). To choose, elect.

Elŏquens, entis, (elŏquor). Eloquent.

Eloquenter, ius, issĭme, adv. (elŏquens). Eloquently.

Eloquentia, ae, f. Eloquence.

E-lŏquor, lŏqui, locūtus sum, dep. To speak out, utter, declare, tell.

Emax, acis, (emo). Eager to buy, fond of buying.

E-mergo, ĕre, mersi, mersum. To emerge, come to light, rise in importance.

Eminentia, ae, f. Eminence, excellence.

Emineo, ĕre, ui. To stand out, be prominent or conspicuous.

E-mitto, ĕre, mīsi, missum. To send forth or away; let go.

Emo, ĕre, emi, emptum. To buy, purchase.

Emolumentum, i, n. Effort, exertion; gain, profit, advantage.

Enim, conj. For, indeed.

E-niteo, ĕre, nitui. To shine forth; be distinguished.

Ennius, ii, n. Ennius, a celebrated Roman poet, (120).

Eo, adv. Thither; therefore; eo usque, so far, to such an extent.

Eo, ire, ivi or ii, ĭtum. To go; walk, sail, ride, pass. 295.

Eōdem, adv. (idem). To the same place.

Epaminondas, ae, m. Epaminondas, a celebrated Theban general, (92, 5).

Ephesius, a, um. Ephesian, relating to Ephesus, of Ephesus, born at Ephesus, (97).

Epigramma, ătis, n. Inscription, epigram. 58, 2.

Epirus, i, f. Epirus, a province in the north of Greece, (180).

Epistŏla, ae, f. A letter, epistle.

Epŭlae, ărum, f. pl. Food, banquet, feast.

Epŭlor, āri, ătus sum, (epŭlae). To feast.

Eques, ĭtis, m. (equus). Horseman. *Pl.* cavalry.

Equester, tris, tre, (eques). Equestrian.

Equĭdem, conj. Indeed, truly, by all means.

Equitātus, us, m. Cavalry.

Equus, i, m. Horse: *ex equo,* from a horse, on horseback.

Eretria, ae, f. Eretria, an important city on the island of Euboea, (16).

Erga, prep. with acc. Towards.

Ergo, adv. Therefore; *as subs. abl.* on account of, for, *with gen.*

Erĭgo, ĕre, erexi, erectum, (e, rego). To raise up, animate.

Eripio, ĕre, eripui, ereptum, (e, rapio). To snatch or take away.

Error, ŏris, m. Error, deception.

Erudio, īre, īvi or ii, ĭtum. To instruct, refine, discipline.

Erudītus, a, um, part. (erudio). Learned, instructed in.

E-rumpo, ĕre, rūpi, ruptum. To break forth, rush forth.

Eruo, ĕre, erui, erŭtum, (e, ruo). To root out, destroy.

Esca, ae, f. Food, bait.

Et, conj. And; *et—et,* both—and.

Et-ĕnim, conj. For, truly, because that, since.

Etiam. Also, even.

Etiam-si. Even if, although.

Etiam-tum, conj. Even then, till then, still.

Etruria, ae, f. Etruria, a country of Central Italy; Tuscany, (190).

Etruscus, i, m. An Etruscan, inhabitant of Etruria, (171).

Et-si. Even if, although, though.

Euboea, ae, f. Euboea, an island in the Aegean sea, (84).   [(144).

Euripĭdes, is, m. An Athenian poet,

Euphrātes, is, m. A river in Asia, (24).

Eurōpa, ae, f. The continent of Europe.

Eurybiădes, is, m. A king of Sparta, (219).

E-vādo, ĕre, vāsi, vāsum. To go out; to turn out, become; escape; evade.

E-venio, īre, vēni, ventum. To come forth, happen; *evēnit, ut,* it chanced, that.

E-verto, ĕre, verti, versum. To pull down, overthrow.

Evŏco, āre, āvi, ātum, (e, voco). To call forth, summon.

Evŏlo, āre, āvi, ātum, (e, volo). To fly *or* flee away, hasten away.

Ex, prep. with abl. From. See *e* or *ex.*

Ex-adversum or ex-adversus, adv., and prep. with acc. Opposite, against.

Ex-anĭmo, āre, āvi, ātum. To deprive of life *or* spirit; kill.

Ex-ardesco, ĕre, arsi. To kindle, be inflamed; break out, *as war.*

Ex-cēdo, ĕre, cessi, cessum. To retire, withdraw.

Ex-cello, ĕre, cellŭi, celsum. To elevate; excel, be eminent.

Excelsus, a, um, (excello). Lofty.

Excidium, ii, n. Destruction, ruin.

Excipio, ĕre, cĕpi, ceptum, (ex, capio). To take out, except.

Ex-cĭto, āre, āvi, ātum. To excite, arouse, awaken, strengthen.

Exclūdo, ĕre, clūsi, clūsum, (ex, claudo). To exclude, shut out, cut off.

Ex-cogĭto, āre, āvi, ātum. To devise, think out.

Excutio, ĕre, cussi, cussum, (ex, quatio). To shake or throw off.

Exemplum, i, n. Example.

Ex-eo, īre, īvi or ii, ĭtum. To go from or forth.

Exerceo, ēre, cui, cĭtum, (ex, arceo). To exercise, practise.

Exercĭtus, us, m. (exerceo). Army, train.

Ex-haurio, īre, hausi, haustum. To exhaust, impoverish.

Ex-horresco, ĕre, horrui. To dread, to tremble at.

Exĭgo, ĕre, ēgi, actum, (ex, ago). To drive out, expel; finish, end; demand.

Exiguus, a, um. Small.

Eximius, a, um. Excellent, choice, remarkable.

Exĭmo, ĕre, ēmi, emptum, (ex, emo). To take away or from; exempt; rescue.

Existimātio, ōnis, f. (existĭmo). An opinion, judgment, supposition; reputation.

Existĭmo, āre, āvi, ātum, (ex, aestĭmo). To judge, think.

Exitium, ii, n. (exeo). End, death, destruction.

Ex-orior, orīri, ortus sum, dep., partly of 3d conj. To arise; be derived from. 288, 2.

Ex-orno, āre, āvi, ātum. To adorn, beautify, embellish, furnish, equip.

Exōsus, a, um. Hating, hated, odious.

Expedio, īre, īvi or ii, ītum. To release, extricate; also to be expedient, or profitable.

Expedĭtio, ōnis, f. (expedio). Expedition.

Ex-pello, ĕre, pŭli, pulsum. To expel, drive away, banish.

Ex-pĕto, ĕre, īvi or ii, ītum. To seek, request.

Ex-pleo, ēre, ēvi, ītum. To fill make full; fulfil.

Ex-plĭco, āre, āvi, ātum. To unfold; adjust; settle.

Explorātor, ōris, m. Explorer, spy.

Ex-pugno, āre, āvi, ātum. To take, conquer, storm.

Ex-scindo, ĕre, scĭdi, scissum. To destroy.

Ex-sculpo, ĕre, sculpsi, sculptum. To erase.

Exsecrabĭlis, e. Detestable.

Exsequiae, ārum, f. pl. Funeral.

Ex-sĕquor, sĕqui, secūtus sum. To prosecute, accomplish, finish; perform.

Exsilium, ii, n. Banishment, exile.

Exspectatio, ōnis, f. (exspecto). Expectation, high hope.

Ex-specto, āre, āvi, ātum. To await, expect.

Ex-stinguo, ĕre, stinxi, stinctum. To extinguish, destroy.

Ex-struo, ĕre, struxi, structum. To build, construct.

Exsul, ŭlis, m. and f. An exile.

Ex-templo, adv. Immediately.

Ex-torqueo, ēre, torsi, tortum. To extort, obtain by force.

Ex-trăho, ēre, traxi, tractum. To extract, draw out, remove; rescue.

F

Fabius, ii, m. Fabius, the name of a distinguished Roman family. *Quintus Fabius Maxĭmus,* the celebrated Roman general who so successfully weakened Hannibal in the first Punic war, (175).

Fabricius, ii, m. Fabricius, a distinguished leader of the Romans in the war against Pyrrhus, (182).

Fabŭla, ae, f. Report, narrative, fable, story, drama.

Facies, ēi, f. A face, appearance.

Facĭle, ius, lĭme, adv. (facĭlis). Easily.

Facĭlis, e, (facio). Easy.

Facĭnus, ŏris, n. Deed, act; wickedness, crime.

Facio, ēre, feci, factum. To do, act, make, compose.

Factio, ŏnis, f. Faction, party.

Facultas, ātis, f. Capacity, ability, resource, opportunity; *plur.* riches, property, resources.

Fallo, ēre, fefelli, falsum. To deceive, foil.

Falsus, a, um. False, spurious.

Fama, ae, f. Fame, report.

Fames, is, f. Hunger, famine.

Familia, ae, f. Retinue of slaves, a family.

Familiarĭtas, ātis, f. Friendship, intimacy.

Famŭla, ae, f. Female slave.

Fannius, ii, m. Fannius, a Roman name, (43).

Fanum, i, n. Temple.

Fascis, is, m. A bundle, parcel.

Fastidio, ire, ivi or ii, ĭtum. To loathe, despise, disdain.

Fatālis, e, (fatum). Fated, fatal.

Fatĭgo, āre, āvi, ātum. To oppress, trouble, weary, importune.

Fatum, i, n. Fate, destiny, oracle.

Fauce, abl. f.; plur. fauces, faucium. Throat, jaws.

Faustŭlus, i, m. Faustulus, the shepherd who brought up Romulus and Remus, (153).

Faveo, ēre, favi, fautum. To favor.

Favor, ŏris, m. (faveo). Favor, kindness.

Felicĭtas, ātis, f. (felix). Felicity, success.

Felicĭter, ius, issĭme, adv. (felix). Happily, prosperously.

Felis, is, f. Cat.

Felix, ĭcis. Happy.

Femĭna, ae, f. Woman, female.

Femur, ŏris, n. Thigh.

Fera, ae, f. Wild beast.

Ferax, ācis. Fertile, fruitful, productive.

Fere, adv. Almost.

Ferme, adv. Almost.

Ferio, ire. To strike, beat.

Fero, ferre, tuli, latum. To bear, endure; raise; say, tell; propose, as law. 292.

Ferox, ōcis. Bold, warlike, savage.

Ferrum, i, n. Iron, sword.

Fertĭlis, e. Fertile, rich.

Ferus, a, um. Wild, rude, cruel; *ferus* and *fera* (subs.), wild animal or beast.

Fessus, a, um. Wearied, exhausted.

Festĭno, āre, āvi, ātum. To hasten.

Festus, a, um. Festal; *festum* (subs.), a festival, feast.

Fidēlis, e, (fides). Faithful, trusty.

Fides, ei, f.   Fidelity, allegiance; protection, confidence, assurance; *in fidem,* under protection.

Fido, ĕre, fisus sum.   To trust, confide.

Fiducia, ae, f.   Trust, confidence.

Filia, ae, f., dat. and abl. pl. *filiābus.* Daughter. 49, 4.

Filius, ii, m.   Son.

Fingo, ĕre, finxi, fictum.   To form, feign, rcpresent.

Finio, ĭre, ĭvi, ĭtum, (finis).   To finish, put an end to.

Finis, is, m. and f.   Limit, end; *pl.* territory.

Finitĭmus, a, um.   Ncighboring; *subs.* a neighbor.

Fio, fiĕri, factus sum, pass. of *facio.* To be made; bccome, happen. 294.

Firme, adv.   Firmly, resolutely.

Firmĭtas, ătis, f. (firmus).   Firmness, strength.

Firmus, a, um.   Strong, secure, firm.

Flagitiōsus, a, um.   Infamous, abandoned.

Flagitium, ii, n.   Disgrace, shame, base deed.

Flagro, āre, āvi, ātum.   To burn, be carried on with zeal.

Flaminius, ii, m.   Flaminius, a Roman consul, defeated by Hannibal at the Lake Trasimenus, (190).

Flamma, ae, f.   Flame.

Flecto, ĕre, flexi, flexum.   To bend, turn.

Fletus, us, m.   Weeping, tears.

Florens, entis, (floreo).   Blooming, youthful, excellent. *Florens aetas,* youth.

Floresco, ĕre, florui, (floreo).   To bloom, flourish, prosper; excel.

Flos, ōris, m.   Blossom, flower.

Flumen, ĭnis, n.   Stream, river.

Fluvius, ii, m.   River.

Foederātus, a, um.   Confederate, allied.

Foedus, ĕris, n.   League, alliance, treaty.

Fons, ontis, m.   Spring, fountain.

Forem, es, etc. = *essem, es,* etc., Might be; *fore = futūrum esse.* See 297, III. 2.

Formo, āre, āvi, ātum.   To form, fashion, adjust.

Fors, fortis, f.   Chance; abl. *forte* as adv., by chance, perchance.

Forsĭtan, (fors, sit, an).   Perhaps.

Fortasse.   Perhaps.

Forte.   See *fors.*

Fortis, e.   Brave, valiant.

Fortĭter, ius, issĭme, adv. (fortis). Bravely.

Fortitūdo, ĭnis, f. (fortis).   Fortitude, bravery.

Fortūna, ae, f.   Fortune.

Forum, i, n.   Market-place, forum.

Fossa, ae, f.   Ditch, trench.

Frango, ĕre, fregi, fractum.   To break.

Frater, tris, m.   Brother.

Fraus, dis, f.   Fraud, deceit.

Frequenter, ius, issĭme, adv.   Frequently, in great numbers.

Fretus, a, um.   Trusting, relying upon.

Fructus, us, m.   Fruit, produce.

Frugalĭtas, ătis, f.   Frugality, integrity.

Frumentum, i, n.   Corn, grain.

Fruor, frui, fruĭtus and *fructus sum,* dep.   To enjoy.

Frustra, adv.   In vain.

Fuga, ae, f.   Flight.

Fugio, ĕre, fugi, fugĭtum. To fly, flee, avoid, shun.

Fugo, āre, āvi, ātum. To rout, put to flight.

Fulgur, ŭris, n. Lightning, thunderbolt.

Fulguratio, ōnis, f. Lightning.

Fulmen, ĭnis, n. Lightning, thunderbolt.

Fundamentum, i, n. Foundation.

Fundĭtus, adv. Utterly, entirely.

Fundo, ĕre, fudi, fusum. To pour out, shed, rout; also to make, cast.

Funestus, a, um, (funus). Deadly, destructive; mournful, sad.

Fungor, fungi, functus sum, dep. To discharge, perform, pay.

Furcŭla, ae, f. Fork. *Furcŭlae Caudīnae; see Caudīnus.*

Furius, ii, m. Furius, a Roman family name, as *Marcus Furius Camillus; see* Camillus.

Furor, ōris, m. Fury, madness.

Furtum, i, n. Theft.

Futūrus, a, um, part. (sum). Future.

G.

Galatia, ae, f. Galatia, a country of Asia Minor, (206).

Gallia, ae, f. The ancient country of Gaul, (209).

Gallĭcus, a, um, (Gallia). Gallic.

Gallīna, ae, f. Hen.

Gallus, i, m. A cock.

Gallus, i, m. (Gallia). A Gaul, a native of Gaul, (39, III.).

Gaudeo, ĕre, gavīsus sum. To rejoice, take pleasure in. 271, 3.

Gaudium, ii, n. Joy, pleasure.

Gemĭnus, a, um. Twin, double.

Gemma, ae, f. Gem.

Gener, ĕri, m. Son-in-law.

Genero, āre, āvi, ātum, (genus). To beget, create, produce.

Genĭtus, a, um, part. (gigno). Born, produced.

Gens, gentis, f. Family, clan, tribe, nation, race. *Ubĭnam gentium,* where in the world?

Genus, ĕris, n. Race, family, people, kind.

Germania, ae, f. Germany, (39, V.).

Germānus, ĭ, m. (Germania). A German, (30).

Gero, ĕre, gessi, gestum. To bear, wear; carry on, perform; wage, *as war.*

Gestio, īre, īvi or *ii, ītum.* To desire, long for.

Gigno, ĕre, genui, genĭtum. To bring forth, beget, produce.

Glaciālis, e. Icy, freezing.

Gladiātor, ōris, m. Gladiator, a fighter at the public games.

Gladiatorius, a, um, (gladiātor). Gladiatorial.

Gladius, ii, m. Sword.

Glisco, ĕre. To grow, spread; rise.

Gloria, ae, f. Glory.

Glorior, āri, ātus sum, dep. To boast, exult, glory.

Gracchus, i, m. Gracchus, a Roman name. *Sempronius Gracchus,* the Roman general defeated by Hannibal at the Trebia, (190). *Gracchi, ōrum,* m. pl. The Gracchi, members of the Gracchus family, but especially the two brothers, *Tiberius Cornelius Gracchus* and *Caius Cornelius Gracchus,* famous in the political history of Rome, (181).

Gradus, us, m. Step, position, stair.

Graece, adv. (Graecus). In the Greek language, in Greek.

Graecia, ae, f. Greece, (210).

Graecus or *Graius, a, um*, (Graecia). Grecian. Subs. *Graecus* or *Graius, i*, m. A Greek, (30, 8).

Grammatica, ae, f. Grammar.

Grammaticus, a, um. Of or belonging to grammar, grammatical.

Grandis, e. Large, great.

Grando, ĭnis, f. Hail.

Gratia, ae, f. Favor, gratitude; *pl.* thanks; *gratiā*, abl. for the sake of.

Gratiis or *gratis*, adv. For nothing, without pay.

Gratulatio, ōnis, f. Gratulation, congratulation.

Gratus, a, um. Pleasing, acceptable, grateful.

Gravis, e, Heavy, severe.

Gravitas, ātis, f. (gravis). Weight; dignity, gravity.

Graviter, ius, issĭme, adv. (gravis). Heavily, severely.

Gravo, āre, āvi, ātum, (gravis). To burden, load.

Grus, gruis, m. and f. Crane.

Gubernator, ōris, m. Pilot, ruler, governor.

Guberno, āre, āvi, ātum. To steer, pilot; direct, manage.

Gylippus, i, m. Gylippus, a Spartan commander in the Sicilian expedition, (223).

H.

Habeo, ēre, ui, ĭtum. To have; regard; keep. *Sermōnem habēre*, to hold a conversation.

Habĭto, āre, āvi, ātum, (habeo). To inhabit, live in, dwell in. 332, L. 2.

Habĭtus, us, m. (habeo). Habit, dress, attire.

Hamilcar, ăris, m. Hamilcar, the father of Hannibal, (186).

Hamus, i, m. Fish-hook, hook.

Hannĭbal, ălis, m. Hannibal, the celebrated Carthaginian general in the second Punic war, (189).

Hanno, ōnis, m. Hanno, a Carthaginian general in the second Punic war, (195).

Hasdrŭbal, ălis, m. Hasdrubal, son of Hamilcar and brother of Hannibal, (192). Another of the same name was the brother-in-law of Hannibal, and the founder of New Carthage, in Spain.

Hasta, ae, f. Spear.

Hastĭle, is, n. Spear.

Hastĭlis, e, (hasta). Belonging to a spear.

Haud, adv. Not.

Haurio, ĭre, hausi, haustum. To drink, draw out, exhaust.

Hector, ŏris, m. Hector, son of Priam and Hecuba, the bravest of the Trojans, (146).

Hedĕra, ae, f. Ivy.

Hellespontus, i, m. Hellespont, the straits of the Dardanelles.

Helvetii, ōrum, m. The Helvetians, a people of Gaul, (42).

Hercŭles, is, m. Hercules, a celebrated Grecian hero, deified after death.

Heres, ĕdis, m. and f. Heir, heiress.

Herennius, ii, m. Herennius, the father of Pontius Thelesinus, who conquered the Romans at the Caudine Forks, (179).

Herodŏtus, i, m. Herodotus, a celebrated Grecian historian, (20).

Heros, ŏis, m. Hero.

Heu ! interj. Oh ! Ah ! Alas !

Hiberna, ŏrum, n. (hibernus). Winter-quarters.

Hic, haec, hoc. This, he, she, it.

Hic, adv. Here, in this place.

Hiems, ĕmis, f. Storm, winter.

Hiĕro, ŏnis, m. Hiero, king of Syracuse at the time of the first Punic war, (185).

Hierosolўma, ae, f. or ŏrum, n. pl. Jerusalem, the capital of Judea, (206).

Hinc, adv. (hic). Hence, on this account, on this side; hinc—hinc, on the one side—on the other side.

Hippias, ae, m. Hippias, son of Pisistratus, tyrant of Athens, (97).

Hispania, ae, f. Spain, (97).

Hispānus, a, um. Spanish; subs. Hispānus, i, m. A Spaniard, (194).

Historia, ae, f. History.

Hodie, adv. To-day.

Hoedus, i, m. A kid, young goat.

Homĕrus, i, m. Homer, the celebrated Greek epic poet, (134).

Homo, ĭnis, m. and f. Human being, man.

Honestas, ătis, f. (honestus). Honor, honesty.

Honeste, ius, issĭme, adv. (honestus). Honorably, nobly, honestly.

Honestus, a, um, (honor). Full of honor, honorable, creditable, worthy, virtuous.

Honor or honos, ŏris, m. Honor, rank, dignity.

Honorifĭce, centius, centissĭme, adv. (honorifĭcus). Honorably. 305.

Honŏro, āre, āvi, ātum, (honor). To honor, reverence.

Hora, ae, f. Hour.

Horreo, ēre, horrui. To shudder, shudder at, dread.

Horatii, ŏrum, m pl. See Curiatii; also note on " Horatiŏrum et Curiatiŏrum, (160).

Horatius, ii, m. See Cocles and Pulvillus.

Hortensius, ii, m. Hortensius, a Roman name. Quintus Hortensius Hortūlus, a celebrated orator in the time of Cicero, (84, 91).

Hortor, āri, ātus sum, dep. To exhort, incite.

Hospĭta, ae, f. Guest.

Hostia, ae, f. Victim.

Hostīlis, e, (hostis). Hostile.

Hostilius, ii, m. Hostilius, a Roman name. Tullus Hostilius, the third king of Rome, (160). Caius Hostilius Mancīnus, a Roman consul, (201).

Hostis, is, m. and f. Enemy.

Humānus, a, um, (homo). Human.

Humĭlis, e. Humble, small, low.

Humo, āre, āvi, ātum. To bury.

Hypānis, is, m. Hypanis, a river of Sarmatia, (85).

I.

Ibĕrus, i, m. Iberus, a river of Spain, now the Ebro, (25).

Ibi, adv. There, in that place.

Ico, ĕre, ici, ictum. To strike; make, ratify.

Idem, eădem, idem. The same; sometimes best rendered by also.

Idoneus, a, um. Suitable, fit.

Igĭtur, conj. Therefore, accordingly.

Ignāvus, a, um. Slothful, indolent.

Ignis, is, m. Fire.

Ignŏro, āre, āvi, ātum. To be ignorant of, not know.

Ignosco, ĕre, ignōvi, ignōtum. To excuse, forgive, overlook.

Ilienses, ium, m. Inhabitants of Ilium, Trojans, (146).

Ilium, ii, n. Ilium, or Troy, sometimes applied to the city, and sometimes to the district, (236).

Ille, a, ud. That; he, she, it.

Illustris, e. Illustrious, famous.

Illustro, āre, āvi, ātum, (illustris). To enlighten, illumine, illustrate, celebrate.

Illyrĭcus, a, um, or *Illyrius, a, um.* Illyrian, of or pertaining to Illyria, a country on the northeastern coast of the Adriatic, (245). Subs. *Illyrĭcus* or *Illyrius, i,* m., an Illyrian.

Imāgo, ĭnis, f. Image, figure, picture.

Imbecillus, a, um, or *imbecillis, e.* Weak, feeble.

Imbuo, ĕre, imbui, imbūtum. To imbue, impress.

Imitātio, ōnis, f. Imitation.

Imĭtor, āri, ātus sum, dep. To imitate, copy, portray, counterfeit.

Immatūrus, a, um, (in, matūrus). Young, immature.

Immĕmor, ŏris, (in, memor). Unmindful, forgetful.

Immitto, ĕre, mĭsi, mĭssum, (in, mit-

to). To send or let in; let go; bring forward.

Immortālis, e, (in, mortālis). Immortal.

Immortalĭtas, ātis, f. (immortālis.) Immortality.

Immunĭtas, ātis, f. Immunity, exemption.

Imo or *immo,* adv. Yes indeed, indeed, by all means.

Impatiens, entis, (in, patiens). Impatient.

Impatienter, ius, issĭme, adv. (impatiens). Impatiently.

Impedimentum, i, n. (impedio). Impediment, obstacle; *pl.* baggage.

Impedio, ĭre, ĭvi or *ii, ĭtum.* To impede, embarrass; hinder, prevent.

Impello, ĕre, pŭli, pulsum, (in, pello). To impel, induce.

Impensa, ae, f. Expense, cost.

Imperātor, ōris, m. (impĕro). Commander, emperor.

Imperītus, a, um, (in, perītus). Unskilled, ignorant.

Imperium, ii, n. (impĕro). Command, power, rule, sway, reign.

Impĕro, āre, āvi, ātum. To command, rule, govern.

Impĕtro, āre, āvi, atum. To accomplish, obtain.

Impĕtus, us, m. Attack, fury.

Impiĕtas, ātis, f. (impius). Want of respect, irreverence, impiety.

Impius, a, um, (in, pius). Undutiful, irreverent, impious, abandoned.

Impōno, ĕre, posui, posĭtum, (in, pono). To place or put in or to; enjoin; impose.

Improbo, āre, āvi, ātum, (in, probo). To reject.

Imprudenter, ius, issime, adv. (imprūdens, *imprudent*). Imprudently.

Impūbes, ĕris. Youthful, young.

Impugno, āre, āvi, ātum, (in, pugno). To assail, attack.

Impulsus, us, m. (impello). Instigation.

In, prep. with acc. or abl. Into, to, for, against, *with acc.*; in, on, *with abl.*

Inānis, e. Empty, void; vain, foolish, useless.

Incendium, ii, n. (incendo). Fire, conflagration.

Incendo, ĕre, cendi, censum. To set on fire, inflame, excite.

In-certus, a, um. Uncertain.

Incesso, ĕre, cessīvi or cessi. To attack.

Inchoo, āre, āvi, ātum. To begin, commence.

Incĭdo, ĕre, cĭdi, cāsum, (in, cado). To fall into or upon, fall in with, happen.

Incīdo, ĕre, cīdi, cīsum, (in, caedo). To cut, destroy.

Incipio, ĕre, cēpi, ceptum, (in, capio). To begin, undertake.

Incitamentum, i. n. (incĭto). Incentive, inducement.

Incitātus, a, um, (incĭto). Running; *equo incitāto,* at full speed.

In-cĭto, āre, āvi, ātum. To incite, hasten, spur on; inspire.

In-clino, āre, āvi, ātum. To incline, bend; *pass.* to sink, go to ruin.

Incŏla, ae, m. and f. (incŏlo). Inhabitant.

In-cŏlo, ĕre, colui, cultum. To dwell, abide in, inhabit.

In-colŭmis, e. Safe, uninjured.

In-credibilis, e. Incredible.

Incrementum, i, n. Growth, increase.

Incursio, ōnis, f. (incurro). Attack, inroad.

Inde, adv. Thence, from that place.

Indecōre, adv. Disgracefully.

India, ae, f. India, an extensive country of Asia, (242).

In-dīco, ĕre, dixi, dictum. To declare, publish, appoint.

Indigeo, ĕre, indigui. To need; part. *indĭgens,* as *adj.* or *subs.* indigent, an indigent person.

Indignatio, ōnis, f. (indignor). Scorn, indignation.

Indignor, āri, ātus sum, (indignus). To disdain, scorn; be indignant.

In-dignus, a, um. Unworthy, harsh, indecent.

In-domĭtus, a, um. Unsubdued, invincible.

In-dubitātus, a, um. Undoubted, certain.

Induciae, or *indutiae, ārum,* f. pl. Truce.

In-dūco, ĕre, duxi, ductum. To induce, lead into, overlay, adorn with, gild.

Indurātus, a, um, (indūro). Obdurate, hardened.

In-dūro, āre, āvi, ātum. To harden.

Industria, ae, f. Industry.

In-eo, īre, īvi or ii, itum. To enter, go into; *gratiam inire,* to obtain the favor of, conciliate. 295.

Inermis, e, (in, arma). Unarmed.

Infamis, e. Infamous, notorious.

Infans, antis, adj. Speechless, dumb; *subs.* an infant.

In-fēlix, ĭcis. Unhappy, unfortunate.

Infensus, a, um. Exasperated, enraged.

Inferior, ius. Inferior. 163, 3.

In-fĕro, ferre, tŭli, illātum. To carry against, wage against. 292, 2.

Infcsto, āre, āvi, ātum, (infestus). To infest, trouble.

Infestus, a, um. Infested, troublesome, hostile.

In-finītus, a, um. Great, infinite, boundless, of unlimited power.

In-flammo, āre, āvi, ātum. To set on fire, burn, inflame, arouse.

Informis, e, (in, forma). Shapeless, deformed.

In-frendo, ĕre, —, fressum, frēsum. To gnash with the teeth.

Infringo, ĕre, frēgi, fractum, (in, frango). To infringe, break.

Infūla, ae, f. Fillet, head-dress, badge of office.

In-gĕmo, ĕre, ui. To groan, lament.

Ingenium, ii, n. Character, genius, intellect, power.

Ingens, entis. Great, mighty.

Ingratiis or ingrātis, adv. Against one's will.

In-grātus, a, um. Disagreeable, offensive, ungrateful.

In-gredior, grĕdi, gressus sum, dep. (in, gradior). To enter, encounter.

In-haereo, ĕre, haesi, haesum. To cleave or stick to, to stick fast, adhere.

In-hio, āre, āvi, ātum. To gape, stand open; desire, long for.

Inhumanĭtas, ātis, f. (inhumānus). Barbarity, incivility, inhumanity.

Inimīcus, a, um, (in, amīcus). Hostile; subs. an enemy.

Inīquus, a, um, (in, aequus). Unfavorable, unjust.

Initium, ii, n. (ineo). Beginning; pl. sacred mysteries.

Injicio, ĕre, jēci, jectum, (in, jacio). To throw in; cause; inspire with.

Injuria, ae, f. Injury, wrong.

Injuste, ius, issĭme, adv. (injustus). Unjustly.

In-justus, a, um. Unjust, oppressive, severe.

In-nŏcens, entis. Innocent.

In-notesco, ĕre, notui. To become known.

In-noxius, a, um. Harmless, innocent.

In-numerabĭlis, e. Innumerable.

In-opinātus, a, um. Sudden, unexpected.

Inquam, defective. To say. See 297, II. 2.

Insania, ae, f. Insanity, folly.

Inscitia, ae, f. Ignorance.

In-sĕquor, sĕqui, secūtus sum. To follow, pursue.

Insidiae, ārum. f, pl. Ambush, treachery, plot.

Insigne, is, n. Mark, sign; pl. badges of office, insignia.

Insignis, e. Distinguished, noted.

In-simŭlo, āre, āvi, ātum. To blame, accuse, charge.

In-sisto, ĕre, stĭti, stĭtum. To persist; urge; entreat.

In-sŏlens, entis. Unusual, insolent.

Insolenter, ius, issĭme, adv. (insŏlens). Insolently.

Inspecto, āre, āvi, ātum. To look at, to look on.

Inspicio, ĕre, spexi, spectum, (in, spe

cio). To consider, inspect, look on.

Instauro, āre, āvi, ātum. To renew.

Instituo, ĕre, stitui, stitūtum, (in, statuo). To institute, establish.

Institūtum, i, n. (instituo). Habit, manner, custom, institution.

In-sto, stāre, stĭti, stătum. To stand in *or* upon a thing, be near to; to urge, insist, beg earnestly.

Instrumentum, i, n. (instruo). Implements, movables, goods.

In-struo, ĕre, struxi, structum. To prepare, build, furnish with, equip.

Insŭla, ae, f. Island.

In-sŭper. Moreover.

In-tactus, a, um. Unharmed.

Intĕger, gra, grum. Whole, entire, unhurt; just, impartial, neutral.

Integrĭtas, ātis, f. (intĕger). Integrity, probity, honesty.

Intelligentia, ae, f. (intellĭgo). Intelligence, discernment, understanding.

Intellĭgo, ĕre, lexi, lectum. To understand, perceive, know.

Inter, prep. with acc. Between, among, in the midst of.

Intercipio, ĕre, cēpi, ceptum, (inter, capio). To catch; intercept, take from.

Interclūdo, ĕre, clūsi, clūsum, (inter, claudo). To prevent, cut off.

Inter-dum, adv. Sometimes.

Inter-ea, adv. In the mean time.

Inter-eo, īre, ĭvi or *ii, ĭtum.* To perish. 295.

Inter-est, impers. It concerns, it is important.

Interfector, ōris, m. (interficio). Murderer.

Interficio, ĕre, fēci, fectum, (inter, facio). To kill, slay.

Intĕrim, adv. In the mean time, meanwhile.

Interĭmo, ĕre, ēmi, emptum, (inter, emo). To deprive of, to kill.

Interior, ius. Interior, inland. 166.

Interĭtus, us, m. (intereo). Destruction.

Interjicio, ĕre, jēci, jectum, (inter, jacio). To place between; *anno interjecto,* at the expiration of a year.

Internecio, ōnis, f. Slaughter.

Inter-nuncius or *internuntius, ii,* m. Messenger.

Interregnum, i, n. An interreign, interregnum.

In-terrĭtus, a, um. Fearless, undismayed.

Inter-rŏgo, āre, āvi, ātum. To ask, question.

Inter-rumpo, ĕre, rūpi, ruptum. To break down, interrupt.

Inter-sĕro, ĕre, serui, sertum. To allege, interpose.

Inter-sum, esse, fui. To be present at, take part in.

Inter-venio, īre, vēni, ventum. To intervene, occur.

Intestīnus, a, um. Intestine, civil.

Intra, adv., and prep. with acc. Within.

Intro, āre, āvi, ātum. To enter.

Intro-eo, īre, ĭvi or *ii, ĭtum.* To enter. 295.

In-tueor, tuēri, tuĭtus sum. To look at, observe.

Intus, adv. Within.

In-usitātus, a, um. Unusual, extraordinary.

In-utĭlis, e. Useless.

In-vādo, ĕre, vāsi, vāsum. To invade, seize.

In-venio, īre, vēni, ventum. To find, invent, devise, meet with.

Inventrix, īcis, f. (inventor). Inventress.

In-vīcem, adv. By turns, one another.

In-victus, a, um. Unconquered, invincible.

In-video, ĕre, vīdi, vīsum. To envy.

Invidia, ae, f. Envy, hatred.

Invīsus, a, um. Odious, hateful.

Invīto, āre, avi, ātum. To invite, allure.

Invītus, a, um. Unwilling.

Ionia, ae, f. Ionia, a country in the western part of Asia Minor, (224).

Iōnes, um, m. pl. The Ionians.

Iphicrătes, is, m. Iphicrates, a celebrated Athenian general. He rose from an humble station to the highest offices of state, (49).

Ipse, a, um. Self, himself, herself, itself.

Ira, ae, f. Anger.

Irascor, irasci, irātus sum, dep. To be angry, be in a rage.

Irātus, a, um, (irascor). Enraged, angry, angered.

Irreparabĭlis, e. Irrecoverable.

Irrideo, ĕre, rīsi, rīsum, (in, rideo). To ridicule, laugh at, laugh.

Irrīto, āre, āvi, ātum. To provoke, irritate, incite.

Irrumpo, ĕre, rūpi, ruptum, (in, rumpo). To rush into, make an incursion into.

Is, ea, id. He, she, it, that, such.

Isocrătes, is, m. Isocrates, a famous orator and teacher of rhetoric at Athens, (45).

Iste, a, ud. That, such; *sometimes used in contempt.*

Ister, tri, m. The river Danube. This name is applied to the lower part of the river, the upper part taking the name Danubius, (215).

Ita, adv. Thus, so; to such an extent.

Italia, ae, f. Italy, (180).

Italīcus or *Itŭlus, a, um.* Italian; subs. *Itŭlus, i,* m., an Italian, (148).

Itŭ-que, adv. Therefore, and thus, accordingly.

Iter, itinĕris, n. Way, march, route, road.

Itĕrum, adv. Again, a second time.

J

Jaceo, ĕre, ui, ĭtum. To lie.

Jacio, ĕre, jĕci, jactum. To throw, hurl; *also,* to lay, place, erect.

Jacŭlum, i, n. (jacio). Dart, javelin.

Jam, adv. Now, already.

Janicŭlum, i, n. Janiculum, a hill on the west side of the Tiber, not one of the *seven hills* of Rome, though included within the wall built by Aurelian in the third century, (148).

Jocus, i, m., also in the pl. *joca, jocōrum.* Joke, jest. 141.

Jubeo, ĕre, jussi, jussum. To order, direct.

Jucundus, a, um. Pleasing, pleasant, delightful.

Judaea, ae, f. Judea, (206).

Judaeus, a, um. Jewish; subs. *Judaeus, i,* m., a Jew, (206).

Judex, īcis, m. and f. (judīco). Judge, arbiter.

Judicium, ii, n. (judex). Judgment, decision, trial.

Judico, āre, āvi, ātum. To judge.

Jugum, i, n. Yoke.

Julius, ii, m. See *Caesar.*

Jungo, ĕre, junxi, junctum. To join, unite; *societātem jungĕre,* to form a partnership.

Junior, ius, (juvĕnis). Younger. 168, 3.

Junius, ii, m. Junius, a Roman name; as *Caius Junius,* consul and dictator, (20, 7). See *Brutus.*

Jupiter, Jovis, m. Jupiter, king of the gods. 66, 3.

Juro, āre, āvi, ātum. To take oath, swear.

Jus, juris, n. Right, justice, authority, control; *jure,* with *or* by right, justly, properly.

Justitia, ae, f. (justus). Justice.

Justus, a, um, (jus). Just.

Juvenca, ae, f. Heifer, cow.

Juvencus, i, m. A young bullock.

Juvĕnis, e. Young; *subs.* a youth. 168, 4.

Juventus, ūtis, f. (juvĕnis). Youth; the period of youth.

Juvo, āre, juvi, jutum. To help, aid, assist, support.

L

L. An abbreviation of *Lucius.*

Labiēnus, i, m. Labienus, a Roman name. *Titus Labiēnus,* the legate of Caesar in Gaul, (56, 14).

Labor, ōris, m. Labor, work.

Labōro, āre, āvi, ātum, (labor). To labor, strive, take pains; toil; suffer.

Lac, lactis, n. Milk.

Lacedaemon, ŏnis, f. The city of Lacedaemon *or* Sparta, the capital of Laconia, (94).

Lacedaemonius, a, um. Lacedaemonian *or* Spartan; *subs. Lacedaemonius, ii,* m., a Lacedaemonian *or* Spartan, (123).

Lacesso, ĕre, ivi or *ii, itum.* To excite, assail, provoke.

Laconia or *Laconica, ae,* f. Laconia, a country of the Peloponnesus, (222).

Laco or *Lacon, ŏnis,* m. A Laconian.

Lacrima or *lacryma, ae,* f. Tear.

Lacrimo or *lacryno, āre, āvi, ātum,* (lacrima). To weep, shed tears.

Lacus, us, m. Lake. 117.

Laelius, ii, m. Laelius, a Roman name. *Caius Laelius,* a celebrated Roman consul and augur, surnamed the Wise. He was the intimate friend of Scipio Africanus the Younger, (65).

Laetitia, ae, f. (laetus). Joy, gladness.

Laetus, a, um. Glad, joyous, pleased.

Laevīnus, i, m. Laevinus, a Roman name. *Publius Valerius Laevīnus,* a Roman consul, (180). *Marcus Valerius Laevīnus,* also a Roman consul and a distinguished commander, (193).

Laevus, a, um. Left, on the left hand.

Lamăchus, i, m. Lamachus, an Athenian general in the Sicilian expedition, (223).

Lamia, ae, m. Lamia, a Roman surname, (71).

Lanio, āre, āvi, ātum. To tear in pieces.

Lassitūdo, inis, f. Fatigue, weariness

Latĕbra, ae, f. Retreat, hiding-place, pretence.

Latīne, adv. (Latinus). In Latin.

Latīnus, i, m. Latinus, an ancient king of the Laurentians in Italy, (149).

Latium, iï, n. Latium, a country of Italy containing Rome, (167).

Latīnus, a, um, adj. Latin; subs. *Latīnus, i,* m., an inhabitant of Latium, a Latin; *pl.* the Latins, (161).

Latro, ōnis, m. Robber.

Latus, a, um. Broad, wide.

Latus, ĕris, n. Side.

Laudabīlis, e, (laudo). Praiseworthy, laudable.

Laudo, āre, āvi, ātum, (laus). To praise.

Laurentia, ae, f. See *Acca.*

Laus, laudis, f. Praise.

Lavinia, ae, f. Lavinia, daughter of Latinus and wife of Aeneas, (149).

Lavinium, ii, n. Lavinium, a town in Latium, a few miles south of Rome, founded by Aeneas, and named by him after his wife Lavinia, (149).

Laxo, āre, āvi, ātum. To relax, loosen.

Lectīto, āre, āvi, ātum, (lego). To read often, with eagerness, to read. 332, I. 3.

Lectus, a, um, (lego). Choice, excellent.

Legatio, ōnis, f. Legation, embassy.

Legātus, i, m. Ambassador, lieutenant, messenger.

Legio, ōnis, f. Legion, a body of soldiers.

Lego, āre, āvi, ātum, (lex). To bequeathe as a legacy.

Lego, ĕre, legi, lectum. To choose, elect; read.

Lentŭlus, i, m. Lentulus, a surname of a distinguished Roman family. *Publius Cornelius Lentŭlus,* a conspirator with Catiline, (97, 15).

Leo, ōnis, m. Lion.

Leonĭdas, ae, m. Leonidas, a Spartan king who fell at Thermopylae, (124).

Lepĭdus, i, m. Lepidus, one of the triumvirs with Octaviānus and Antony, (83, 212).

Lesbos or *Lesbus, i,* f. Lesbos, a celebrated island in the Aegean Sea, (49, 12).

Letālis, e, (letum). Deadly, mortal.

Letum, i, n. Death.

Leuctra, ōrum, n. pl. Leuctra, a small town in Boeotia, celebrated for the victory of Epaminondas over the Lacedaemonians, (229).

Leuctrīcus, a, um. Of or belonging to Leuctra; Leuctrian, (230).

Levis, e. Light, easy.

Levĭter, ius, issīme, adv. (levis). Lightly, slightly.

Lex, legis, f. Law, condition, terms.

Liber, bri, m. Book.

Liber, ĕra, ĕrum. Free.

Libĕri, ōrum, m. pl. Children.

Libĕro, āre, āvi, ātum, (liber). To liberate, free.

Libertas, ātis, f. (liber). Liberty, freedom.

Licet, impers. It is lawful, is permitted.

Licet, conj. Although, though.

Licinius, ii, m. Licinius, a Roman name. *Publius Licinius,* a Roman consul and commander in the war with Perseus, (198). *Marcus Lĭ-*

cinius Crassus, proconsul in the war of the gladiators, (204).

Ligneus, a, um. Wooden, of wood.

Ligūres, um, m. pl. The Ligurians, inhabitants of Liguria in the western part of Italy, (190).

Lilybaeum, i, n. Lilybaeum, a promontory on the southwestern coast of Sicily, (188).

Lis, litis, f. Strife, quarrel, lawsuit.

Littĕrae, ārum, f. pl. Letter, letters; literature. 132.

Litus, ŏris, n. Shore, sea-shore.

Locuplēto, āre, āvi, ātum. To enrich, make rich.

Locus, i, m., pl. *loci* or *loca*, n. Place. 141.

Longe, ius, issĭme, adv. (longus). Much, greatly, by far.

Longinquus, a, um. Remote, distant, long.

Longitūdo, ĭnis, f. (longus). Length.

Longus, a, um. Long.

Loquor, loqui, locūtus sum. To speak, converse.

Lorīca, ae, f. Coat-of-mail.

Lucius, ii, m. Lucius, a name common among the Romans; as, *Lucius Tarquinius Priscus*, (162).

Lucretius, ii, m. Lucretius, a Roman name. *Spurius Lucretius*, the colleague of Publicola in the consulship, (170).

Lucrum, i, n. Gain, profit, advantage.

Lucus, i, m. Grove.

Ludus, i, m. Game, play, sport, school.

Lugeo, ēre, luxi. To grieve, mourn, weep for.

Lumen, ĭnis, n. A light; the eye.

Luna, ae, f. Moon.

Luo, ĕre, lui, luĭtum or *lutum.* To pay; expiate, atone for.

Lupa, ae, f. A she-wolf.

Lupus, i, m. A wolf.

Lustratio, ōnis, f. (lustro). Expiatory sacrifice; review attended with sacrifices.

Lustro, āre, āvi, ātum. To purify, review.

Lusus, us, m. Play, game; jest, sport, fun.

Lutatius, ii, m. See *Catŭlus.*

Lux, lucis, f. Light, light of day.

Luxuria, ae, f. Luxury, excess.

Lycurgus, i, m. Lycurgus, the celebrated law-giver of Sparta, (95).

Lydia, ae, f. Lydia, a country in Asia Minor, (225).

Lydus, a, um. Lydian, pertaining to Lydia; *subs.* a Lydian, (33).

Lysander, dri, m. Lysander, a celebrated Spartan general, (225).

M

M. An abbreviation of *Marcus.*

Macedonia, ae, f. Macedonia, Macedon, a country north of Thessaly, (193).

Macĕdo, ŏnis, m. A Macedonian, (230).

Macedonĭcus, a, um, adj. Macedonian, (197).

Magis, comp. adv. More. See the superlative, *maxĭme.*

Magister, tri, m. Master, leader, teacher.

Magistra, ae, f. Instructress, teacher.

Magistrātus, us, m. Magistracy, magistrate.

Magnif'ĭce, centius, centissĭme, adv. (magnifĭcus). Magnificently, splendidly. 305.

Magnificenter, ius, issĭme, adv. =
    magnifĭce.
Magnificentia, ae, f. (magnifĭcus).
    Magnificence, costliness.
Magnifĭcus, a, um ; comp. *magnifi-*
    centior, superl. *magnificentissĭmus.*
    Splendid ; stately ; high-minded,
    magnificent. 164.
Magnitūdo, ĭnis, f. (magnus). Great-
    ness, size.
Magnŏpĕre, adv. (magnus, opus).
    Greatly, earnestly.
Magnus, a, um ; comp. *major,* su-
    perl. *maxĭmus.*   Great, large ;
    in comp. and superl. sometimes
    older, oldest, elder, eldest : *ma-*
    jōres, forefathers, ancestors ; *ma-*
    jōres natu, elders. 165.
Magus, i, m. Generally plur. *Magi,*
    ŏrum. A wise man, *particularly*
    among the Persians.
Majestas, ātis, f. Majesty, dignity.
Major. See *magnus.*
Male, comp. *pejus,* superl. *pessĭme,*
    adv. (malus). Badly, with ill
    success. 305.
Male-dico, ĕre, dixi, dictum. To speak
    evil of, revile, abuse, rail at.
Malefĭcus, a, um, (male, facio.)
    Evil-doing, vicious, wicked, hurt-
    ful. 164.
Malo, malle, malui, irregular. To
    prefer. 293.
Malum, i, n. Misfortune, evil.
Malus, a, um ; comp. *pejor,* superl.
    pessĭmus.   Bad, poor, wicked.
    165.
Mancīnus, i, m. Mancinus, a Ro-
    man consul in the war with the
    Numantians, (201).
Mando, āre, āvi, ātum. To bid, en-
    join, intrust.

Maneo, ēre, mansi, mansum.   To
    remain.
Manifesto, āre, āvi, ātum. To show,
    manifest.
Manius, ii, m. Manius, a Roman
    name ; as, *Manius Manlius.*
Manlius, ii, m. Manlius, a Roman
    name. *Manius Manlius,* a Roman
    consul in the third Punic war,
    (199). *Titus Manlius,* a Roman
    youth, surnamed *Torquātus* for
    his achievements in the Gallic
    war, (177).
Mantinēa, ae, f. A city of Arcadia,
    in the Peloponnesus, (142).
Manumitto, ĕre, mīsi, missum, (ma-
    nus, mitto). To release from one's
    power, emancipate, make free.
Manus, us, f. Hand ; force.
Marăthon, ōnis, m.   Marathon, a
    town and plain in Attica, cele-
    brated for the victory of Miltiades
    over the Persians, (216).
Marathonius, a, um.   Marathonian ;
    of or belonging to Marathon, (97).
Marcius, ii, m.   Marcius, a Roman
    name. See *Ancus, Censorīnus.*
Marcellus, i, m. Roman gen'l, (193).
Marcus, i, m.   Marcus, a Roman
    name, (186).
Mardonius, ii, m. Mardonius, a Per-
    sian general, defeated by Pausa-
    nias in the battle of Plataea, (221).
Mare, is, n. Sea.
Marinus, a, um, (mare). Marine,
    of the sea, from or by the sea.
Marius, ii, m. Marius, a Roman
    name. *Caius Marius,* a distin-
    guished Roman general, the con-
    queror of Jugurtha, and leader in
    the civil war against Sulla. He
    was consul seven times, (202).

Mars, Martis, m. Mars, the god of war; sometimes put for war itself, (152, 226).

Massa, ae, f. Mass, lump.

Mater, tris, f. Mother.

Materia, ae, f., or *materies, ēi,* f. Material.

Matricidium, ii, n. Matricide.

Matrimonium, ti, n. Marriage.

Matrōna, ae, f. Matron.

Maxime, adv. Especially, in the highest degree. See *magis.*

Maximus, a, um; superlative of *magnus.* Greatest.

Maximus, i, m. Maximus, a Roman surname; as, *Quintus Fabius Maximus,* the famous dictator in the second Punic war, (175).

Medicus, i, m. Physician.

Medius, a, um. Middle, midst of, middle of. 441, 6.

Medius, ii, m. Medius, a Thessalian, friend of Alexander the Great, (243).

Medus, a, um. Median, Assyrian,(53).

Mehercŭle, adv. By Hercules, truly, indeed.

Mel, mellis, n. Honey.

Melior, ius. Better. See *bonus.*

Membrum, i, n. Member, limb.

Memini, isti, defect. To remember. 297.

Memor, ŏris. Mindful, endowed with memory, remembering readily, remembering.

Memorabĭlis, e. Memorable.

Memoria, ae, f. Memory, recollection.

Memphis, is, f. Memphis, a city of Egypt, (239).

Menander, dri, m. Menander, a Roman name, (67).

I

Mendacium, ii, n. Untruth, falsehood, lie.

Menenius, ii, m. See *Agrippa.*

Mens, mentis, f. Mind, reason.

Mensis, is, m. Month.

Mentio, ōnis, f. Mention.

Mentior, īri, ītus sum, dep. To speak falsely, lie, cheat, deceive.

Merces, ēdis, f. (mereo). Reward, price, wages.

Mercor, āri, ātus sum, dep. To trade, buy, purchase.

Mercurius, ii, m. Mercury, the son of Jupiter and Maia, the god of eloquence, and the messenger of the gods, (19).

Mereo, ēre, ui, ĭtum. To deserve, merit.

Mereor, ēri, ĭtus sum, dep. To deserve, earn, merit.

Mergo, ĕre, mersi, mersum. To merge, sink; destroy.

Merĭto, adv. (merĭtum). With good reason, with reason, deservedly.

Merĭtum, i, n. Reward, merit.

Merum, i, n. Wine, pure wine.

Mesopotamia, ae, f. Mesopotamia, a country of Asia, between the Euphrates and Tigris, (24, 10).

Metallum, i, n. Metal, mine.

Metellus, i, m. Metellus, a Roman name; as, *Metellus Pius,* (138).

Metior, īri, mensus sum, dep. To measure, estimate.

Metius, ii, m. See *Suffetius.*

Meto, ĕre, messui, messum. To reap, mow.

Metuo, ĕre, ui. To fear.

Metus, us, m. Fear, dread.

Meus, a, um, voc. sing. masc. *mi.* My, mine. 185.

Migro, ăre, āvi, ătum. To migrate, remove.

Miles, ĭtis, m. Soldier.

Militāris, e, (miles). Military.

Militia, ae, f. (miles). Warfare, military service, military affairs.

Milĭto, āre, āvi, ătum, (miles). To serve as a soldier, to serve.

Mille, subs. and adj. Thousand; *millia,* subs., a thousand, a thousand men.

Milliarium, ii, n. Milestone, mile.

Miltĭădes, is, m. Miltiades, a celebrated Athenian general, conqueror at Marathon, (39, IV.)

Minerva, ae, f. Goddess of wisdom, (22).

Minĭme, adv. Least. See *parum.*

Minĭmus, a, um, (parvus). Smallest, least.

Minĭtor, āri, ātus sum, dep. To threaten, menace.

Minor, ŏris. See *Armenia.*

Minor, us, (parvus). Smaller, less.

Minŭo, ĕre, ŭi, ūtum. To lessen, diminish.

Minus, adv. Less. See *parum.*

Mirabĭlis, e, (miror). Wonderful.

Mirifĭcus, a, um, (mirus, facio). Causing wonder, wonderful, marvellous.

Miror, āri, ātus sum, dep. To wonder, admire.

Mirus, a, um. Wonderful, surprising.

Miser, ĕra, ĕrum. Unfortunate, unhappy, worthless, miserable, sad.

Misereo, ēre, ui, ĭtum. To pity; often impersonal; *misĕret me,* I pity.

Misereor, ēri, misertus or *miserĭtus sum,* dep. To pity.

Miseria, ae, f. (miser). Misery, affliction.

Misericordia, ae, f. Compassion.

Mithridātes, is, m. Mithridates, a celebrated king of Pontus, (202).

Mithridatĭcus, a, um. Mithridatic; of or belonging to Mithridates, (202).

Mitis, e. Mild, gentle, placid.

Mitto, ĕre, misi, missum. To send

Moderāte, ius, issĭme, adv. (moderātus). With moderation.

Moderatio, ōnis, f. Moderation, self-control.

Moderātus, a, um. Discreet, moderate.

Modius (or *um,* n.), *ii,* m. Measure, a little more than a peck.

Modo, adv. Now, only, but, provided that; *modo—modo,* sometimes—sometimes.

Modus, i, m. Manner, measure, limits.

Moenia, ium, n. pl. Walls of a city, city.

Moles, is, f. Mole, dam.

Molestus, a, um. Unwelcome, irksome, oppressive, troublesome, painful.

Molitio, ōnis, f. Undertaking, preparation.

Mollio, īre, īvi or *ii, ītum.* To soften.

Momentum, i, n. Weight, influence.

Moneo, ēre, ŭi, ĭtum. To advise, warn, admonish.

Monĭtus, us, m. (moneo). Advice.

Mons, montis, m. Mountain, mount.

Monstro, āre, āvi, ātum. To show.

Mora, ae, f. Delay.

Morbus, i, m. Disease.

Morior, ĭri or *i, mortŭus sum,* dep. To die. 283.

Moror, āri, ātus sum, dep. (mora). To delay, tarry.

Mors, mortis, f. Death.

Morsus, us, m. Bite.

Mortālis, e. Mortal, deadly; *subs.* mortal, man.

Mortĭfer, ĕra, ĕrum, (mors and fero). Deadly, mortal.

Mos, moris, m. Custom, manner; *pl.* character, morals.

Motus, us, m. Motion; commotion, revolt.

Moveo, ēre, movi, motum. To move, excite.

Mox, adv. Presently, soon.

Mucius, ii, m. Mucius, a Roman name. *Mucius Scaevōla,* a Roman youth who attempted to assassinate Porsena, (172).

Mucro, ōnis, m. Point of sword, sword.

Muliĕbris, e, (mulier). Belonging to women, womanly, woman's.

Mulier, ĕris, f. Woman.

Multitūdo, ĭnis, f. (multus). Multitude.

Mullo, āre, āvi, ātum. To punish, deprive of by way of punishment; to fine.

Multo, adv. (multus). By far, much.

Multus, a, um; comp. *plus,* n., superl. *plurĭmus.* Much, many. 165.

Mundus, i, m. World, universe.

Munia, ium, n. pl. Duties, functions of office.

Munificentia, ae, f. Munificence, beneficence.

Munimentum, i, n. Fortification, defence, covering.

Munio, ĭre, ĭvi or *ii, ītum.* To fortify, defend.

Munitio, ōnis, f. Fortification, rampart.

Munītus, a, um, part. (munio). Fortified.

Munus, ĕris, n. Reward, present; service, office.

Munychia, ae, f. The Athenian harbor Munychia and the hill which rises above it, (228).

Murus, i, m. Wall.

Mus, muris, m. Mouse.

Mutatio, ōnis, f. (muto). Change.

Muto, āre, āvi, ātum. To change, alter.

Mutuus, a, um. Mutual.

Mycăle, es, f. Mycale, a high promontory or mountain of Ionia, in Asia Minor, (221).

Myndii, ōrum, m. pl. Myndians, inhabitants of Myndus, (135).

Myndus or *os, i,* f. Myndus, a city of Caria, in Asia Minor, now Mendes, (135).

N

Nam, conj. For.

Nam-que, conj. For, but.

Nanciscor, nancisci, nactus sum, dep. To obtain, take advantage of.

Narro, āre, āvi, ātum. To relate, narrate.

Nascor, nasci, natus sum, dep. To be born, be produced, to arise.

Natālis, e, (nascor). Of *or* belonging to one's birth, natal; *natālis dies,* birth-day.

Natio, ōnis, f. Nation, people.

Natu, defective, abl. sing. (nascor). By birth, in age: *maxĭmus natu,* eldest. 134.

9

Natūra, ae, f. Nature, creation.

Natus, a, um, part. (nascor). Born, having been born.

Naturālis, e, (natūra). Natural.

Naufragium, ii, n. (navis, frango). Shipwreck.

Nautius, ii, m. Nautius, a Roman name; as, *Caius Nautius,* the consul, (19, 11).

Navalis, e, (navis). Naval.

Navigatio, ōnis, f. Navigation, sailing.

Navīgo, āre, āvi, ātum. To sail, sail upon, navigate.

Navis, is, f. Ship.

Ne, adv., and conj. used with imperative and subj. Not, that not, lest; *after verbs of fearing,* that, lest; *nequīdem,* or *ne—quidem,* not even.

Ne, interrog. particle. 346, II. 1.

Nec or *neque,* adv. and conj. Neither, nor; and not, not; *nec—nec, neque—neque,* neither—nor.

Necessarius, a, um. Necessary.

Necesse, adj. neut. *used chiefly in this form.* Necessary, inevitable.

Neco, āre, āvi, ātum. To slay, kill.

Neglīgens, entis, (neglīgo). Negligent, neglectful.

Neglīgo, ěre, lexi, lectum. To neglect, disregard.

Nego, āre, āvi, ātum. To deny, refúse.

Negotium, ii, n. Business, difficulty; undertaking, work, enterprise.

Nemo, (*ĭnis,* gen. not in good use). No one, nobody.

Nepos, ōtis, m. Grandson.

Neptūnus, i, m. Neptune, the god of the sea, (155).

Neque. See *Nec.*

Nequeo, īre, īvi, or *ii, ĭtum,* irreg. like *eo.* To be unable, not to be able. 296.

Nequīdem. See *Ne.*

Nequis or *ne quis, qua, quod,* or *quid.* That no one.

Nervii, ōrum, m. Nervians, a people of Belgic Gaul, (28).

Nescio, īre, īvi or *ii, ĭtum,* (ne, scio). To be ignorant, not to know.

Nescius, a, um, (nescio). Ignorant, unknown.

Nicias, ae, m. Nicias, an Athenian statesman and general, (223).

Nicomēdes, is, m. Nicomedes, king of Bithynia, (43).

Niger, gra, grum. Dark, black, dusky.

Nigrans, antis. Black, dusky.

Nihil, n. indec. Nothing; *adv.* not, in nothing. 128.

Nihīlum, i, n. Nothing.

Nilus, i, m. The river Nile in Egypt, (211).

Nimis, adv. Exceedingly, too much.

Nimius, a, um. Excessive, too much, too great.

Nisi, conj. Unless, if not, except.

Niteo, nitēre, nitui, (nix). To shine, glitter, glisten.

Nitor, niti, nisus or *nixus sum,* dep. To strive, attempt; to depend *or* rely upon.

Nix, nivis, f. Snow.

Nobīlis, e. Noble, famous.

Nobilītas, ātis, f. (nobīlis). Fame, nobleness; nobility, nobles.

Nobilīto, āre, āvi, ātum, (nobīlis). To render famous; to ennoble; improve.

Noceo, ĕre, ui, ĭtum. To hurt, harm, injure.

Noctu, abl. By night.

Nocturnus, a, um. Nocturnal, occurring at night.

Nolo, nolle, nolui, irreg. To be unwilling. 293.

Nomen, ĭnis, n. Name.

Nomĭnŏ, ăre, ăvi, ătum, (nomen). To name, call.

Non, adv. Not; *nonnĭsi,* only.

Nonagesĭmus, a, um. Ninetieth.

Nonaginta, indec. Ninety.

Non-dum, adv. Not yet.

Nonne, interrog. particle. Whether, *expecting answer* yes. 346, II. 1.

Nonnullus, a, um, (declined like *nullus*). Some.

Nonus, a, um. Ninth.

Nosco, ĕre, novi, notum. To know, understand, learn.

Noster, tra, trum. pron. Our.

Notitia, ae, f. (notus). Celebrity, note; acquaintance, knowledge.

Notus, a, um. part. (nosco). Known.

Novem, indecl. Nine.

Noverca, ae, f. Step-mother.

Novo, ăre, ăvi, ătum, (novus). To renew, change; revolutionize.

Novus, a, um. New; *novae res,* revolution.

Nox, noctis, f. Night.

Nubes, is, f. Cloud.

Nubo, ĕre, nupsi, nuptum. To veil one's self, to marry, *applied to the bride as she was covered with a veil.*

Nudus, a, um. Naked, uncovered, destitute of.

Nullus, a, um. No one, no. 151.

Num, interrog. particle. Whether,

used both in direct and in indirect questions. See 346, II. 1.

Numa, ae, m. Numa. *Numa Pompilius,* the second king of Rome, (159).

Numantia, ae, f. Numantia, a city of Spain, (201).

Numantĭni, ŏrum, m. pl. Numantians, the inhabitants of Numantia, (201).

Numen, ĭnis, n. A god, deity.

Numĕro, ăre, ăvi, ătum, (numĕrus). To count, reckon, number.

Numĕrus, i, m. Number, quantity.

Numĭda, ae, m. A Numidian, inhabitant of Numidia in Africa, (48).

Numitor, ŏris, m. Numitor, a king of Alba, grandfather of Romulus and Remus, (154).

Nummus, i, m. Money, a piece of money, a coin.

Nunc. Now.

Nuncŭpo, ăre, ăvi, ătum. To call, name.

Nunquam. Never.

Nuntio (or *cio*), *ăre, ăvi, ătum,* (nuntius). To announce, relate.

Nuntius, ii, m. Message, news, messenger.

Nuptiae, ārum, f. pl. Marriage, nuptials.

Nutrio, ĭre, ĭvi or *ii, ĭtum.* To nourish, support.

Nutrix, ĭcis, f. Nurse.

Nympha, ae, f. Nymph, spouse.

Nysa, ae, f. Nysa, a city in India, (242).

O.

O, interj. O!

Ob, prep. with acc. On account of, for.

Ob-dūco, ĕre, duxi, ductum. To draw over, overspread, cover.

Obedio, īre, īvi or ii, ītum. To obey, serve; be subject to.

Ob-eo, īre, īvi or ii, ītum. To meet; die. 295.

Objecto, āre, āvi, ātum, (objicio). To expose, set forth; endanger. 332, I.

Objicio, ĕre, jēci, jectum, (ob, jacio). To expose, offer, present.

Oblecto, āre, āvi, ātum. To delight, divert, please.

Ob-līgo, āre, āvi, ātum. To bind, oblige, put under obligation.

Oblītus, a, um, part. (obliviscor). Having forgotten, forgetful.

Oblivio, ōnis, f. (obliviscor). Forgetfulness, oblivion.

Obliviscor, oblivisci, oblītus sum, dep. To forget.

Ob-ruo, ĕre, rui, rŭtum. To destroy, overwhelm.

Obscūrus, a, um. Obscure, hidden; mean.

Obsĕcro, āre, āvi, ātum, (ob, sacro). To beseech, implore.

Obses, ĭdis, m. and f. Hostage.

Obsideo, ĕre, sēdi, sessum, (ob, sedeo). To besiege, invest.

Obsidio, ōnis, f. (obsideo). Siege, blockade.

Ob-sum, obesse, obfui. To be hurtful, be injurious, to injure.

Ob-sto, stāre, stĭti, stātum. To oppose, prevent.

Obtemperatio, ōnis, f. Submission, obedience.

Ob-tĕro, ĕre, trīvi, trītum. To crush, wear down.

Obtineo, ĕre, tinui, tentum, (ob, teneo). To obtain, hold, prevail.

Obtingo, ĕre, tĭgi, tactum, (ob, tango). To befall, happen to.

Ob-trunco, āre, āvi, ātum. To slaughter.

Occaeco, āre, āvi, ātum, (ob, caeco). To darken, obscure, blind, dazzle.

Occasio, ōnis, f. Opportunity, occasion.

Occāsus, us, m. The setting of the heavenly bodies; setting, evening; the west.

Oc-cĭdo, ĕre, cĭdi, cāsum, (ob, cado). To fall down, fall; to set; to perish, die, be ruined.

Occĭdo, ĕre, cĭdi, cīsum, (ob, caedo). To kill, slay.

Occulte, ius, issĭme, adv. (occultus). In secret, secretly.

Occultus, a, um. Secret, hidden; reserved, dissembling.

Occŭpo, āre, āvi, ātum. To occupy, take possession of.

Occurro, ĕre, curri (cucurri), cursum, (ob, curro). To meet, attack. 273, I. 2.

Ocĕānus, i, m. Ocean.

Octaviānus, i, m. (Caesar). Octavianus, the first Roman emperor usually called Augustus after his victory at Actium, (213).

Octāvus, a, um, (octo). Eighth.

Octingenti, ae, a. Eight hundred.

Octo, indecl. Eight.

Octogesĭmus, a, um. The eightieth.

Octoginta, indec. (octo). Eighty.

Ocŭlus, i, m. Eye.

Odi, odisse, defect. To hate; dislike. 297.

Odium, ii, n. Hatred, enmity.

Oenomaus, i, m. Oenomaus, a celebrated gladiator, (204).

Offendo, ĕre, fendi, fensum. To offend, injure.

Offensus, a, um, (offendo). Offended, hostile.

Offĕro, ferre, obtŭli, oblātum, (ob, fero). To offer, show; *se offerre,* to present one's self, to offer one's self, *sometimes* as an antagonist, to oppose; expose one's self.

Offīcium, ii, n. Office, duty, kindness, kind office.

Olim, adv. Formerly.

Olympiăcus, Olympĭcus or *Olympius, a, um.* Olympic, (134).

Olynthus, i, f. Olynthus, a city of Thrace.

Olynthii, ōrum, m. pl. The Olynthians, (231).

Omen, ĭnis, n. Omen, sign.

Omitto, ĕre, misi, missum, (ob, mitto). To let go, omit, neglect, disregard.

Omnis, e. All, every, whole.

Oneraria, ae, f. (onus). Ship of burden.

Onĕro, āre, āvi, ātum, (onus). To burden, load, oppress.

Onustus, a, um, (onus). Laden, full of.

Opĕra, ae, f. Pains, work, labor; care, attention; means.

Opīmus, a, um. Rich, fertile.

Oportet, impers. It behooves, one ought. 299.

Opperior, opperīri, oppertus or *opperītus sum,* dep. To wait for, await.

Oppidānus, a, um, (oppĭdum). Inhabitant of a town, citizen.

Oppĭdum, i, n. Town, city.

Opportunĭtas, ātis, f. (opportūnus). Opportunity, fitness.

Opportūnus, a, um. Suitable, fit.

Opprĭmo, ĕre, pressi, pressum, (ob, premo). To put down, defeat, overcome; suppress; oppress.

Oppugno, āre, āvi, ātum, (ob, pugno). To attack, storm, take by storm.

(*Ops*), *opis,* f., nom. sing. not used. Power, resources, wealth, force, aid.

Optabĭlis, e, (opto). Wished for, desirable.

Optĭmus, a, um, superl. (bonus). Best, most excellent.

Optio, ōnis, f. Choice, option.

Opto, āre, āvi, ātum. To wish, desire; ask.

Opŭlens, entis, or *opulentus, a, um,* adj. Wealthy, rich.

Opus, ĕris, n. Work.

Opus, nom. and accus. Need, necessary thing, necessary.

Ora, ae, f. The shore, coast.

Oracŭlum, i, n. Response, oracle.

Oratio, ōnis, f. (oro). Oration, speech, language.

Orător, ōris, m. (oro). Orator, messenger.

Orbis, is, m. Circle, world; *orbis terrārum,* the world.

Ordĭno, āre, āvi, ātum, (ordo). To arrange, establish.

Ordo, ĭnis, m. Row, rank, order; bank *as of oars; extra ordĭnem,* out of the common course.

Orestes, is, and *ae,* m. Orestes, son

of Agamemnon and Clytemnestra, (43).

Oriens, entis, (orior). Rising; the morning, the east, the countries of the east, the Orient, (213).

Origo, inis, f. Origin, source.

Orior, oriri, ortus sum, dep. To rise, appear, dawn. 288, 2.

Ornamentum, i, n. Equipage, ornament, jewel.

Orno, are, avi, atum. To adorn, equip.

Oro, are, avi, atum. To beg, ask, speak.

Ortus, us, m. (orior). A rising; place of rising, the east; birth; beginning.

Os, ossis, n. Bone.

Osculor, ari, atus sum. To kiss.

Ostendo, ere, di, sum or *tum*. To show.

Ostentum, i, n. (ostendo). Prodigy.

Ostia, ae, f. Ostia, a town at the mouth of the Tiber, (161).

Ostium, ii, n. Mouth, door.

Otium, ii, n. Leisure, rest, ease, idleness.

Ovis, is, f. Sheep.

Ovum, i, n. Egg.

P.

P. An abbreviation of *Publius*.

Paco, are, ave, atum (pax). To subdue.

Pactum, i, n. Bargain, contract; *abl. pacto*, way, manner.

Padus, i, m. River Po in Italy, (55).

Paene, adv. Almost.

Paenitet, ere, paenituit, impers. It causes regret; *paenitet me*, it causes me to repent, I repent, am sorry for, regret.

Palam, adv. Openly.

Palatium, ii, n. Palace.

Pallium, ii, n. Cloak, coat, garment.

Pango, ere, pepigi, pactum. To contract, ratify.

Papirius, ii, n. See *Cursor*.

Par, paris, adj. Equal, a match for, competent for.

Paratus, a, um, (paro). Prepared, ready.

Parco, ere, peperci or *parsi, parsum*. To spare.

Parens, entis, m. and f. Parent.

Parento, are, avi, atum, (parens). To sacrifice in honor of parents or friends.

Pareo, ere, ui, itum. To obey, be subject to.

Pario, ere, peperi, partum. To bear, bring forth, produce, lay, accomplish, procure.

Paro, are, avi, atum. To prepare, equip.

Pars, partis, f. Part, portion; party.

Parsimonia, ae, f. Frugality, parsimony.

Particeps, participis, (pars, capio). Sharing, partaking, participant.

Partim. Partly, in part; *partim—partim*, some—others, either—or.

Partior, iri, itus sum, dep. To divide, share.

Parum, comp. *minus*, superl. *minime*, adv. Too little, little, not enough. 305.

Parvus, a, um, comp. *minor*, superl. *minimus*. Small, little, unimportant.

Pasco, ere, pavi, pastum. To feed, graze.

Pascor, pasci, pastus sum, dep. To feed, graze, graze upon.

Passer, ĕris, m. Sparrow.

Passus, us, m. Pace; *mille passus,* a mile.

Pastor, ōris, m. (pasco). Shepherd.

Patefacio, ĕre, fĕci, factum, (pateo, facio). To disclose, lay open, open.

Pateo, ĕre, ui. To lie open, be exposed.

Pater, tris, m. Father, *sometimes* senator.

Paternus, a, um, (pater). Paternal.

Patior, pati, passus sum, dep. To permit, keep, endure.

Patria, ae, f. Country, native country.

Patrimonium, ii, n. Estate, patrimony.

Patrius, a, um, (pater). Fatherly.

Patruus, i, m. Uncle by the father's side, paternal uncle.

Pauci, ae, a. Few.

Paulātim, adv. By degrees, gradually.

Paulus or *Paullus, i,* m. Paulus, a surname in the Aemilian gens or tribe. *Lucius Aemilius Paulus,* the name of two Roman consuls, one of whom fell in the battle of Cannae, (191); the other conquered Perseus at Pydna, (198).

Paulo, adv. (paulus). A little, by a little.

Paulus, a, um. Little, small.

Pauper, ĕris. Poor, without means; scanty, meagre.

Pausanias, ae, m. Pausanias, the leader of the Spartans in the battle of Plataea, (221).

Pax, pacis, f. Peace.

Pectus, ŏris, n. Breast.

Pecunia, ae, f. Money, sum of money.

Pecus, ŏris, n. Flock, herd, cattle.

Pedes, ĭtis, m. Foot-soldier; *plur.* infantry.

Pedester, tris, tre. Pedestrian, on foot, on land; *pedestres copiae,* infantry forces.

Pellicio, ĕre, lexi, lectum. To allure, cajole.

Pellis, is, f. Skin, hide.

Pello, ĕre, pepŭli, pulsum. To drive.

Pelopĭdas, ae, m. Pelopidas, a celebrated Theban general, (230).

Penarius, a, um. Of *or* for provisions; *cella penaria,* granary.

Pendeo, ĕre, pependi. To hang, be suspended.

Penĕtro, āre, āvi, ātum. To penetrate.

Penĭtus, adv. Inwardly; fully, entirely.

Per, prep. with acc. Through, by, during.

Percurro, ĕre, percucurri or *percurri, cursum.* To run through, pass over.

Percussor, ōris, m. Assassin, murderer.

Perdiccas or *Perdicca, ae,* m. Perdiccas, one of the most distinguished generals of Alexander the Great, (97).

Perdĭtus, a, um, (perdo). Lost, abandoned, desperate.

Per-do, ĕre, dĭdi, dĭtum. To destroy, waste, lose.

Per-dūco, ĕre, duxi, ductum. To conduct, bring to, to extend, build, make.

Perennis, e, (per, annus). Continual, perpetual.

Per-eo, ire, ivi or *ii, itum.* To perish. 295.

Per-exiguus, a, um. Very small, very little.

Per-fěro, ferre, tŭli, lātum. To carry through ; bear ; suffer.

Perfidia, ae, f. Perfidy.

Pergo, ěre, rexi, rectum, (per, rego). To go on *or* to, persevere.

Pericles, is, m. Pericles, a celebrated Athenian orator and statesman, (222).

Periculōsus, a, um, (pericŭlum). Dangerous.

Pericŭlum, i, n. Danger, peril.

Peritus, a, um. Skilled in, skilful.

Per-magnus, a, um. Very great.

Per-mitto, ěre, misi, missum. To send ; grant, permit ; *permittitur,* impers., it is permitted.

Per-multus, a, um. Very much, very many.

Permutatio, ōnis, f. Exchange, barter.

Per-paucus, a, um. Few, very few.

Per-pětro. āre, āvi, ātum. To finish, achieve.

Perpetuo, adv. (perpetuus). Constantly, ever.

Perpetuus, a, um. Perpetual, constant.

Persa, ae. or *Perses, ae,* m. A Persian, (44, II. ; 126).

Per-sěquor, sěqui, secūtus sum, dep. To follow, pursue, carry on, prosecute.

Perseus, i, or *Perses, ae,* m. Perseus *or* Perses, the last king of Macedonia, (198).

Persevěro, āre, āvi, ātum. To persevere, persist.

Persicus, a, um. Persian, (50, 13).

Persōna, ae, f. Part, character, person.

Perspicio, ěre, spexi, spectum, (per, specio). To perceive.

Per-stringo, ěre, strinxi, strictum. To graze, wound slightly.

Per-suadeo, ěre, suāsi, suāsum. To persuade.

Per-terreo, ěre, ui, itum. To terrify greatly.

Pertineo, ěre, tinui, (per, teneo). To pertain to, tend.

Per-turbo, āre, āvi, ātum. To disturb, throw into confusion, route, embarrass.

Per-utilis, e. Very useful.

Per-venio, ire, věni, ventum. To reach, come to.

Perverse, adv. Perversely, wrongly.

Pes, pědis, m. Foot.

Peto, ěre, ivi or *ii, itum.* To seek, ask ; aim at ; attack.

Phaëthon, ontis, m. Phaethon, fabled son of Helios the sun, (71).

Phalěrae, ārum, f. pl. Trappings, ornaments for horses.

Phalērum, i, n. Phalerum, the oldest harbor of Athens ; often called *Phalericus portus.*

Pharnāces, is, m. Pharnaces, son of Mithridates, (205).

Pharsālus, i, f. Pharsalus, a city in Thessaly, where Pompey was defeated by Caesar, (210). The district was called Pharsalia.

Philippi, ōrum, m. pl. Philippi, a city in Macedonia, (213).

Philippus, i, m. Philip, the name of several Macedonian kings, the most celebrated of whom was the father of Alexander the Great, (140, 230).

Philosophia, ae, f. Philosophy.

Philosophus, i, m. Philosopher.

Phyle, es, f. Phyle, a castle in Attica, (228).

Picēnum, i, n. Picenum, a district in the eastern part of Italy.

Picēnus, a, um, (Picēnum). Of or belonging to Picenum, Picene, (23, 19).

Piētas, ātis, f. Dutiful conduct, sense of duty; affection; loyalty; piety.

Piget, ēre, piguit or *pigītum est,* impers. It irks, grieves, displeases. 299.

Pingo, ēre, pinxi, pictum. To paint, depict.

Piraeus, or *Piraeeus, i, m.* The Piraeus, the celebrated port of Athens, (228).

Pirāta, ae, m. Pirate.

Piscis, is, m. A fish.

Pius, i, m. See *Metellus Pius,* (138).

Placeo, ēre, ui, ītum. To please, be pleasing to; be determined.

Placīdus, a, um, (placeo). Quiet, gentle.

Placo, āre, āvi, ātum. To quiet, soothe, calm, appease.

Plancus, i, m. Plancus, a Roman name, (42, 9).

Plataeae, ārum, f. pl. Plataea, a city in Boeotia, (221).

Plataeenses, ium, m. pl. The Plataeans, the inhabitants of Plataea, (216).

Plato, ōnis, m. Plato, one of the most celebrated Grecian philoso-

phers, disciple of Socrates, and instructor of Aristotle, (81).

Plebs, bis, f. Common people, people.

Plenus, a, um. Full, possessed of, rich in.

Plerumque, adv. (plerusque). Commonly, generally, frequently.

Plerusque, āque, umque. Most, many.

Plurīmus. See *Multus.*

Plus, adv. More.

Plus, uris, n. adj. More, *pl.* many, several. See *Multus.*

Pocŭlum, i, n. Cup.

Poēma, ătis, n. Poem.

Poena, ae, f. Punishment.

Poenus, i, m. A Carthaginian, (185).

Poēta, ae, m. Poet.

Polliceor, ēri, ītus sum, dep. To promise, offer.

Pollux, ūcis, m. Pollux, a celebrated pugilist, brother of *Castor,* (63, 9). According to some authorities, he was the son of Tyndarus, but according to others, he was the son of Jupiter. See *Castor.*

Polycrātes, is, m. Polycrates, a celebrated tyrant of Samos, (24, 12).

Pompa, ae, f. Pomp, public procession, procession.

Pompeius, ii, m. Pompey, the name of a Roman gens. *Cnaeus Pompeius,* a Roman consul and a distinguished commander, defeated by Caesar at Pharsalia, (205). *Quintus Pompeius,* also consul and commander, defeated in several engagements by the Numantines, (201).

Pompeiānus, a, um, adj. (Pompeius).

Pompeian, of or belonging to Pompey, (211).

Pompilius, ii, m. See *Numa.*

Pondus, ĕris, n. Weight.

Pono, ĕre, posŭi, posĭtum. To place, build, pitch.

Pons, Pontis, m. Bridge.

Pontius, ii, m. Pontius, a Roman name. *Pontius Thelesinus,* a general of the Samnites, who conquered the Romans at the Caudine Forks, (179).

Pontus, i, m. Pontus, a province in Asia Minor, south of the Black Sea, (202).

Populatio, ōnis, f. (popŭlo). Pillaging, booty; people, population.

Popŭlo, āre, āvi, ātum, (popŭlus). To depopulate, devastate, pillage; *popŭlor,* dep. = popŭlo.

Popŭlus, i, m. People, nation, tribe.

Porrĭgo, ĕre, rexi, rectum. To extend, stretch.

Porsĕna, ae, m. Porsena, a king of Etruria in Italy, (171).

Porta, ae, f. Gate.

Portendo, ĕre, tendi, tentum. To portend.

Portio, ōnis, f. Portion, share.

Portus, us, m. Port, harbor.

Posco, ĕre, poposci. To demand, ask.

Possessio, ōnis, f. (possideo). Possession.

Possideo, ĕre, sēdi, sessum. To possess.

Possum, posse, potui, irreg. To be able. 289.

Post, adv., and prep. with acc. Afterwards, after, behind, since.

Post-ea, adv. Afterwards.

Posterĭtas, ātis, f. (postĕrus). Posterity.

Postĕrus, a, um; comp. *posterior,* superl. *postrēmus, postĭmus.* Following, ensuing; *postĕri,* posterity, descendants; *postrēmo, ad postrēmum,* at last. 163, 3.

Post-fĕro, ferre. To place after, esteem less; sacrifice.

Post-pōno, ĕre, posŭi, posĭtum. To put after, esteem less, postpone; disregard, neglect.

Post-quam, or *post quam,* conj. After, after that.

Postrēmo, adv. (postrēmus). At last, finally.

Postrēmus, a, um. The last; *ad postrēmum,* at last, finally. See *postĕrus.*

Postridie, adv. On the following day.

Postŭlo, āre, āvi, ātum. To demand.

Postumius, ii, m. Postumius, the name of a Roman gens or clan. *Aulus Postumius,* a Roman in whose consulship the first Punic war was brought to a close, (89, 188). *Spurius Postumius,* a Roman consul, defeated by the Samnites at the Caudine Forks, (179).

Potens, entis, (possum). Able, powerful.

Potentĭa, ae, f. Might, force, power, ability.

Potestas, ātis, f. (potens). Power.

Potior, potīri, potītus sum, dep. To obtain, get possession of.

Potis, e, comp. *potior,* superl. *potissĭmus.* Able, capable, possible.

Potius, potissĭme, adv. (potis); positive not used. Rather than.

Prae, prep. with abl. Before, for, on account of, in comparison with.

Praebeo, ēre, ui, ĭtum. To show, furnish.

Prae-cēdo, ēre, cessi, cessum. To precede, surpass, outstrip.

Praeceptor, ōris, m. (praecipio). Preceptor, commander, teacher.

Praeceptum, i, n. (praecipio). Maxim, rule, precept.

Praecipio, ēre, cēpi, ceptum (prae, capio). To admonish, advise, order.

Praecipitium, ii, n. Precipice.

Praecipĭto, āre, āvi, ātum. To throw down, precipitate.

Praecipuus, a, um. Remarkable, prominent, special.

Praeclārē, ius, issĭme, adv. (preclārus). Excellently, nobly.

Prae-clārus, a, um. Excellent, noble, distinguished, illustrious.

Praeclūdo, ēre, clūsi, clūsum, (prae, claudo). To hinder, preclude, cut off.

Praeco, ōnis, m. Herald, crier.

Praeda, ae, f. Prey, booty.

Prae-dĭco, ēre, dixi, dictum. To predict, forewarn.

Praedictum, i, n. (praedĭco). Prediction, warning.

Praedĭtus, a, um. Endued with, possessed of.

Praedor, āri, ātus sum, (praeda). To plunder.

Prae-fāri, defective. To predict, prophesy; say. 297, II. 3.

Praefectus, i, m. Commander, prefect.

Prae-fĕro, ferre, tŭli, latum. To prefer, choose; carry or bear before.

Praeficio, ēre, fēci, fectum, (prae, facio). To place over, put in command.

Prae-lēgo, ēre, lēgi, lectum. To read to another, to read aloud, to lecture.

Prae-mitto, ēre, mĭsi, missum. To send forward, send in advance.

Praemium, ii, n. Reward, premium.

Praeneste, is, n. Praeneste, a town in Latium, (182).

Prae-pōno, ēre, posui, posĭtum. To place over, intrust with.

Praesens, entis. Present; *praesentia, ōrum,* n. pl. present things, the present.

Praesentia, ae, f. (praesens). Presence.

Praeses, ĭdis, adj. Presiding, ruling, chief; *subs.* head, chief, ruler, governor.

Praesidium, ii, n. Guard, garrison.

Praestabĭlis, e. Preëminent, distinguished, excellent.

Praestans, antis, (praesto). Excellent, eminent.

Praestantia, ae, f. Superiority, preeminence.

Praesto, āre, stĭti, ĭtum, (prae, sto). To surpass, be superior to; furnish, do, pay, render (as service); evince, show, give.

Prae-sum, esse, fui. To preside over, command.

Prae-tendo, ēre, tendi, tentum. To pretend, allege.

Praeter, prep. with acc. Except, besides.

Praeter-ea, adv. Besides, moreover.

Praeter-eo, ĭre, ĭvi or *ii, ĭtum.* To pass by, omit. 295.

Praeterĭtus, a, um, (praetereo). Gone by, past; *praeterĭta, ōrum,* n. pl. the past.

Praeter-vĕhor, vĕhi, vectus sum, dep.

To be borne over *or* by ; to drive *or* sail by ; to pass by.

Praetorius, a, um, (praetor). Praetorian, belonging to a praetor *or* general ; *praetorius,* subs. one who has been praetor.

Prae-vidĕo, ĕre, vīdi, vīsum. To foresee.

Pratum, i, n. Meadow, pasture.

Pravus, a, um. Depraved, bad.

Preces, um, f. pl. *dat. acc.* and *abl. sing.* also occur. Prayers, entreaties.

Precor, āri, ātus sum. To beseech, pray.

Premo, ĕre, pressi, pressum. To press, urge.

Pretium, ii, n. Price, worth.

Pridie, adv. On the day before.

Primo, primum, adv. (primus). At first, first ; *quam primum,* as soon as possible.

Primus, a, um, superl. (prior). First. 166.

Princeps, ĭpis, m. Prince, ruler ; chief man.

Principātus, us, m. Sovereignty, imperial power.

Principium, ii, n. Beginning.

Prior, us. Former, previous. 166.

Priscus, i, m. Priscus, the surname of *Lucius Tarquinius,* the fifth king of Rome, (162).

Pristīnus, a, um. Ancient, pristine.

Prius, adv. Before, first ; *priusquam* or *prius quam,* before that, before.

Privātus, a, um. Private, personal, *subs.* a private citizen.

Pro, prep. with abl. Before, in front of; for, in behalf of, instead of, as ; *pro hoste,* as an enemy.

Probatio, ōnis, f. Approbation, proof.

Probātus, a, um, (probo). Tried, tested, proved, approved.

Probĭtas, ātis, f. (probus). Honesty, probity, integrity.

Probo, āre, āvi, ātum, (probus). To prove, show ; approve.

Probus, a, um. Upright, honest.

Procas, ae, m. Procas, a Roman name. *Silvius Procas,* a king of Alba, (151).

Pro-cēdo, ĕre, cessi, cessum. To step forth, to advance, proceed, come on, succeed.

Procillus, i, m. Procillus, a young man sent by Caesar to Ariovistus, (52).

Pro-clāmo, āre, āvi, ātum. To cry out, proclaim.

Pro-consul, ŭlis, m. Proconsul, one with the authority of consul.

Procul, adv. At a distance, far off.

Pro-cūro, āre, āvi, ātum. To attend to, have the care of.

Pro-curro, ĕre, curri (cucurri), *cursum.* To run forth, project.

Proditio, ōnis, f. (prodo). Treachery, treason.

Prodĭtor, ōris, m. (prodo). Traitor.

Pro-do, ĕre, dĭdi, dĭtum. To disclose, betray.

Pro-dūco, ĕre, duxi, ductum. To lead forth, produce.

Proelium, ii, n. Battle, conflict.

Profecto, adv. Indeed, truly.

Proficiscor, proficisci, profectus sum. To depart, set out, go.

Proflīgo, āre, āvi, ātum, (pro, fligo). To overthrow, ruin.

Pro-fundo, ĕre, fūdi, fūsum. To

pour out, spend; throw away, lavish, dissipate.

Progredior, grĕdi, gressus sum, dep. (pro, gradior). To proceed, advance.

Prohibeo, ēre, ui, ĭtum, (pro, habeo). To prohibit, prevent.

Promissus, a, um, (promitto). Growing long, long.

Pro-mitto, ĕre, misi, missum. To send forth, promise.

Promontorium, ii, n.   Promontory.

Promptus, a, um.   Prompt, ready.

Pro-nuntio, āre, āvi, ātum. To publish, proclaim, announce; recite, declaim; act, tell, narrate.

Propago, āre, āvi, ātum.   To propagate; prolong.

Prope, adv., and prep. with acc. Near, nearly, near to, close by, near.

Propĕro, āre, āvi, ātum. To hasten.

Propior, ius.   Nearer.   See 166.

Propius, adv.   Nearer.

Pro-pōno, ĕre, posui, posĭtum. To set forth, state, propose.

Proprius, a, um.   Peculiar, proper, one's own, characteristic of.

Propter, prep. with acc.   For, on account of.

Propter-ea, adv.   Therefore, on that account.

Pro-pulso, āre, āvi, ātum. To repel, ward off.

Prora, ae, f.   Prow, forepart of a ship.

Prorsus, adv.   Uninterruptedly, straight on, absolutely.

Pro-rumpo, ĕre, rūpi, ruptum. To rush or break forth.

Pro-scrĭbo, ĕre, scripsi, scriptum. To proscribe, outlaw.

Prosilio, īre, ii or ui, (pro, salio). To leap up, spring forth.

Prospēre, ius, rime, adv. (prospĕrus). Happily, prosperously.

Prospĕrus, a, um.   Favorable, fortunate, prosperous.

Prospicio, ĕre, spexi, spectum, (pro, specio). To look forward, look; see; look out for, take care of, provide for; discern, descry.

Prosterno, ĕre, strāvi, strātum, (pro, sterno). To prostrate, overthrow.

Pro-sum, prodesse, profui. To profit, avail, be useful.

Protĭnus, adv.   Directly, immediately after.

Pro-video, ēre, vīdi, vīsum. To provide, be on one's guard.

Provīdus, a, um, (provideo). Foreseeing, prudent, cautious, provident.

Provincia, ae, f.   Province.

Provocatio, ōnis, f. (provŏco). Challenge, appeal.

Provŏco, āre, āvi, ātum. To challenge, appeal.

Proxĭmus, a, um.   Nearest, next. 166.

Prudens, entis. Prudent, wise, learned, skilled.

Prudentia, ae, f. (prudens).   Prudence.

Ptolemaeus, i, m.   Ptolemy, the name of several kings of Egypt, (211).

Publicŏla, ae, m.   Publicola, the surname of *Valerius*, one of the first consuls at Rome, (169).

Publĭcus, a, um.   Public.

Publius, ii, m.   Publius, a Roman name; as, *Publius Rutilius Rufus*, (139).

Pudet, ēre, puduit, pudītum est, impers. It shames ; *pudet me*, it shames me, I am ashamed.

Pudor, ōris, m. Regard, respect, modesty, awe, shame.

Puella, ae, f. Girl.

Puer, ĕri, m. Boy.

Puerīlis, e, (puer). Boyish, youthful.

Pueritia, ae, f. (puer). Boyhood.

Pugio, ōnis, m. Dagger, poniard.

Pugna, ae, f. Battle.

Pugno, āre, āvi, ātum. To fight.

Pulcher, chra, chrum. Beautiful.

Pulvillus, i, m. Pulvillus. *Horatius Pulvillus*, a Roman consul in the first year after the banishment of Tarquin, (170).

Pumilio, ōnis, m. and f. Dwarf, pigmy.

Punĭcus, a, um, (Poeni). Punic, Carthaginian, belonging to Carthage or the Carthaginians. (196).

Punio, īre, īvi, ītum. To punish.

Pupillus, i, m. Pupil.

Puppis, is f. The stern, the hinder part of a ship.

Pusillus, a, um. Small, weak; little.

Puto, āre, āvi, ātum. To think, imagine, esteem.

Pydna, ae, f. Pydna, a town of Macedonia, celebrated for the victory of Paulus over Perseus, (198).

Pyrenaeus, i, m. The Pyrenees, a range of mountains between France and Spain, (190).

Pyrrhus, i, m. Pyrrhus, a king of Epirus, (183).

Pythagŏras, ae, m. Pythagoras, a celebrated philosopher of Samos, (94).

Pythia, ae, f. Pythia, the priestess of Apollo, at Delphi, (217).

Q.

Q. or Qu. An abbreviation of *Quintus*.

Quadragesĭmus, a, um, (quadraginta). Fortieth.

Quadraginta, indecl. Forty.

Quadrīga, ae, f. Chariot, four-horse chariot.

Quadringentesĭmus, a, um, (quadringenti). The four hundredth.

Quadringenti, ae, a. Four hundred.

Quaero or *quaeso, ĕre, quaesīvi, quaesītum*. To seek, inquire, ask, implore. *Quaerĭtur*, impers. It is asked, the question is asked.

Qualis, e. What, what sort ; *talis —qualis*, such—as.

Quam, adv. and conj. How; as, than, after : *quam multi*, how many ; *with superl.* intensive, *quam maxĭmus*, as great as possible.

Quam-diu, adv. How long, as long as.

Quam-quam, conj. Although, though.

Quam-vis. However, however much, though.

Quantus, a, um. How great, how much ; *tantus—quantus*, so great as ; *quanto*, by how much, as.

Qua-re. Wherefore, whereby.

Quartus, a, um. Fourth.

Quasi. As if.

Quaterni, ae, a, distributive. Four by four, four at a time, four each 174, 2.

Quatio, *ĕre, quassi, quassum.* To shake.

Quatriduum, *i,* n. (quattuor, dies). Space of four days, four days.

Quattuor, indecl. Four.

Quattuordĕcim, indecl. (quattuor, decem). Fourteen.

̦Que, appended to another word. And. 587, I. 3.

Quem-ad-mŏdum, adv. In what manner, how, as.

Querēla, *ae,* f. (queror). Complaint.

Queror, *queri, questus sum,* dep. To complain.

Qui, *quae, quod,* rel. and interrog. Who, which, what.

Quia, conj. Because.

Quicŭnque (or cumque) *quaecunque, quodcunque.* Whoever, whatever.

Quidam, *quaedam, quoddam* or *quiddam.* A certain one, certain.

Quidem. Indeed.

Quies, *ētis,* f. Rest, quiet.

Quiesco, *ĕre, quiĕvi, quiĕtum,* (quies). To rest, repose, keep quiet.

Quiētus, *a, um,* (quiesco). Quiet, at rest.

Qui-lĭbet, *quaelĭbet, quodlĭbet,* indef. pron. Any one, any.

Quin. That not, but that, that.

Quinctius, *ii,* m. Quinctius. *Titus Quinctius,* a Roman general at the time the city was threatened by the Gauls, 321 B. C. (177). *Titus Quinctius Flaminius* gained the victory at Cynoscephalae, (197).

Quindĕcim, indecl. Fifteen.

Quingentĕsĭmus, *a, um,* (quingenti). The five hundreth.

Quingenti, *ae, a.* Five hundred.

Quinquagesĭmus, *a, um,* (quinquaginta). Fiftieth.

Quinquaginta, indecl. Fifty.

Quinque, indecl. Five.

Quinquennium, *ii,* n. Five years, space of five years.

Quintus, *a, um.* Fifth.

Quintus, *i,* m. Quintus, a common Roman name; as, *Quintus Mucius Scaevŏla,* (172).

Quippe, conj. Indeed.

Quis, *quae, quid ?* interrog. pron. Who, which, what ?

Quis, *quae, quid,* indef. pron. Some one, any one. 190, 1.

Quisnam or *quinam, quaenam, quodnam* or *quidnam.* Who, which, what.

Quispiam, *quaepiam, quodpiam,* and subs. *quidpiam* or *quippiam,* indef. pron. Any one, any body, any; some one, some thing, some.

Quis-quam, *quaequam, quidquam* or *quicquam.* Any, any one.

Quis-que, *quaeque, quodque* or *quidque.* Every, every one, whoever, whatever; *with superl., intensive, primo quoque tempŏre,* on the *very* first opportunity.

Quis-quis, *quaequae, quidquid* or *quicquid.* Whoever, whatever.

Quo. Where, whither, that, in order that.

Quo-ad. Till, until, as long as, as far as.

Quod, conj. That, because.

Quomĭnus, (quo, minus). That not, from.

Quomŏdo, adv. (quo, modo). How, by what means.

Quondam, adv. Formerly.

Quoque. Also, too.

Quot, adj. pl. indec. How many, as many, as; all.

Quot-annis. Every year, yearly.

Quotidie. Daily, every day.

Quotus, a, um. Of what number, how many; what, *often applied to the hour of the day.*

Quum or *cum.* When, since; though; *quum—tum,* not only—but also, both—and; *rarely* either —or.

R.

Rabies, ei, f. Madness, rage.

Radix, icis, f. Root, foot, base, *as of a mountain.*

Ramus, i, m. Branch.

Rapina, ae, f. Rapine, plunder.

Rapio, ere, rapui, raptum. To rob, carry off.

Raptor, oris, m. (rapio). Robber, plunderer.

Raro, adv. (rarus). Rarely, seldom.

Rarus, a, um. Rare, uncommon.

Ratio, onis, f. A calculating, thinking; reason, understanding; plan, method, kind.

Ratis, is, f. Raft.

Re-bello, are, avi, atum. To rebel.

Re-cedo, ere, cessi, cessum. To withdraw, recede, retire.

Recens, entis. Recent, fresh, young, new.

Recipio, ere, cepi, ceptum, (re, capio). To receive, recover, resume; *se recipere,* to betake one's self, withdraw.

Recito, are, avi, atum, (re, cito). To repeat, recite.

Recognosco, ere, novi, nitum, (re, cognosco). To recognize.

Recordatio, onis, f. (recordor). Recollection, remembrance.

Recordor, ari, atus sum, dep. To recollect.

Recte, ius, issime, adv. (rectus). Rightly.

Rector, oris, m. (rego). Director, ruler.

Rectum, i, n. (rectus). Right.

Rectus, a, um, (rego). Straight, right, correct.

Recupero, are, avi, atum. To regain.

Red-do, ere, didi, ditum. To restore, return; make; render, repeat, recite, give up, resign; assign.

Red-eo, ire, ivi or ii, itum. To go back, return. 295.

Redigo, ere, egi, actum, (red, ago). To force, reduce, compel.

Redimo, ere, emi, emptum, (red, emo). To ransom.

Reditus, us, m. (redeo). Return, revenue.

Re-duco, ere, duxi, ductum. To lead back, reduce.

Red-undo, are, avi, atum. To overflow; to abound.

Re-fercio, ire, fersi, fertum, (re, farcio). To fill, stuff, cram.

Re-fero, ferre, tuli, latum, (re-fero). To bring back, requite, return, render, place among, refer; *refert,* imps. it concerns, matters.

Refertus, a, um, part. (refercio). Filled.

Reficio, ere, feci, fectum, (re, facio). To repair, restore; recover.

Refluo, ere, fluxi, fluxum, (re, fluo). To flow back.

Re-fugio, ěre, fūgi, fugĭtum. To retreat.

Regīna, ae, f. Queen.

Regio, ōnis, f. Region, country.

Regius, a, um, (rex). Royal.

Regno, āre, āvi, ātum, (regnum). To reign, rule.

Regnum, i, n. (rex). Kingdom, sovereignty, government.

Rego, ěre, rexi, rectum. To direct, rule, manage.

Regredior, grědi, gressus sum, dep. (re, gradior). To return.

Regŭla, ae, f. (rego). Rule, pattern, model.

Regŭlus, i, m. Regulus. *Marcus Atilius Regŭlus,* a distinguished Roman consul taken prisoner by the Carthaginians in the first Punic war, (186).

Religio, ōnis, f. Religion, obligation.

Re-linquo, ěre, lĭqui, lictum. To leave, desert.

Reliquiae, ārum, f. pl. Remnant, those who escaped.

Relĭquus, a, um. The rest, remaining, the other. *Relĭquum est,* it is left, it remains.

Re-maneo, ěre, mansi, mansum. To remain.

Remedium, ii, n. Remedy.

Reminiscor, ci, dep. To remember.

Re-mitto, ěre, mĭsi, missum. To send back.

Re-moveo, ěre, mōvi, mōtum. To take away, remove.

Remus, i, m. Oar.

Remus, i, m. Remus, the brother of Romulus, (152).

Re-nŏvo, āre, āvi, ātum, (re, novo). To renew.

Re-nuntio, āre, āvi, ātum. To report, announce.

Repăro, āre, āvi, ātum, (re, paro). To renew, repair.

Re-pello, ěre, pŭli, pulsum. To repel, drive back.

Repente, adv. Suddenly.

Repentīnus, a, um. Unexpected, sudden.

Reperio, īre, pěri, pertum, (re, pario). To find.

Re-pleo, ēre, ēvi, ētum. To fill, fill again.

Re-pōno, ěre, posui, posĭtum. To replace, restore, lay up.

Re-porto, āre, āvi, ātum. To gain, bear off.

Reprehendo, ěre, prehendi, prehensum, (re, prehendo). To blame, censure.

Repudio, āre, āvi, ātum. To reject, divorce.

Re-pugno, āre, āvi, ātum. To resist.

Re-quīro, ěre, quisīvi or ii, quisītum (re, quaero). To seek, demand, require.

Res, rei, f. Thing; affair; state; deed, reality, battle; *res gestae,* exploits; *res publĭca,* republic.

Re-scrībo, ěre, scripsi, scriptum. To write back, reply in writing.

Resideo, ēre, sēdi, (re, sedeo). To sit, remain, sit down.

Resisto, ěre, stĭti, stĭtum. To oppose, resist.

Respectus, us, m. (respicio). Respect, regard.

Respicio, ěre, spexi, spectum, (re, spe cio). To look back; regard, respect.

Re-spondeo, ēre, spondi, sponsum. To reply.

Responsum, i. n. (respondeo). Answer, response.

Res publica, rei publicae, or *respublica, reipublicae,* f. Republic. 126.

Re-spuo, ĕre, spui. To cast out, eject ; reject, refuse, dislike.

Restituo, ĕre, stitui, stitūtum, (re, statuo). To restore.

Re-tardo, āre, āvi, ātum. To detain, retard, check.

Retineo, ĕre, tinui, tentum, (re, teneo). To retain.

Reus, i, m. Criminal, defendant.

Reverentia, ae, f. Reverence.

Re-verto, ĕre, verti, versum ; revertor, dep. To come back, return.

Re-vŏco, āre, āvi, ātum. To recall.

Rex, regis, m. King.

Rhea, ae, f. Rhea. *Rhea Silvia,* the daughter of Numitor and the mother of Romulus and Remus, (152).

Rhenus, i, m. The river Rhine, (208).

Rhodănus, i, m. The river Rhone, in Gaul, (208).

Rhodius, a, um, (Rhodos, *the island of Rhodes*). Rhodian, of or belonging to Rhodes. *Rhodius, ii,* m. A Rhodian, (143).

Rideo, ēre, si, sum. To laugh, to laugh at.

Ripa, ae, f. Bank, *or of a river.*

Rite, adv. Rightly, in due form.

Robur, ŏris, n. Strength.

Robustus, a, um, (robur). Robust, strong.

Rogatio, ōnis, f. (rogo). An asking, question ; entreaty, request.

Rogo, āre, āvi, ātum. To ask, question.

Roma, as, f. Rome, (27).

Romānus, a, um, adj. (Roma). Roman ; subs. *Romānus, i,* m. a Roman, (26).

Romŭlus, i, m. Romulus, the founder of Rome, (154).

Roscius, ii, m. Roscius, a Roman name. *Lucius Roscius,* a celebrated tribune of the people and friend of Cicero, (51).

Rotundus, a, um. Round, spherical.

Rufus, i, m. Rufus, a Roman surname ; as, Publius Rutilius Rufus, (139).

Ruina, ae, f. Ruin, fall.

Rullianus, i. m. Rullianus, a Roman name. *Quintus Fabius Rullianus,* master of the cavalry (*magister equitum*) under the dictator *Papirius Cursor,* (178).

Rumpo, ĕre, rupi, ruptum. To break.

Ruo, ĕre, rui, ruitum or *rutum.* To run, rush forth.

Rupes, is, f. Rock, cliff.

Rursus (or *um*), adv. Back, again.

Rus, ruris, n. Country, *as opposed to city.*

Rusticus, i, m. Countryman, farmer, peasant, husbandman.

Rutilius, ii, m. Rutilius, a Roman name. *Publius Rutilius Rufus,* a Roman consul, slain in the Social war, (139).

S.

S. An abbreviation for *Sextus, Sp* for *Spurius.*

Sabini, ōrum, m. pl. The Sabines. a people of Italy, bordering upon Latium, (157).

Sacer, sacra, sacrum. Sacred.

Sacerdos, ōtis, m. and f. (sacer). Priest, priestess.

Sacrificium, ii, n. Sacrifice.

Sacro, āre, āvi, ātum, (sacer). To consecrate.

Sacrum, i, n. Sacred rite *or* institution; sacrifice.

Saepe, ius, issime, adv. Often.

Saevio, īre, īvi or *ii, ītum.* To rage, be cruel.

Sagacitas, ātis, f. Sagacity, acuteness, shrewdness.

Sagax, ācis. Acute, sagacious.

Sagitta, ae, f. Arrow.

Saguntum, i, n. Saguntum, a town in Spain, on the Mediterranean, (189).

Saguntini, ōrum, m. pl. The Saguntines, citizens of Saguntum, (189).

Salāmis, is or *īnis,* f. (acc. *Salamīna*), or *Salamina, ae,* f. The island of Salamis, off the coast of Attica, (217).

Salūber, bris, bre, (salus). Healthful; salubrious.

Salus, ūtis, f. Safety; *Salus* personified, the Roman goddess, *Salus,* (20, 7).

Salutāris, e, (salus). Healthful, wholesome.

Salūto, āre, āvi, ātum, (salus). To salute.

Salve, def. verb. Hail. See 297, III. 1.

Salvus, a, um. Safe, unhurt.

Samnites, ium, m. pl. The Samnites, the inhabitants of Samnium, in Italy, (178).

Samus or *Samos, i,* f. The island Samos, on the coast of Asia Minor.

Sancte, ius, issime, (sanctus, *sacred, pure*), adv. Chastely, purely, conscientiously.

Sanguis, īnis, m. Blood.

Sannio, ōnis, m. Sannio, a proper name, (35).

Sapiens, entis. Wise; *subs.* a wise man.

Sapienter, ius, issime, adv. (sapiens). Wisely.

Sapientia, ae, f. (sapiens). Wisdom.

Sapio, ĕre, īvi or *ui.* To taste; to have sense, to know, understand, be wise.

Sardes, ium, f. Sardis, the ancient capital of Lydia.

Sardinia, ae, f. The island of Sardinia, west of Italy, (188).

Satelles, ītis, m. and f. Lifeguard, attendant.

Satio, āre, āvi, ātum. To fill, satisfy, content.

Satis, adv., adj., subs. Enough, sufficient, sufficiently; *satis habēre,* to have enough, be content.

Saturnia, ae, f. Saturnia, the town and citadel built by Saturn, (148).

Saturnus, i, m. Saturn, the most ancient king of Latium, (148).

Saucius, a, um. Wounded, injured, hurt, sick, intoxicated.

Saxum, i, n. Rock, stone.

Scaevōla, ae, m. See *Mucius,* (172).

Scelestus, a, um, (scelus). Wicked, criminal, infamous.

Scelus, ĕris, n. Crime, wickedness.

Scena, ae, f. Scene, stage.

Schola, ae, f. Leisure devoted to learning; a place of learning, a school; a lecture, dissertation.

Scientia, ae, f. (scio). Knowledge, science, skill, expertness.

Scio, scīre, scivi, scitum. To know, understand, have knowledge.

Scipio, ōnis, m. Scipio, the name of a distinguished Roman family. See *Africānus,* (190).

Scriba, ae, m. (scribo). Scribe, clerk.

Scribo, ĕre, scripsi, scriptum. To write, prepare.

Scutum, i, n. Shield.

Scythia, ae, f. Scythia, an extensive country in the north of Europe and Asia, (215).

Scythae, ārum, m. pl. The Scythians, (215).

Se-cēdo, ĕre, cessi, cessum. To retire, withdraw.

Secundum, adv., and prep. with acc. After, behind, next to; according to, by the side of, along.

Secundus, a, um. Second, favorable, prosperous.

Sed, conj. But.

Sedĕcim, indec. (sex, decem). Sixteen.

Sedeo, ĕre, sedi, sessum. To sit, stay.

Sedes, is, f. Seat, abode, residence.

Seditio, ōnis, f. Quarrel, sedition.

Seditiōsus, a, um, (seditio). Mutinous, seditious.

Sedo, āre, āvi, ātum. To allay, quiet.

Segnis, e. Slothful, inactive.

Segnĭter, ius, issĭme, adv. (segnis). Slothfully.

Seleucia, ae, f. Seleucia, a city of Syria on the Orontes, (206).

Semel, adv. Once.

Sementis, is, f. Seed; sowing.

Semianĭmis, e. Half-alive, half-dead.

Semper, adv. Always, ever.

Sempiternus, a, um, (semper). Everlasting, imperishable.

Sempronius, ii, m. See *Gracchus,* (190).

Senātor, ōris, m. (senex). Senator.

Senātus, us, m. (senex). Senate.

Senectus, ūtis, f. (senex). Old age, age.

Senesco, ĕre, senui. To grow old, become aged; *senescens, entis,* becoming old, aged.

Senex, senis. Old, aged. 168, 3.

Senex, senis, m. and f. An old man, an aged person.

Senōnes, um, m. pl. The Senones, a powerful people in Gaul, (176).

Sensim, adv. (sentio). Sensibly; slowly, gradually, by degrees.

Sensus, us, m. Sensation, sense, perception.

Sententia, ae, f. Opinion, sentence, sentiment, maxim, axiom, purpose, decision.

Sentio, īre, sensi, sensum. To perceive, feel, experience; think, judge.

Sepelio, īre, pelīvi or *ii, pultum.* To bury.

Sepio, īre, sepsi, septum. To guard, shelter.

Septem, indecl. Seven.

Septĭmus, a, um, (septem). Seventh.

Septingentesĭmus, a, um, (septingenti). The seven hundredth.

Septingenti, ae, a. Seven hundred.

Septuagesĭmus, a, um, (septuaginta). Seventieth.

Septuaginta, indecl. Seventy.

Sepulcrum, i, n. (sepelio). Grave tomb, sepulchre.

Sepultūra, ae, f. (sepelio). Burial.

Sequāni, ōrum, m. The Sequani, a Gallic people, dwelling on the river Sequana, (28, 15).

Sequor, sequi, secûtus sum, dep. To follow, succeed.

Sergius, ii, m. See *Catilina,* (207).

Sermo, ōnis, m. Speech, discourse, conversation.

Sero, ius, issīme, adv. (serus). Late, too late.

Serpo, ĕre, serpsi, serptum. To spread, extend.

Serus, a, um. Late.

Servilius, ii, m. Servilius, a Roman name.

Servio, īre, īvi or *ii, ītum.* To be a slave, to serve, be subject to.

Servĭtus, ūtis, f. (servio). Servitude, slavery.

Servius, ii, m. Servius, a Roman name. *Servius Tullius,* the sixth king of Rome, (164).

Servo, āre, āvi, ātum. To observe, keep; preserve.

Servus, i, m. Slave.

Seu. Whether; *seu—seu,* whether —or.

Sex, indecl. Six.

Sexagesĭmus, a, um, (sexaginta). Sixtieth.

Sexaginta, indecl. Sixty.

Sexcentesĭmus, a, um, (sexcenti). Six hundredth.

Sexcenti, ae, a. Six hundred.

Sextus, a, um, (sex). Sixth.

Si, conj. If.

Sic, adv. Thus, so.

Siccus, a, um. Dry.

Sicilia, ae, f. The island of Sicily, (185).

Sidus, ĕris, n. A group of stars, a constellation.

Significo, āre, āvi, ātum, (signum, facio). To show, indicate, mean, signify.

Signum, i, n. Mark, sign, indication, standard.

Silentium, ii, n. Silence, stillness, quiet, repose.

Sileo, ēre, ui. To be silent, still, quiet; to pass over in silence, not to speak of.

Silvia, ae, f. See *Rhea,* (152).

Silvius, ii, m. Silvius, the name of several kings of Alba, the first of whom was the son of *Aeneas,* (150, 151).

Similis, e. Similar, like. 163, 2.

Similĭter, ius, īme, adv. (similis). In like manner, similarly, in a similar way. 305, 2.

Simonĭdes, is, m. Simonides, a celebrated lyric poet of Cea, (132).

Simul, adv. At the same time.

Simulātio, ōnis, f. An assumed appearance, pretence, simulation, deceit, hypocrisy.

Sin, conj. But if.

Sine, prep. with abl. Without.

Singulāris, e. Single, singular, remarkable.

Singŭlus, a, um. Single, one by one.

Sinister, tra, trum. Left, on the left.

Sino, ĕre, sivi, situm. To permit; allow; *situs,* put, placed, situated.

Sinus, us, m. Bosom, bay.

Si-quis or *siqui, siqua, siquid* or *siquod,* indef. pron. If any, if any one.

Sitis, is, f. Thirst, desire.

Sobrius, a, um. Sober, temperate, moderate, reasonable.

Socer, ĕri, m. Father-in-law.

Sociālis, e, (socius). Social, friendly.

Socĭĕtas, ātis, f. (socius). League, alliance, partnership, society.

Socius, ii, m. Ally, confederate.

Socrātes, is, m.   Socrates, a celebrated Grecian philosopher, (20, 8).

Sol, solis, m. Sun.

Solemnis, e.   Stated, established;
religious, solemn.

Solemnĭter, adv. (solemnis).   Sol-
emnly, in due form.

Soleo, ēre, ĭtus sum. To be accustomed, be wont. 271, 3.

Solĭdus, a, um. Solid.

Solitūdo, ĭnis, f. (solus). Solitude.

Solĭtus, a, um, (soleo). Usual.

Sollertia, ae, f. Sagacity, shrewdness.

Solon, ŏnis, m.   Solon, a celebrated
Athenian law-giver and one of the
seven wise men of Greece, (128).

Solum, adv. (solus). Only, alone.

Solus, a, um. Alone. 151.

Solūtus, a, um, (solvo). Unrestrain-
ed, dissolute.

Solvo, ēre, solvi, solūtum. To loose,
unbind; to pay.

Somnio, āre, āvi, ātum, (somnium).
To dream.

Somnium, ii, n. Dream.

Somnus, i, m. Sleep.

Sonĭtus, us, m. (sono). Sound, noise.

Sono, āre, ui, ĭtum. To sound, utter, speak, call, express, mean.

Sonus, i, m. (sono). Sound.

Sophŏcles, is and *i,* m. Sophocles,
a celebrated Grecian tragic poet,
(55).

Sordĭdus, a, um. Sordid, soiled,
filthy, base, mean.

Soror, ōris, f. Sister.

Sors, sortis, f. Lot.

Sparta, ae, f. Sparta, the capital of
Laconia, in the Peloponnesus;
also called Lacedaemon.

Spartānus, a, um, adj. (Sparta).
Spartan; subs. *Spartānus, i,* m.,
a Spartan, (222).

Spartăcus, i, m. Spartacus, a celebrated gladiator who waged war
against the Romans, (204).

Spatium, ii, n. Space.

Species, ēi, f. Appearance, guise.

Spectacŭlum, i, n. (specto). Specta-
cle, show.

Specto, āre, āvi, ātum. To view,
witness. *Spectātus, a, um.* Tried,
proved, illustrious.

Sperno, ēre, sprēvi, sprētum.   To
despise, reject, contemn, scorn,
spurn.

Spero, āre, āvi, ātum. To expect,
hope; flatter one's self.

Spes, ei, f. Hope.

Spolio, āre, āvi, ātum, (spolium). To
rob; spoil; despoil.

Spolium, ii, n.   Plunder, spoil,
booty.

Spontis, gen. *sponte,* abl. sing. Of
or for himself, itself, of one's own
accord, on one's own account, voluntarily, spontaneously.

Spurius, ii, m.   See *Postumius* and
Lucretius.

Stabilĭtas, ātis, f.   Immovability,
steadfastness, stability.

Stadium, ii, n.   A stade *or* stadium,
a measure equal to 606 English
feet; race-course, race-ground.

Statim, adv. (sto). At once, immediately.

Statio, ŏnis, f. (sto). Station, post;
residence.

Statua, ae, f. (statuo). Statue.

Statuo, ēre, ui, ūtum, (status, *from*
sto).   To determine; appoint,
place.

Statūra, ae, f. (status, from sto).
Height, size of the body, stature.

Status, us, m. (sto). State, condition.

Stella, ae, f. Star.

Sterno, ĕre, stravi, stratum. To
prostrate.

Sto, stare, steti, statum. To stand.

Strages, is, f. Slaughter, defeat.

Strangŭlo, āre, āvi, ātum. To
strangle.

Strenue, adv. (strenuus). Vigor-
ously, carefully.

Strenuus, a, um. Active, valiant.

Studeo, ĕre, ui. To study, favor, be
attached to; to devote one's self
to; be zealous.

Studiōse, ius, issĭme, adv. (studiōsus). Diligently, earnestly.

Studiōsus, a, um, (studium). Eager,
desirous, zealous; friendly, stu-
dious.

Studium, ii, n. Zeal, study, desire,
pursuit.

Stultitia, ae, f. (stultus). Folly, fool-
ishness, simplicity.

Stultus, a, um. Foolish, simple,
silly.

Suadeo, ĕre, suasi, suasum. To advise.

Sub, prep. with acc. or abl. Under,
at the foot of.

Sub-dūco, ĕre, duxi, ductum. To take
away, withdraw.

Subĭgo, ĕre, ĕgi, actum, (sub, ago).
To subdue, conquer.

Subĭto, adv. (subĭtus, from subeo).
Suddenly, unexpectedly.

Sublīme, adv. (sublimis). Aloft,
loftily, on high.

Sublīmis, e. High, on high.

Sub-mergo, ĕre, mersi, mersum. To
dip or plunge under; to sink,
overwhelm, submerge. Pass. To
be overwhelmed, to sink.

Sub-rideo, ĕre, risi, risum. To smile,
laugh.

Subsidium, ii, n. The reserve; aid,
reinforcement.

Sub-silio, ĭre, silui and silii, (sub,
salio). To leap or jump up, leap,
jump.

Sub-sum, esse, fui. To be at hand
or near, be under.

Subter, prep. with acc. or abl. Below, beneath, under.

Sub-trăho, ĕre, traxi, tractum. To
take away, remove, subtract.

Sub-venio, ĭre, vēni, ventum. To
come to; to aid, relieve.

Sub-verto, ĕre, verti, versum. To
overturn, overthrow, destroy, sub-
vert.

Succēdo, ĕre, cessi, cessum, (sub,
cedo). To succeed, come after.

Successio, ōnis, f. (succēdo). Succession.

Successor, ōnis, m. (succēdo). Successor.

Successus, us, m. (succēdo). Success.

Suc-cumbo, ĕre, cubui, cubĭtum. To
yield, submit to.

Suffetius, ii, m. Suffetius. Metius
Suffetius, dictator of the Albans.
Having been summoned to aid
the Romans against the Veientines, he drew off his forces at the
very moment of battle, and awaited the issue of the engagement.
For this perfidy he was put to
death by order of Tullius Hostilius (160).

Sufficio, ĕre, fēci, fectum, (sub, facio). To substitute; be sufficient,
suffice.

J

Suffundo, ĕre, fūdi, fusum, (sub, fundo). To spread over, pour through; suffuse.

Sui, sibi. Himself, herself, itself.

Sulla, ae, m. Sulla, a distinguished Roman dictator and general, (202).

Sum, esse, fui. To be.

Summa, ae, f. (summus). Supreme power.

Summoveo, ĕre, mōvi, mōtum, (sub, moveo). To remove, displace.

Summus. See *Supĕrus.*

Sumo, ĕre, sumpsi, sumptum. To take, inflict.

Sumptus, us, m. (sumo). Expense, cost.

Super, prep. with acc. or abl. Over, above, upon; of, concerning, at, at the time of.

Superbia, ae, f. (superbus). Pride, haughtiness.

Superbus, a, um. Proud.

Superbus, i, m. Superbus, the surname of Tarquin, the last king of Rome, (167).

Supĕro, āre, āvi, ātum, (supĕrus). To surpass; conquer; pass by, cross.

Superstitio, ōnis, f. (supersto). Superstition.

Super-sum, esse, fui. To remain, be left, survive.

Supĕrus, a, um ; comp. *superior ;* superl. *suprēmus* or *summus.* High, above; past, former. 163, 3.

Super-venio, īre, vēni, ventum. To come to, surprise.

Supplementum, i, n. Supplies, reinforcement.

Supplex, ĭcis, (sub, plico). Humbly begging, submissive, beseeching, suppliant ; *subs.* a suppliant.

Supplicium, ii, n. Punishment.

Supra, prep. with acc. Above, upon.

Suprēmus. See *Supĕrus.*

Surripio, ĕre, ripui, reptum, (sub, rapio). To snatch away; to steal, pilfer, purloin.

Suscipio, ĕre, cēpi, ceptum, (sub, capio). To bear, endure ; receive; undertake, engage in.

Suspendo, ĕre, pendi, pensum, (sub, pendo). To suspend, hang up.

Suspensus, a, um, (suspendo). Uncertain, undecided ; anxious.

Suspicio, ōnis, f. (suspĭcor). Suspicion.

Suspicio, ĕre, spexi, spectum, (sub, specio). To suspect.

Suspĭcor, āri, ātus sum, (suspicio), dep. To suspect.

Sustento, āre, āvi, ātum, (sustineo). To hold up, support, sustain ; endure, suffer; delay. 332, L.

Sustineo, ĕre, tinui, tentum, (sub, teneo). To sustain, withstand ; endure, endure the thought of.

Suus, a, um. His, her, its, their; *pl. often,* one's party, friends.

Syracūsae, ārum, f. pl. Syracuse, a city in Sicily, (185).

Syracusāni, ōrum, m. pl. The Syracusans, the citizens of Syracuse, (223).

T.

T. An abbreviation of *Titus.*

Tabernacŭlum, i, n. Tent.

Taceo, ĕre, tacui, tacĭtum. To be silent, not to speak, to pass over in silence.

Tacĭtus, a, um. Silent, secret, tacit.

Tactus, us, m. Touch.

Taedĕt, ĕre, taeduit or *taesum est,* impers. It disgusts, wearies.

Talentum, i, n. Talent, sum of money, somewhat more than $1,000.

Talis, e, such.

Tam. So; *tam—quam,* so—as.

Tamen, conj. Yet, nevertheless.

Tametsi, conj. (tamen, etsi). Notwithstanding that, although, though.

Tanăquil, ĭlis, f. Tanaquil, the wife of Tarquinius Priscus, (165).

Tandem, adv. At length.

Tanquam, adv. As, just as.

Tantum. Only.

Tantus, a, um. Such, so great, so much; *tanti esse,* to be worth the while.

Tarentum, i, n. Tarentum, a town of Lower Italy, (184).

Tarentīni, ōrum, m. pl. The Tarentines, the inhabitants of Tarentum, (180).

Tarpeia, ae, f. Tarpeia, a Roman maiden, who betrayed the citadel of Rome to the Sabines, (156).

Tarpeius, ii, m. Tarpeius, one of the seven hills of Rome, also called *Capitolīnus.* The Capitol was erected upon it. Afterwards the term *Tarpeius* was applied to the southern summit of the hill, (157).

Tarquinii, ōrum, m. pl. Tarquinii, an ancient town of Etruria, (49, 10).

Tarquinius, ii, m. Tarquin, the name of the fifth king of Rome and of his descendants, as *Tar-*

quinius *Superbus,* the last king of Rome; and *Tarquinius Collatīnus,* the colleague of Brutus in the consulship, (169).

Tectum, i, n. (tego). Covering, roof; house, edifice.

Tego, ĕre, texi, tectum. To cover.

Telum, i, n. Weapon.

Temĕre, adv. Rashly.

Temerĭtas, ātis, f. Rashness, indiscretion, temerity.

Tempestas, ātis, f. (tempus). Time; tempest, storm.

Tempestīve, adv. (tempestīvus, timely). Seasonably, just at the time, opportunely.

Templum, i, n. Temple.

Tempus, ŏris, n. Time. *Tempŏra,* times, seasons, events.

Temulentus, a, um. Drunk, intoxicated.

Teneo, ĕre, ui, tentum. To hold, keep, occupy; obtain, retain, as in the memory.

Tento, āre, āvi, ātum, (tendo). To try; attack. 332, I.

Tenus, prep. with abl. Up to, as far as.

Terentius, ii, m. See *Varro,* (191).

Ter-gemĭnus, a, um. Threefold; *tergemĭni,* three brothers born at a birth.

Tergum, i, n. Back.

Termĭno, āre, āvi, ātum, (termĭnus). To limit, bound.

Termĭnus, i, m. Limit, boundary; end.

Terra, ae, f. Earth, land, country.

Terreo, ĕre, ui, ĭtum. To terrify.

Terrester, tris, tre, (terra). Terrestrial, on land, land (*as adj.*).

Territorium, ii, n. Territory.

Terror ŏris, m. (terreo). Terror, alarm; fear of.

Tertius, a, um. Third.

Testamentum, i, n. Testament, will.

Testis, is, m. and f. Witness.

Testor, āri, ātus sum, (testis). To affirm; call to witness.

Testūdo, ĭnis, f. Tortoise.

Thales, is, m. Thales, a celebrated Grecian philosopher of Miletus, one of the seven wise men, (114).

Theātrum, i, n. Theatre.

Thebae, ārum, f. pl. Thebes, the capital of Boeotia in Greece, (230).

Thebānus, a, um, adj. (Thebae). Theban, (229); subs. *Thebānus, i*, m., a Theban.

Thelesīnus, i, m. See *Pontius*, (28, 10).

Themistŏcles, is, m. Themistocles, a celebrated Athenian commander, (132—134).

Theocrĭtus, i, m. Theocritus, a celebrated Grecian poet, (130).

Theophrastus, i, m. Theophrastus, a Grecian philosopher, a disciple of Plato and Aristotle, (129).

Thermopȳlae, ārum, f. pl. Thermopylae, the famous defile *or* pass between Locris and Thessaly, where Leonidas fell, (218).

Thessalia, ae, f. The country of Thessaly, in Greece, south of Macedonia, (210).

Thessălus, a, um, adj. Thessalian; subs. *Thessălus, i*, m., a Thessalian, (243).

Thessălus, i, m. Thessalus, a native of Thesprotia, in Epirus, who is said to have formed a settlement in Thessaly, and to have given his name to the country.

Thorax, ăcis, m. Breastplate, coat-of-mail, corselet.

Thracia, ae, f. The country of Thrace, east of Macedonia, (231).

Thrasybūlus, i, m. Thrasybulus, an Athenian who liberated the city from the Thirty Tyrants, (130, 228).

Thucydīdes, is, m. Thucydides, celebrated Greek historian, (77).

Tibĕris, is, m. The river Tiber, in Italy, (153).

Tiberius, ii, m. Tiberius, the second Roman emperor, (145).

Ticīnus, i, m. Ticinus, a river in Cisalpine Gaul, famous for the victory of Hannibal over the Romans, (190, 194).

Tigrānes, is, m. Tigranes, son-in-law of Mithridates and king of Armenia, (205).

Timeo, ĕre, ui. To fear.

Timĭdus, a, um, (timeo). Cowardly, timid.

Timoleon, ontis, m. Timoleon, a Corinthian general, (51).

Timotheus, ei, m. Timotheus, an Athenian general, son of Conon, (49, 12).

Tintinnabŭlum, i, n. Bell.

Tiresias, ae, m. Tiresias, a celebrated blind soothsayer of Thebes, (24, 11).

Tissaphernes, is, m. Tissaphernes, a distinguished Persian satrap of Lower Asia, under Darius; afterwards general in the service of Artaxerxes, (225).

Titus, i, m. Titus, a Roman emperor, (141). See also *Quinctius*, (177).

Tollo, ĕre, sustŭli, sublātum. To

raise, take up, elate; take away; destroy; discard.

Tondeo, ēre, totondi, tonsum. To shear, clip, crop; graze, browse; pluck, gather.

Torquātus, i, m. Torquatus, surname of *Titus Manlius* and his descendants, (177).

Torquis, is, m. and f. Collar, chain for the neck.

Tot, indecl. So many.

Totĭdem, indecl. Just as many, the same number.

Totus, a, um. All, the whole, *sometimes best rendered by adv.* wholly, entirely. 151, 443.

Tracto, āre, āvi, ātum. To use, treat, manage.

Trado, ĕre, dĭdi, dĭtum, (trans, do). To deliver, give, consign to; *also* to relate, say; *traditur* (when impers.), it is said.

Tradūco, ĕre, duxi, ductum, (trans, duco). To lead across, transport.

Tragoedia, ae, f. Tragedy.

Tragoedus, i, m. Tragedian.

Traho, ĕre, traxi, tractum. To draw; protract, delay, detain, derive, influence.

Trajicio, ĕre, jēci, jectum, (trans, jacio). To throw over; to cross; conduct over, lead over.

Trano, āre, āvi, ātum, (trans, no). To swim over.

Trans, prep. with acc. Across, beyond.

Trans-dūco = tradūco.

Trans-eo, īre, ivi or *ii, ĭtum.* To go over, to cross. 295, 3.

Trans-fĕro, ferre, tūli, lātum. To transport, transfer, translate.

Trans-figo, ĕre, fixi, fixum. To transfix, to thrust through, to pierce through.

Transgredĭor, grĕdi, grĕssus sum, dep. (trans, gradior). To go or pass over.

Transĭgo, ĕre, ēgi, actum, (trans, ago). To accomplish, finish, pass, spend.

Transilio, īre, ĭi, ii or *ui,* (trans, salio). To leap *or* pass over.

Transĭtus, ūs, m. (transeo). Passage.

Trans-marīnus, a, um. Transmarine, over the sea.

Trans-no = trano.

Trans-porto, āre, āvi, ātum. To carry *or* convey from one place to another, carry across, transport.

Trasimēnus, i, m. Lake Trasimenus in Etruria, (190).

Trebia, ae, f. The river Trebia in Cisalpine Gaul, (190).

Trecentesĭmus, a, um, (trecenti). The three hundredth.

Trecenti, ae, a. Three hundred.

Tredĕcim, indecl. Thirteen.

Tremo, ĕre, tremui. To shake, quake, tremble, quiver.

Trepĭdus, a, um. Alarmed; in terror.

Tres, tria. Three.

Tribūnus, i, m. Tribune.

Tribuo, ĕre, ui, ūtum. To bestow, impute, award.

Tributarius, a, um. Tributary.

Tribūtum, i, n. (tribuo). Tax, tribute.

Tricesĭmus, a, um. The thirtieth.

Triennium, ii, n. The space of three years, three years.

Trigemĭnus = tergemĭnus.

Trigesĭmus = tricesĭmus.

Triginta, indecl. Thirty.

Triplex, ĭcis. Triple, threefold.

Tripudio, āre, āvi. To leap, dance.

Tripus, ŏdis, m. Tripod.

Trirēmis, is, f. (tres, remus). Galley with three banks of oars.

Trirēmis, e, adj. Having three banks of oars.

Tristis, e. Sad.

Triumpho, āre, āvi, ātum, (triumphus). To triumph, have a triumphal procession.

Triumphus, i, m. Triumph.

Troezen, ēnis, f. (acc. *Troezēna*). Troezen, an ancient city of Argolis, (217).

Troja, ae, f. The city of Troy, (33, 6).

Trojāni, ōrum, m. pl. (Troja). The Trojans, (149).

Trojānus, a, um, (Troja). Trojan, (236).

Tropaeum, i, n. Trophy, victory.

Trucīdo, āre, āvi, ātum, (trux, caedo). To slay, massacre.

Trux, trucis. Fierce, stern.

Tu, tui. Thou, you.

Tuba, ae, f. Trumpet.

Tubĭcen, ĭnis, m. Trumpeter.

Tueor, ēri, tuĭtus or *tutus sum,* dep. To look upon; preserve, defend.

Tullia, ae, f. Tullia, the daughter of Servius Tullius, and wife of Tarquinius Superbus, (166).

Tullius, ii, m. See *Servius,* (164).

Tullus, i, m. See *Hostilius,* (160).

Tum. Then; *tum—tum,* not only —but also; both—and.

Tumultuo, āre, āvi, ātum, (tumultus). To make a noise *or* tumult.

Tumultus, us, m. Tumult, sedition.

Tumŭlus, i, m. Tomb, grave.

Tunc, adv. Then ; *tunc tempŏris,* then. 396, 2, 4.

Tunīca, ae, f. Tunic, coat, a garment worn under the toga.

Turba, ae, f. Crowd, throng, multitude.

Turbo, āre, āvi, ātum, (turba). To disturb, throw into confusion.

Turgesco, ĕre, turgui. To swell, to swell with passion.

Turpĭter, ius, issĭme, adv. (turpis, base). Basely, disgracefully, in disgrace.

Turris, is, f. Tower.

Tuscŭlum, i, n. Tusculum, an ancient town in Latium, (172).

Tutor, ōris, m. Tutor, guardian.

Tutus, a, um. Safe.

Tuus, a, um, adj. pron. (tu). Thy, thine, your, yours.

Tyrannis, ĭdis, f. (tyrannus). Tyranny.

Tyrannus, i, m. Tyrant, monarch.

U

Uber, ĕris, n. Udder, dug.

Ubertas, ātis, f. Richness, fertility.

Ubi, adv. Where, when, *sometimes interrog.*

Ubii, ōrum, m. pl. The Ubii, an ancient Germanic people dwelling on the Rhine, (94).

Ubĭnam, adv. Where, in what part of ?

Ubĭque. Everywhere.

Ullus, a, um. Any, any one. 151.

Ulterior, us ; superl. *ultĭmus.* Further, more remote; *superl.* last. 166.

Ultio, ōnis, f. Revenge.

Ultra, adv., and prep. with acc. Beyond, more than.

Ultro, adv. Voluntarily, of one's own accord.

Ulŭlo, āre, āvi, ātum. To howl, to cry aloud, to shriek.

Umbra, ae, f. Shade, shadow.

Unde, adv. Whence, *also interrog.* whence ?

Undĕcim, indecl. Eleven.

Undequinquaginta, indecl. Forty-nine.

Undevicesĭmus, a, um. Nineteenth.

Undĭque, adv. From all quarters or sides.

Unguentum, i, n. Ointment, perfume.

Unguis, is, m. Nail, claw, talon.

Ungŭla, ae, f. Claw, talon, hoof.

Universus, a, um. Whole, entire; all together.

Unquam, adv. At any time, ever.

Unus, a, um. One, alone. 175.

Unus-quisque, unaquaeque, etc. (unus, quisque, *both parts declined*). Each, each one.

Urbs, urbis, f. City.

Urgeo, ēre, ursi. To urge, drive; press upon.

Usque, adv. So far as; *usque ad,* even to; *usque eo,* to such an extent.

Usurpo, āre, āvi, ātum. To usurp, assume.

Usus, us, m. Use, service; experience; need.

Ut or uti, conj. That, as; *after verbs of fearing,* that not.

Utcumque or utcunque, adv. However, somewhat.

Uter, tra, trum, adj. Which? which of the two? 151.

Uterque, utrăque, utrumque, like *uter.* Both, each. 151, 4.

Utilis, e. Useful.

Utilĭtas, ātis, f. (utilis). Utility, service, advantage.

Utor, uti, usus sum. To use.

Utrinque or utrinque, adv. On both sides.

Utrum, in double questions. Whether.

Uva, ae, f. A bunch of grapes, a grape.

Uxor, ōris, f. Wife.

V

Vaco, āre, āvi, ātum. To be empty, vacant, to have leisure for; be free from.

Vacuus, a, um. Vacant, empty, free from.

Vadum, i, n. Ford, shallow water.

Vagĭtus, us, m. Crying.

Vagor, āri, ātus sum. To wander about.

Vagus, a, um. Wandering, doubtful, uncertain, vague.

Valeo, ēre, ui, ĭtum. To have strength, avail, be well.

Valerius, ii, m. Valerius, a Roman name. See *Publicŏla, Laevīnus,* (169, 180).

Valetūdo, ĭnis, f. (valeo). Habit, state of the body, health, state of health.

Vanus, a, um. Empty, vain, false.

Variĕtas, ātis, f. (varius). Variety, change.

Varius, a, um. Various.

Varro, ōnis, m. Varro, a Roman name. *Caius Terentius Varro,* a Roman consul defeated at Cannae, (191).

Vas, vasis, n. Vessel, dish, vase.

Vasto, āre, āvi, ātum, (vastus). To lay waste, devastate, pillage.

Vastus, a, um. Waste, desert, vast.

Vates, is, m. and f. Prophet, prophetess.

Vectīgal, ālis, n. Tax, income, revenue.

Veho, ĕre, vexi, vectum. To carry, bear.

Veientes, um, or *Veientāni, ōrum,* m. pl. The Veientians, *or* Veientines, the inhabitants of Veii in Etruria, (175).

Vel, conj. Or, even ; *vel—vel,* either—or.

Velox, ōcis. Swift, rapid, fleet.

Vel-ut, or *vel-ŭti,* adv. As, like as, as if.

Vendālis, e. To be sold, for sale, purchasable.

Vendo, ĕre, dĭdi, dĭtum. To sell; *sub corōna vendĕre,* to sell as slaves.

Venēnum, i, n. Poison.

Venio, īre, veni, ventum. To come.

Venor, āri, ātus sum, dep. To hunt, chase, pursue.

Venter, tris, m. Belly, stomach.

Ventus, i, m. Wind.

Venus, ĕris, f. Venus, the goddess of love, (28).

Verbum, i, n. Word.

Vereor, ēri, verītus sum, dep. To fear, to be afraid.

Verītas, ātis, f. Truth.

Vero, adv. and conj. (verus). Truly, indeed ; but.

Verres, is, m. Verres, a Roman name. *Caius Cornelius Verres* rendered himself notorious by his abuse of power in Sicily, (43).

Verso, āre, āvi, ātum, or *versor,* dep. (verto). To turn ; busy one's self, be occupied with. 832, I. 2.

Versus, us, m. A verse.

Vertex, ĭcis, m. (verto). Summit, top.

Verto, ĕre, verti, versum. To turn.

Verum, conj. But.

Verus, a, um. True, real.

Vescor, vesci. To enjoy, feed upon, live upon, to eat.

Vesper, ĕris or *ĕri,* m. Evening.

Vespĕra, ae, f. Evening.

Vesperasco, ĕre, vesperāvi, (vesper). To become evening.

Vesta, ae, f. Vesta, the goddess of the hearth, to whom a perpetual fire was kept burning, (152).

Vestālis, e, adj. (Vesta). Vestal, relating to Vesta, (152).

Vester, tra, trum. Your.

Vestibŭlum, i, n. Vestibule, entrance.

Vestio, īre, īvi, ītum, (vestis). To clothe.

Vestis, is, f. Garment.

Veterānus, a, um, (vetus). Veteran.

Veto, āre, ui, ītum. To forbid.

Veturia, ae, f. Veturia, the mother of Coriolanus, (174).

Veturius, ii, m. Veturius, a Roman name. *Titus Veturius,* a Roman consul defeated by the Samnites at the Caudine Forks, (179).

Vetus, ĕris. Old, of long standing, ancient.

Vetustas, ātis, f. (vetus). Antiquity, age.

Vetustus, a, um. Old, ancient.

Via, ae, f. Way.

Viātor, ōris, m. Traveller.

Vicesĭmus, a, um. Twentieth.

Vicīnus, a, um. Neighboring.

Vicis, gen. f. Change, reverse, al

ternation, requital; fate, fortune; *in vicem* or *vicem*, in turn, place. 133, 1.

Vicissitūdo, *ĭnis*, f. (vicis). Change, alternation, vicissitude, succession.

Victor, *ōris*, m. (vinco). Conqueror.

Victoria, *ae*, f. Victory.

Victus, *a*, *um*, part. (vinco). Conquered, vanquished.

Vicus, *i*, m. Village.

Video, *ēre*, *di*, *sum*. To see; *pass. videor*, etc., to be seen; to seem.

Vigeo, *ēre*, *ui*. To flourish, thrive, be in force.

Vigilantia, *ae*, f. Wakefulness, vigilance.

Viginti, indec. Twenty.

Vilis, *e*. Low, cheap, base, vile.

Vincio, *ĭre*, *vinxi*, *vinctum*. To bind.

Vinco, *ēre*, *vici*, *victum*. To conquer.

Vinculum or *vinclum*, *i*, n. Fetter, chain.

Vindex, *ĭcis*, m. and f. Defender.

Vindĭco, *āre*, *āvi*, *ātum*. To claim; rescue, defend; punish, avenge.

Vinolentus, *a*, *um*, (vinum). Full of wine, intoxicated with wine.

Vinum, *i*, n. Wine.

Viŏlo, *āre*, *āvi*, *ātum*. To violate, do violence to; profane, harm.

Vir, *viri*, m. Man, hero, husband.

Virga, *ae*, f. Rod, twig.

Virgo, *ĭnis*, f. Virgin, maiden.

Virgŭla, *ae*, f. Small rod, rod.

Virtus, *ūtis*, f. (vir). Manliness, bravery, virtue.

Vis, *vis*, f.; pl. *vires*. Power, strength, force; forces; abundance.

Viscus, *ĕris*, n. Vitals, bowels.

Viso, *ĕre*, *si*, *sum*. To view, see, visit.

Vita, *ae*, f. Life.

Vitis, *is*, f. Vine.

Vitium, *ii*, n. Fault, vice, crime.

Vitupĕro, *āre*, *āvi*, *ātum*. To censure, blame, find fault with.

Vivo, *ĕre*, *vixi*, *victum*. To live.

Vivus, *a*, *um*. Living, alive.

Vocabŭlum, *i*, n. Désignation, name, word.

Voco, *āre*, *āvi*, *ātum*, (vox). To call, name.

Volo, *āre*, *āvi*, *ātum*. To fly.

Volo, *velle*, *volui*, irreg. To will, be willing, wish, desire; *sibi velle*, to mean. 293; 389, 2.

Volsci, *ōrum*, m. pl. The Volsci or Volscians, a people of Latium, (174).

Volŭcer, *cris*, *cre*, (volo). Flying, winged; swift, rapid; *subs.* a bird.

Volumnia, *ae*, f. Volumnia, the wife of Coriolanus, (174).

Voluntarius, *a*, *um*, (voluntas). Voluntary, willing, spontaneous.

Voluntas, *ātis*, f. (volo). Wish, inclination, good will.

Voluptas, *ātis*, f. Pleasure.

Voveo, *ēre*, *vovi*, *votum*. To vow, dedicate, consecrate.

Vox, *vocis*, f. Voice, word.

Vulgus, *i*, n. Populace, common people.

Vulnĕro, *āre*, *āvi*, *ātum*, (vulnus). To wound.

Vulnus, *ĕris*, n. Wound.

Vulpes, *is*, f. Fox.

Vultus, *us*, m. Countenance.

X

Xanthippus, i, m. Xanthippus, a Spartan commander, who took Regulus prisoner in the first Punic war, (186).

Xerxes, is, m. Xerxes, a celebrated Persian king, (137, 217).

Xenophon, ontis, m. Xenophon, a Greek historian, and the leader of the Greeks in the famous retreat of the ten thousand, (142).

Z

Zama, ae, f. Zama, a town of Numidia, in Africa, famous for the victory of Scipio over Hannibal, (196).

A

PRACTICAL INTRODUCTION

TO

LATIN COMPOSITION.

FOR

SCHOOLS AND COLLEGES.

BY

ALBERT HARKNESS, Ph.D.,

PROFESSOR IN BROWN UNIVERSITY.

AUTHOR OF

"A LATIN GRAMMAR," "AN INTRODUCTORY LATIN BOOK," "A LATIN READER,"
"A FIRST GREEK BOOK," ETC.

PART I.

NEW YORK:

D. APPLETON AND COMPANY,

1, 3, AND 5 BOND STREET.

LONDON: 16 LITTLE BRITAIN.

1881.

CONTENTS.

PART FIRST.

Grammatical Forms and Rules.

Lesson		Page
I.	Declension of Nouns.	1
II.	Adjectives and Pronouns.	3
III., IV.	Verbs.	6
V.	Agreement of Nouns. — Nominative and Vocative.	10
VI., VII.	Use of the Accusative.	11
VIII.	Use of the Dative.	15
IX., X.	Use of the Genitive.	17
XI.—XIV.	Use of the Ablative.	20
XV.	Adjectives. Pronouns.	26
XVI.	Agreement of Verbs. — Indicative.	28
XVII.—XIX.	Tenses and Use of the Subjunctive.	30
XX.	Imperative. Infinitive.	36
XXI.	Gerunds, Supines, Participles. — Particles.	37
XXII., XXIII.	Gender. Formation of Cases.	39
XXIV.—XXVII.	Synopsis of Conjugation. Formation of the Parts of the Verb.	41
XXVIII.—XXX.	Irregular, Defective, and Impersonal Verbs.	46

EXPLANATION OF REFERENCES AND ABBRE-VIATIONS.

ALL reference numerals in the "Lessons from the Grammar," and those marked "G" in other parts of the work, refer to the author's Latin Grammar. The other references are to articles in this work.

The following abbreviations occur: —

abl. . . . . . ablative.	indec. . . . . indeclinable.
abl. abs. . . ablative absolute.	lit. . . . . . literally.
acc. . . . . . accusative.	m. . . . . . masculine.
act. . . . . . active.	n. . . . . . . neuter.
adj. . . . . . adjective.	part. . . . . participle.
adv. . . . . . adverb.	pass. . . . . passive.
comp. . . . . comparative.	plur., or pl. . plural.
conj. . . . . conjunction.	pred. . . . . predicate.
Conj. . . . . conjugation.	prep. . . . . preposition.
dat. . . . . . dative.	pron. . . . . pronoun.
dep. . . . . . deponent.	relat. . . . . relative.
distrib. num. distributive numeral.	sing. . . . . singular.
f. . . . . . . feminine.	subj. . . . . subjunctive.
gen. . . . . . genitive.	subs. . . . . substantive.
ger. . . . . . gerund.	superl. . . . superlative.
impers. . . . impersonal.	trans. . . . . transitive.

(xi)

PART FIRST.

GRAMMATICAL FORMS AND RULES.

LESSON I.

DECLENSION OF NOUNS.
[1-6.] [1]

1. LESSON FROM THE GRAMMAR. [2]

I. First Declension. 48.

II. Second Declension. 51.

III. Third Declension. 55-66.

IV. Fourth Declension. 116.

V. Fifth Declension. 120.

VI. Agreement of Appositives. Rule II. 363.

VII. Genitive with Nouns. Rule XVI. 395.

VIII. Cases with Prepositions. Rule XXXII. 432-435.

---

[1] In Part First the enclosed numerals standing at the beginning of each lesson refer to the sections in the Reader which the lesson is intended to follow. Thus [1-6] shows that this lesson is to be learned after the pupil has read the first six sections in the Reader.

[2] The lessons from the Grammar contain the grammatical points involved in the Exercises, and should be carefully learned, or reviewed, in the Grammar itself. The references are all to the author's Latin Grammar, the Revised Edition.

(1)

2. MODELS.

I. Tigranes the king.	I. *Tigrănes rex.*
II. The love of glory.	II. *Amor gloriae.*
III. Before light.	III. *Ante lucem.*

3. REMARKS.

I. Tigranes the king.

1. TIGRANES. Looking in the vocabulary for the corresponding Latin, we find *Tigrănes*, the same as in English.

2. THE. The English article, *a, an, the,* has no Latin equivalent. It must therefore be omitted in translating into Latin. See Gram. 48, 6.

3. KING. The corresponding Latin is *rex*, which must be in the Nominative, in apposition with *Tigrănes*, according to Rule II.

4. The Appositive generally follows its subject, as in English. Hence

Tigrănes rex.

II. The love of glory.

1. THE LOVE, *amor ;* THE — not translated.

2. OF, sign of the Genitive.

3. GLORY, *gloria.* Of glory, *gloriae ;* Gen. Sing.

4. The Genitive may either precede or follow its noun, but seems more frequently to follow when not emphatic. See Gram. 598. Hence we have

Amor gloriae.

III. Before light.

1. BEFORE, *ante.* No Latin case expresses the relation *before.* Hence a preposition must be used.

2. LIGHT, *lux.* But the preposition *ante* is used only with the Accusative. Hence *lucem,* and not *lux,* must be used. See Gram. 433. Hence

Ante lucem.

4. VOCABULARY.

Art, *ars, artis,* f.	Boy, *puer, puĕri,* m.
Bird, *avis, avis,* f.	Chariot, *currus, us,* m.
Book, *liber, libri,* m.	Cicero, *Cicĕro, ŏnis,* m.

Concerning, *de*, prep. with abl.

Eagle, *aquĭla, ae*, f.

Friend, *amĭcus, i*, m.

Friendship, *amicitia, ae*, f.

Hope, *spes, spei*, f.

Orator, *orātor, ōris*, m.

Prize, *praemĭum, ii*, n.

War, *bellum, i*, n.

Wisdom, *sapientia, ae*, f.

5. EXERCISE.

1. The eagle, the eagles. 2. Of an eagle, of the eagles. 3. For an eagle, for eagles. 4. Of friendship, of wisdom. 5. For friendship, for wisdom. 6. With friendship, with wisdom. 7. The friend, the friends. 8. Of the friend, of the friends. 9. For the friend, for the friends. 10. The books, the prizes. 11. The boy's book.

12. Of the bird, of the birds. 13. For the bird, for the birds. 14. The art of war. 15. The arts of war. 16. With the arts of war. 17. The chariot, of the chariots. 18. Of hope, with hope. 19. Cicero the orator. 20. Concerning Cicero the orator.

LESSON II.

ADJECTIVES AND PRONOUNS.
[7–10.]

6. LESSON FROM THE GRAMMAR.

I. Declension of Adjectives. 146–158.

II. Comparison of Adjectives. 160–162.

III. Agreement of Adjectives. Rule XXXIII. 438.

IV. Declension of Pronouns. 182–191.

V. Agreement of Pronouns. Rule XXXIV. 445; 445, 1.

7. MODELS.

I. The Roman people.	I. *Popŭlus Romānus.*
II. *True* [1] friendships.	II. *Verae amicitiae.*
III. An animal which.	III. *Anĭmal quod.*
IV. This state.	IV. *Haec civĭtas.*

8. REMARKS.

I. The Roman people.

1. In translating a noun and its adjective into Latin, we must begin with the noun, because the gender and case of the noun will determine the ending of the adjective, which must agree with it.

2. THE PEOPLE, *popŭlus ;* THE — not translated.

3. ROMAN, *Romānus, a, um.* But as *popŭlus* is in the Nom. Sing. Masc., the adjective must be in the same case, gender, etc., according to Rule XXXIII. Hence *Romānus.*

4. The adjective may either precede or follow its noun, but seems more frequently to follow when not emphatic. See Gram. 598. Hence

Popŭlus Romānus.

II. True friendships.

1. FRIENDSHIPS. *Friendship* (for which you must look, not *friendships*) is *amicitia ;* FRIENDSHIPS is *amicitiae,* the plural of *amicitia.*

2. TRUE, *verus, a, um.* But as *amicitiae* is in the Nom. Plur. Fem., the adjective must be in the same case, etc.; hence *verae.*

3. In *true* friendships, as opposed to *false* friendships, *true* is emphatic. Hence *verae* must precede its noun. See Gram. 598, 2.

Verae amicitiae.

III. An animal which.

1. AN ANIMAL, *anĭmal ;* AN — not translated.

2. WHICH, *qui, quae, quod.* But as *anĭmal* is in the Neut. Sing., the relative must be in the same gender and number, according to Rule XXXIV.; hence *quod.*

Anĭmal quod.

IV. This state.

1. STATE, *civĭtas.*

2. THIS, *hic, haec, hoc.* But as *civĭtas* is in the Nom. Sing. Fem., the

---

[1] In the Models and Exercises, *italicized* English words are emphatic.

demonstrative which agrees with it as an adjective must be in the same case, etc. See Gram. 445, 1; hence *haec*.

Haec civitas.

9. VOCABULARY.

Acceptable, *gratus, a, um.*	My, *meus, a, um.* G. 185.
Beautiful, *pulcher, chra, chrum.*	Present, *donum, i,* n.
Certain, a certain, *quidam, quae-dam, quoddam* and *quiddam.*	Pupil, *discipulus, i,* m.
	This, *hic, haec, hoc.*
Crown, *corōna, ae,* f.	Thou, you, *tu, tui.*
Diligent, *diligens, entis.*	True, *verus, a, um.*
High, *altus, a, um.*	Useful, *utilis, e.*
Himself, herself, itself, *sui.*	Who, which, what, interrog., *qui,*
I, *ego, mei.*	*quae, quod,* adj.; *quis, quae,*
Kind, *benignus, a, um.*	*quid,* subs.
Law, *lex, legis,* f.	Your, *tuus, a, um; vester, tra,*
Mountain, *mons, montis,* m.	*trum.* G. 185.

10. EXERCISE.

1. A *kind* friend, of a *kind* friend. 2. Kind friends, of kind friends. 3. *True* friendship, of *true* friendships. 4. An acceptable present, with acceptable presents. 5. The beautiful books, the beautiful crowns, the beautiful presents. 6. Useful laws, of the useful laws.

7. A high mountain, a higher mountain, the highest mountain. 8. The most diligent pupils. 9. Of me, of you,[1] of himself, of whom? 10. With my books, with your[1] books. 11. This mountain, this crown, this present. 12. A certain book.

---

[1] In the Exercises the pronoun *you* may be treated as singular, unless it is marked (pl.), or is shown by the sense to be plural. In like manner, *your* may be treated as referring to one person, unless the sense shows that two or more persons are addressed.

LESSON III.

VERBS. — SUM. FIRST AND SECOND CONJUGATIONS.
[11-13.]

11. LESSON FROM THE GRAMMAR.

I. Verb Sum. 204.

II. First Conjugation. 205, 206.

III. Second Conjugation. 207, 208.

IV. Subject Nominative. Rule III. 367.

V. Agreement of Verb with Subject. Rule XXXV. 460.

VI. Predicate Nouns. Rule I. 362.

VII. Direct Object. Rule V. 371.

12. MODELS.

I. God made the world.	I. *Deus mundum aedificāvit.*
II. Cincinnatus was dictator.	II. *Cincinnātus dictātor fuit.*

13. REMARKS.

I. God made the world.

1. GOD, *Deus.* As subject it must be in the Nominative, according to Rule III.

2. MADE. Look for the present *make*, not for *made;* MAKE, BUILD, *aedifĭco* (I make); I MADE, *aedificāvi.* But as *Deus*, the subject, is in the Third Pers. Sing., the verb must be in the same person and number, according to Rule XXXV.; hence *aedificāvit.*

3. WORLD, *mundus.* But as direct object of *aedificāvit*, it must be in the Accus.; hence *mundum.*

4. The order is — Subject, Object, Verb. See Gram. 593.

    Deus mundum aedificāvit.

II. Cincinnatus was dictator.

1. CINCINNATUS, *Cincinnātus*, the same as in English. As subject it must be in the Nominative.

2. WAS. The verb *to be* is *sum*, I am. I WAS, *fui;* but according to Rule XXXV., the verb must agree with its subject, *Cincinnātus;* hence *fuit.*

3. DICTATOR, *dictātor*, the same as in English. As predicate noun, it must agree in case with *Cincinnātus*, according to Rule I., hence in the Nom.

4. The Predicate Noun may either precede or follow the verb. Placing it before the verb, we have

Cincinnātus dictātor fuit.

14. VOCABULARY.

Accuse, *accūso, āre, āvi, ātum.*	Grieve, *doleo, ēre, ui, ītum.*
Advise, *moneo, ēre, ui, ītum.*	Happy, *beātus, a, um.*
Be, *sum, esse, fui.*	Praise, *laudo, āre, āvi, ātum.*
Blame, *vitupēro, āre, āvi, ātum.*	That, *ille, a, ud.*

15. EXERCISE.

1. This law is useful. 2. That law was useful. 3. These laws will be useful. 4. We may be happy. 5. You (pl.)[1] might have been happy. 6. I praise, we praise. 7. He was blaming, they were blaming. 8. I shall praise, we shall praise. 9. He accuses, he is accused. 10. He will accuse, he will be accused.

11. They praised Cicero. 12. We will praise Cicero. 13. Cicero has been praised. 14. I grieve, we grieve. 15. He was grieving, they were grieving. 16. I shall grieve, we shall grieve. 17. He advises, he is advised. 18. He was advising, he was advised. 19. You will advise the boys. 20. The boys have been advised.

---

[1] See foot note page 5.

Lesson IV.

VERBS. — THIRD AND FOURTH CONJUGATIONS. DE-PONENT VERBS. PERIPHRASTIC CONJUGATION.
[14–18.]

16. Lesson from the Grammar.

I. Third Conjugation. 209, 210 ; 213–215.

II. Fourth Conjugation. 211, 212.

III. Deponent Verbs. 225–230.

IV. Periphrastic Conjugation. 231–233.

V. Use of Adverbs. Rule LI. 582.

17. Models.

I. The wise live happily.	I. *Sapientes feliciter vivunt.*
II. Diligence should be culti-vated.	II. *Diligentia colenda est.*

18. Remarks.

I. The wise live happily.

1. The wise. Wise, *sapiens ;* the wise, *sapientes*, Nom. Plur. See Gram. 441, 1.

2. Live. I live, *vivo.* But the verb must agree with the subject, *sapientes ;* hence *vivunt.* Third Pers. Plur.

3. Happily, *feliciter.* But the adverb in Latin generally precedes the verb, though it generally follows it in English. See Gram. 600.

Sapientes feliciter vivunt.

II. Diligence should be cultivated.

1. Diligence, *diligentia.* Nom. Sing.

2. Should be cultivated, is to be cultivated. The duty or neces-

sity denoted by *should be, is to be, ought,* may be expressed by the Second Periphrastic conjugation. See Gram. 232. I cultivate, *colo.* Periphrastic conjugation, *colendus sum.* But the verb must agree with *diligentia* in number and person, and the participle in gender, number, and case. See Gram. 460, 1. Hence we have *colenda est.*

Diligentia colenda est.

19. Vocabulary.

Always, *semper,* adv.	Instruct, *erūdio, īre, īvi, ītum.*
City, *urbs, urbis,* f.	Lead, *duco, ĕre, duxi, ductum.*
Father, *pater, tris,* m.	Our, *noster, tra, trum.*
Follow, *sequor, i, secūtus sum,* dep.	Rule, *rego, ĕre, rexi, rectum.*
Fortify, *munio, īre, īvi, ītum.*	Saguntum, *Saguntum, i,* n.
Hannibal, *Hannĭbal, ălis,* m.	Sleep, *dormio, īre, īvi, ītum.*
His, her, its, their, *suus, a, um.*	Take, *capio, ĕre, cepi, captum.*
Imitate, *imĭtor, āri, ātus sum,* dep.	

20. Exercise.

1. He leads, he is led.   2. He will rule, he will be ruled.   3. They have ruled, they have been ruled.   4. Hannibal took Saguntum.   5. Saguntum was taken.   6. The cities had been taken.   7. He sleeps, they sleep. 8. He will sleep, they will sleep.   9. He may sleep, they may sleep.   10. Your father instructed you.   11. These boys have been instructed.

12. The boy imitates his father.   13. We will imitate our fathers.   14. You have always imitated your father. 15. We will follow you.   16. The boys followed their father.   17. We were about to praise you.   18. Diligent pupils must be praised.   19. They were about to fortify the city.   20. These cities must be fortified.

K

LESSON V.

AGREEMENT OF NOUNS. — NOMINATIVE AND VOCATIVE.
[19–22.]

21. LESSON FROM THE GRAMMAR.

I. Predicate Nouns.   Rule I. 362.
II. Appositives.   Rule II. 363.
III. Subject Nominative.   Rule III. 367.
IV. Case of Address.   Rule IV. 369.

22. MODELS.

I. Hear, citizens.   I. *Audite, cives.*
II. For other models, see under Lessons I. and III.

23. REMARKS.

1. HEAR.   I hear, *audio ;* hear, hear ye, *audite*, Imperative Second Pers. Plur.   The subject *vos*, ye, is omitted.   See Gram. 367, 2.
2. CITIZENS.   Citizen, *civis ;* citizens, *cives*, Voc. Plur.   See Rule IV.
3. The Vocative generally, though not always, stands after one or more words.   See Gram. 602, VI.

24. VOCABULARY.

Brother, *frater, tris*, m.
Brutus, *Brutus, i*, m.
Consul, *consul, ŭlis*, m.
Diligence, *diligentia, ae*, f.
Greatly, *valde*, adv.
Herodotus, *Herodŏtus, i*, m.
History, *historia, ae*, f.

Letter, *epistŏla, ae*, f.
Many, *multi, ae, a*, plur.
Philosopher, *philosŏphus, i*, m.
Save, *servo, āre, āvi, ātum.*
Socrates, *Socrātes, is*, m.
Soldier, *miles, ĭtis*, m.
Write, *scribo, ĕre, scripsi, scriptum.*

25. Exercise.

1. Cicero was an orator. 2. The consul was an orator.
3. Cicero the consul was an orator. 4. Brutus had been
consul. 5. Brutus was consul. 6. Cicero the orator
wrote many letters. 7. The letters of Cicero the orator
have been greatly praised. 8. Socrates was a philosopher.
9. Your brother will be an orator. 10. Herodotus was
the father of history. 11. The orator praises Herodotus
the father of history. 12. Pupils, your diligence will be
praised. 13. Your diligence, boys, must be praised. 14.
The city has been fortified. 15. The city must be saved.

Lesson VI.

USE OF THE ACCUSATIVE.
[23–25.]

26. Lesson from the Grammar.

I. Accusative as Direct Object. Rule V. 371.

II. Two Accusatives — Same Person. Rule VI. 373.

III. Two Accusatives — Person and Thing. Rule VII. 374.

27. Models.

I. They called the council Senate.	I. *Consilium appellavē-runt Senātum.*
II. He asked me my opinion.	II. *Me sententiam rogāvit.*

III. For Model for Direct Object, see under Lesson III.

28. Remarks.

I. They called the council Senate.

1. **They called.** I call, *appello ;* they called, *appellavērunt* (appel-

larunt), Perf. Indic. Third Pers. Plur. The subject is omitted, being implied in the ending *erunt*. See Gram. 367, 2.

2. THE COUNCIL, *consilium*, Accus. See Rule VI.

3. SENATE, *Senatus ;* Accus. *Senatum.* See Rule VI.

4. The verb, whose usual place is at the end of the sentence, may stand between the two Accusatives, as in this Model.

II. He asked me my opinion.

1. HE ASKED. I ask, *rogo ;* he asked, *rogavit*, Perf. Indic. Third Pers. Sing. The subject is omitted. See Gram. 367, 2.

2. ME. I, *ego ;* me, *me*, Accus. See Rule VII.

3. MY OPINION. Opinion, *sententia ;* Accus. *sententiam.* See Rule VII. The possessive *my* in this Model is not expressed in Latin, because it can be readily supplied from the context; *my opinion*, not the opinion of another. See Gram. 447.

29. VOCABULARY.

Ask, *rogo, are, avi, atum.*

Call, *appello, are, avi, atum.*

Catiline, *Catilina, ae,* m.

Delight, *delecto, are, avi, atum.*

Enemy, *hostis, is,* m. and f.

Island, *insula, ae,* f.

Judge, *judico, are, avi, atum.*

Modesty, *verecundia, ae,* f.

Opinion, *sententia, ae,* f.

Preceptor, *praeceptor, oris,* m.

Rome, *Roma, ae,* f.

Sicily, *Sicilia, ae,* f.

Teach, *doceo, ere, docui, doctum.*

Virtue, *virtus, utis,* f.

30. EXERCISE.

1. Your letter delights me. 2. This letter will delight your father. 3. Who wrote that letter? 4. My brother wrote that letter. 5. They call the island Sicily. 6. The island is called Sicily. 7. Sicily is an island. 8. They called Herodotus the father of history. 9. We judge you, O Catiline, an enemy. 10. You, O Catiline, will be judged an enemy. 11. We teach boys modesty. 12. We will teach our pupils wisdom. 13. The preceptor will ask you your opinion. 14. The city was called Rome. 15. Virtue must be praised.

Lesson VII.

ACCUSATIVE — Continued.
[26–29.]

31. Lesson from the Grammar.

I. Accusative of Time and Space.   Rule VIII. 378.

II. Accusative of Limit.   Rule IX. 379.

III. Accusative of Specification.   Rule X. 380.

IV. Accusative in Exclamations.   Rule XI. 381.

V. Interrogative Sentences.   346, II.

32. Models.

I. He lived thirty years.	I. *Triginta annos vixit.*
II. Plato came to Tarentum.	II. *Plato Tarentum venit.*
III. They are not at all moved.	III. *Nihil moventur.*
IV. O *deceptive* hope!	IV. *O fallācem spem!*

33. Remarks.

I. He lived thirty years.

1. He lived. I live, *vivo;* he lived, *vixit.* See Gram. 367, 2.

2. Thirty, *triginta*, indeclinable.

3. Years. Year, *annus;* years, Accus. Plur. *annos.* See Rule VIII.

II. Plato came to Tarentum.

1. Plato, *Plato*, Nom. See Rule III.

2. Came. I come, *venio;* came, he came, *venit.* See Gram. 287.

3. To Tarentum. Tarentum, *Tarentum;* to Tarentum, Accus. *Tarentum.* See Rule IX.

III. They are not at all moved.

1. They are moved. I move, *moveo;* am moved, *moveor;* they are moved, *moventur*, Pres. Indic. Pass. Third Pers. Plur.

2

2. Not at all, *nihil.* See Rule X.

IV. O deceptive hope!

1. O hope. Hope, *spes;* O hope, *O spem.* Rule XI.

2. Deceptive, *fallax;* Acc. Sing. *fallācem.* Rule XXXIII. 438.
It is emphatic, and accordingly precedes its noun. See Gram. 598, 2.

34. Vocabulary.

Athens, *Athēnae, ārum,* f. pl.	Not, *non,* adv.; interrog., *nonne.*
Come, *venio, īre, veni, ventum.*	G. 346, II. 1.
Day, *dies, diēi,* m.	Not at all, *nihil,* indeclinable. G.
Forty-three, *tres (tria) et quadra-*	128.
ginta. G. 174.	Numa, *Numa, ae,* m.
Hour, *hora, ae,* f.	Reign, *regno, āre, āvi, ātum.*
How many, *quot,* indeclinable.	Send, *mitto, ĕre, misi, missum.*
In, *in,* prep. with abl.	Seven, *septem,* indeclinable. G.
Italy, *Italia, ae,* f.	176.
Messenger, *nuntius, ii,* m.	Two, *duo, ae, o.* G. 175.
Month, *mensis, mensis,* m.	Wonderful, *admirabilis, e.*
Move, *moveo, ēre, movi, motum.*	Year, *annus, i,* m.

35. Exercise.

1. How many years did *Numa* reign? 2. Numa reigned forty-three years. 3. Were you (pl.) not two years in *Italy?* 4. We were *in Italy* seven months. 5. The consul came to Rome. 6. He was in that city seven days. 7. Was he not asked his opinion? 8. He was asked his opinion. 9. You, consul, have saved the city. 10. O wonderful virtue! 11. You will not move the consul *at all.* 12. Did you not send a messenger to Athens? 13. I sent two messengers to Athens. 14. How many hours did you sleep? 15. I slept seven hours.

Lesson VIII.

USE OF THE DATIVE.
[30–38.]

36. Lesson from the Grammar.

I. Dative with Verbs. Rule XII. 384.

II. Two Datives — To Which and For Which. Rule XIII. 390.

III. Dative with Adjectives. Rule XIV. 391.

IV. Dative with Derivatives. Rule XV. 392.

37. Models.

I. They serve the king.	I. *Regi serviunt.*
II. It *is* a care to me.	II. *Est mihi curae.*
III. Country is dear to all.	III. *Patria omnĭbus cara est.*
IV. Obedience to laws.	IV. *Obtemperatio legĭbus.*

38. Remarks.

I. They serve the king.

1. They serve, *serviunt.*

2. The king. King, *rex ;* Dat. *regi.* Rule XII.

II. It is a care to me (to me for a care).

1. It is, *est.* It is placed at the beginning of the sentence because it is emphatic. See Gram. 594, I.

2. To me. I, *ego ;* to me, *mihi.* Rule XIII.

3. A care = for a care. Care, *cura ;* for a care, *curae,* Dat. Rule XIII.

III. Country is dear to all.

1. Country, *patria.*

2. Is, *est.*

3. **Dear.** Dear, *carus*; Fem. *cara*, to agree with *patria*.

4. **To all.** All, *omnis*; Dat. Plur. *omnibus.* Rule XIV.

5. Observe the order of the words in the model, though much freedom is allowable in this respect.

IV. Obedience to laws.

1. **Obedience,** *obtemperatio.*

2. **To laws.** Law, *lex*; to laws, *legibus*, Dat. Plur. Rule XV.

39. Vocabulary.

All, *omnis, e.*

Award, *tribuo, ĕre, ui, ūtum.*

Citizen, *civis, civis,* m. and f.

Country, one's country, *patria, ae,* f.

Dear, *carus, a, um.*

Ever = always, *semper,* adv.

General, *imperător, ōris,* m.

Give, *do, dare, dedi, datum.*

Glory, *gloria, ae,* f.

Good, *bonus, a, um.*

Have, *sum, esse, fui,* with dat. G. 387.

Honor, *honor, ōris,* m.

Industry, *industria, ae,* f.

Learning, *doctrina, ae,* f.

Obedience, *obtemperatio, ōnis,* f.

Obey, *pareo, ĕre, ui, ītum.*

Praiseworthy, *laudabĭlis, e.*

Prefer, *praefĕro, ferre, tŭli, lātum.* G. 292, 2.

Roman, *Romānus, a, um.*

Wealth, *divitiae, ārum,* f. pl.

40. Exercise.

1. *Good* citizens will obey the laws. 2. The Romans awarded honors to their generals. 3. Industry is an honor to a pupil. 4. Virtue is a glory to all. 5. I prefer virtue to learning. 6. We prefer learning to wealth. 7. I will give you that book as a present. 8. I have seven beautiful books. 9. Will not this present be acceptable to you? 10. That present will be acceptable to me. 11. Is not the country dear to you? 12. The country has ever been very dear to me. 13. Obedience to the laws is praiseworthy.

Lesson IX.

USE OF THE GENITIVE.
[39, 40.]

41. Lesson from the Grammar.

I. Genitive with Nouns. Rule XVI. 395.
II. Genitive with Adjectives. Rule XVII. 399.

42. Models.

I. The love of truth.	I. *Amor veritātis.*
II. Desirous of truth.	II. *Veritātis cupĭdus.*

43. Vocabulary.

Athenian, *Atheniensis, is,* m. and f.
Celebrated, distinguished, *clarus, a, um.*
Demosthenes, *Demosthĕnes, is,* m.
Desirous of, *cupĭdus, a, um.*
Fond of, *amans, amantis.*
King, *rex, regis,* m.
Love, *amor, ŏris,* m.

Man, *homo, ĭnis; vir,*[1] *viri,* m.
Money, *pecunia, ae,* f.
Often, *saepe,* adv.
Oration, *oratio, ŏnis,* f.
Pleasure, *voluptas, ātis,* f.
Praise, *laus, laudis,* f.
Precept, *praeceptum, i,* n.
Skilled in, *perītus, a, um.*

44. Exercise.

1. The orations of Cicero have often been praised. 2. You have often praised the orations of Cicero the orator.

---

[1] *Homo* is the ordinary term for *man* as a member of the human family; while *vir* is a term of respect, a *hero*, a *man* in the full sense of the word.

3. The orations of Demosthenes, the *celebrated* orator, will always be praised.   4. Boys are fond of pleasure. 5. The pupils are fond of praise.   6. The king was desirous of glory.   7. Men are fond of money.   8. The love of country is an honor to a citizen.   9. The precepts of the *philosophers* were useful to the Athenians.   10. The general is skilled in *war*.

LESSON X.

GENITIVE — CONTINUED.
[41–43.]

45. LESSON FROM THE GRAMMAR.

I. Predicate Genitive.   Rule XVIII. 401.

II. Genitive with certain Verbs.   Rule XIX. 406.

III. Accusative and Genitive.   Rule XX. 410.

46. MODELS.

I. It is of small value.	I. *Parvi pretii est.*
II. He remembers *the past.*	II. *Meminit praeteritōrum.*
III. You accuse men of crime.	III. *Viros scelĕris arguis.*

47. REMARKS.

1. MODEL I. — OF SMALL VALUE, *parvi pretii.* Rule XVIII.

2. MODEL II. — THE PAST = past things, events, *praeteritōrum*, Gen. Plur. Neut. of *praterĭtus*, from *praetereo*. Rule XIX. *Praeteritārum rerum* should not be used for *praeteritōrum*, except to avoid real ambiguity, as it is less euphonious.

Praeteritōrum would regularly precede the verb, but is made emphatic by being placed at the end of the sentence. See Gram. 594, II.

3. Of CRIME, *scelĕris*, Gen. of *scelus*. Rule XX.

48. Vocabulary.

Already, *jam*, adv.

Concerns, it concerns, *refert*, retŭlit, impers.

Esteem, *aestĭmo*, *āre*, *āvi*, *ātum*.

Favor, *beneficium*, *ĭi*, n.

Folly, *stultitia*, *ae*, f.

Forget, *obliviscor*, *i*, *oblĭtus sum*, dep.

Goodness, *bonĭtas*, *ātis*, f.

Grain, *frumentum*, *i*, n.

Great, *magnus*, *a*, *um*.

Greatly, with *intĕrest* and *refert*, *magni*.

High, at a high price, *magno*, or *magni*; with verbs of valuing, *magni*; very highly, *maxĭmi*.

Integrity, *integrĭtas*, *ātis*, f.

Interests, it interests, *intĕrest*, *interfuit*, impers.

Never, *nunquam*, adv.

Pity, *misereor*, *ēri*, *erĭtus sum*, dep.

Poor, *pauper*, *ĕris*.

Remember, *memĭni*, *isse*. G. 297, I.

Repent, I repent, *me paenĭtet*, *paenituit*. G. 299.

Sell, *vendo*, *ĕre*, *dĭdi*, *dĭtum*.

Theft, *furtum*, *i*, n.

Value, price, *pretium*, *ĭi*, n.

49. Exercise.

1. Virtue is a characteristic of a good man. 2. Integrity is of great value. 3. Goodness must be highly esteemed. 4. We esteem goodness very highly. 5. This book will be of great value to us. 6. We pity the poor. 7. I remember your favors. 8. We do not forget our friends. 9. We shall never forget you. 10. They accuse the boy of theft. 11. I have already repented of my folly. 12. He sells grain at a high price. 13. This greatly interests us.

Lesson XI.

USE OF THE ABLATIVE.
[44, 45.]

50. Lesson from the Grammar.

I. Ablative of Cause, Manner, Means.   Rule XXI.   414.

II. Ablative of Price.   Rule XXII.   416.

51. Models.

I. He is led by glory.

II. You purchased the house at a high price.

I. *Gloria ducĭtur.*

II. *Domum magno emis-ti.*

52. Remarks.

1. Model I. — By glory, *gloria*, Abl.   Rule XXI.

2. Model II. — At a high price, *magno*, Abl.   Rule XXII.   The Abl. of the adjective is sometimes thus used, *pretio* being understood.

53. Vocabulary.

By, *a, ab*, prep. with abl. G. 434, 3.

Glory in, *glorior, āri, ātus sum*, dep.

Gold, *aurum, i*, n.

Happiness, success, *felicĭtas, ātis*, f.

Horse, *equus, equi*, m.

Judge, *judex, ĭcis*, m.

Mina, *mina, ae*, f.

Not, with imperatives, *ne*, adv.

One, *unus, a, um*.   G. 175.

Proud, *superbus, a, um*.

Purchase, *emo, ĕre, emi, emptum*.

Rejoice, *gaudeo, ēre, gavīsus sum*. G. 271, 3.

Scipio, *Scipio, ōnis*, m.

Study, *studium, ii*, n.

Talent, *talentum, i*, n.

Thirty, *triginta*, indecl.

Valor, *virtus, ātis*, f.

54. EXERCISE.

1. Socrates has often been praised for (because of) his wisdom. 2. They glory in their wealth. 3. This philosopher glories in his wisdom. 4. The pupils rejoice in their studies. 5. We are delighted with the precepts of the *philosophers*. 6. Wisdom is not purchased with gold. 7. Do not sell happiness for gold. 8. The judge has purchased a horse for one talent. 9. I will sell this horse for thirty minae. 10. He is proud of his wealth. 11. Scipio was proud of his country.

LESSON XII.

ABLATIVE — CONTINUED.
[46–48.]

55. LESSON FROM THE GRAMMAR.

I. Ablative with Comparatives. Rule XXIII. 417.

II. Ablative of Difference. Rule XXIV. 418.

III. Ablative in Special Constructions. Rule XXV. 419.

56. MODELS.

I. Nothing is more lovely than virtue.

I. *Nihil est amabilius virtūte,* or *Nihil est amabilius quam virtus.*

II. He preceded me by two days.

II. *Biduo me antecessit.*

III. We enjoy very many things.

III. *Plurĭmis rebus fruĭmur.*

IV. Safety rests upon truth.

V. I do not need a *remedy*.

VI. They are *worthy* of friendship.

VII. We need your *authority*.

IV. *Salus veritāte nitĭtur.*

V. *Non egeo medicīna.*

VI. *Digni sunt amicitia.*

VII. *Auctoritāte tua nobis opus est.*

57. Remarks.

1. Model I. — Than virtue, *quam virtus* or *virtāte*. Rule XXIII. 417, 1. The Abl. *virtāte* may either follow or precede the comparative, *amabilius*.

2. Model II. — By two days, *biduo*, Abl. of Dif. Rule XXIV.

3. Model III. — Very many, *plurĭmis*, Superl. See G. 160.

4. Things, *rebus*, Abl. Rule XXV. *Rebus* is necessary to avoid ambiguity, because, though *plurĭma* may be used substantively, in the sense of very many things, *plurĭmis* would be ambiguous, as it would not distinguish *things* from *persons*.

5. Models IV. V. VI. — Upon truth, a remedy, of friendship, *veritāte, medicīna, amicitia*, Abls. Rule XXV.

6. *Medicīna* would regularly precede its verb, but is here emphatic. The regular order in Model VI. would be, *Amicitia digni sunt*, but as *digni* is emphatic, it is placed at the beginning of the sentence. See G. 594, I.

7. Model VII. — We need = there is need to us, *nobis opus est*. See G. 419, 3. Authority, *auctoritāte*, Abl. Rule XXV. *Auctoritāte* is emphatic, and is accordingly placed at the beginning of the sentence.

58. Vocabulary.

Abound in, *abundo, āre, āvi, ātum.*

Cato, *Cato, ōnis*, m.

Discharge, fulfil, *fungor, i, functus sum*, dep.

Duty, *officium, ii*, n.

Enjoy, *fruor, i, fructus* or *fruĭtus sum*, dep.

Five, *quinque*, indecl.

Learned, *doctus, a, um.*	Relying upon, *fretus, a, um.*
Much, with comparatives, *multo,* adv.	Trust in, *confido, ĕre, fisus sum.*
	Use, *utor, uti, usus sum*, dep.
Need, there is need, *opus est, fuit.*	Wisely, *sapienter*, adv.
Older, *major, ōris,* or *major natu.*	Worthy, *dignus, a, um.*

59. Exercise.

1. Cicero was more learned than Cato. 2. You are more diligent than your brother. 3. Virtue is better than wisdom. 4. Wisdom is better than gold. 5. Wisdom is dearer to us than gold. 6. You are five years older than I. 7. Your father uses his wealth wisely. 8. We enjoy our studies. 9. We will discharge our duties. 10. This city abounds in wealth. 11. We do not trust in wealth. 12. Your pupils are worthy of praise. 13. I rely (am relying) upon your friendship. 14. *We* need friends.

Lesson XIII.

ABLATIVE — Continued.
[49-51.]

60. Lesson from the Grammar.

I. Ablative of Place. Rule XXVI. 421.

II. Ablative of Source and Separation. Rule XXVII. 425.

III. Ablative of Time. Rule XXVIII. 426, 427.

61. Models.

I. In the forum.	I. *In foro.*
II. He was at Rome.	II. *Romae fuit.*
III. I ward off slaughter from you.	III. *Caedem a vobis depello.*

IV. He died in his *eightieth* year.	IV. *Octogesimo anno est mortuus.*

62. Remarks.

1. Model II. — At Rome, *Romae;* why *Romae*, rather than *Roma?* See G. 421, II.

2. Model IV. — In —year, *anno.* Rule XXVIII. Why not *in anno?* See G. 426, 2. *Octogesimo* is emphatic, and accordingly precedes its noun. See G. 598, 2.

63. Vocabulary.

Ago, *abhinc*, adv.	Receive, *accipio, ěre, cěpi, ceptum.*
Corinth, *Corinthus, i,* f.	Reside, *habito, ăre, ăvi, ătum.*
Danger, *periculum, i,* n.	See, *video, ěre, vidi, visum.*
Flee, *fugio, ěre, fugi, fugitum.*	Sunset, *solis occăsus, us,* m.
Free from, *libero, ăre, ăvi, ătum.*	Temple, *templum, i,* n.
From, *a, ab,* prep. with abl.	Three, *tres, tria.*
Garden, *hortus, i,* m.	Time, *tempus, ŏris,* n.
Greece, *Graecia, ae,* f.	Where, *ubi,* adv.
Keep from, keep off, *arceo, ěre, cui, ctum.*	Whole, *totus, a, um.*　G. 151.
	Winter, *hiems, ěmis,* f.

64. Exercise.

1. There were beautiful cities *in Greece.*　2. Were you in Corinth?　3. We were in *Corinth* the whole winter.　4. In *Athens* we saw beautiful temples.　5. Does not your friend reside at Rome?　6. He resides in Athens.　7. He fled from Rome to Athens.　8. I have received two letters *from your father.*　9. The city has been freed from great dangers.　10. Where were you at *sunset?*　11. I was in the garden *at that time.*　12. I was in Rome three years ago.　13. We will keep the enemy from the city.

Lesson XIV.

ABLATIVE — Continued.
[52–55.]

65. Lesson from the Grammar.

I. Ablative of Characteristic. Rule XXIX. 428.

II. Ablative of Specification. Rule XXX. 429.

III. Ablative Absolute. Rule XXXI. 430, 431.

IV. Cases with Prepositions. Rule XXXII. 432–435.

66. Models.

I. Piso, a man of the *highest* virtue.	I. *Piso, vir summa virtute.*
II. Piso was a man of the *highest* virtue.	II. *Piso summa virtute fuit.*
III. They are similar in character.	III. *Moribus similes sunt.*
IV. They flourished in the reign of Servius.	IV. *Servio regnante viguērunt.*
V. I have written to a friend.	V. *Ad amicum scripsi.*

67. Remarks.

1. Model I. — A man of the highest virtue, *vir summa virtute;* but in the predicate, as in the second model, Piso was a man, etc., *vir* is omitted. See G. 428. 1, 2). As *summa* is emphatic, it is placed before its noun. See G. 598. 2.

2. Model III. — In character. Character, manners, *mores;* in character, *moribus;* Abl. of Specification. Rule XXX.

8. Model IV. — In the reign of Servius = Servius reigning, *Servio regnante;* Abl. Absol. Rule XXXI.

68. Vocabulary.

Ancus, *Ancus*, i, m.

Before, *ante*, prep. with acc.

Conspiracy, *conjuratio, ōnis*, f.

Courage, *virtus, ûtis*, f.

Eloquence, *eloquentia, ae*, f.

Form, make, *facio, ĕre, feci, factum.*

Greek, *Graecus, i*, m.

Light, *lux, lucis*, f.

Marcius, *Marcius, ii*, m.

Remarkable, *singulāris, e.*

Spain, *Hispania, ae*, f.

Surpass, *supĕro, āre, āvi, ātum*.

Tarquin, *Tarquinius, ii*, m.

To, *ad*, prep. with acc.

69. Exercise.

1. The general, a man of *remarkable* courage, will save the city. 2. The general is a man of remarkable courage. 3. Cicero, a man of remarkable eloquence, was consul. 4. The Greeks surpassed the Romans in learning. 5. The Romans surpassed the Greeks in valor. 6. Tarquin came to Rome in the reign of Ancus Marcius. 7. A conspiracy was formed in Rome when Cicero was consul. 8. Scipio was in Spain. 9. Tarquin came into Italy. 10. The boy came to me *before light.*

Lesson XV.

ADJECTIVES. PRONOUNS.
[56–62.]

70. Lesson from the Grammar.

I. Agreement of Adjectives. Rule **XXXIII.** 438, 439.

II. Agreement of Pronouns. Rule **XXXIV.** 445.

    Personal and Possessive Pronouns. 446–449.

    Demonstrative Pronouns. 450–452.

Relative Pronouns. 453.

Interrogative Pronouns. 454.

Indefinite Pronouns. 455–459.

71. MODELS.

I.	Fortune is blind.	I.	*Fortūna caeca est.*
II.	I who encourage you.	II.	*Ego qui te confirmo.*
III.	Wash your hands.	III.	*Manus lava.*
IV.	He loves himself.	IV.	*Se diligit.*
V.	The guardian of this city.	V.	*Custos hujus urbis.*
VI.	Who am I?	VI.	*Quis ego sum?*
VII.	A certain rhetorician.	VII.	*Quidam rhetor.*

72. REMARKS.

1. MODEL I. — BLIND, *caeca*, Fem. Sing. Nom. to agree with *fortūna.* Rule XXXIII.

2. MODEL II. — ENCOURAGE, *confirmo*, First Pers. to agree with *qui*, which is of the First Pers. to agree with the antecedent *ego.* Rule XXXIV.

3. MODEL III. — YOUR HANDS, *manus.* The possessive, *tuas*, your, is omitted. See G. 447.

4. MODEL V. — OF THIS CITY. This city, *haec urbs;* of this city, *hujus urbis.*

5. MODEL VI. — WHO, *quis!* Why not *qui!* See G. 454.

73. VOCABULARY.

Have, *habeo, ĕre, ui, ĭtum.*

Instructor, *praeceptor, ōris,* m.

Make, *facio, ĕre, feci, factum.*

Modest, *modestus, a, um.*

Peace, *pax, pacis,* f.

Some one, a certain one, *quidam, quaedam, quiddam* or *quoddam.* G. 191.

Yesterday, *heri*, adv.

74. EXERCISE.

1. Peace will be acceptable to us.   2. The city will be beautiful.   3. I have seen *beautiful* cities.   4. The pupils are diligent.   5. Your friendship delights me.   6. Your instructor praises you.   7. Which book have you?   8. I have *your* book.   9. *True* wisdom makes men modest.   10. This precept will be useful to me.   11. The precepts of your instructor will be useful to you.   12. Some boys praise themselves.   13. The letter which you wrote yesterday will delight your father.

LESSON XVI.

AGREEMENT OF VERBS. — INDICATIVE.
[63–67.]

75. LESSON FROM THE GRAMMAR.

I. Agreement of Verb with Subject.   Rule **XXXV**. 460–463.

II. Use of Indicative.   Rule **XXXVI**. 474.

   Present. 466, 467.

   Imperfect. 468, 469.

   Future and Future Perfect. 470, 473.

   Perfect and Pluperfect. 471, 472.

76. MODELS.

I. Cato praised this law.

I. *Cato hanc legem lau davit.*

II. Cicero and I are well.

    II. *Ego et Cicĕro valēmus.*

III. I will write to you.

    III. *Scribam ad te.*

77. REMARKS.

1. MODEL I. — PRAISED, *laudāvit*, Historical Perfect (G. 471, II.), Third Pers. Sing. to agree with *Cato*. Rule XXXV.

2. MODEL II. — CICERO AND I, *ego et Cicĕro*. In Latin the First Pers. stands before the Second.

3. ARE WELL, *valēmus*, First Pers. Plur. to agree with *ego et Cicĕro*. See G. 463, 1.

4. MODEL III. — I WILL WRITE, *scribam*, Fut. Why not *ego scribam?* See G. 367, 2; 446.

5. TO YOU, *ad te*. This may stand either before or after the verb, though the modifiers of verbs more frequently stand before them. See G. 600.

78. VOCABULARY.

At, *ad*, or *apud*, prep. with accus.

Conquer, *vinco, ĕre, vici, victum.*

For his (her, its) own sake, *propter sese* (*se*).

Love, *amo, āre, āvi, ātum.*

Macedonia, *Macedonia, ae*, f.

Perseus, *Perseus, i*, m.

Pydna, *Pydna, ae*, f.

Servius, *Servius, ii*, m.

Ten, *decem*, indecl.

To-morrow, *cras*, adv.

Tried, *spectātus, a, um.*

Wise, *sapiens, entis.*

79. EXERCISE.

1. By whom was *Saguntum* taken? 2. This city was taken by Hannibal. 3. How many books have you? 4. *I* have ten good books. 5. Cato was a man of *tried* virtue. 6. We rejoice in your happiness. 7. Who was reigning at that time? 8. King Servius was reigning at Rome. 9. Will you not write to me? 10. I will write

to you to-morrow. 11. Virtue must be loved for its own sake. 12. Socrates was judged the wisest of men. 13. Herodotus has been called the father of history. 14. Perseus, the king of Macedonia, was conquered at Pydna.

Lesson XVII.

TENSES AND USE OF THE SUBJUNCTIVE.
[68–74.]

80. Lesson from the Grammar.

I. Sequence of Tenses. Rule XXXVII. 480, 481.

II. Potential Subjunctive. Rule XXXVIII. 485, 486.

III. Subjunctive of Desire. Rule XXXIX. 487, 488.

IV. Subjunctive of Purpose or Result. Rule XL. 489–492; 494; 497–500.

81. Models.

I. Perhaps you may inquire.	I. *Forsĭtan quaerātis.*
II. Who doubts?	II. *Quis dubĭtet?*
III. Let us *love* our country.	III. *Amēmus patrĭam.*
IV. He strives that he may conquer.	IV. *Enitĭtur ut vincat.*
V. I allowed *no day* to pass without giving something.	V. *Nullum intermīsi diem quin alĭquid darem.*

82. Remarks.

1. Model I. — You may inquire, *quaerātis*, Subj. Rule XXXVIII. Subject *vos*, omitted. See G. 367, 2.

2. MODEL II. — WHO DOUBTS, or would doubt? = no one doubts, *quis dubltet !* question of appeal, Subj. See G. 486, II.

3. MODEL III. — LET US LOVE, *amēmus*, Subj. of Desire. Rule **XXXIX.** The verb is made emphatic by standing at the beginning of the sentence. See G. 594, I.

4. OUR COUNTRY, *patriam*, possessive omitted. See G. 447.

5. MODEL IV. — THAT HE MAY CONQUER, *ut vincat*, Subj. of Purpose. Rule **XL.** Present tense, because it depends upon a Principal tense, *enilltur.* Rule **XXXVII.**

6. MODEL V. — I ALLOWED — TO PASS, *intermlst.*

7. WITHOUT GIVING SOMETHING = but that I gave something, *quin allquid darem. Darem*, Subj. with *quin*, Imperfect tense, dependent upon *intermlst.* See G. 498, 3; 481, II. 1.

8. *Nullum — diem* are made emphatic by separation. See G. 594, III.

83. VOCABULARY.

Doubt, *dublto, āre, āvi, ātum.*
So, *tam ; ita*, adv.

That, expressing purpose or result, *ut*, conj.
That = but that, *quin*, conj.

84. EXERCISE.

1. He praises you (pl.) that he may be praised by you.
2. He praised you (pl.) that he might be praised by you.
3. They will praise us that they may be praised by us. 4. I do not doubt that you (pl.) have been diligent. 5. We did not doubt that you (pl.) had been diligent. 6. The judge may be accused of folly. 7. Let us obey the laws. 8. May our pupils love virtue. 9. May they be diligent. 10. The pupils are so diligent that they are praised by their preceptor. 11. Let us praise virtue. 12. Let virtue be praised.

Lesson XVIII.

SUBJUNCTIVE — Continued.
[75–82.]

85. Lesson from the Grammar.

I. Subjunctive of Condition. Rule XLI. 503–513.

II. Subjunctive of Concession. Rule XLII. 515, 516.

III. Subjunctive of Cause. Rule XLIII. 517–520.

IV. Subjunctive of Time with Cause. Rule XLIV. 521–523.

86. Models.

I. If this is a state, I am a citizen.

II. The day would fail me, if I should recount.

III. Wisdom would not be sought, if it accomplished nothing.

IV. Though he may deride.

V. Since life is full of fear.

VI. You are waiting till he speaks.

I. *Si haec civitas est, civis sum ego.*

II. *Dies deficiat, si numĕrem.*

III. *Sapientia non expeterētur, si nihil efficĕret.*

IV. *Licet irrideat.*

V. *Quum vita metus plena sit.*

VI. *Exspectas dum dicat.*

87. Remarks.

1. Model I. — In *civis sum ego*, regularly *ego sum civis*, or *ego civis sum*, *civis* is emphatic, and is accordingly placed at the beginning of the clause. See G. 594, I.

2. Model II. — Would fail, should recount, *deficiat, numĕrem*, Subj. Rule XLI. 509.

3. MODEL III. — WOULD BE SOUGHT, ACCOMPLISHED, *expeterĕtur*, *efficĕret*, Subj. Rule XLI. 510, Imperfect, 510, 1.

4. MODEL IV. — MAY DERIDE, *irrideat*, Subj. of Concession. Rule XLII.

5. MODEL V. — SINCE — IS, *quum — sit*, Subj. of Cause. Rule XLIII.

6. MODEL VI. — TILL HE SPEAKS, that he may speak; *dum dicat*, Subj. of Cause and Time. Rule XLIV.

88. VOCABULARY.

Although, *quamquam ; licet, etsi,* conj.	Read, *lego, ĕre, legi, lectum.*
Because, *quod,* conj.	Until, *dum, donec,* conj.
However, *quamvis,* adv.	Wait, *exspecto, āre, āvi, ātum.*
If, *si,* conj.	When, *quum,* conj.
Just, *justus, a, um.*	Yet, *tamen,* adv.

89. EXERCISE.

1. If they are good, they are happy. 2. If you will be diligent, you will be praised. 3. If you would be diligent, you would be praised. 4. If you (pl.) were diligent, you would be praised. 5. If they had been good, they would have been happy. 6. Although the judge is just, he is yet often blamed. 7. However just he may be, he will often be blamed. 8. You will be praised, because you are diligent. 9. The citizens will praise the judge, because (on the ground that) he is just. 10. We will wait until you read the letter (i. e. that you may read it). 11. We saw beautiful temples, when we were in Rome.

L

LESSON XIX.

SUBJUNCTIVE — CONTINUED.
[83–85.]

90. LESSON FROM THE GRAMMAR.

I. Subjunctive in Indirect Questions.   Rule XLV. 525.

II. Subjunctive by Attraction.   Rule XLVI. 527.

III. Subjunctive in Indirect Discourse.   Rule XLVII. 529.

91. MODELS.

I. What a day may bring forth is uncertain.

I. *Quid dies ferat, in certum est.*

II. I fear I shall increase the *labor,* while I wish to diminish it.

II. *Vereor ne, dum minuĕre velim labōrem, augeam.*

III. He boasted that he had made the *ring* which he wore.

III. *Gloriātus est, annŭlum quem habēret se confecisse.*

92. REMARKS.

1. MODEL I. — MAY BRING FORTH, *ferat,* Subj.   Rule XLV.

2. UNCERTAIN, *incertum,* Nom. Sing. Neut., to agree with the clause *quid — ferat.*   See G. 438, 3; 42, III.

3. MODEL II. — I SHALL INCREASE = lest I may increase, *ne augeam,* Subj.   See G. 492, 4.

4. WHILE I WISH, *dum velim.   Velim* is attracted into the Subjunctive by the Subjunctive *augeam.*   Rule XLVI.

5. In the arrangement of words and clauses in Model II., observe (1) that the clause *dum — labōrem* is inserted in the clause *ne — augeam* (G. 604, I.), and (2) that the object *labōrem* is expressed in the in-

serted clause, *dum — labōrem*, but omitted after *augeam*. A literal rendering of the Latin would be, *I fear lest, while I wish to diminish the labor, I may increase* (*it*). Emphasis places *labōrem* at the end of the clause. See G. 594, II.

6. MODEL III. — THAT HE HAD MADE, *se confecisse*, Infinitive with Subject Accusative, depending upon *gloriātus est*. See G. 550. *Se*, not *eum*, must be used, according to G. 449, I.

7. WHICH HE WORE, had, *quem habēret*. *Habēret*, Subj., because in Indirect Discourse. Rule XLVII. The Imperfect is used, because it depends upon an Historical tense, *gloriātus est*, and denotes Incomplete action. See G. 481, II. 1. In the language of the one who made the boast, the Indicative would be used, *quem habeo*.

8. The object *annŭlum* would regularly follow the subject *se*, but is here placed at the beginning of the clause because it is emphatic.

93. VOCABULARY.

Ask (a question), *interrŏgo, āre, āvi, ātum*.	Please, *placeo, ēre, ui, ĭtum*, dat. G. 385.
Do, *facio, ēre, feci, factum*.	Say, *dico, ēre, dixi, dictum*.
Know, *scio, ire, ivi, itum*.	Whether, *num*, adv. G. 526, I.
Not to know, *nescio, ire, ivi, ĭtum*.	Who, which (relative), *qui, quae, quod*.

94. EXERCISE.

1. What did your father say? 2. I do not know what he said. 3. He asks what I have done. 4. He asked what I had done. 5. They ask what I am doing. 6. They asked what I was doing. 7. He asked me to read the letter which he had received. 8. The preceptor praises the pupils, because they are diligent. 9. He says that he praises the pupils, because they are diligent. 10. Did not that letter please your father? 11. I asked whether that letter pleased your father.

LESSON XX.

IMPERATIVE. INFINITIVE.
[86-91.]

95. LESSON FROM THE GRAMMAR.

I. Imperative. Rule XLVIII. 535.

II. Subject of Infinitive. Rule XLIX. 545.

III. Infinitive as Subject. 549.

IV. Infinitive as Object. 550.

96. MODELS.

I. Practise justice.

II. That a *citizen should be bound,* is a crime.

III. I find that Plato came to Tarentum.

I. *Justitiam cole.*

II. *Facīnus est vincīri ci. vem.*

III. *Platōnem Tarentum venisse reperio.*

97. REMARKS.

1. MODEL II. — THAT A CITIZEN SHOULD BE BOUND, *vincīri civem,* or *civem vincīri.* The latter is the common order, but in the former *vincīri* and *civem* are made emphatic. *Vincīri civem* is the subject of *est* (G. 549), and *civem* is the subject of *vincīri.* Rule XLIX.

2. MODEL III. — THAT PLATO CAME TO TARENTUM, *Platōnem Tarentum venisse,* object of the active verb, *reperio.* See G. 550.

3. TO TARENTUM, *Tarentum.* Rule IX.

98. VOCABULARY.

Ancient, *antīquus, a, um.*

Break, offend against, *viŏlo, āre, āvi, ātum.*

Guard, *custōdio, īre, īvi, ītum.*

Parent, *parens, entis,* m. and f.

People = nation, *popŭlus, i,* m.

Practise, *colo, ēre, colui, cultum.* | See that, take care that, *curo, āre,*
Safe, *salvus, a, um.* | *āvi, ātum.*

99. EXERCISE.

1. Boys, obey the laws, love your parents, imitate the good. 2. Soldiers, see that you guard the city. 3. Remember the ancient valor of the Roman people. 4. It is the part of a *good* citizen to obey the laws. 5. It is the part of a wise man to practise virtue. 6. Ancus was reigning. 7. They say that Ancus was reigning. 8. We know that the city is safe. 9. Do not break the laws. 10. Imitate your father. 11. They say that the city has been taken. 12. It is true that *good* laws are useful.

LESSON XXI.

GERUNDS, SUPINES, PARTICIPLES. — PARTICLES.
[92–99.]

100. LESSON FROM THE GRAMMAR.

   I. Gerunds and Gerundives.   559–566.
  II. Supines.   567–570.
 III. Supine in *um.*   Rule L. 569.
  IV. Participles.   571–581.
   V. Use of Adverbs.   Rule LI. 582–585.
  VI. Use of Conjunctions.   587, 588.

101. MODELS.

   I. The art of living.   I. *Ars vivendi.*
  II. We are inclined to learn.   II. *Ad discendum propensi sumus.*

3

III. For cultivating the fields.	III. *Ad colendos agros.*
IV. By reading the orators.	IV. *Legendis oratorĭbus.*
V. He has come to congratulate you.	V. *Venit tibi gratulātum.*
VI. Plato died while writing.	VI. *Plato scribens mortuus est.*
VII. Laelius was living happily.	VII. *Laelius beāte vivēbat.*
VIII. You and Tullia are well.	VIII. *Tu et Tullia valētis.*

102. Remarks.

1. Model I. — Of living, *vivendi*, Gen. of Gerund, depending upon *ars.* Rule XVI.

2. Model III. — For cultivating the fields, *ad colendos agros ; colendos*, Gerundive agreeing with *agros*. See G. 562. *Ad colendum agros* should not be used. See G. 562, 3 ; 565, 2.

3. Model IV. — *Legendis* is Gerundive, agreeing with *oratorĭbus. Legendo oratōres* may also be used.

4. Model V. — To congratulate, *gratulātum*, Sup. Rule L.

5. Model VI. — While writing, *scribens*, Participle, G. 578, I.

6. Model VIII. — Are well, *valētis*, Second Pers. Plur., G. 463, 1.

103. Vocabulary.

Act, *ago, ĕre, egi, actum.*

Agreeable, *jucundus, a, um.*

Ambassador, *legātus, i*, m.

And, *et ; atque ; que*, enclitic. G. 587, I. 2.

Ask for, seek, *peto, ĕre, petīvi, petītum.*

Either — or, *aut — aut*, conj.

Happily, *beāte*, adv.

Hear, *audio, īre, īvi, ītum.*

Inclined, *propensus, a, um.*

Learn, *disco, ĕre, didĭci.*

Live, *vivo, ĕre, vixi, victum.*

Neither — nor, *neque — neque ; nec — nec.*

Play, *ludo, ĕre, lusi, lusum.*

Terrify, *terreo, ĕre, ui, ĭtum.*

104. Exercise.

1. We are desirous of living happily. 2. The art of reading will be useful to us. 3. Are you (pl.) not desirous of learning wisdom? 4. We are desirous of learning wisdom. 5. Boys are inclined to play. 6. Men are inclined to act. 7. We learn by teaching. 8. They will send ambassadors to ask for *peace*. 9. This is agreeable *to hear*. 10. The soldiers, being terrified, fled. 11. Let us imitate the good and wise. 12. He is either in Rome or in Athens. 13. They were neither in Rome nor in Athens.

Lesson XXII.

GENDER. FORMATION OF CASES.
[100–111.]

105. Lesson from the Grammar.

I. Gender. 48, 51, 99–116, 120.

II. Formation of Cases. 62–65 ; 69–98.

106. Models.

I. He yields to the time.	I. *Tempŏri cedit.*
II. In winter and summer.	II. *Hiĕme et aestāte.*
III. *Cato's* orations.	III. *Catōnis oratiōnes.*

107. Remarks.

1. Model I. — To the time, *tempŏri*, Dat. Rule XII.

2. Model II. — In winter, *hiĕme*, Abl. Rule XXVIII.

3. Model III. — Cato's, *Catōnis*, Gen. Rule XVI. The Genitive

more commonly follows its noun, but may precede, especially when emphatic. G. 598, 2.

4. Give the Gender of all the nouns in the Models.

108. Vocabulary.

Battle, *proelium, ii,* n.

Brave, *fortis, e.*

Demand, *postŭlo, ăre, ăvi, ătum.*

Despair of, *despero, ăre, ăvi, ătum,* with acc., or *de* with abl.

From, *a* or *ab; e* or *ex.*

Incite, *incĭto, ăre, ăvi, ătum.*

Incursion, *incursio, ōnis,* f.

Reward, *merces, ĕdis,* f.

Safe, secure, *tutus, a, um.*

Safety, *salus, ūtis,* f.

Small, *parvus, a, um.*

Timid, *timĭdus, a, um.*

Trumpeter, *tubĭcen, ĭnis,* m.

109. Exercise.

1. The trumpeter incites the brave soldiers to battle. 2. The brave soldiers are incited to battle by the trumpeter. 3. The citizens have despaired of safety. 4. Let us not despair *of safety.* 5. *Timid* men often despair of safety. 6. *Brave* soldiers will never despair of their country. 7. The citizens are safe from the incursions of the enemy. 8. Let us not be timid in danger. 9. A reward must be demanded. 10. We will demand a small reward.

Lesson XXIII.

GENDER AND FORMATION OF CASES — Continued.
[112–147.]

110. Vocabulary.

Admonish, *admŏneo, ēre, ui, ĭtum.*

Another, *alius, a, ud; alter, altĕ-*

ra, altĕrum. G. 151.

Bravely, *fortĭter,* adv.

Common, *commŭnis, e.*

Content, *contentus, a, um.*

Easy, *facĭlis, e.*

Ennius, *Ennius, ii, m.*

Fight, *pugno, āre, āvi, ātum.*

Herald, *praeco, ōnis, m.*

Hope, *spes, spei, f.*

Liberate, *libĕro, āre, āvi, ātum.*

Name, *nomen, ĭnis, n.*

Not yet, *nondum,* adv.

Poem, *poēma, ătis, n.*

Proclaim, *proclāmo, āre, āvi, ātum.*

Rule, *dominatio, ōnis, f.*

Son, *filius, ii, m.* G. 52.

Tyrant, *tyrannus, i, m.*

Victor, *victor, ōris, m.*

Xenophon, *Xenŏphon, ontis, m.*

111. Exercise.

1. Hope is common to all men. 2. It is easy to admonish another. 3. The *brave* soldiers fought most bravely. 4. The son of Xenophon fought bravely. 5. Xenophon heard that his son had fought bravely. 6. Herald, proclaim the name of the *victor.* 7. The names of the *victors* will be proclaimed by the heralds. 8. Have you not read the poems of Ennius? 9. I have not yet read them. 10. They liberated the city from the rule of the *tyrants.* 11. Let us be content with our books.

Lesson XXIV.

SYNOPSIS OF CONJUGATION. FORMATION OF THE PARTS OF THE VERB.
[148–168.]

112. Lesson from the Grammar.

I. Synopsis of Conjugation. 216–230.

II. Formation of the Parts of the Verb. 213–215; 241–258.

113. MODELS.

I. I will write to you what I think.	I. *Ad te scribam quid sentiam.*
II. He *will conquer* his disposition and command himself.	II. *Vincet anĭmum sibīque imperābit.*

114. REMARKS.

1. MODEL I. — I THINK, *sentiam*, Subj. in Indirect Question. See G. 525.

2. MODEL II. — HIS. The possessive should here be omitted in Latin. See G. 447.

3. Give the Principal Parts and the Synopsis of the Verbs in the Models.

115. VOCABULARY.

Alba Longa, *Alba Longa, Albae Longae*, f.

Ascanius, *Ascanius, ii*, m.

Citadel, *arx, arcis*, f.

Early, ancient, *antiquus, a, um*.

Enlarge, *amplio, āre, āvi, ātum*.

Found, *condo, ĕre, dĭdi, dĭtum*.

Priscus, *Priscus, i*, m.

Romulus, *Romŭlus, i*, m.

Saturnia, *Saturnia, ae*, f.

Succeed, *succēdo, ĕre, cessi, cessum*, dat. G. 386.

Tullius, *Tullius, ii*, m.

116. EXERCISE.

1. The citadel was called Saturnia. 2. Did not Ascanius found a city in Italy? 3. He founded a city in *very early* times. 4. He is said to have founded a city in very early times. 5. They say that he founded a city. 6. The city was called Alba Longa. 7. Who founded Rome? 8. Romulus founded Rome. 9. Who enlarged

the city? 10. King Ancus enlarged the city. 11. Whom did *Servius Tullius* succeed? 12. King Servius succeeded Tarquinius Priscus.

Lesson XXV.

FORMATION OF THE PARTS OF VERBS — Continued.
[169–184.]

117. Vocabulary.

Against, *contra*, *in*, prep. with acc.

Camillus, *Camillus*, *i*, m.

Conspire, *conjūro*, *āre*, *āvi*, *ātum*.

Fable, *fabŭla*, *ae*, f.

Field, *ager*, *agri*, m.

Fire, *ignis*, *ignis*, m.

Lay waste, *vasto*, *āre*, *āvi, ātum*.

Porsena, *Porsēna*, *ae*, m.

Relate, *narro*, *āre*, *āvi*, *ātum*.

Sword, *ferrum*, *i*, n., lit. *iron;* with fire and sword, *ferro ignēque*.

With, *cum*, prep. with abl.

Youth, *juvĕnis*, *is*, m. and f.

118. Exercise.

1. What ought to be done? 2. I will ask my father what ought to be done. 3. Ask your father what ought to be done. 4. Who conquered the enemy? 5. Camillus is said to have conquered the enemy. 6. They were conquered in a great battle. 7. The youths conspired against king Porsena. 8. Will you (pl.) not make peace with the enemy? 9. We are making peace with the enemy. 10. I will relate to you this fable. 11. The enemy will lay waste the fields with fire and sword.

LESSON XXVI.

FORMATION OF THE PARTS OF VERBS — CONTINUED.
[185–200.]

119. VOCABULARY.

Be subject to, obey, *pareo, ĕre, ui, ĭtum,* dat.

Cannae, *Cannae, ārum,* f. pl.

Carthaginian, *Poenus, i,* m.; *Carthaginiensis, is,* m. and f.

Fight, battle, *pugna, ae,* f.

Formerly, *quondam,* adv.

Friendly, *amĭcus, a, um.*

In vain, *frustra,* adv.

Naval, *navālis, e;* naval battle,

naval engagement, *pugna navālis.*

New Carthage, *Carthăgo Nova, Carthagĭnis Novae,* f.

Once, *semel,* adv.

Publius, *Publius, ii,* m.

State, *civĭtas, ātis,* f.

Try, *tento, āre, āvi, ātum.*

Victory, *victoria, ae,* f.

Village, *vicus, i,* m.

120. EXERCISE.

1. Who took New Carthage? 2. Publius Scipio is said to have taken that city. 3. Peace will be tried in vain. 4. We will try peace once. 5. They called the village Cannae. 6. Many states of Italy were formerly subject to the Romans. 7. Saguntum was friendly to the Romans. 8. The Romans conquered the Carthaginians in (by) a naval battle. 9. This victory was most acceptable to the soldiers. 10. Victory is always acceptable to soldiers.

Lesson XXVII.

FORMATION OF THE PARTS OF VERBS—Continued.
[201-214.]

121. Vocabulary.

Among, *inter*, prep. with acc.	Egypt, *Aegyptus, i,* f.
Booty, *praeda, ae,* f.	Find, *invĕnio, ĭre, vēni, ventum.*
Caesar, *Caesar, ăris,* m.	Golden, *aureus, a, um.*
Capua, *Capua, ae,* f.	Mithridates, *Mithridātes, is,* m.
Cleopatra, *Cleopătra, ae,* f.	Nile, *Nilus, i,* m.
Coat of mail, *lorĭca, ae,* f.	Ptolemy, *Ptolemaeus, i,* m.
Come to the relief of, *subvĕnio,*	Queen, *regĭna, ae,* f.
ĭre, vēni, ventum.	School, *ludus, i,* m.
Divide, *divĭdo, ĕre, vīsi, vīsum.*	Sulla, *Sulla, ae,* m.

122. Exercise.

1. Will you not come to the relief of your country?
2. We ask you to come to the relief of your country. 3.
He says that he will come to the relief of his country. 4.
By whom was *Mithridates* conquered? 5. He was conquered in many battles by Sulla. 6. He was conquered
in Greece. 7. This school was at Capua. 8. Cleopatra
was queen of Egypt. 9. The soldiers will divide the
booty among themselves. 10. Ptolemy, king of Egypt,
was conquered by Caesar. 11. The king's golden coat of
mail was found in the Nile.

LESSON XXVIII.

IRREGULAR, DEFECTIVE, AND IMPERSONAL VERBS.
[215–221.]

123. LESSON FROM THE GRAMMAR.

   I. Irregular Verbs. 289–296.

  II. Defective Verbs. 297.

III. Impersonal Verbs. 298–301.

124. MODELS.

I. Who proposed the law ?	I. *Quis legem tulit ?*
II. I should prefer to be Phidias.	II. *Ego me Phidiam esse mallem.*
III. They began to be credulous.	III. *Credūli esse coepērunt.*
IV. It is proper that this should be done.	IV. *Hoc fĭĕri oportet.*

125. REMARKS.

   1. MODEL II. — SHOULD PREFER, *mallem*, Potential Subj. See G. 485.

   2. To BE = that I should be, *me esse*, depending upon *mallem*. See G. 551, II.

   3. MODEL III. — CREDULOUS, *credŭli*, Nom., agreeing with the subject of *coepērunt*. See G. 547, I.

   4. MODEL IV. — THAT THIS SHOULD BE DONE, *hoc fĭĕri*, subject of *oportet*. See G. 549, 1.

   5. Give the Synopsis of the Irregular, Defective, and Impersonal Verbs in the Models.

126. Vocabulary.

Approve, *probo, āre, āvi, ātum.*

Be able, can, *possum, posse, potui.*

Forces, *copiae, ārum,* f. pl.

From, out of, *e, ex,* prep. with abl. G. 434, 8.

Gaul, the country, *Gallia, ae,* f.

Gaul, a Gaul, *Gallus, i,* m.

Lacedaemonian, *Lacedaemonius, ii,* m.

Lead out, *edūco, ĕre, duxi, ductum.*

Leonidas, *Leonĭdas, ae,* m.

Occupy, *occŭpo, āre, āvi, ātum.*

Plan, *consilium, ii,* n.

Renew, *instauro, āre, āvi, ātum.*

Return, go back, *redeo, īre, ii, ītum.*

So, so greatly, to such an extent, *adeo,* adv.

Thermopylae, *Thermopȳlae, ārum,* f. pl.

Wage against, *infĕro, ferre, tŭli, illātum.*

127. Exercise.

1. Caesar was waging war against the Gauls. 2. War has been waged against us. 3. Caesar had returned from Gaul to Rome. 4. Leonidas was king of the Lacedaemonians. 5. The Lacedaemonians sent their king Leonidas to occupy Thermopylae. 6. We led out our forces from the city. 7. The enemy were so terrified that they fled. 8. Were they able to renew the war? 9. They were not able to renew the war. 10. Do you (pl.) not approve my plan? 11. We approve it. 12. It will be approved by all.

LESSON XXIX.

IRREGULAR, DEFECTIVE, AND IMPERSONAL VERBS —
CONTINUED.
[222–229.]

128. VOCABULARY.

Begin, *coepi, coepisse.*

Engagement, fight, *proelium, ii,* n., *pugna, ae,* f.

Finish, bring to a close, *finio, ire, ivi, itum.*

Leuctra, *Leuctra, ōrum,* n. pl.

Observe, *servo, āre, āvi, ātum.*

Six, *sex,* indecl.

Wish, *volo, velle, volui.*

129. EXERCISE.

1. Did not the enemy fortify the city? 2. They began to fortify the city. 3. Do you (pl.) not *wish* to fortify the city? 4. We *wish* to fortify it. 5. *Shall* we not *be able* to fortify it? 6. You (pl.) *will be able* to fortify it. 7. The war was brought to a close (finished) by a *naval* engagement. 8. Will you (pl.) not give me this book as a present? 9. We will give you *six books* as a present. 10. This peace will be observed many years. 11. The Lacedaemonians were conquered at Leuctra.

LESSON XXX.

IRREGULAR, DEFECTIVE, AND IMPERSONAL VERBS —
CONTINUED.
[230–245.]

130. VOCABULARY.

Agis, *Agis, ĭdis,* m.

Chaeronea, *Chaeronēa, ae,* f.

Conceal, *celo, āre, āvi, ātum.*

Joy, *gaudium, ii,* n.

Liberty, *libertas, ātis,* f.

Pericles, *Perīcles, is,* m.

Philip, *Philippus, i,* m.

Prefer, would rather, *malo, malle, malui.*

Present, *dono, āre, āvi, ātum.*

Preside over, *praesum, esse, fui.*

Recover, *recupĕro, āre, āvi, ātum.*

Republic, *res publĭca, rei publĭcae,* f.

131. Exercise.

1. Pericles at that time presided over the republic. 2. He is said to have presided over the republic many years. 3. Philip wished to wage war against the Athenians. 4. War was waged by Philip against the Athenians. 5. Philip conquered the Athenians at Chaeronea. 6. The victor wished to conceal his joy. 7. Many wish to rule. 8. I prefer to obey. 9. The Athenians wished to present the general with a golden crown. 10. The Lacedaemonians wished to recover their liberty.

NOTES.

15. — 1. **Is useful,** *utīlis est,* or *est utīlis.* In this exercise, the
learner will adopt the former order. — 11. **Cicero;** for the position
of the object in Latin, see 13, I. 4. — **Cicero,** the most celebrated
of the Roman orators. — 7

20. — 4. **Hannibal,** a celebrated Carthaginian general. — **Sa-**
guntum, a town in Spain. — 16. **Their,** *suum.* Remember that the
Number, as well as the *Gender* and *Case,* of the possessive, is determined, not by the noun to which it refers, but by that to which it
belongs. Here *suum,* their, refers to *puĕri,* boys, which is in the
plural, while it belongs to *patrem,* father, which is in the singular. — 9

25. — 2. **Consul.** Under the Roman commonwealth, two *con-*
suls were annually chosen as joint presidents. — 8. **Socrates,** a
celebrated Athenian philosopher. — 10. **Herodotus,** a Greek historian. — 11

30. — 9. **Catiline,** the notorious conspirator against the Roman
government. — 12. **Our pupils;** omit the possessive *our* in rendering into Latin: so also *your,* in the next sentence. See G. 447. — 12

35. — 1. **Numa.** The emphatic subject should be placed at the
end of the sentence. See G. 594, II. — **Numa,** the second king of
Rome. — 12. **Athens,** the capital of Attica, in Greece. — 14

40. — 3. **Is an honor to,** Lat. idiom, *is for an honor to.* See
G. 390. — 7. **As a present** = *for a present.* — 8. **I have** = *there*
are to me. — 16

44. — 2. **The orator,** *oratōris.* See G. 48, 6; 363. — 3. **De-**
mosthenes, the greatest of Athenian orators. — 17

49. — 1. **Is a characteristic of,** Lat. idiom, *is of.* See G. 402,
I. — 8. **Our friends;** omit *our* in rendering. — 13. **Us,** *nostra.*
See G. 408, 1, 2). — 19

54. — 8. **Talent,** *talentum,* a sum of money somewhat more than
$1000. It consisted of sixty *minae.* — 10. **Proud of** = *proud be-*
cause of. — 11. **Scipio,** a celebrated Roman general. — 21

23   **59.** — 1. **Cato,** the name of several distinguished Romans. The most celebrated was Marcus Porcius Cato, the Censor. — 6. **Five years older** = *older by five years.*

24   **64.** — 1. **There were,** *fuĕrunt,* or *erant.* — **There** — omitted in rendering into Latin. The Perf. *fuĕrunt* simply states the historical fact, that *there were cities;* while the Impf. *erant* gives prominence to the continued existence of these cities. — 2. **Were you?** *fuistine?* a question for information. See G. 346, II. 1. — **Corinth,** a beautiful city in Greece.

26   **69.** — 6. **Tarquin.** Tarquinius Priscus, the fifth king of Rome, is meant. He came from Tarquinii, a city of Etruria. — **In the reign of Ancus,** Lat. idiom, *Ancus reigning.* See G. 431, 2. Ancus Marcius was the fourth king of Rome. 7. **When Cicero was consul** = *in the consulship of Cicero.* See G. 431, 2.

29   **79.** — 1. **Saguntum.** Place the emphatic subject at the end of the sentence. See G. 594, II. — 3. **How many books have you** = *how many books are there to you?* — 5. **Was a man of,** Lat. idiom, *was of.* See G. 402, III. — 6. **In your happiness** = *because of,* etc. — 8. **Servius.** Servius Tullius, the sixth king of Rome, is meant. — 14. **Pydna,** a town in Macedonia. — **At Pydna,** *ad Pydnam.*

35   **94.** — 7. **He had received,** *accepisset,* Subj. by Attraction. See G. 527. — 8. **Because they are diligent,** *quod diligentes sunt,* — a positive reason on the authority of the narrator. Hence the Indic. *sunt.* See G. 520, I. But in 9, where the Indirect Discourse is used, *sunt* becomes *sint.* See G. 531.

37   **99.** — 1. **Boys,** *puĕri.* Place the Vocative after the first clause. See G. 602, VI. — **The good.** See G. 441, 1. — 3. **Of the Roman people.** For the position of the Genitive, see G. 598, 3. — 4. **Is the part of,** Lat. idiom, *is of.* See G. 402, I.

39   **104.** — 5. **Inclined to play,** Lat. idiom, *inclined to playing.* — 8. **To ask for** = *to seek,* Supine in *um.* See G. 569.

41   **111.** — 2. **Another,** *alter;* as only two persons are mentioned. See G. 459, 3. — 4. **Xenophon,** a celebrated Greek historian. — 8. **Ennius,** a Roman poet. — 11. **Let us be content.** See G. 487.

42   **116.** — 1. **Saturnia,** an ancient citadel on the Capitoline Hill, the fabled beginning of Rome. — 2. **Ascanius,** the son of Aeneas, and founder of the city of Alba Longa in Italy.

43   **118.** — 2. **What ought?** etc. See G. 232; 525. — 5. **Camillus,** a distinguished Roman general. — 7. **Porsena,** a king of Etruria in Italy.

44   **120.** — 1. **New Carthage,** a town in Spain. — 5. **Cannae** a

village in Apulia, famous for the victory of Hannibal over the Romans. — 6. **Many states of Italy.** See G. 598, 3. — 8. **Carthaginians**, the citizens of ancient Carthage in Northern Africa.

122. — 1. **Your country**, *patriae tuae*, or *patriae*. See G.   45
447; 385. — 2. **To come.** See G. 492, 2. — 4. **Mithridates**, a
celebrated king of Pontus. — 5. **Sulla**, a distinguished Roman general. — 7. **Capua**, the chief city of Campania in Italy. — 10. **Caesar.** Julius Caesar, a distinguished Roman general and statesman, is
meant. — 11. **Nile**, a river in Egypt.

127. — 1. **Gauls**, the inhabitants of ancient Gaul, embracing   47
modern France. — 4. **Lacedaemonians**, the inhabitants of Lacedaemon, or Sparta, a celebrated city in Greece. — 5. **Their king
Leonidas**, *regem Leonidam*. Place these words after the verb,
directly before the Relative. — **To occupy**, *qui occuparet*. See G.
500. — **Thermopylae**, the celebrated pass in Greece where Leonidas fell.

129. — 8. **As a present.** See G. 390, II. — 10. **Many years.**   48
See G. 378. — 11. **Leuctra**, a town in Boeotia.

131. — 1. **Pericles**, a celebrated Athenian statesman. — 3.   49
Philip, a king of Macedonia. — 5. **Chaeronea**, a town in Boeotia.

ENGLISH-LATIN VOCABULARY.

A.

Abandon. *Relinquo, ĕre, līqui, lictum.*

Able, be able. *Possum, posse, potui.* G. 290.

Abound in. *Abundo, āre, āvi, ātum.*

About. To be about to, rendered by the Act. Periphras. Conj. G. 281.

Above. *Supra,* adv.

Absurd. *Absurdus, ā, um.*

Abundance. *Copia, ae,* f.

Academy. *Academĭa, ae,* f.

Acceptable. *Acceptus, a, um; gratus, a, um.* See 216. Make acceptable, *probo, āre, āvi, ātum.*

Accommodate one's self to. *Obsĕquor, i, secūtus sum,* dep.

Accomplish. *Confĭcio, effĭcio, ĕre, fĕci, fectum; assĕquor, i, secūtus sum,* dep. Achievements are accomplished, *res geruntur.*

Accordance, in accordance with. *Ex, e,* prep. with abl. G. 434, 3.

According to one's desire. *Ex sententia.* See 339.

Account, on account of. *Propter,* prep. with acc.

Accumulate (trans.). *Augeo, ĕre, auxi, auctum.*

Accusation. *Crimen, ĭnis,* n.

Accuse. *Accūso, āre, āvi, ātum.*

Achieve. *Ago, ĕre, egi, actum.*

Achievement. *Res gesta.* See 474. Achievements are accomplished, *res geruntur.*

Achilles. *Achĭlles, is,* m.

Acquaintance, experience. *Usus, us,* m. A very intimate acquaintance, *summus usus.*

Acquainted, be, become, acquainted with. *Cognosco, ĕre, nōvi, nĭtum.*

Acquire. *Paro, āre, āvi, ātum.*

Acquit. *Absolvo, ĕre, solvi, solūtum.*

Across. *Trans,* prep. with acc.

Act. *Ago, ĕre, egi, actum; facio, ĕre, feci, factum.*

Action, deed. *Factum, i,* n.

Adjacent, nearest. *Proxĭmus, a, um.*

Administer. *Gero, ĕre, gessi, gestum.*

Admiration, a feeling of admiration. *Admĭratio, ōnis,* f.

Admire. *Mīror, admīror, āri, ātus sum,* dep.

Admit, confess. *Confiteor, ēri, fessus sum,* dep. Admit, concede, *concēdo, ĕre, cessi, cessum.*

Admitted, it is admitted. *Constat, constĭtit.*

Admonish. *Moneo, admŏneo, ĕre, ui, ĭtum.*

Admonition. *Admonĭtio, ōnis,* f.

13

Adorn. *Exorno, āre, āvi, ātum.*
Adorn, clothe, *vestio, īre, īvi* and *ii, ītum.*

Advantage. *Emolumentum, i,* n.; *commŏdum, i,* n.; *utilītas, ātis,* f.

Adversary. *Adversarius, ii,* m. See 504.

Adversity. *Res adversae,* f. pl. G. 441, 4.

Advice. *Consilium, ii,* n. To give advice, *suadeo, ēre, suasi, suasum.* G. 385.

Advise. *Moneo, ēre, ui, ītum ; suadeo, ēre, suasi, suasum.*

Adviser. *Auctor, ōris,* m.

Aeduans. *Aedui, ōrum,* m. pl.

Affair, thing. *Res, rei,* f. Military affairs, *res militāris,* sing.

Affect. *Afficio, ēre, fēci, fectum.* Affect, prompt, *commŏveo, ēre, mōvi, mōtum.*

Affection. *Amor, ōris,* m. Dutiful affection, *piĕtas, ātis,* f.

Affluent, rich, copious. *Uber, ĕris.*

Africa. *Africa, ae,* f.

Africanus. *Africānus, i,* m.

After. *Post,* prep. with acc.

Afterwards. *Post,* adv.

Again and again. *Etiam atque etiam.*

Against. *Contra ; in ;* prep. with acc.

Age, period of life. *Aetas, ātis,* f. Old age, *senectus, ūtis,* f. At the age of, *natus, a, um,* with acc. of time. See 400.

Aged, old. *Senex, senis.*

Agency — through one's agency. *Per,* prep. with acc. See 232, 5.

Agis. *Agis, īdis,* m.

Ago. *Abhinc,* adv.

Agreeable. *Jucundus, a, um.* See 216.

Ahala. *Ahāla, ae,* m.

Aid. *Auxilium, ii,* n.; *adjumentum, i,* n. Means, *opes, opum,* f. pl. G. 133, 1.

Aid, to aid. *Adjŭvo, āre, jūvi, jūtum.*

Aim — propose to one's self no other aim. *Sibi nihil aliud nisi*

proponĕre *(propōno, ēre, posui, positum).* See 444.

Alba Longa. *Alba Longa, Albae Longae,* f.

Alexander. *Alexander, dri,* m.

Alive. *Vivus, a, um.*

All. *Omnis, e.* Each, every, *quisque, quaeque, quodque* and *quicque* or *quidque.* All together, *cunctus, a, um.* At all, *omnīno,* adv. Not at all, *nihil.* G. 380, 2.

Allobroges. *Allobrŏges, um,* m. pl.

Allow. *Concĕdo, ēre, cessi, cessum.* Allow to pass, *intermitto, ēre, misi, missum.*

Ally. *Socius, ii,* m.

Alone. *Solus, a, um.* G. 151. Without exception, *unus, a, um.* G. 151.

Already. *Jam,* adv.

Also. *Etiam,* adv. I, you, he, &c., also, *idem, eădem, idem.* See 350.

Although. *Etsi ; licet ; etiamsi ; quamquam ; quamvis.* G. 515, 516.

Always. *Semper,* adv.

Ambassador. *Legātus, i,* m.

Among. *Inter,* prep. with acc Among, with, near to, *apud,* prep. with acc.

Amount, quantity. *Vis, vis,* f.

Ample. *Amplus, a, um.*

Ancient. *Antiquus, a, um ; pristīnus, a, um.* See 162.

Ancus. *Ancus, i,* m.

And. *Et ; que ; atque* or *ac,* conj. G. 587, I. 2, 3. And yet = and, *et.* And not, *neque,* conj. And that too, *et is ; et is quidem (is ea, id).*

Anger. *Iracundia, ae,* f.

Annoyance. *Molestia, ae,* f.

Another. *Alius, a, ud.* G. 151 ; 151, 3. Another (of two), a fellow-creature, *alter, ĕra, ĕrum.* G. 151 ; 151, 2. Another's, *aliēnus, a, um.*

Antioch. *Antiochīa, ae,* f.

Antiochus. *Antiŏchus, i,* m.

Antipater. *Antipāter, tri,* m.

Antony. *Antonius, ii,* m.

Any. *Ullus, a, um ;* G. 151; *aliqui, qua, quod.* Any one, *quis.* Any thing, *quid.* G. 189. If any, *si quis.* G. 190, 1.

Apollo. *Apollo, ĭnis,* m.

Apparel. *Vestītus, us,* m.

Appear, seem. *Videor, ēri, vīsus sum.* See 577.

Appius. *Appius, ii,* m.

Apply to. *Confĕro, ferre, tŭli, collātum, in* with acc. Apply one's self to, *se conferre ad* with acc. (*confĕro, ferre, tŭli, collātum*); *se applicāre ad* with acc. (*applĭco, āre, āvi, ātum*).

Appoint. *Constĭtuo, ĕre, ui, ŭtum.*

Approach. *Appropinquo, āre, āvi, ātum ; accēdo, ĕre, cessi, cessum.*

Appropriate, take. *Sumo, ĕre, sumpsi, sumptum.* Appropriate to, apply to, *confĕro, ferre, tŭli, collātum, in* with acc.

Approve. *Probo, āre, āvi, ātum.*

Aquitanians. *Aquitāni, ōrum,*m.pl.

Arar. *Arar, aris,* m.; acc. *Ardrim.*

Archytas. *Archȳtas, ae,* m.

Arganthonius. *Arganthonius,ii,*m.

Ariovistus. *Ariovistus, i,* m.

Arise, become. *Exsisto, ĕre, stĭti, stĭtum.*

Aristotle. *Aristotĕles, is,* m.

Armenian. *Armenius, ii,* m.

Arms. *Arma, ōrum,* n. pl. G. 131, 1, 4).

Army. *Exercĭtus, us,* m.; *agmen, ĭnis,* n.; *acies, ēi,* f. See 178. Army on the march, *agmen, ĭnis,* n.

Around. *Circum,* adv., and prep. with acc.

Arouse. *Erĭgo, ĕre, rexi, rectum.*

Arrange (a line of battle). *Instruo, ĕre, struxi, structum.* Arrange with reference to, *refĕro, ferre, tŭli, lātum, ad* with acc. See 534.

Arrive. *Pervĕnio, īre, vēni, ventum.* Arrive, come, *venio, īre, veni, ventum.*

Arrogance. *Arrogantia, ae,* f.

Art. *Ars, artis,* f.

As. *Ut,* adv. As = since, *quum,* conj. As, after *tam, quam,* adv. As = for, *pro,* prep. with abl. As to, after *ita, ut,* conj. with subjunct. As — as possible, *quam,* adv. with superlat. See 449. As much, *quantus, a, um.* As much — as, *tantus, a, um — quantus, a, um.* See 527. As soon as, *quum primum.* As, relative, especially after *idem,* etc., *qui, quae, quod.* As = that which, a thing which, *id quod.* See 267; also G. 445, 7.

Ascanius. *Ascanius, ii,* m.

Ascertain. *Cognosco, ĕre, nōvi, nĭtum.*

Ashamed, be ashamed. *Pudet, puduit* and *pudĭtum est.* See 228; also G. 299; 410, III.

Asia. *Asia, ae,* f.

Ask. *Rogo, āre, āvi, ātum.* Ask (a question), *interrŏgo, āre, āvi, ātum.* Ask, inquire, *quaero, ĕre, quaesīvi* and *ii, quaesītum.* Ask for, *peto, ĕre, īvi* and *ii, ītum.* It is asked, *quaerĭtur, quaesītum est.*

Assemble. *Convĕnio, īre, vēni, ventum.* Multitudes assemble, *concursus fit.* See 606.

Assembly. *Concio, ōnis,* f.

Assiduously. *Studiōse,* adv.

Assign. *Tribuo, ĕre, ui, ūtum.*

Associate. *Socius, ii,* m.

Astyages. *Astyăges, is,* m.

At. *Apud, ad,* prep. with acc. At the age of, *natus, a, um,* with acc. of time. See 400. At the suggestion of, *auctor,* in abl. abs. At all, *omnĭno,* adv. Not at all, *nihĭl.* G. 380, 2. At length, *tandem,* adv. At once, *jam,* adv. At times, *interdum,* adv.

Athenian. *Atheniensis, is,* m. and f.

Athens. *Athēnae, ārum,* f. pl.

Attack. *Adorĭor, īri, ortus sum,* dep.

M

Attain. *Consĕquor, assĕquor, i, secūtus sum*, dep.; *adipiscor, i, adeptus sum*, dep.

Attempt. *Conor, āri, ātus sum*, dep.; *tento, āre, āvi, ātum*.

Attend to, serve. *Servio, ire, ivi, itum*. G. 385.

Attendance, with the attendance of. *Comes, Itis*, in abl. abs.

Attendant. *Comes, Itis*, m. and f.

Attention, study. *Studium, ii*, n. Attention, exertion, work, *opĕra, ae*, f.

Attentive. *Attentus, a, um*.

Atticus. *Attĭcus, i*, m.

Attract. *Allĭcio, ĕre, lexi, lectum*.

Audacity. *Audacia, ae*, f.

Author. *Auctor, ōris*, m. and f.

Authority. *Auctorĭtas, ātis*, f.

Avail. *Valeo, ēre, ui, ĭtum*.

Avaricious. *Avārus, a, um*.

Avoid. *Vito, āre, āvi, ātum*.

Await. *Exspecto, āre, āvi, ātum*.

Award. *Tribuo, ĕre, ui, ūtum*.

Aware — be aware. *Scio, scire, scivi, scitum*.

B.

Banish, throw off. *Abjĭcio, ĕre, jēci, jectum*. Banish, expel, *expello, ĕre, pŭli, pulsum*.

Base. *Turpis, e*.

Battle. *Proelium, ii*, n. A battle is fought, *pugnātur, ātum est*, impers.

Be. *Sum, esse, fui*. Be a characteristic of. See 426. Be a lawgiver, *leges scribo, ĕre, scripsi, scriptum*. See 438. Be a statesman, *rei publĭcae praesum, esse, fui*. See 438. Be a warrior, *bellum gero, ĕre, gessi, gestum*. See 444. Be able, *possum, posse, potui*. Be about to, Act. Periphrast. Conj. Be acquainted with, *cognosco, ĕre, nōvi, nĭtum*. Be ashamed, *pudet, puduit* and *pudĭtum est*. See 228; also G. 410, III. Be aware, *scio, scire, scivi, scitum*. Be born, *nascor,*

i, natus sum. Be busy, *occupatiōne distinēri (distĭneo, ēre, ui, tentum)*. See 631. How very busy one is, *quanta occupatiōne*, etc. Be conducive to, *condūco, ĕre, duxi, ductum*. See 289. Be consistent with one's self, *sibi consentīre*, with *ipse, a, um*, in agreement with subject (*consentio, ire, sensi, sensum*). Be delighted with, *gaudeo, ēre, gavīsus sum*. Be destitute of, need, *egeo, indĭgeo, ēre, ui*. See 239, I. Be elated, *effĕror, ferri, elātus sum*. See 295. Be eminent, *unus, a, um, emĭneo, ēre, ui*, or *emineo* alone. Be engaged in, *sum, esse, fui, in* with abl. See 534. Be evident, *consto, āre, stĭti, stātum*. Be expected to, Act. Periphrast. Conj. Be free from, be without, *vaco, āre, āvi, ātum; careo, ēre, ui, ĭtum; egeo, ēre, ui*. See 239, I. Be grateful, *gratiam habeo, ēre, ui, ĭtum*. See 548. Be held = to be, *sum, esse, fui*. Be ignorant of, *ignōro, āre, āvi, ātum*. Be in command of, *praesum, esse, fui*. G. 386. Be in force, *vigeo, ēre, vigui*. Be intimate with, *familiarĭter utor, i, usus sum*, dep. G. 419, I. Be mad, *furo, ĕre, ui*. Be needful, there needs, is need of, *opus est, fuit*. G. 419, 3. Be on one's guard, *caveo, ēre, cavi, cautum*. Be one's intention, *in anĭmo sum, esse, fui*. See 206. Be subject to, obey, *pareo, ēre, ui, ĭtum*. G. 385. Be sufficient, be able, *possum, posse, potui*. Be the duty, mark, part, &c., of, often rendered by the Pred. Gen. See 426. Be the result, *evĕnio, ire, vēni, ventum*. Be the slave of, *servio, ire, ivi* and *ii, itum*. G. 385. Be unable, *non possum, posse, potui*. Be unwilling, *nolo, nolle, nolui*. Be useful, *utĭlis, e, sum, esse, fui; utilĭta-*

tem affĕro, ferre, attŭli, allātum.
See 444. Be willing, *volo, velle, volui.* Be without. See *Be free from.* Be wont, *soleo, ĕre, solĭtus sum.*

Bear. *Fero, ferre, tuli, latum.* Bear, suffer, *patior, pati, passus sum,* dep. Bear, support, *sustĭneo, ĕre, ui, tentum.*

Beautiful. *Pulcher, chra, chrum.*

Beauty. *Pulchritūdo, ĭnis, f.*

Because. *Quod, quia,* conj. See Lesson LXXX. Because of, *propter,* prep. with acc.

Become. *Fio, fĭĕri, factus sum.* Become acquainted with, *cognosco, ĕre, nōvi, nĭtum.*

Befall. *Accĭdo, ĕre, i.*

Before. *Ante,* adv., and prep. with acc.

Begin. *Coepi, isse.* G. 297, I.

Beginning. *Initium, ii, n.*

Behalf, in behalf of. *Pro,* prep. with abl.

Behooves — it behooves. *Oportet, uit.*

Belgians. *Belgae, ārum,* m. pl.

Believe. *Credo, ĕre, dĭdi, dĭtum.* G. 385.

Beneficence. *Beneficentia, ae, f.*

Best. *Optĭmus, a, um.* G. 165. In the best manner, *optĭme,* adv.

Bestow. *Impertio, ĭre, ĭvi* and *ii, ĭtum.* Bestow upon, *confĕro, ferre, tŭli, collātum.*

Betake one's self. *Se conferre (confĕro, ferre, tŭli, collātum); se recipĕre (recĭpio, ĕre, cēpi, ceptum).*

Better. *Melior, ius.* G. 165. Better, preferable, *satius.* See 527.

Between. *Inter,* prep. with acc.

Bird. *Avis, avis, f.*

Bitterly. *Acerbe,* adv.

Blame. *Vitupĕro. āre, āvi, ātum.*

Blessing, good. *Bonum, i, n.*

Blind. *Caecus, a, um.*

Boast. *Glōrior, āri, ātus sum,* dep.

Book. *Liber, bri, m.*

Booty. *Praeda, ae, f.*

Borders, territory. *Fines, ium,* m. pl.

Born for. *Natus, a, um,* with dat., or *ad* with acc.

Both — and. *Et — et.*

Boy. *Puer, puĕri,* m.

Boyhood. See 408. From boyhood, *a puĕro.*

Branch of learning. *Doctrīna, ae,* f.

Brave. *Fortis, e.*

Bravely. *Fortĭter,* adv.

Break, offend against. *Viŏlo, āre, āvi, ātum.*

Bring. *Affĕro, ferre, attŭli, allātum.* Bring, bear, *fero, ferre, tuli, latum.* Bring to, *addūco, ĕre, duxi, ductum.* Bring to a close, *finio, ĭre, ĭvi* and *ii, ĭtum.*

Britain — of or from Great Britain, British. *Britannĭcus, a, um.*

Brother. *Frater, tris,* m.

Brutus. *Brutus, i,* m.

Build, make. *Facio, ĕre, feci, factum.*

Burn, burn up. *Exūro, ĕre, ussi, ustum.* Burn, set fire to, *incendo, ĕre, cĕndi, censum.*

Business. *Negotium, ii,* n. To have business, *negotium esse,* with dat. of possessor.

Busy, be busy. *Occupatiōne distinĕri (distĭneo, ĕre, ui, tentum).* See 631. How very busy one is, *quanta occupatiōne,* etc.

But. *Sed ; autem ; vero.* G. 587, III. 2. But not, and not, *neque.*

By. *A, ab,* prep. with abl. By = from, in accordance with, *e, ex,* prep. with abl. By = through, *per,* prep. with acc. By letter, *per littĕras.* By myself, yourself, &c., *mecum,* etc. See 568. By no means, *minĭme,* adv. See 586.

C.

Caesar. *Caesar, ăris,* m.

Caius. *Cāius, ii,* m.

Calamity. *Calamĭtas, ātis,* f.

Call. *Nomĭno, voco, appello, āre, āvi, ātum.* See 184. Call to mind, *commemŏro, āre, āvi, ātum.*

Camillus. *Camillus, i,* m.

Camp. *Castra, ōrum*, n. pl.

Can, could. *Possum, posse, potui.*

Cannae. *Cannae, ārum*, f. pl.

Capable. *Capax, ācis.*

Capture. *Capio, ĕre, cēpi, captum.*

Capua. *Capua, ae,* f.

Care — take care. *Caveo, ĕre, cavi, cautum.*

Care, care for. *Curo, āre, āvi, ātum.*

Carefully. *Diligenter,* adv.

Caria. *Caria, ae,* f.

Carry. *Porto, āre, āvi, ātum.*

Carthage. *Carthāgo, ĭnis,* f.

Carthaginian. *Poenus, i,* m.; *Carthaginiensis, is,* m. and f.

Cassius. *Cassius, ii,* m.

Catiline. *Catilīna, ae,* m.

Cato. *Cato, ōnis,* m.

Catulus. *Catūlus, i,* m.

Cause. *Causa, ae,* f.

Cavalry. *Equitātus, us,* m.

Celebrated. *Clarus, a, um; celĕber, bris, bre.* See 233.

Celestial. *Coelestis, e.* Celestial bodies, *coelestia, ium,* n. pl.

Celts. *Celtae, ārum,* m. pl.

Censor. *Censor, ōris,* m.

Censorship. See 409.

Censure. *Reprehendo, ĕre, di, sum.*

Census — take the census of, *censeo, ĕre, ui, censum.* See 490.

Certain. *Certus, a, um.* A certain, *quidam, quaedam, quoddam* and *quiddam.*

Certainly. *Certe,* adv.

Ceus, of Ceus. *Ceus, a, um.*

Chaeronea. *Chaeronēa, ae,* f.

Change. *Muto, āre, āvi, ātum.*

Characteristic. See 426.

Chariot. *Currus, us,* m.

Cheerfulness. *Hilarĭtas, ātis,* f.

Chief. *Summus, a, um.* G. 163, 3.

Children. *Libĕri, ōrum,* m. pl.

Choice. *Conquisitĭus, a, um.*

Choose, select. *Elĭgo, ĕre, lēgi, lectum.*

Cicero. *Cicĕro, ōnis,* m.

Cimbrian. *Cimbrĭcus, a, um.* A victory over the Cimbrians, *Cimbrĭca victoria.*

Citadel. *Arx, arcis,* f.

Citizen. *Civis, civis,* m. and f.

City. *Urbs, urbis,* f. City walls, walls of the city, *moenia, ium,* n. pl. Founding of the city, *urbs condĭta.* G. 580.

Civil. *Civĭlis, e.* Civil, domestic, *domestĭcus, a, um.* Civil, belonging to the city, *urbānus, a, um.*

Claudius. *Claudius, ii,* m.

Clear. *Clarus, a, um; perspicuus, a, um.*

Cleopatra. *Cleopātra, ae,* f.

Clodius. *Clodius, ii,* m.

Close — bring to a close. *Finio, ĭre, ĭvi* and *ii, ĭtum.*

Coat of mail. *Lorīca, ae,* f.

Collatinus. *Collatīnus, i,* m.

Colleague. *Collēga, ae,* m.

Come. *Venio, ĭre, veni, ventum.* Come to the relief of, *subvĕnio, ĭre, vēni, ventum.* G. 386. To come, future, *futūrus, a, um.*

Command. *Impĕro, āre, āvi, ātum.* G. 385. Be in command of, *praesum, esse, fui.* G. 386. At the command of, Pres. Part. of *impĕro* in abl. abs.

Commander. *Imperātor, ōris,* m.

Commend, make acceptable. *Probo, āre, āvi, ātum.*

Commit, do. *Facio, ĕre, feci, factum.* Commit one's self, *se tradĕre; trado, ĕre, dĭdi, dĭtum.* Commit, commit to memory, *edisco, ĕre, didĭci.* Commit to writing, *littĕris mando, āre, āvi, ātum.*

Common. *Commūnis, e.*

Commonwealth. *Res publĭca, rei publicae,* f.

Communicate, relate. *Trado, ĕre, dĭdi, dĭtum.* Communicate, converse, *collŏquor, i, locūtus sum,* dep.

Companions — my, &c., companions. *Mei,* etc. G. 441, 1.

Compare. *Confĕro, ferre, tūli, collātum.*

Compel. *Cogo, ĕre, coēgi, coactum.*

Complain. *Queror, i, questus sum,* dep.

Completely conquer. *Devinco, ěre, vĭci, victum.*

Conceal. *Celo, āre, āvi, ātum; occulto, āre, āvi, ātum.*

Concede. *Concēdo, ěre, cessi, cessum.*

Concerning. *De,* prep. with abl.

Concerns, it concerns. *Refert, tŭlit.* G. 408.

Condemn. *Damno, condemno, āre, āvi, ātum.*

Condition, state. *Status, us,* m.

Conducive — be conducive to. *Condūco, ěre, duxi, ductum.* See 289.

Conduct. *Perdūco, ěre, duxi, ductum.* Conduct one's self, *se gerěre (gero, ěre, gessi, gestum).*

Confess. *Confiteor, ěri, fessus sum,* dep.

Confidence. *Fides, ěi,* f.

Confirm. *Confirmo, āre, āvi, ātum.*

Connected. *Contĭnens, entis.*

Connection — no connection. *Nihil conjunctum.* See 637.

Conquer. *Vinco, ěre, vici, victum.* Conquer completely, *devinco, ěre, vĭci, victum.*

Conscript Fathers. *Patres Conscripti,* m. pl.

Consider. *Cogĭto, āre, āvi, ātum.* Consider as, *arbĭtror, āri, ātus sum,* dep. Consider, judge, *existĭmo, āre, āvi, ātum.*

Consistent—be consistent with one's self. *Sibi consentĭre,* with *ipse, a, um,* in agreement with subject *(consentio, ĭre, sensi, sensum).*

Consistently. *Convenienter,* adv.

Conspiracy. *Conjuratio, ōnis,* f.

Conspirators. *Conjurāti, ōrum,* m. pl.

Conspire. *Conjūro, āre, āvi, ātum.*

Constantly. *Assiduus, a, um.* G. 443.

Consternation. *Formĭdo, ĭnis,* f. See 305.

Consul. *Consul, ŭlis,* m.

Consulship. See 409.

Consult, consult for, consult for the interest of. *Consŭlo, ěre, ui, sultum.* G. 335, 3.

Contemplate. *Contemplor, āri, ātus sum,* dep.

Contend. *Decerto, āre, āvi, ātum; contendo, ěre, di, tum.*

Content. *Contentus, a, um.* G. 419, IV.

Contract. *Contraho, ěre, traxi, tractum.*

Contracted, small. *Angustus, a, um.*

Contrary to. *Contra, praeter,* prep. with acc.

Conversation. *Sermo, ōnis,* m.

Convict. *Convinco, ěre, vĭci, victum.*

Corinth. *Corinthus, i,* f.

Correctly. *Recte,* adv.

Costly. *Pretiōsus, a, um.*

Could, can. *Possum, posse, potui.*

Counsel. *Consilium, ii,* n.

Country. *Patria, ae,* f.; *rus, ruris,* n.; *ager, agri,* m. See 245. From the country, in the country. G. 424, 2.

Courage. *Virtus, ūtis,* f.; *anĭmus, i,* m.

Course — to follow this course. *Hoc sequor, i, secūtus sum,* dep.

Cover, clothe. *Vestio, ĭre, ĭvi* and *ii, ĭtum.*

Crassus. *Crassus, i,* m.

Credit. *Fides, ěi,* f.

Crime. *Scelus, ěris,* n.

Cross. *Transeo, ĭre, ii, ĭtum.*

Crotona. *Croto, ōnis,* m. and f.

Crown. *Corōna, ae,* f.

Cruelty. *Crudelĭtas, ātis,* f.

Cultivate. *Colo, ěre, colui, oul tum.*

Culture. *Cultus, us,* m.

Curio. *Curio, ōnis,* m.

Curtius. *Curtius, ii,* m.

Custom, habit. *Consuetūdo, ĭnis,* f.; *mos, moris,* m. See 167.

Cypselus. *Cypsĕlus, i,* m.

D.

Daily. *In dies, in dies singŭlos ; quotidie.* See 399.

Danger. *Pericŭlum, i,* n.

Dare. *Audeo, ēre, ausus sum.*

Dated. *Datus, a, um.* See 366.

Day. *Dies, ēi,* m. and f. G. 120. Day before, *pridie,* adv. First day of the month, *calendas, ārum,* f. pl. Fifth day of the month (generally), *nonae, ārum,* f. pl. G. 708, I. 2. Seventh day of the month in March, May, July, and October, *nonae, ārum,* f. pl. G. 708, I. 2. Three days, *triduum, ui,* n. From day to day, *in dies.*

Dear. *Carus, a, um.*

Death. *Mors, mortis,* f. Put to death, *occīdo, ēre, cīdi, cīsum ; interfĭcio, ēre, fēci, fectum.*

Debt. *Aes aliēnum,* n. See 454.

Decree. *Consultum, i,* n.

Deed. *Factum, i,* n. Deed, thing, *res, rei,* f. Good deed, *recte factum.* See 366.

Defence. *Praesidium, ii,* n.

Defend. *Defendo, ēre, di, sum.* Defend, guard, *tueor, ēri, ĭtus sum,* dep.

Defendant. *Reus, i,* m.

Define. *Defĭnio, īre, īvi, ītum.*

Delight. *Delecto, oblecto, āre, āvi, ātum.*

Delightful. *Dulcis, e.*

Deliver, give over. *Trado, ēre, dĭdi, dĭtum.* Deliver (an oration), *habeo, ēre, ui, ĭtum.*

Delphic. *Delphĭcus, a, um.*

Demand. *Postŭlo, āre, āvi, ātum.*

Demaratus. *Demarātus, i,* m.

Demosthenes. *Demosthĕnes, is,* m.

Deny. *Nego, āre, āvi, ātum.*

Depart, depart from. *Discēdo, ēre, cessi, cessum.* Depart, go from, *exeo, īre, ii, ĭtum.* Depart, set out, *proficiscor, i, profectus sum.* Depart, go, *eo, ire, ivi, itum.*

Depend upon. *Posĭtus, a, um, esse, in* with abl. See 560.

Desert. *Desĕro, ēre, serui, sertum.*

Deserve. *Mereo, ēre, ui, ĭtum ; mereor, ēri, ĭtus sum,* dep. Deserve is often rendered by the Pass. Per. Conj. See G. 232.

Design. *Consilium, ii,* n.

Desirable. *Optabĭlis, e.*

Desire. *Cupidĭtas, ātis,* f. ; *libĭdo, ĭnis,* f. According to one's desire, *ex sententia.* See 339.

Desire, to desire. *Cupio, ēre, īvi, ītum ; opto, āre, āvi, ātum ; volo, velle, volui.* See 618.

Desirous of. *Cupĭdus, a, um ; studiōsus, a, um.* Very desirous, greedy, *avĭdus, a, um.* See 222.

Despair of. *Despĕro, āre, āvi, ātum,* with acc., or *de* with abl.

Despise. *Contemno, ēre, tempsi, temptum.*

Destitute of. *Expers, tis.* To be destitute of, *egeo, indigeo, ēre, ui.* See 239.

Destroy. *Deleo, ēre, ēvi, ētum.*

Deter. *Deterreo, ēre, ui, ĭtum.*

Detriment. *Detrimentum, i,* n.

Devise. *Invĕnio, īre, vēni, ventum.*

Devote one's self to. *Studeo, ēre, ui ;* G. 385 ; *incumbo, ēre, cubui, cubĭtum, in* with acc. Devote one's self to, apply one's self to, *se conferre in* or *ad* with acc. (*confĕro, ferre, tŭli, collātum*).

Dictate. *Dicto, āre, āvi, ātum.*

Die. *Morior, i, mortuus sum,* dep.

Difference — there is a difference. *Intĕrest, fuit.*

Differently. *Aliter,* adv.

Difficult. *Difficĭlis, e.*

Dignity. *Dignĭtas, ātis,* f.

Diligence. *Diligentia, ae,* f.

Diligent. *Dilĭgens, entis.*

Diligently. *Diligenter,* adv.

Diminish. *Minuo, ēre, ui, ūtum.*

Dine. *Coeno, āre, āvi, ātum.*

Dinner. *Coena, ae,* f.

Dion. *Dio* or *Dion, ōnis,* m.

Dionysius. *Dionysius, ii.* m.

Disagree. *Dissentio, īre, sensi, sensum.*

Discharge, fulfil. *Fungor, i, functus sum,* dep.

Discord. *Discordia, ae,* f.

Discourse. *Oratio, ōnis,* f.

Disgraceful. *Turpis, e.*

Disguise. *Dissimŭlo, āre, āvi, ātum.*

Displease. *Displĭceo, ēre, ui, ĭtum.* G. 385.

Dissension. *Dissidium, ii,* n.

Distinguished. *Clarus, a, um.* See 233.

Distrusting. *Diffĭsus, a, um.* See 625.

Divide. *Divĭdo, ĕre, vīsi, vīsum.*

Divine. *Divīnus, a, um.*

Do. *Facio, ĕre, feci, factum;* ago, *ĕre, egi, actum.* Do, perform, *gero, ĕre, gessi, gestum.* Is doing, is done, *agĭtur, gerĭtur.*

Domestic. *Domestĭcus, a, um.*

Doubt — there is no doubt. *Non dubium est.* See 322.

Doubt, to doubt. *Dubĭto, āre, āvi, ātum.*

Doubtful. *Dubius, a, um.*

Dream. *Somnium, ii,* n.

Drive. *Pello, ĕre, pepŭli, pulsum.* Drive, cast out, *ejĭcio, ĕre, jēci, jectum.*

Due — one's due. *Suum, i,* n. G. 441.

Duillius. *Duillius, ii,* m.

Dumnorix. *Dumnŏrix, ĭgis,* m.

During, in. *In,* prep. with abl.

Dutiful affection. *Pĭĕtas, ātis,* f.

Duty. *Officium, ii,* n. To be the duty of, often rendered by the Pred. Gen. See 426; also G. 404, 1.

E.

· Each, every. *Quisque, quaeque, quodque* and *quicque* or *quidque.* One each, *singŭli, ae, a.* Each topic, *quidque.*

Eager. *Alăcer, cris, cre;* studiōsus, a, um; avĭdus, a, um. See 222.

Eagerly. *Cupĭde;* vehementer, adv.

Eagle. *Aquĭla, ae,* f.

Ear. *Auris, auris,* f.

Early, ancient. *Antĭquus, a, um.* Early in the morning, *mane,* adv.

Easily. *Facĭle,* adv.

Easy. *Facĭlis, e.*

Eclipse. *Defectio, ōnis,* f.

Edifice. *Aedes, is,* f. G. 132.

Egypt. *Aegyptus, i,* f.

Eighth of November. *Ante diem sextum idus Novembres (a. d. VI. id. Nov.).* G. 708.

Eighty. *Octoginta,* indecl.

Either — or. *Aut — aut; vel — vel.* G. 587, II. 2.

Elated — be elated. *Effĕror, ferri, elātus sum,* pass. of *effĕro.*

Elegance. *Elegantia, ae,* f.

Elegantly. *Polĭte,* adv.

Eloquence. *Eloquentia, ae,* f.

Eloquent. *Elŏquens, entis.*

Eminent, excelling. *Excellens, entis.* To be eminent, *unus, a, um, emĭnec, ĕre, ui;* or *emineo* alone.

Emolument. *Emolumentum, i,* n.

Empire. *Imperium, ii,* n.

Enact. *Sancio, īre, sanxi, sanctum.* Enact, write, *scribo, ĕre, scripsi, scriptum.*

Encamp. *Castra pono, ĕre, posui, posĭtum.*

Encounter. *Subeo, obeo, īre, ii, ĭtum; oppĕto, ĕre, petīvi* or *ii, ĭtum.*

Endeavor. *Conor, āri, ātus sum,* dep.

Endowed with. *Praedĭtus, a, um.* G. 419, III.

Endure. *Fero, ferre, tuli, latum.*

Enemy. *Hostis, is,* m. and f.; *inimĭcus, i,* m. See 344.

Engaged — be engaged in. *Sum, esse, fui, in* with abl. See 534.

Engagement, fight. *Proelium, ii,* n.; *pugna, ae,* f. See 256. Naval engagement, *pugna navālis.*

Enjoy. *Fruor, i, fructus* and *fruĭtus sum,* dep. G. 419, I.

Enjoyment. *Delectatio, ōnis,* f.

Enlarge. *Amplio, āre, āvi, ātum.*

Ennius. *Ennius, ii,* m.

Entertain, hold. *Teneo, ĕre, ui,*

tentum. Entertain gratitude, *gratiam habeo, ēre, ui, ĭtum.* See 548. Entertain the same sentiments, *eādem sentio, īre, sensi, sensum.*

Entertainment. *Convivium, ii,* n.

Entirely. *Omnīno,* adv.; *totus, a, um.* G. 151; 443.

Entitle. *Inscrĭbo, ēre, scripsi, scriptum.*

Envy, to look upon with envy. *Invĭdeo, ēre, vīdi, vīsum.*

Epaminondas. *Epaminondas, ae,* m.

Ephesus. *Ephēsus, i,* f.

Epicurus. *Epicūrus, i,* m.

Equal. *Par, paris.*

Equity. *Aequĭtas, ātis,* f.

Erudition. *Eruditio, ōnis,* f.

Escape. *Effŭgio, ēre, fūgi.*

Especially. *Maxĭme, praesertim,* adv.

Establish. *Firmo, confirmo, āre, āvi, ātum.*

Established — firmly established. *Firmus, a, um.*

Esteem. *Aestĭmo, āre, āvi, ātum; facio, ēre, feci, factum.* Esteem lightly, despise, *contemno, ēre, tempsi, temptum.*

Eternal. *Sempiternus, a, um.*

Etruria. *Etruria, ae,* f.

Even. *Etiam,* adv. Even if, *etiamsi,* conj. G. 516, III.

Evening. *Vesper, ĕris,* m. In the evening, *vespĕri.*

Event, issue. *Eventus, us,* m. Event, thing, *res, rei,* f.

Ever. *Unquam,* adv. Ever = always, *semper,* adv. For ever, *in perpetuum.*

Every. *Quisque, quaeque, quodque* and *quicque* or *quidque; omnis, e.*

Evident — be evident. *Consto, āre, stĭti, stătum.*

Evil. *Malum, i,* n.

Exalted, most exalted. *Summus, a, um.* G. 163, 8.

Example. *Exemplum, i,* n.

Exceedingly. *Vehementer, valde,* adv.

Excel. *Excello, ēre, cellui, celsum.*

Excellence, goodness. *Bonĭtas, ātis,* f.

Excellent. *Praeclārus, a, um.* Excellent, good, *bonus, a, um.*

Excellently. *Excellenter,* adv.

Excelling. *Excellens, entis.*

Except. *Praeter,* prep. with acc.

Exception — without exception. *Unus, a, um.* G. 175, 1.

Excessive. *Nimius, a, um.*

Excite. *Excĭto, āre, āvi, ātum.*

Exercise. *Exerceo, ēre, ui, ĭtum.*

Exertion, zeal. *Studium, ii,* n. Exertion, attention, *opĕra, ae,* f.

Exhort. *Hortor, cohortor, āri, ātus sum,* dep.

Exile. *Exsilium, ii,* n.

Exist. *Sum, esse, fui.*

Expect. *Exspecto, āre, āvi, ātum.* To be expected to; rendered by the Act. Periphrast. Conj. G. 231.

Expectation, opinion. *Opinio, ōnis,* f.

Expel. *Expello, ēre, pŭli, pulsum.*

Experience. *Usus, us,* m.

Expose one's self. *Se opponĕre (oppōno, ēre, posui, posĭtum).*

Express, utter. *Elōquor, i, locūtus sum,* dep. Express opinion, think, *censeo, ēre, ui, censum.* See 576. Express thanks, *gratias ago, ēre, egi, actum.* See 548.

Extol. *Extollo, ēre,* with *laudĭbus* or *laudando.*

Eye. *Ocŭlus, i,* m.

F.

Fabius. *Fabius, ii,* m.

Fable. *Fabŭla, ae,* f.

Fabricius. *Fabricius, ii,* m.

Faesulae. *Faesŭlae, ārum,* f. pl.

Fail. *Defĭcio, ēre, fēci, fectum.*

Faith. *Fides, ĕi,* f.

False. *Falsus, a, um.*

Familiarly. *Familiarĭter,* adv.

Famous. *Clarus, a, um.* The

famous, sometimes rendered by *ille, a, ud.* G. 450, 4.

Far — so far. *Tantum,* adv. So far am I from, *tantum abest ut* with subj. See 498. Thus far, *adhuc,* adv.

Father. *Pater, tris,* m. Conscript Fathers, *Patres Conscripti,* m. pl.

Fault. *Culpa, ae,* f.

Favor. *Beneficium, ii,* n. To requite a favor, *gratiam refĕro, ferre, tŭli, lātum.* See 548.

Favor, to favor. *Faveo, ĕre, favi, fautum.* G. 385.

Fear. *Metus, us,* m.; *timor, ōris,* m. See 305.

Fear, to fear. *Metuo, ĕre, ui; timeo, ĕre, ui; vereor, ĕri, verĭtus sum,* dep. Fear greatly, *pertimesco, ĕre, timui.*

Feast. *Epŭlae, ārum,* f. pl.

Feel the need of. *Indĭgeo, ĕre, ui.* See 239, I.; also G. 419, III.; 409, 1.

Feeling of admiration. *Admiratio, ōnis,* f.

Few. *Pauci, ae, a,* pl.

Fidelity. *Fidelĭtas, ātis,* f.; *fides, ĕi,* f.

Field. *Ager, agri,* m.

Fifth. *Quintus, a, um.* Fifth day of the month (generally), *Nonae, ārum,* f. pl. G. 708, I. 2.

Fiftieth. *Quinquagesĭmus, a, um.*

Fight, battle. *Pugna, ae,* f.

Fight, to fight. *Pugno, āre, āvi, ātum.* Fight (a battle), lit. *make, facio, ĕre, feci, factum.* See 257. A battle is fought, *pugnātur, ātum est.*

Fill. *Compleo, ĕre, ĕvi, ĕtum.*

Find, by accident. *Invĕnio, ĭre, vēni, ventum.* Find, by search, *repĕrio, ĭre, pĕri, pertum.*

Finish, bring to a close. *Finio, ĭre, ĭvi and ii, ĭtum.*

Fire. *Ignis, is,* m. Set fire to, *inflammo, āre, āvi, ātum; incendo, ĕre, di, sum.* With fire and sword, *ferro ignĕque.* See 117.

Firmly established. *Firmus, a, um.*

First. *Primus, a, um.* First, for the first time, *primum,* adv. First day of the month, *Calendae, ārum,* f. pl.

Fitting — it is fitting. *Oportet, uit,* impers.

Five. *Quinque,* indecl.

Flaccus. *Flaccus, i,* m.

Flee. *Fugio, ĕre, fugi, fugĭtum; profŭgio, ĕre, fūgi.*

Flight. *Fuga, ae,* f.

Flourishing. *Florens, entis.*

Flow into. *Influo, ĕre, fluxi, fluxum.*

Foe. *Inimĭcus, i,* m.

Follow. *Sequor, consĕquor, i, secūtus sum,* dep. Follow this course, *hoc sequor.*

Folly. *Stultĭtia, ae,* f. Surpass the folly of, *esse dementior.* See 480.

Fond of. *Amans, antis; cupĭdus, a, um; dilĭgens, entis.*

Foolish. *Demens, entis.*

For, prep. *Pro,* prep. with abl. For = about, concerning, *de,* prep. with abl. For = against, *in,* prep. with acc. For — because of, *propter,* prep. with acc. For = during, *per,* prep. with acc. For = to secure, *ad,* prep. with acc. For after *idoneus, parātus,* etc., *ad,* prep. with acc. For ever, *in perpetuum.* For his, &c., own sake, *propter sese (se).* For my, &c., sake, *mea causa,* etc. G. 414, 2, 3). For the purpose of, for the sake of, *causa* or *gratia* with gen. G. 414, 2, 3). For a long time, *jamdūdum; jamprĭdem.* G. 467, 2. For the first time, *primum,* adv. For the reason that, *propterea quod.*

For, conj. *Enim, nam,* conj.

Force. *Vis, vis,* f.; frequently used in pl. *vires, ium.* A force, forces, *copiae, ārum,* f. pl. To be in force, *vigeo, ĕre, vigui.*

Forced marches. *Magna itinĕra,* n. pl. See 246.

Ford. *Vadum, i,* n.

Forefathers. *Majōres, um,* pl.

Forget. *Oblīviscor, i, oblītus sum,* dep. G. 406, II.

Form, make. *Facio, ĕre, feci, factum.*

Formerly. *Quondam, antea,* adv.

Forth — set forth. *Exprōmo, ĕre, prompsi, promptum.* Set forth views, state, *praedĭco, āre, āvi, ātum.*

Fortify. *Munio, īre, īvi and ii, ītum.*

Fortitude. *Fortitūdo, ĭnis,* f.

Fortunate. *Fortunātus, a, um.*

Fortune. *Fortūna, ae,* f. To be one's good fortune, *contingo, ĕre, tĭgi, tactum.*

Forty. *Quadraginta,* indecl.

Forum. *Forum, i,* n.

Forward — look forward to. *Exspecto, āre, āvi, ātum.*

Found. *Condo, ĕre, dĭdi, dĭtum.*

Founding of the city. *Urbs condĭta.* G. 580.

Four. *Quattuor,* indecl.

Fourth. *Quartus, a, um.*

Free. *Liber, ĕra, ĕrum.* To be free from, *vaco, āre, āvi, ātum; careo, ĕre, ui, ĭtum; egeo, ĕre, ui.* See 239, I.

Free from. *Libĕro, āre, āvi, ātum.* G. 425, 3, 2).

Frequently. *Saepe, crebro,* adv.; *frequens, entis.* G. 443.

Friend. *Amīcus, i,* m. My, &c., friends, *mei, ōrum,* etc., m. pl. G. 441, 1. Friend of the people, *populāris, is,* m. and f.

Friendly. *Amīcus, a, um.*

Friendship. *Amicitia, ae,* f.

From. *A, ab; e, ex;* prep. with abl. G. 434, 3. From, after verbs of hindering, *quomĭnus,* conj. G. 499. From boyhood, *a puĕro.* From day to day, *in dies.* From that place, thence, *inde,* adv.

Fulfil. *Fungor, i, functus sum,* dep. G. 419, I.

Full, in full numbers. *Frequens, entis.*

Fully — more fully. *Plurĭbus verbis.* See 514.

Furnish. *Orno, āre, āvi, ātum.*

G.

Gain. *Emolumentum, i,* n.

Game. *Ludus, i,* m.

Garden. *Hortus, i,* m.

Gate. *Porta, ae,* f.

Gaul. *Gallia, ae,* f.

Gaul, a Gaul. *Gallus, i,* m.

General. *Imperātor, ōris,* m.

Geneva. *Genēva, ae,* f.

Genius. *Ingenium, ii,* n.

German. *Germānus, i,* m.

Gift. *Donum, i,* n.

Give. *Do, dare, dedi, datum.* Give, deliver, *trado, ĕre, dĭdi, dĭtum.* Give, confer, *confĕro, ferre, tūli, collātum.* Give advice, *suadeo, ēre, suasi, suasum.* G. 385. Give heed, *opĕram do, dare, dedi, datum.* Give precepts, *praecĭpio, ĕre, cēpi, ceptum.*

Gladly. *Laete,* adv.

Glorious. *Gloriōsus, a, um.*

Glory. *Gloria, ae,* f.

Glory in. *Glorior, āri, ātus sum,* dep.

Go. *Eo, ire, ivi and ii, itum.* Go from, *exeo, īre, ii, ītum.*

God. *Deus, i,* m. G. 51, 5.

Gold. *Aurum, i,* n.

Golden. *Aureus, a, um.*

Good. *Bonus, a, um.* Good deed, *recte factum,* n. See 366. Good will, *benevolentia, ae,* f. To be one's good fortune, *contingo, ĕre, tĭgi, tactum.*

Good, a good. *Bonum, i,* n.

Goodness. *Bonĭtas, ātis,* f.

Gorgias. *Gorgias, ae,* m.

Govern. *Guberno, āre, āvi, ātum; rego, ĕre, rexi, rectum.*

Government. *Regnum, i,* n.

Gracchus. *Gracchus, i,* m.

Grain. *Frumentum, i,* n.

Grandson. *Nepos, ōtis,* m.

Grateful — be grateful. *Gratiam habeo, ēre, ui, ītum.* See 548.

Gratitude. *Gratia, ae,* f. To entertain gratitude, *gratiam habeo, ēre, ui, ītum.*

Gravity. *Gravĭtas, ātis,* f.

Great. *Magnus, a, um.* Great, illustrious, *amplus, a, um.* Great, severe, *gravis, e.* How great, *quantus, a, um.* So great, *tantus, a, um.*

Great Britain — of or from Great Britain. *Britannĭcus, a, um.*

Greater. *Major, us.* G. 165. Of greater value, *pluris.* G. 402, III. 1. To render a greater service, *plus prosum, prodesse, profui.* G. 290.

Greatest. *Maxĭmus, a, um.* G. 165. Greatest (in rank), highest, *summus, a, um.* G. 163, 3.

Greatly. *Valde, magnopĕre,* adv. Greatly, with *intĕrest* and *refert, magni.* G. 408, 8.

Greece. *Graecia, ae,* f.

Greedy. *Avĭdus, a, um.*

Greek. *Graecus, a, um.*

Greek, a Greek. *Graecus, i,* m.

Greek, in Greek. *Graece,* adv.

Grieve. *Doleo, ēre, ui, ītum.*

Guard — be on one's guard. *Caveo, ēre, cavi, cautum.*

Guard, to guard. *Custōdio, īre, īvi* and *ii, ītum.* Guard, defend, *tueor, ēri, ītus sum,* dep.

Guidance — under the guidance of. *Dux, ducis,* in abl. abs.

Guide. *Dux, ducis,* m. and f.

H.

Habit. *Consuetūdo, ĭnis,* f. See 167.

Hand. *Manus, us,* f.

Hannibal. *Hannĭbal, ălis,* m.

Happen. *Fio, fĭĕri, factus sum,* dep. Happen, of desirable occurrences, *contingo, ĕre, tĭgi, tactum.* Of undesirable, *accĭdo, ĕre, cĭdi.* See 624.

Happily. *Beāte, felicĭter,* adv.

Happiness, success. *Felicĭtas, ātis,* f.

Happy. *Beātus, a, um.*

Harm. *Injuria, ae,* f.

Harmony. *Concordia, ae,* f.

Hasten. *Contendo, ĕre, di, tum.*

Hate. *Odi, odisse.* G. 297, I.

Hatred. *Odium, ii,* n.

Have. *Habeo, ēre, ui, ītum; sum, esse, fui,* with dat. of possessor. To have business, *negotium esse,* with dat. of possessor. To have confidence in, *fidem habeo, ēre, ui, ĭtum* with dat. To have a prosperous voyage, *ex sententia navĭgo, āre, āvi, ātum.* See 339. To have reference to, *refĕror, ferri, lātus sum, ad* with acc. See 577.

He, she, &c. *Is, ea, id.* He himself, &c., *ipse, a, um.* He, &c., he also = the same, *idem, eădem, idem.* He, &c. = this one, *hic, haec, hoc.*

Health. *Valetūdo, ĭnis,* f.

Hear. *Audio, īre, īvi, ītum.*

Hearer. *Audiens, entis,* m. and f.; *auditor, ōris,* m.; *is qui audit.* See 438.

Hearing, in the hearing of, pres. part. of *audio* in abl. absol. See 555.

Heaven, heavens. *Caelum, i,* n.

Heavy. *Gravis, e.*

Heed, give heed to. *Opĕram do, dare, dedi, datum.*

Held, to be held = to be. *Sum, esse, fui.*

Helvetian. *Helvetius, a, um.*

Helvetians. *Helvetii, ōrum,* m. pl.

Herald. *Praeco, ōnis,* m.

Here. *Hic,* adv.

Hero. *Vir, viri,* m.

Herodotus. *Herodŏtus, i,* m.

Hesitate. *Dubĭto, āre, āvi, ātum.*

High. *Altus, a, um.* High, ample, *amplus, a, um.* High, great (price), *magnus, a, um.* At a high price, *magno.* G. 416.

Highest, of the highest degree. *Summus, a, um.* G. 163, 3.

Highest results, *summa, ōrum,* n. pl. G. 441, 1. Highest welfare of the state, highest public welfare, *summa res publīca.*

Highly, with verbs of valuing. *Magni.* Very highly, *maxīmi.* More highly, *plurīs.* How highly, *quanti.* G. 402, III. 1.

Himself. *Sui, sibi.* Himself, intensive, *ipse, a, um.* By himself, *secum.*

Hippias. *Hippias, ae,* m.

His. *Suus, a, um;* not reflexive, *ejus.* See 468, 2. His own things, productions, *sua, ōrum,* n. pl. G. 441, 1.

History. *Historia, ae,* f.

Hold. *Teneo, ēre, ui, tentum.* Have, *habeo, ēre, ui, ītum.*

Home. *Domus, i,* f. G. 117, 1.

Homer. *Homērus, i,* m.

Honestly. *Honeste,* adv.

Honor. *Honor, ōris,* m.; *honestas, ātis,* f.

Honorable. *Honestus, a, um.*

Hope. *Spes, spei,* f.

Hope, to hope. *Spero, āre, āvi, ātum.*

Horse. *Equus, equi,* m.

Hortensius. *Hortensius, ii,* m.

Hostile. *Inimīcus, a, um.*

Hostility, enmity. *Odium, ii,* n.

Hour. *Hora, ae,* f.

House, one's house. *Domus, us* and *i,* f. G. 119, 1. Walls of my, &c., house, *mei pariētes,* etc. See 378.

How. *Quam,* adv. How great, how large, *quantus, a, um.* How highly, with verbs of valuing, *quanti.* G. 402, III. 1. How long, *quousque,* adv. How many, *quot,* indecl. How very busy one is, *quanta occupatiōne distinētur (distĭneo, ēre, ui, tentum).* See 631.

However. *Quamvis,* adv. However much, *quantumvis,* adv.

Hundred. *Centum,* indecl.

I.

I. *Ego, mei.* I, emphatic, *egŏmet.* G. 184, 6. I myself, *ipse, a, um.* I would that, *utinam,* adv. G. 488, 1.

Ides. *Idus, uum,* f. pl. G. 708, I. 3.

If. *Si,* conj. See Lesson LXXVII. If only, *dummŏdo,* conj. If any, *si quis.* G. 190, 1.

Ignorance — keep in ignorance. *Celo, āre, āvi, ātum.* G. 374, 2, 1); 3, 1).

Ignorant — be ignorant of. *Ignōro, āre, āvi, ātum.* To keep ignorant of, in regard to, *celo, āre, āvi, ātum, de* with abl. G. 374, 3, 1).

Illustrious. *Illustris, e.* Most illustrious, highest, *summus, a, um.* G. 163, 3.

Imitate. *Imĭtor, āri, ātus sum,* dep.

Immediately. *Jam,* adv.

Immense. *Ingens, entis.*

Immortal. *Immortālis, e.*

Impel. *Impello, ēre, pūli, pulsum.* Impel, incite, *concĭto, āre, āvi, ātum.*

Impious. *Impius, a, um.*

Implore. *Oro, āre, āvi, ātum.*

Important, great. *Magnus, a, um.* It is important, *intĕrest, fuit.* G. 408.

Impose upon. *Impōno, ēre, posui, posĭtum.*

Impudence. *Impudentia, ae,* f.

In. *In,* prep. with abl. In accordance with, *e, ex,* prep. with abl. In behalf of, *pro,* prep. with abl. In regard to, *de,* prep. with abl.; sometimes rendered by the gen. In = situated in, *posĭtus, a, um, in* with abl. In the censorship, consulship, life, reign, etc., of. See 409. In the presence of, *apud,* prep. with acc. In the vicinity of, *ad,* prep. with acc. In a spirited manner, *acrĭter,* adv. In full numbers, *frequens, entis.* In vain, *frustra; nequidquam,* adv. See 888.

Inaction, inactivity. *Inertia, ae, f.*
Incite. *Incĭto, āre, āvi, ātum.*
Inclined. *Propensus, a, um.*
Increase, intrans. *Cresco, ĕre, crĕvi, cretum ;* trans., *augeo, ĕre, auxi, auctum.*
Incursion. *Incursio, ōnis, f.*
Indeed. *Quidem ; enim ; tandem ;* adv. See 606. Indeed I, &c. See 514.
Individual, one. *Unus, a, um.* G. 175, 1.
Induce. *Indŭco, ĕre, duxi, ductum.*
Industry. *Industria, ae, f.*
Infer. *Collĭgo, ĕre, lēgi, lectum.*
Influence. *Indŭco, addŭco, ĕre, duxi, ductum.*
Inform. *Certiōrem facio, ĕre, feci, factum.* See 527. Inform, teach, *doceo, ĕre, ui, doctum.*
Inhabitant. *Incŏla, ae, m. and f.*
Injure. *Noceo, ĕre, ui, ĭtum.* G. 385.
Injury. *Injuria, ae, f.*
Inner. *Interior, ius.* G. 166.
Innocence. *Innocentia, ae, f.*
Innumerable. *Innumerabĭlis, e.*
Inquire. *Quaero, ĕre, quaesivi, ĭtum.*
Inscribe. *Inscrĭbo, ĕre, scripsi, scriptum.*
Insolence. *Insolentia, ae, f.*
Instance, thing. *Res, rei, f.*
Instruct. *Erŭdio, ĭre, īvi and ii, ĭtum.* Instruct, teach, *doceo, ĕre, docui, doctum.*
Instructor. *Praeceptor, ōris, m.*
Integrity. *Integrĭtas, ātis, f.*
Intention — be one's intention. *In anĭmo sum, esse, fui,* with dat. of possessor. See 206.
Interest — object of interest. *Quod visendum est.* See 527.
Interests, advantage. *Utilĭtas, ātis, f.*
Interests, it interests. *Intĕrest, fuit.* G. 408.
Interrupt. *Interpello, āre, āvi, ātum.*
Intimate—a very intimate acquaint-

ance. *Summus usus.* To be intimate with, *familiarĭter utor, i, usus sum,* dep. G. 419, I.
Into. *In,* prep. with acc.
Introduce, bring in. *Indŭco, ĕre, duxi, ductum.*
Invent, devise. *Fingo, ĕre, finxi, fictum.* See 605.
Invention. *Inventum, i, n.*
Invite. *Voco, āre, āvi, ātum ;* see 184, 2 ; *invĭto, āre, āvi, ātum.*
Is doing, is done. *Agĭtur ; gerĭtur.*
Island. *Insŭla, ae, f.*
Isocrates. *Isocrătes, is, m.*
It. *Is, ea, id ; ille, a, ud.* It itself, *ipse, a, um.* It, the same thing, *idem, eădem, idem.* Its, *suus, a, um ; ejus.* See 468, 2.
Italy. *Italia, ae, f.*
Itself. *Sui, sĭbi ;* intensive, *ipse, a, um.*

J.

Journey. *Iter, itinĕris, n.*
Joy. *Gaudium, ii, n.; laetitia, ae, f.* See 294.
Joyful. *Laetus, a, um.*
Judge. *Judex, ĭcis, m.*
Judge, to judge. *Judĭco, āre, āvi, ātum.* Judge, consider, *existĭmo, āre, āvi, ātum.*
July — sixth of July. *Pridie Nonas Quintiles.* G. 708 ; 437, 1.
July — of July. *Quintĭlis, e.*
June — of June. *Junius, a, um.*
Junius. *Junius, ii, m.*
Jupiter. *Jupĭter, Jovis, m.*
Just. *Justus, a, um.* Just, with numbers, *ipse, a, um.* G. 452, 3.
Justice. *Justitia, ae, f.*
Justly. *Juste,* adv.

K.

Keep. *Servo, āre, āvi, ātum.*
Keep from, *prohĭbeo, ĕre, ui, ĭtum.* Keep from, keep off, *arceo, ĕre, ui, arctum.* G. 425, 2, 2). Keep in ignorance, *celo,*

āre, āvi, ātum. G. 374, 2, 1);
3, 1). Keep ignorant of, in regard to, *celo, āre, āvi, ātum, de*
with abl. G. 374, 3, 1).

Kill. *Enĕco, āre, ui, nectum.*

Kind. *Benignus, a, um.*

Kind, class. *Genus, ĕris, n.* Every
kind, *omne genus,* n.

Kindness. *Benignĭtas, ātis, f.*

King. *Rex, regis, m.*

Know, know how. *Scio, scire, scivi,
scitum.* Know, be acquainted
with, *cognosco, ĕre, nōvi, nĭtum.*
Know, comprehend, *percĭpio,
ĕre, cĕpi, ceptum.* Know, understand, *intellĭgo, ĕre, lexi, lectum.*
Not to know, *nescio, īre, īvi* and
ii, ītum.

Knowledge. *Scientia, ae, f.* See
also Note on 638, 7, page 276.
Practical knowledge, *usus, us,* m.

Known — well known, sometimes
rendered by *ille, a, ud.* G.
450, 4.

L.

Labienus. *Labiēnus, i,* m.

Labor. *Labor, ōris,* m.

Lacedaemonian. *Lacedaemonius,
ii,* m.

Laelius. *Laelius, ii,* m.

Lake. *Lacus, us,* m.

Land. *Terra, ae,* f. On sea and
land, *terra marĭque.*

Language, tongue. *Lingua, ae,* f.

Large. *Magnus, a, um.* How large,
quantus, a, um.

Lasting. *Sempiternus, a, um.*

Latin, in Latin. *Latĭne,* adv.

Law. *Lex, legis,* f.; *jus, juris,* n.
See 405. Civil law, *jus civile.*
The law of nations, *jus gentium.*

Lawful — it is lawful. *Licet, licuit*
and *licĭtum est,* impers.

Lawgiver. *Is qui leges scribit*
(*scribo, ĕre, scripsi, scriptum*).
See 438.

Lay waste. *Vasto, āre, āvi, ātum.*

Lead. *Duco, ĕre, duxi, ductum.*
Lead across, *tradŭco, ĕre, duxi,*
ductum. Lead on, *addŭco, ĕre,
duxi, ductum.* Lead out, *edŭco,
ĕre, duxi, ductum.* Lead (a life),
live, *vivo, ĕre, vixi, victum.*

Leader. *Dux, ducis,* m. and f.

Learn. *Disco, ĕre, didĭci.* Learn,
receive, hear, *accĭpio, ĕre, cĕpi,
ceptum.*

Learned. *Doctus, a, um.* Learned,
of learning, *doctrīnae.* See
440, 2.

Learning. *Doctrīna, ae,* f.; *eruditio, ōnis,* f. Branch of learning, *doctrīna, ae,* f.

Least. *Minĭmus, a, um;* G. 165;
minĭme, adv.

Leisure. *Otium, ii,* n. At leisure,
otiōsus, a, um.

Leisure, unoccupied. *Vacuus,a,um.*

Lemannus. *Lemannus, i,* m.

Length — at length. *Tandem,* adv.

Leonidas. *Leonĭdas, ae,* m.

Leontini — of Leontini, Leontine.
Leontīnus, a, um.

Less. *Minor, us;* G. 165; *minus,*
adv.

Let = cause that. *Facio, ĕre, feci,
factum, ut* with subj.

Letter of the alphabet. *Littĕra,
ae,* f. Letter, epistle, *epistŏla,
ae,* f.; *littĕrae, ārum,* f. pl. See
200. By letter, *per littĕras.* Letter from me, &c., *mea epistŏla,*
or *epistŏla a me,* etc. See 366.
Letters, literature, *littĕrae,ārum,*
f. pl.

Leuctra. *Leuctra, ōrum,* n. pl.
Of Leuctra, Leuctrian, *Leuctrĭ-
cus, a, um.*

Liberal. *Liberālis, e.*

Liberality. *Liberalĭtas, ātis,* f.

Liberate. *Libĕro, āre, āvi, ātum.*
G. 425, 3, 2).

Liberty. *Libertas, ātis,* f.

Life. *Vita, ae,* f. Period of life,
aetas, ātis, f.

Light. *Lux, lucis,* f.

Lighten. *Levo, āre, āvi, ātum.*

Lightly. *Levĭter,* adv. Esteem
lightly, despise, *contemno, ĕre,
tempsi, temptum.*

Like. *Similis, e.*

Line of battle. *Acies, ei,* f.

Lines — these lines, these things. *Haec,* n. pl.

Literary = of letters. *Litterārum.* See 440, 2.

Literature, letters. *Littěrae, ārum,* f. pl.

Little—think little of, despise. *Contemno, ěre, tempsi, temptum.*

Live. *Vivo, ěre, vixi, victum.* One lives, men live, *vivǐtur, victum est,* impers.

Live, living. *Vivus, a, um.*

Load, to pile up. *Exstruo, ěre, struxi, structum.*

Long. *Longus, a, um.* Long continued, very long, *perdiuturnus, a, um.* For a long time, *jamdūdum, jampridem.* G. 467, 2. How long, *quousque,* adv.

Long for. *Expěto, ěre, petivi* and *ii, ǐtum.*

Look — look forward to. *Exspecto, āre, āvi, ātum.* Look upon, *suspǐcio, ěre, spexi, spectum.* Look upon with envy, *invǐdeo, ěre, vidi, visum.* G. 385.

Lose. *Amitto, ěre, misi, missum.*

Loss. Rendered by the Perf. Pass. Part. of *amitto, ěre, misi, missum.* G. 580.

Lost, engaged, busy. *Impedǐtus, a, um.*

Loud, great. *Magnus, a, um.* With a loud voice, *magna voce.*

Love. *Amor, ōris,* m.

Love, to love. *Amo, āre, āvi, ātum.*

Lucius. *Lucius, ii,* m.

Lucullus. *Lucullus, i,* m.

Lycurgus. *Lycurgus, i,* m.

Lysis. *Lysis, ǐdis,* m.

M.

Macedon — of Macedon, a Macedonian. *Macědo, ōnis,* m.

Macedonia. *Macedonia, ae,* f.

Mad — be mad. *Furo, ěre, ui.*

Madness. *Furor, ōris,* m.

Maelius. *Maelius, ii,* m.

Magian, pl. the Magi. *Magus, i,* m.

Magistrate. *Magistrātus, us,* m.

Magnificent. *Magnifĭcus, a, um.*

Maiden. *Virgo, ǐnis,* f.

Mail, coat of mail. *Lorĭca, ae,* f.

Make. *Facio, ěre, feci, factum; effĭcio, ěre, fēci, fectum.* Make acceptable, *probo, āre, āvi, ātum.* Make a boast, *glorior, āri, ātus sum,* dep. Make use of, *utor, i, usus sum,* dep. G. 419, I.

Man. *Homo, ǐnis,* m. and f.; *vir, viri,* m. See 239, II.

Manifest. *Apertus, a, um.*

Manilius. *Manilius, ii,* m.

Manius. *Manius, ii,* m.

Manner. *Modus, i,* m. In a spirited manner, *acriter,* adv. In the best manner, *optǐme,* adv.

Mantinea. *Mantinēa, ae,* f.

Many, many of the. *Multi, ae, a,* pl. How many, *quot,* indecl. So many, *tot,* indecl.

March. *Iter, itinĕris,* n. Forced marches, *magna itinĕra.* See 246. On the march, *in itinĕre.*

March—of March. *Martius, a, um.*

Marcius. *Marcius, ii,* m.

Marcus. *Marcus, i,* m.

Marius. *Marius, ii,* m.

Mark. See 426.

Mars. *Mars, Martis,* m.

Master. *Magister, tri,* m.

Mausolus. *Mausōlus, i,* m.

May, it may be that. *Fiěri potest ut,* with subj.

May — of May. *Maius, a, um.*

Mean. *Volo, velle, volui,* with ethical dat. G. 389, 2.

Means, property. *Res, rei,* f. Means, resources, *opes, opum,* f. pl. By no means, *minǐme,* adv. See 586.

Measure. *Metior, iri, mensus sum,* dep.

Memory. *Memoria, ae,* f.

Mention. *Commemŏro, āre, āvi, ātum; dico, ěre, dixi, dictum.*

Mercury. *Mercurius, ii,* m.

Messenger. *Nuntius, ii,* m.

Miletus — of Miletus, Milesian. *Milesius, a, um.*

Military. *Militāris, e.* Military, pertaining to war, *bellīcus, a, um.* Military affairs, military science, *res militāris.*

Milo. *Milo* and *Milon, ŏnis,* m.

Mina. *Mina, ae,* f.

Mind. *Anĭmus, i,* m.; *mens, mentis,* f. See 355. To occupy the mind, *in anĭmo versor, āri, ātus sum,* dep. See 454. To call to mind, *commemŏro, āre, āvi, ātum.* To recall to mind, *recordor, āri, ātus sum,* dep. G. 406, II.

Minister. *Minister, tri,* m.; *ministra, ae,* f.

Minister to. *Minister, tra, sum, esse, fui,* with gen. See 560.

Mithridates. *Mithridātes, is,* m.

Modest. *Modestus, a, um.*

Modesty. *Verecundia, ae,* f.

Money, sum of money. *Pecunia, ae,* f. Money, copper, *aes, aeris,* n.

Month. *Mensis, is,* m.

Monument. *Monumentum, i,* n.

Moral worth. *Honestas, ātis,* f.; *virtus, ūtis,* f.

More. *Plus, pluris;* G. 165, 1; *magis,* adv. More highly, with verbs of valuing, of more value, *pluris.* G. 402, III. 1. More fully, *plurĭbus verbis.* See 514.

Morning, early in the morning. *Mane,* adv.

Most exalted. *Summus, a, um.* G. 163, 3.

Mother. *Mater, tris,* f.

Mountain. *Mons, montis,* m.

Mourn over. *Maereo, ēre.*

Move. *Moveo, commŏveo, ēre, mōvi, mōtum.* Move, affect, *afficio, ēre, fēci, fectum.*

Much. *Multum,* adv. Much, exceedingly, *valde,* adv. Much, with comparatives, *multo,* adv. Very much, *plurĭmum,* adv. However much, *quantumvis,* adv.

Mucius. *Mucius, ii,* m.

Multitude. *Multitūdo, ĭnis,* f. Mul-

titudes assemble, *concursus fit.* See 606.

Muse. *Musa, ae,* f.

Must. See 557.

My. *Meus, a, um.*

Myself, reflexive, not intensive. *Ego, mei;* intensive, *ipse, a, um.* By myself, *mecum.*

N.

Name. *Nomen, ĭnis,* n.

Name, to name. *Nomĭno, appello, āre, āvi, ātum.* See 184.

Narrow. *Angustus, a, um.*

Nasica. *Nasica, ae,* m.

Nation. *Gens, gentis,* f.; *popŭlus, i,* m. The law of nations, *jus gentium.*

Native talent. *Ingenium, ii,* n.

Nature. *Natūra, ae,* f.

Naval. *Navālis, e.* A naval battle, naval engagement, *pugna navālis.*

Near. *Prope (propius, proxĭme),* adv. Near, near to, *ad, apud,* prep. with acc.

Nearest. *Proxĭmus, a, um.* G. 166.

Nearly. *Paene,* adv.

Necessary. *Necessarius, a, um.* It is necessary, *necesse est, fuit.*

Necessity. *Necessĭtas, ātis,* f.

Need—there is need of, there needs. *Opus est, fuit.* G. 419, 3. To need, *egeo, indĭgeo, ēre, ui.* See 239, I. To feel the need of, *indĭgeo, ēre, ui.*

Needful — to be needful (there needs, is need of). *Opus est, fuit.* G. 419, 3.

Neglect. *Neglĭgo, ēre, lexi, lectum.*

Negligent. *Neglĭgens, entis.*

Neither — nor. *Neque* or *nec — neque* or *nec.*

Never. *Nunquam,* adv.

New. *Novus, a, um.* New Carthage, *Carthāgo Nova,* f.

Night. *Nox, noctis,* f.

Nile. *Nilus, i,* m.

Nineteen. *Undēvigintī,* indecl.

Ninetieth. *Nonagesĭmus, a, um.*

No. *Nullus, a, um ;* G. 151; *non,* adv. No one, *nemo, ĭnis,* m. and f. G. 457, 2. That no one, in clauses denoting purpose, *ne quis.* G. 190, 1. By no means, *minĭme,* adv. See 586. To no purpose, *nequidquam,* adv.

Noble. *Nobĭlis, e.* Noble-minded, honorable, *honestus, a, um.*

Nomination—without a nomination from the people. *Injussu popŭli.* G. 414, 2, 3).

Nones. *Nonae, ārum,* f. pl. G. 708, I. 2.

Nor. *Neque* or *nec,* conj.; with imperatives, *neve,* conj.

Not. *Non,* adv.; interrog., *nonne;* G. 346, II. 1; with imperatives, *ne,* adv. Not at all, not = not at all, *nihil.* G. 380, 2. Not, followed by either — or = neither — nor, *neque* or *nec — neque* or *nec.* Not even, *ne quidem.* See 577. Not only — but also, *non solum* or *non modo — sed etiam.* Not very, *non ita,* adv. Not yet, *nondum,* adv. And not, but not, *neque* or *nec.* Not to know, *nescio, ĭre, ĭvi* and *ii, ĭtum.* To say — not = to deny, *nego, āre, āvi, ātum.*

Nothing. *Nihil,* n. indecl.

Nourish. *Alo, ĕre, ui, altum* and *alĭtum.*

Novel. *Novus, a, um.*

Now. *Nunc,* adv. Now, already, *jam,* adv.

Numa. *Numa, ae,* m.

Numantia. *Numantia, ae,* f.

Number. *Numĕrus, i,* m. In full numbers, *frequens, entis.* G. 443.

Numitor. *Numĭtor, ōris,* m.

O.

O, oh that. *Utĭnam,* adv. G. 488, 1.

Obedience. *Obtemperatio, ōnis,* f.

Obey. *Pareo, ēre, ui, ĭtum.* G. 385.

Object, thing. *Res, rei,* f. Object of interest, *quod visendum est.* See 527.

Observe, keep. *Servo, āre, āvi, ātum.* Observe, retain, *teneo, ēre, ui, tentum.*

Obstinacy. *Pertinacia, ae,* f.

Obtain. *Potior, ĭri, ĭtus sum,* dep.; G. 419, I.; *nanciscor, i, nactus sum,* dep. Obtain, find, *invĕnio, ĭre, vēni, ventum.*

Occasion—there is occasion. *Opus est, fuit.* G. 419, 3.

Occult. *Occultus, a, um.*

Occupy. *Occŭpo, āre, āvi, ātum.* To occupy the mind, *in anĭmo versor, āri, ātus sum,* dep. See 454.

Of, concerning. *De,* prep. with abl. Of, from, *a, ab,* prep. with abl. Out of, *e, ex,* prep. with abl. Of, after superlatives=among, *inter,* prep. with acc. Of, before proper nouns. See 435, 436. Of greater value, *pluris.* G. 402, III. 1.

Offend. *Offendo, ĕre, di, sum.* G. 385, 1. Offend against, *vĭolo, āre, āvi, ātum.*

Offer. *Affĕro, ferre, attŭli, allātum.*

Often. *Saepe,* adv.

Oh that. *Utĭnam.* G. 488, 1.

Old. *Senex, senis ;* as substant., old man. Old age, *senectus, ūtis,*f.

Older. *Major, ōris,* or *major natu.*

Olive tree. *Olea, ae,* f.

Olympia. *Olympia, ae,* f.

Olympus. *Olympus, i,* m.

On = concerning, on the subject of. *De,* prep. with abl. On account of, *propter,* prep. with acc. On the part of, often rendered by the gen. On sea and land, *terra marĭque.* On the march, *in itinĕre.*

Once. *Semel,* adv. Once, formerly, *quondam,* adv. At once, *jam,* adv.

One. *Unus, a, um.* G. 175, 1. One, any one, any thing, *quis.*

See 500, III.; also G. 190. One's self, *sui*, *sibi*. One's, one's own, *suus*, *a*, *um*. No one, *nemo*, *ĭnis*, m. and f. G. 457, 2. That no one, in clauses denoting purpose, *ne quis*. G. 190, 1. One each, *singŭli*, *ae*, *a*, pl.

Only. *Modo*, adv.

Open, to open. *Apĕrio*, *ĭre*, *ui*, *pertum*.

Open. *Apertus*, *a*, *um*. Open adversary, *palam adversarius*, *ii*, m.

Openly. *Palam*, adv.

Opinion. *Sententia*, *ae*, f.; *opinio*, *ōnis*, f. To express opinion, *censeo*, *ĕre*, *ui*, *censum*.

Opponent. *Adversarius*, *ii*, m.

Oppose. *Obsisto*, *ĕre*, *stĭti*, *stĭtum*; *obsto*, *āre*, *stĭti*, *stātum*. To oppose one's self, *se opponĕre* (*oppōno*, *ĕre*, *posui*, *posĭtum*).

Opulent. *Opulentus*, *a*, *um*.

Or. *Aut*, conj.; in questions, *an*, conj. Or not, usually *annon* in direct questions, *necne* in indirect.

Oration. *Oratio*, *ōnis*, f.

Orator. *Orātor*, *ōris*, m.

Oratory. *Dicendi*, *o*, gerund of *dico*.

Order. *Jubeo*, *ĕre*, *jussi*, *jussum*.

Orgetorix. *Orgetŏrix*, *ĭgis*, m.

Other. *Alius*, *a*, *ud*. G. 151; 459. The other, the second of two, *alter*, *ĕra*, *ĕrum*. G. 151; 151, 2; 459. The others, the rest, *cetĕri*, *ae*, *a*, pl. Of others, another's, *aliēnus*, *a*, *um*.

Ought. *Debeo*, *ĕre*, *ui*, *ĭtum*. Also rendered by the Pass. 1 eriphrast. Conj. G. 232.

Our. *Noster*, *tra*, *trum*. Our own things, productions, *nostra*, -*rum*, n. pl. G. 441, 1.

Out of. *E*, *ex*, prep. with abl. G. 434, 3. To set out, *proficiscor*, *i*, *profectus sum*, dep.

Overcome. *Vinco*, *ĕre*, *vici*, *victum*.

Overthrow of. Rendered by the perf. pass. part. of *everto*, *ĕre*, *verti*, *versum*. See 439; also G. 580.

Overthrow, to overthrow. *Everto*, *ĕre*, *verti*, *versum*.

Owe. *Debeo*, *ĕre*, *ui*, *ĭtum*.

Own, often expressed by the possessive, or when more emphatic by the gen. of *ipse*, *a*, *um*, with the possessive. G. 452, 4.

Ox. *Bos*, *bovis*, m. G. 66.

P.

Pain. *Dolor*, *ōris*, m.

Paint. *Pingo*, *ĕre*, *pinxi*, *pictum*.

Painting. *Tabŭla picta*, f. See 378.

Panathenaicus. *Panathenaĭcus*, *i*, m.

Parent. *Parens*, *entis*, m. and f.

Part. *Pars*, *partis*, f. On the part of, to be the part of, often rendered by the gen. See 426.

Pass — allow to pass. *Intermitto*, *ĕre*, *mĭsi*, *missum*.

Past. *Praeterĭtus*, *a*, *um*.

Path. *Semĭta*, *ae*, f.

Pay one's respects to. *Salūto*, *āre*, *āvi*, *ātum*.

Peace. *Pax*, *pacis*, f. To reduce to a state of peace, *paco*, *āre*, *āvi*, *ātum*.

Peculiar to. *Proprius*, *a*, *um*.

Penalty. *Poena*, *ae*, f.

People, a people. *Popŭlus*, *i*, m. Friend of the people, *populāris*, *is*, m. and f. Without a nomination from the people, *injussu popŭli*. G. 414, 2, 3).

Perceive. *Percĭpio*, *ĕre*, *cēpi*, *ceptum*; *perspĭcio*, *ĕre*, *spexi*, *spectum*; *sentio*, *ĭre*, *sensi*, *sensum*. Perceive, discern, *cerno*, *ĕre*.

Perfect. *Perfectus*, *a*, *um*.

Perform. *Ago*, *ĕre*, *egi*, *actum*; *gero*, *ĕre*, *gessi*, *gestum*.

Perhaps. *Forsĭtan*, *fortasse*, adv.; sometimes rendered by *haud scio an* with subj. See 586.

Pericles. *Perĭcles*, *is*, m.

Peril. *Pericŭlum*, *i*, n.

Perishable. *Caducus, a, um.*

Permitted — it is permitted. *Licet, licuit* and *licitum est,* impers.

Perpetual. *Perpetuus, a, um.*

Perseus. *Perseus, ei,* m.

Personal, of one's self alone, gen. of *solus, a, um.* G. 151; 397, 3.

Persuade. *Persuadeo, ere, si, sum.* G. 385.

Pertain to. *Pertineo, ere, ui, tentum.*

Pharsalian, of Pharsalus, or Pharsalia. *Pharsalius, a, um.*

Philip. *Philippus, i,* m.

Philo. *Philo* or *Philon, onis,* m.

Philosopher. *Philosophus, i,* m.

Philosophy. *Philosophia, ae,* f.

Pity. *Misereor, eri, itus sum,* dep.; G. 406, 1; *miseret, uit,* impers. G. 410, III. See 228.

Place. *Locus, i,* m. G. 141. From that place, *inde,* adv. To take place, *fio, fieri, factus sum.* G. 294.

Plan. *Consilium, ii,* n.

Plato. *Plato* and *Platon, onis,* m.

Plautus. *Plautus, i,* m.

Play. *Ludo, ere, lusi, lusum.*

Please. *Placeo, ere, ui, itum.* G. 385.

Pleased — be pleased, rejoice. *Laetor, ari, atus sum,* dep.

Pleasure. *Voluptas, atis,* f. Pleasure, enjoyment, *delectatio, onis,*f.

Plunder. *Diripio, ere, ui, reptum.*

Poem. *Poema, atis,* n.

Poet. *Poeta, ae,* m.

Point, thing. *Res, rei,* f.

Pompey. *Pompeius, eii,* m.

Poor. *Pauper, eris.* Poor, with limited means, *inops, opis.*

Popilius. *Popilius, ii,* m.

Porsena. *Porsena, ae,* m.

Possess. *Possideo, ere, sedi, sessum.* Possess, have, *habeo, ere, ui, itum.*

Possessed of. *Praeditus, a, um.* G. 419, III.

Possession. *Possessio, onis,* f. Possessions, things, *res, rerum,* f. pl.

Possible — as . . . as possible. *Quam,* adv. with superlat. See 449.

Power. *Potentia, ae,* f. Regal power, *regnum, i,* n.

Powerful. *Potens, entis.*

Practical knowledge. *Usus, us,* m.

Practice. See Note on 638, 7, page 276.

Practise. *Colo, ere, colui, cultum.*

Praetor. *Praetor, oris,* m.

Praetorship. See 409.

Praise. *Laus, laudis,* f.

Praise, to praise. *Laudo, are, avi, atum.*

Praiseworthy. *Laudabilis, e.*

Pray, I pray, parenthetical. *Quaeso.*

Precept. *Praeceptum, i,* n. To give precepts, *praecipio, ere, cepi, ceptum.*

Preceptor. *Praeceptor, oris,* m.

Preceptress. *Praeceptrix, icis,* f.

Predict. *Praedico, ere, dixi, dictum.*

Prefer. *Praefero, ferre, tuli, latum;* antepono, ere, posui, positum.* Prefer, would rather, *malo, malle, malui.* G. 293.

Preferable. *Satius.* See 527.

Prepared. *Paratus, a, um.*

Presence — in the presence of. *Apud,* prep. with acc.

Present. *Donum, i,* n.

Present, to present. *Dono, are, avi, atum.* To present one's self, *se praebere (praebeo, ere, ui, itum).*

Present, at hand. *Praesens, entis.*

Preserve. *Servo, conservo, are, avi, atum.*

Preside over. *Praesum, esse, fui.* G. 386.

Presume. *Credo, ere, didi, ditum.*

Pretend. *Simulo, are, avi, atum.*

Price. *Pretium, ii,* n.

Pride. *Superbia, ae,* f.

Prince. *Princeps, ipis,* m.

Princely. *Regalis, e.*

Principal. *Princeps, ipis,* m. and f

Priscus. *Priscus, i,* m.

Prize. *Praemium, ii,* n.

Prize, to prize. *Aestĭmo, āre, āvi, ātum.*

Proceed. *Pergo, ĕre, perrexi, per-rectum.*

Proclaim. *Proclāmo, āre, āvi, ātum.*

Prodicus. *Prodĭcus, i, m.*

Produce, bear. *Fero, ferre, tuli, latum.*

Profess. *Profĭteor, ēri, fessus sum,* dep.

Profit. *Utĭlĭtas, ātis, f.*

Profit, to profit. *Condūco, ĕre, duxi, ductum.* See 289.

Profitable. *Fructuōsus, a, um.*

Promise. *Promissum, i, n.*

Promise, to promise. *Pollĭceor, ēri, pollĭcĭtus sum,* dep.

Prompt, affect. *Commŏveo, ĕre, mōvi, mōtum.*

Pronounce, speak. *Dico, ĕre, dixi, dictum.*

Proof. *Testimonium, ii, n.*

Properly, worthily enough. *Satis digne,* adv.

Property, means. *Res, rei, f.*

Propose to one's self no other aim. *Nihĭl sibi aliud nisi proponĕre (propōno, ĕre, posui, posĭtum).* See 444.

Prosperity. *Res secundae, f. pl.* G. 441, 4.

Prosperous. *Felix, ĭcis; beātus, a, um.* See 393. To have a prosperous voyage, *ex sententia navĭgo, āre, āvi, ātum.* See 339.

Protection — to receive under protection. *In deditiōnem accĭpio, ĕre, cēpi, ceptum.*

Proud. *Superbus, a, um.*

Prove. *Probo, āre, āvi, ātum.*

Provide for. *Provĭdeo, ĕre, vĭdi, vĭsum.* G. 386.

Province. *Provincia, ae, f.*

Prudence. *Prudentia, ae, f.*

Ptolemy. *Ptolemaeus, i, m.*

Public. *Publĭcus, a, um.* Highest public welfare, *summa res publĭca, f.*

Publius. *Publius, ii, m.*

Punic. *Punĭcus, a, um.*

Punishment. *Supplicium, ii, n.* Punishment, penalty, *poena, ae, f.*

Pupil. *Discipŭlus, i, m.*

Purchase. *Emo, ĕre, emi, emptum.*

Purpose, wish. *Sententia, ae, f.* For the purpose of, *causa* with gen. G. 414, 2, 3). To no purpose, *nequidquam,* adv.

Pursue. *Sequor, i, secūtus sum,* dep.

Pursuit, study, exertion. *Studium, ii, n.*

Put to death. *Occĭdo, ĕre, di, sum; interfĭcio, ĕre, feci, fectum.*

Pydna. *Pydna, ae, f.*

Pythagoras. *Pythagŏras, ae, m.*

Pythagorean. *Pythagorēus, a, um.*

Q.

Queen. *Regīna, ae, f.*

Question. *Quaestio, ōnis, f.*

Quickly. *Celerĭter,* adv.

Quiet. *Otium, ii, n.*

Quintus. *Quintus, i, m.*

R.

Raise, conduct. *Perdūco, ĕre, duxi, ductum.*

Ranks in line of battle. *Acies, ēi, f.*

Rare. *Rarus, a, um.*

Rather, more. *Magis,* adv. Would rather, *malo, malle, malui.* G. 293.

Read. *Lego, ĕre, legi, lectum.*

Readily. *Facĭle,* adv.

Reason. *Ratio, ōnis, f.* For the reason that, *propterea quod,* conj.

Recall, mention. *Commemŏro, āre, āvi, ātum.* Recall to mind, *recordor, āri, ātus sum,* dep. G. 406, II.

Receive. *Accĭpio, ĕre, cēpi, ceptum.*

Recollection. *Memoria, ae, f.*

Record. *Perscrĭbo, ĕre, scripsi, scriptum.*

Recover. *Recupĕro, āre, āvi, ātum.* Recover, restore, *recreo, āre, āvi, ātum.*

Reduce to a state of peace. *Paco, āre, āvi, ātum.*

Reference — to arrange with reference to. *Refĕro, ferre, tūli, lātum, ad* with acc. See 534. To have reference to, *refĕror, ferri, lātus sum, ad* with acc. See 577.

Refinement. *Humanĭtas, ātis,* f. Refinements, culture, *cultus, us,* m.

Refute. *Refūto, āre, āvi, ātum; refello, ĕre, felli.*

Regal power. *Regnum, i,* n.

Regard — in regard to. *De,* prep. with abl.; sometimes rendered by gen. See 577.

Regard, hold. *Habeo, ĕre, ui, ĭtum.* Think, regard as, *puto, āre, āvi, ātum; statuo, ĕre, ui, ūtum.*

Reign — in the reign of. Pres. Part. of *regno,* in abl. abs. (*regno, āre, āvi, ātum*).

Reign, to reign. *Regno, āre, āvi, ātum.*

Rejoice, rejoice in. *Gaudeo, ĕre, gavīsus sum; laetor, āri, ātus sum,* dep.

Rejoicing, joy. *Laetitia, ae,* f.

Relate. *Narro, āre, āvi, ātum; fero, ferre, tuli, latum; trado, ĕre, dĭdi, dĭtum.*

Release. *Libĕro, āre, āvi, ātum.* G. 425, 3, 2).

Relief — to come to the relief of. *Subvĕnio, ĭre, vĕni, ventum.* G. 386.

Relying upon. *Fretus, a, um.* G. 419, IV.

Remain. *Maneo, ĕre, mansi, mansum.* It remains, *relĭquum est, fuit, ut* with subj.

Remarkable. *Singulāris, e.*

Remember. *Memĭni, meminisse;* G. 297, I.; 406, II.; *reminiscor, i.* G. 406, II.

Remissness. *Nequitia, ae,* f.

Remove, take away. *Tollo, ĕre, sustŭli, sublātum.*

Render service. *Prosum, prodesse,*

profui. See 606; also G. 290; 386.

Renew. *Instauro, āre, āvi, ātum.*

Repeat. *Reddo, ĕre, dĭdi, dĭtum.*

Repent. *Paenĭtet, uit,* impers. G. 410, III. See 228.

Reply. *Respondeo, ēre, di, sum.*

Report. *Rumor, ōris,* m.

Repose. *Tranquillĭtas, ātis,* f.

Republic. *Res publĭca, rei publĭcae,* f.

Request. *Rogātus, us,* m.

Require, compel. *Cogo, ĕre, coēgi, coactum.*

Requite a favor. *Gratiam refĕro, ferre, tūli, lātum.* See 548.

Rescue. *Erĭpĭo, ĕre, ripui, reptum.*

Reside. *Habĭto, āre, āvi, ātum.*

Resources, means. *Opes, opum,* f. pl.

Respects — pay one's respects to. *Salūto, āre, āvi, ātum.*

Rest. *Quies, ētis,* f.; *requies, ētis,* f. See 283.

Rest upon, be situated in. *Posĭtus, a, um, sum, esse, fui, in* with abl.

Rest, the rest. *Cetĕri, ae, a,* pl.

Restore. *Recreo, āre, āvi, ātum.*

Restrain. *Arceo, ēre, ui, arctum.*

Result. *Exĭtus, us,* m. Highest results, *summa, ōrum,* n. pl. See 415. To be the result, *evĕnio, ĭre, vĕni, ventum.*

Retain. *Teneo, ēre, ui, tentum.*

Return. *Redeo, ĭre, ii, ĭtum.* Return, turn back, *revertor, i, versus sum,* dep. G. 273, III., *verto.*

Revolution. *Res novae,* f. pl. See 228.

Reward. *Praemium, ii,* n. Reward, wages, *merces, ēdis,* f.

Rhetorician. *Rhetor, ōris,* m.

Rhine. *Rhenus, i,* m.

Rhone. *Rhodănus, i,* m.

Rich. *Dives, ĭtis.* G. 165, 2.

Riches. *Divitiae, ārum,* f. pl.

Right. *Rectus, a, um.* Right, the right, *fas,* n. indecl. See 405, 1. The right, integrity, *honestas, ātis,* f.

Rightly. *Recte*, adv.
River. *Flumen*, *Inis*, n.
Road. *Via*, *viae*, f.
Robber. *Praedo*, *ŏnis*, m.
Roman. *Romānus*, *a*, *um*.
Roman, a Roman. *Romānus*, *i*, m.
Rome. *Roma*, *ae*, f.
Romulus. *Romŭlus*, *i*, m.
Roscius. *Roscius*, *ii*, m.
Rout. *Pello*, *ĕre*, *pepŭli*, *pulsum*.
Route. *Iter*, *itinĕris*, n.
Ruin, demolish. *Diruo*, *ĕre*, *ui*, *ŭtum*.
Rule. *Dominatio*, *ŏnis*, f.
Rule, to rule. *Rego*, *ĕre*, *rexi*, *rectum* ; *impĕro*, *āre*, *āvi*, *ātum*. G. 385.
Rumor. *Rumor*, *ōris*, m.

S.

Sabine. *Sabīnus*, *a*, *um*.
Sacred. *Sanctus*, *a*, *um* ; *sacer*, *cra*, *crum*.
Sacrifice, to spend. *Profundo*, *ĕre*, *fūdi*, *fūsum*.
Sad. *Tristis*, *e*.
Safe. *Salvus*, *a*, *um*. Safe, secure, *tutus*, *a*, *um*. See 321.
Safety. *Salus*, *ūtis*, f.
Saguntum. *Saguntum*, *i*, n.
Sail. *Navĭgo*, *āre*, *āvi*, *ātum*.
Sake — for the sake of. *Causa* or *gratia* with gen. G. 414, 2, 3). For my, &c., sake, *mea causa*, etc.
Salute. *Salūto*, *āre*, *āvi*, *ātum*.
Same. *Idem*, *eădem*, *idem*. To entertain the same sentiments, *eădem sentio*, *ĭre*, *sensi*, *sensum*.
Satisfy. *Satisfacio*, *ĕre*, *fĕci*, *factum*. G. 25, 8, 2) ; 385.
Saturnia. *Saturnia*, *ae*, f.
Save. *Servo*, *conservo*, *āre*, *āvi*, *ātum*.
Say. *Dico*, *ĕre*, *dixi*, *dictum*. Say, relate, *fero*, *ferre*, *tuli*, *latum*. They say, *ferunt*. Say — not, deny, *nego*, *āre*, *āvi*, *ātum*.
Scaevola. *Scaevŏla*, *ae*, m.

Scarcely, scarcely yet. *Vixdum*, adv.
School. *Ludus*, *i*, m. ; *schola*, *ae*, f.
Science, learning. *Doctrina*, *ae*, f. Military science, *res militāris*, f.
Scipio. *Scipio*, *ōnis*, m.
Sea. *Mare*, *maris*, n. On sea and land, *terra marīque*.
Second, another. *Alter*, *ĕra*, *ĕrum*. G. 151 ; 151, 2. A second time, *itĕrum*, adv.
Secure, safe. *Tutus*, *a*, *um*. See 321.
Secure, to secure, conciliate. *Concĭlio*, *āre*, *āvi*, *ātum*.
Sedition. *Seditio*, *ōnis*, f.
See. *Video*, *ĕre*, *vidi*, *visum*. See that, take care that, *curo*, *āre*, *āvi*, *ātum*.
Seek. *Quaero*, *ĕre*, *quaesīvi*, *quaesītum* ; *peto*, *appĕto*, *expĕto*, *ĕre*, *petīvi* and *ii*, *ītum*. Seek, pursue, *sequor*, *i*, *secūtus sum*, dep.
Seem. *Videor*, *ĕri*, *visus sum*. See 577.
Seize. *Rapio*, *ĕre*, *ui*, *raptum*.
Select. *Elĭgo*, *ĕre*, *lĕgi*, *lectum*.
Select, selected. *Exquisītus*, *a*, *um*.
Self, one's self, reflexive. *Sui*, *sibi* ; intensive, *ipse*, *a*, *um*.
Sell. *Vendo*, *ĕre*, *dĭdi*, *dĭtum*.
Senate. *Senātus*, *us*, m.
Senator. *Senātor*, *ōris*, m.
Send. *Mitto*, *ĕre*, *misi*, *missum*.
Sense. *Sensus*, *us*, m.
Sentiments — entertain the same sentiments. *Eădem sentio*, *ĭre*, *sensi*, *sensum*.
Serve. *Servio*, *ĭre*, *ĭvi* and *ii*, *ĭtum*. G. 385.
Service — render service. *Prosum*, *prodesse*, *profui*. See 606 ; also G. 290 ; 386.
Servilius. *Servilius*, *ii*, m.
Servitude. *Servĭtus*, *ūtis*, f.
Servius. *Servius*, *ii*, m.
Set, set before. *Propōno*, *ĕre*, *posui*, *posĭtum*. Set fire to, *inflammo*, *āre*, *āvi*, *ātum* ; *incendo*, *ĕre*, *cendi*, *censum*. Set forth, *exprōmo*, *ĕre*, *prompsi*, *promp-*

tum. Set forth views, state, *prae-dīco, āre, āvi, ātum.* Set out, *proficiscor, i, profectus sum,* dep.

Seven. *Septem,* indecl.

Seventh time. *Septĭmum,* adv.

Seventh day of the month, — in March, May, July, and October. *Nonae, ārum,* f. pl. G. 708, I. 2.

Several. *Complūres, a* or *ia,* pl.

Severe. *Sevērus, a, um.* Severe, grievous, *gravis, e.*

Sextus. *Sextus, i,* m.

Share. *Communĭco, āre, āvi, ātum.*

Sharply. *Acrĭter,* adv.

Short, brief. *Brevis, e.*

Shoulder. *Humĕrus, i,* m.

Show. *Ostendo, ĕre, di, sum* and *tum; monstro, demonstro, āre, āvi, ātum.*

Sicily. *Sicilia, ae,* f.

Silent. *Mutus, a, um.*

Silver. *Argentum, i,* n.

Since, as. *Quum, quoniam,* conj. Since, ago, *abhinc,* adv.

Six. *Sex,* indecl.

Six hundredth. *Sexcentesĭmus, a, um.*

Sixth. *Sextus, a, um.* Sixth of July, *pridie Nonas Quintĭles.* G. 708, III.; 437, 1.

Sixtieth. *Sexagesĭmus, a, um.*

Skilled in, skilful in. *Perĭtus, a, um.*

Slave — be the slave of. *Servio, ĭre, ĭvi* and *ii, ĭtum.* G. 385.

Slay. *Interfĭcio, ĕre, fēci, fectum; occīdo, ĕre, cīdi, cīsum.*

Sleep. *Dormio, ĭre, ĭvi, ĭtum.*

Small. *Parvus, a, um.* Small, contracted, *angustus, a, um.*

So. *Tam, ita,* adv.; sometimes rendered by *is, ea, id.* See 444. In such a manner, *sic,* adv. So greatly, to such an extent, *adeo,* adv. So — as, with adjectives, *tam — quam,* adv.; with verbs, *sic — ut,* adv. So far, *tantum,* adv. So far am I from, *tantum abest, ut* with subj. See 498. So great, *tantus, a, um.* So many, *tot,* indecl. So much, *tantus, a, um; tantopĕre,* adv. So that,

ut, conj. Not so much, *non tam,* adv.

Socrates. *Socrătes, is,* m.

Soldier. *Miles, ĭtis,* m. and f.

Solon. *Solo* and *Solon, ōnis,* m.

Some. *Nonnulli, ae, a,* pl. Some, any, *aliqui, qua, quod.* Some one, a certain one, *quidam, quaedam, quoddam.* Somebody, something, *aliquis.* G. 191. At some time, *aliquando,* adv.; *aliquo tempŏre.* G. 426. Some — others, *alii — alii.* G. 459.

Sometime. *Aliquando,* adv.

Sometimes. *Interdum,* adv.

Son. *Filius, ii,* m.

Soul. *Anĭmus, i,* m.

Sovereignty. *Imperivm, ii,* n.

Spain. *Hispania, ae,* f.

Sparta. *Sparta, ae,* f.

Speak. *Dico, ĕre, dixi, dictum; loquor, i, locūtus sum,* dep.

Spend. *Consūmo, ĕre, sumpsi, sumptum.* Of time, *ago, ĕre, egi, actum.*

Spirit, courage. *Anĭmus, i,* m.

Spirited, in a spirited manner. *Acrĭter,* adv.

Spurius. *Spurius, ii,* m.

Squander. *Profundo, ĕre, fūdi, fūsum.*

Stadium. *Stadium, ii,* n.

Start, set out. *Proficiscor, i, profectus sum,* dep.

State, condition. *Status, us,* m. To reduce to a state of peace, *paco, āre, āvi, ātum.* The state, *civĭtas, ātis,* f. State, commonwealth, *res publĭca, rei publĭcae,* f. The highest welfare of the state, *summa res publĭca.*

State, say. *Dico, ĕre, dixi, dictum.*

Statesman. *Is qui rei publĭcae praeest (praesum, esse, fui).* See 438.

Station, to place. *Collŏco, āre, āvi, ātum.*

Stator. *Stator, ōris,* m.

Statue. *Signum, i,* n.

Stoic. *Stoĭcus, i,* m.

Strengthen. *Alo, ĕre, alui, alĭtum* and *altum.*

14

Strife. *Pugna, ae,* f.
Strive. *Nitor, niti, nisus* and *niz-us sum,* dep.
Strong, ample. *Amplus, a, um.* In the strongest terms, *amplissimis verbis.*
Strongly. *Valde,* adv.
Student of. *Studiōsus, a, um.*
Studiously. *Studiōse,* adv.
Study. *Studium, ii,* n.
Subject, thing. *Res, rei,* f. On the subject of, concerning, *de,* prep. with abl.
Subject — to be subject to. *Pareo, ēre, ui, ītum.* G. 385.
Succeed. *Succēdo, ēre, cessi, cessum.* G. 386.
Success. *Felicĭtas, ātis,* f.
Successful. *Secundus, a, um.*
Such. *Talis, e;* sometimes rendered by *qui, quae, quod.* Such, so great, *tantus, a, um.* Such — as, *talis, e — qualis, e; is, ea, id — qui, quae, quod; tantus, a, um — quantus, a, um.* See 534.
Sudden. *Subĭtus, a, um.*
Suffer. *Patior, i, passus sum,* dep.
Suffering, pain. *Dolor, ōris,* m.
Sufficient — to be sufficient, be able. *Possum, posse, potui.*
Sufficiently. *Satis,* adv.
Suggestion — at the suggestion of. *Auctor,* in abl. absol. See 504.
Suitable. *Idoneus, a, um.*
Suitably = worthily enough. *Satis digne,* adv.
Sulla. *Sulla, ae,* m.
Sum of money. *Pecunia, ae,* f.
Sumptuous. *Sumptuōsus, a, um.*
Sun. *Sol, solis,* m.
Sunset. *Solis occāsus, us,* m.
Superbus. *Superbus, i,* m.
Supplicate. *Supplĭco, āre, āvi, ātum.*
Suppose, think. *Arbĭtror, āri, ātus sum,* dep.; *puto, āre, āvi, ātum.*
Suppress. *Comprĭmo, ēre, pressi, pressum.*
Supreme. *Summus, a, um.* G. 163, 3

Sure. *Certus, a, um.*
Surely. *Certe,* adv.
Surpass. *Supēro, āre, āvi, ātum.* To surpass the folly of = to be more foolish than, *sum, esse, fui, dementior, ius.*
Surround. *Circumdo, āre, dēdi, dătum; cingo, ĕre, cinxi, cinctum.*
Sword. *Ferrum, i,* n. See 117. With fire and sword, *ferro ignĕque.*
Syllable. *Syllăba, ae,* f.
Syracuse. *Syracūsae, ārum,* f. pl. Of Syracuse, Syracusan, *Syracusius, a, um.*

T.

Table. *Mensa, ae,* f.
Tablet. *Tabŭla, ae,* f.
Take, take up. *Capio, ĕre, cepi, captum.* Take, appropriate, *sumo, ĕre, sumpsi, sumptum.* Take, carry, *porto, āre, āvi, ātum.* Take away, *tollo, ĕre, sustŭli, sublātum.* Take care, *caveo, ĕre, cavi, cautum.* Take place, *fio, fiĕri, factus sum.* Take the census of, *censeo, ēre, ui, censum.* See 490.
Talent, native talent. *Ingenium, ii,* n. Talent, mental ability, *mens, mentis,* f. Talent, a sum of money, *talentum, i,* n.
Tarentum. *Tarentum, i,* n.
Tarquin, Tarquinius. *Tarquinius, ii,* m.
Tarquinii. *Tarquinii, ōrum,* m. pl.
Tarry. *Commŏror, āri, ātus sum,* dep.
Teach. *Doceo, ēre, ui, doctum.* Teach, instruct, *erūdio, īre, īvi* and *ii, ītum.* Teach, train up, *instituo, ĕre, ui, ūtum.* See 585.
Teacher. *Doctor, ōris,* m.; *magister, tri,* m. See 423.
Tear. *Lacrĭma, ae,* f.
Tedious, long. *Longus, a, um.*
Tell. *Dico, ĕre, dixi, dictum.*
Temperate. *Tempĕrans, antis.*

Temple. *Templum, i,* n.; *aedes,* *is,* f.; *fanum, i,* n. See 871.

Ten. *Decem,* indecl.

Terms — in the strongest terms. *Amplissimis verbis.*

Terrify. *Terreo, ēre, ui, ĭtum.*

Territory. *Fines, ium,* m. pl.

Thales. *Thales, is,* m.

Than. *Quam,* conj.

Thank. *Gratias ago, ĕre, egi, actum.* See 548.

Thanks. *Gratiae, ārum,* f. pl. G. 132. To express thanks, *gratias ago, ĕre, egi, actum.*

That. *Ille, a, ud ; is, ea, id,* less strongly demonstrative than *ille.* And that too, *et is ; et is quidem.* G. 451, 2.

That, in that. *Quod,* conj. That, expressing purpose or result, *ut,* conj. with subj. That, expressing purpose, when the dependent clause contains a comparative, *quo,* conj. with subj. That = but that, *quin,* conj. with subj. G. 498.

The = that, emphatic. *Ille, a, ud ;* not emphatic, *is, ea, id.* The — the, with comparatives, *quo — eo.* See 454.

Theban, of Thebes. *Thebānus, a, um.*

Theft. *Furtum, i,* n.

Their, theirs. *Suus, a, um ;* not reflexive, *eōrum, eārum.* See 468, 2. Their own things, productions, *sua, ōrum,* n. pl. G. 441, 1.

Themistocles. *Themistōcles, is,* m.

Then. *Tum,* adv.

There. *Illic,* adv.

Thermopylae. *Thermopȳlae, ārum.* f. pl.

Thing. *Res, rei,* f.

Think. *Sentio, ĭre, sensi, sensum ; puto, āre, āvi, ātum ; arbĭtror, āri, ātus sum,* dep. Think, be of opinion, *censeo, ēre, ui, censum.* See 576. Think, ponder, *cogĭto, āre, āvi, ātum.* Think out, *commentor, āri, ātus sum,* dep.

Think little of, despise, *contemno, ĕre, tempsi, temptum.*

Third. *Tertius, a, um.*

Thirty. *Triginta,* indecl.

Thirty-eight. *Duodequadraginta,* indecl.

This. *Hic, haec, hoc.* This = that, not strongly demonstrative, *is, ea, id.*

Thou, you. *Tu, tui.* Thou thyself, you yourself, intensive, *ipse, a, um.*

Though. See Lesson LXXVIII.

Thought, opinion. *Sententia, ae,* f. Thought, reflection, *cogitatio, ōnis,* f.

Thousand. *Mille.* G. 178.

Three. *Tres, tria.* Three days, *triduum, ui,* n.

Three hundred. *Trecenti, ae, a,* pl.

Through. *Per,* prep. with acc.

Thus. *Sic,* adv. Thus far, *adhuc,* adv.

Thy, your. *Tuus, a, um.*

Thyself, yourself, emphatic or reflexive, not intensive. *Tu, tui.* By thyself, by yourself, *tecum.*

Tiberius. *Tiberius, ii,* m.

Tigranes. *Tigrānes, is,* m.

Till. *Colo, ĕre, colui, cultum.*

Time. *Tempus, ŏris,* n. At some time, *aliquando,* adv.; *alĭquo tempŏre.* G. 426. At times, *interdum,* adv. For the first time, *primum,* adv. The second time, *itĕrum,* adv. The seventh time, *septĭmum,* adv. For a long time, *jamdūdum ; jamprĭdem,* adv. G. 467, 2. In the time of. See 255, 2.

Timid. *Timĭdus, a, um.*

To. *Ad,* prep. with acc. To, towards, of friendly feelings and conduct towards a person, *erga,* prep. with acc. To no purpose, *nequidquam,* adv.

Toil, labor. *Labor, ōris,* m.

To-morrow. *Cras,* adv.

Tongue. *Lingua, ae,* f.

Too. *Nimis,* adv.; often expressed by the comparative. See 448.

N

And that too, *et is; et is quidem* (*is, ea, id*). G. 451, 2.

Topic — each topic, each thing. *Quidque.*

Torture. *Crucio, āre, āvi, ātum.*

Touch. *Tango, ĕre, tetĭgi, tactum.*

Towards. *Adversus, versus,* prep. with acc.; *versus,* adv. G. 433, 2. Towards, of friendly feelings and conduct towards a person, *erga,* prep. with acc.

Town. *Oppĭdum, i,* n.

Treachery, treason. *Prodĭtio, ōnis,* f.

Treasures, things. *Res, rerum,* f. pl.

Tried. *Spectātus, a, um.*

Troublesome. *Molestus, a, um.*

True. *Verus, a, um.*

Trumpeter. *Tubĭcen, ĭnis,* m.

Trust, to hope. *Spero, āre, āvi, ātum.* Trust in, *confīdo, ĕre, fīsus sum.* G. 419, II.; 4, 2).

Truth. *Verĭtas, ātis,* f.; *verum, i,* n. G. 441, 2.

Try. *Tento, āre, āvi, ātum.*

Tullius. *Tullius, ii,* m.

Twenty. *Vigintī,* indecl.

Twice. *Bis,* adv.

Two. *Duo, duae, duo.* G. 175.

Tyranny. *Tyrannis, ĭdis,* f.

Tyrant. *Tyrannus, i,* m.

U.

Unable, be unable. *Non possum, posse, potui.*

Unbridled. *Effrenātus, a, um.*

Uncertain. *Incertus, a, um.*

Under. *Sub,* prep. with acc. and abl. G. 435. Under the guidance of, *dux, ducis,* in abl. abs.

Understand. *Cognosco, ĕre, nōvi, nĭtum.*

Understanding. *Mens, mentis,* f.

Undertake. *Suscĭpio, ĕre, cēpi, ceptum.*

Unfriendly. *Inimīcus, a, um.*

Unhappy. *Infēlix, īcis.*

Unharmed. *Incolŭmis, e; sine injuria.* See 504.

Unimpaired. *Intĕger, gra, grum.*

Unless. *Nisi,* conj. G. 507.

Unmindful. *Immĕmor, ŏris.*

Unnecessary. *Non necessarius, a, um.*

Unpopularity. *Invidia, ae,* f.

Until. *Dum, donec,* conj. G. 522.

Unusual. *Inusitātus, a, um.*

Unwilling — to be unwilling. *Nolo, nolle, nolui.* G. 293.

Unwillingly. *Invītus, a, um.* G. 443.

Upon. *In,* prep. with acc. and abl. G. 435. Upon, concerning, *de,* prep. with abl.

Upright. *Probus, a, um.*

Urge. *Impello, ĕre, pŭli, pulsum.*

Use, make use of. *Utor, i, usus sum,* dep. G. 419, I.

Useful. *Utĭlis, e.* To be useful, *utĭlis, e, sum, esse, fui; utilitātem affĕro, ferre, attŭli, allātum.* See 444.

Usefulness. *Utilĭtas, ātis,* f.

Useless. *Inutĭlis, e.*

Utter. *Elōquor, i, locūtus sum,* dep.

Utterly. *Fundĭtus,* adv.

V.

Vain — in vain. *Frustra, nequidquam,* adv. See 838.

Valor. *Virtus, ūtis,* f.

Value, price. *Pretium, ii,* n. Of greater value, of more value, *pluris.* G. 402, III. 1.

Vender. *Vendĭtor, ōris,* m.

Verres. *Verres, is,* m.

Verse. *Versus, us,* m.

Very. *Valde;* often rendered by the superlative. See 448. Very, with nouns, *ipse, a, um.* G. 452, 2. Very much, *plurĭmum,* adv. Very highly, with verbs of valuing, *maxĭmi.* G. 402, III. 1). Not very, *non ita,* adv. How very busy one is, *quanta occupatiōne distinētur.* See 631.

Viands. *Epŭlae, ārum,* f. pl.

Vice. *Vitium, ii,* n.

Vicinity — in the vicinity of, near. *Ad,* prep. with acc.

Victor. *Victor, ōris,* m.

Victory. *Victoria, ae,* f. Victory over the Cimbrians, *Cimbrica victoria.*

Views — set forth views, state. *Praedĭco, āre, āvi, ātum.*

Vigilant. *Vigĭlans, antis.*

Vigilantly, sharply. *Acrĭter,* adv.

Village. *Vicus, i,* m.

Violate. *Viŏlo, āre, āvi, ātum.*

Virtue. *Virtus, ūtis,* f.

Visit. *Viso, ĕre, visi, visum.*

Voice. *Vox, vocis,* f. A feeble voice, *vocŭla, ae,* f.

Voyage — have a prosperous voyage. *Ex sententia navĭgo, āre, āvi, ātum.* See 339.

W.

Wage. *Gero, ĕre, gessi, gestum.* Wage against, *infĕro, ferre, tŭli, illātum.* G. 386.

Wait. *Exspecto, āre, āvi, ātum.*

Walk. *Ambŭlo, āre, āvi, ātum.* Walk, go along, *ingrĕdior, i, ingressus sum,* dep.

Wall. *Murus, i,* m.; *moenia, ium,* n. pl.; *paries, ĕtis,* m. See 377. Walls of the city, city walls, *moenia, ium,* n. pl. Walls of my, &c., own house, *mei,* etc., *parietes.* See 378.

War. *Bellum, i,* n.

Warrior. *Is qui bellum gerit (gero, ĕre, gessi, gestum).* See 444.

Watch. *Vigĭlo, āre, āvi, ātum.*

Way, manner. *Modus, i,* m. In no way, *nullo modo;* in no thing, *nulla re.*

Wealth. *Divitiae, ārum,* f. pl.

Wealthy. *Dives, ĭtis.*

Weary. *Defatīgo, āre, āvi, ātum.*

Weep at. *Illacrĭmor, āri, ātus sum,* dep. G. 386.

Weighty. *Gravis, e.*

Welfare, advantage. *Commŏdum,*

i, n. Highest welfare of the state, highest public welfare. *summa res publĭca.*

Well. *Bene,* adv. Well known, sometimes rendered by *ille, a, ud.* G. 450, 4.

What, interrog. *Qui, quae, quod,* adj.; *quis, quae, quid,* substant.

Whatever. *Quisquis, quaequae, quodquod* and *quicquid* or *quidquid.* Whatever = that which, *is, ea, id — qui, quae, quod.*

When. *Quum,* adv. *When* and *while* are sometimes rendered by the abl. abs., by a participle, by an adjective, or by an appositive. See Lesson LXXIX.; also G. 431, 1 and 2, (1); 578, I.; 442; 363, 3. When, interrog., *quando,* adv.

Where. *Ubi,* adv.

Whether. *Num,* conj.; in double questions, *utrum; num; ne,* enclit. conj. Whether — not, *nonne.* Whether — or, *utrum — an.* G. 346, II. 2.

Which, relat. *Qui, quae, quod;* interrog., *qui, quae, quod,* adj., *quis, quae, quid,* substant. Which one, of two, *uter, utra, utrum.* G. 149.

While. *Dum,* conj. G. 522. When, *quum,* conj. See also "When."

Who, which, what, relat. *Qui, quae, quod;* interrog., *qui, quae, quod,* adj., *quis, quae, quid,* substant.

Whoever. *Quisquis, quaequae, quodquod* and *quicquid* or *quidquid.* Whoever = he, etc. — who, *is, ea, id — qui, quae, quod.*

Whole, the whole of. *Totus, a, um;* G. 151; *cunctus, a, um; omnis, e; universus, a, um.*

Wholly, whole. *Totus, a, um.* G. 151; 443.

Why. *Quare; cur;* adv.; *quid.* G. 454, 2.

Wicked. *Scelerātus, a, um;* *imprŏbus, a, um.*

Wickedness. *Scelus, ĕris,* n.

Will — good will. *Benevolentia, ae,* f.

Willing — be willing. *Volo, velle, volui.* G. 293.

Willingly. *Libenter,* adv.

Winter. *Hiems, ĕmis,* f. Winter quarters, *hiberna, ōrum,* n. pl.

Wisdom. *Sapientia, ae,* f.

Wise. *Sapiens, entis.*

Wisely. *Sapienter,* adv.

Wish. *Volo, velle, volui.* G. 293.

With. *Cum,* prep. with abl. With, among, near to, at the house of, *apud,* prep. with acc. *With* is sometimes rendered by the abl. abs. With the attendance of, *comes, ĭtis,* in abl. abs. With each other, *inter se.* G. 448, 1. With fire and sword, *ferro ignē-que.* See 117.

Withdraw, call off. *Avŏco, āre, āvi, ātum.* Withdraw, retire, *se re-movēre (remŏveo, ēre, mōvi, mō-tum); decēdo, ēre, cessi, cessum.*

Within. *Intra,* prep. with acc.

Without. *Sine,* prep. with abl.; sometimes rendered by *nullus, a, um,* G. 151, in agreement with noun; sometimes by *quin,* conj. with subj. See 571; also G. 498, 3. Without exception, alone, *unus, a, um.* G. 175, 1. With-out a nomination from the peo-ple, *injussu popŭli.* G. 414, 2, 3). To be without, *vaco, āre, āvi, ātum; careo, ēre, ui, ĭtum; egeo, ēre, ui.* See 239, I.

Witness. *Testis, is,* m. and f.

Witness, to witness. *Specto, āre, āvi, ātum.*

Wonder, wonder at. *Miror, āri, ātus sum,* dep.

Wonderful. *Mirabĭlis, e; admi-rabĭlis, e; mirus, a, um.*

Wont, be wont. *Soleo, ēre, solĭtus sum.*

Word. *Verbum, i,* n. Word for word, *ad verbum.* See 361.

Work, monument. *Monumentum, i,* n.

World. *Mundus, i,* m.

Worship. *Venĕror, āri, ātus sum,* dep.

Worth, moral worth. *Honestas, ātis,* f.; *virtus, ūtis,* f.

Worthily. *Digne,* adv.

Worthy. *Dignus, a, um.*

Would rather. *Malo, malle, malui.* G. 293.

Would that. *Utĭnam,* adv. G. 488, 1.

Write. *Scribo, ĕre, scripsi, scrip-tum.*

Writing. *Scriptum, i,* n. To com-mit to writing, *littĕris mando, āre, āvi, ātum.*

Wrong. *Pravus, a, um.*

Wrong, crime. *Nefas,* n. indecl.

X.

Xenophon. *Xenŏphon, ontis,* m.

Xerxes. *Xerxes, is,* m.

Y.

Year. *Annus, i,* m.

Yesterday. *Heri,* adv.; *hesterno die.* G. 426. Yesterday's, of yesterday, *hesternus, a, um.*

Yet. *Tamen,* adv.

Yoke. *Jugum, i,* n.

You, thou. *Tu, tui.* You your-self, *ipse, a, um.*

Young man. *Adolescens, entis,* m.; *juvĕnis, is,* m.

Your. *Vester, tra, trum.* Your, thy, *tuus, a, um.* Your companions, &c., *vestri, ōrum; tui, ōrum;* m. pl. G. 441, 1.

Yourself, emphatic, not intensive. *Tu, tui;* intensive, *ipse, a, um.* By yourself, *tecum.*

Youth. *Juvĕnis, is,* m. and f.

Z.

Zeal. *Studium, ii,* n.

Arnold's Latin Course:

I. FIRST AND SECOND LATIN BOOK AND PRACTICAL GRAMMAR. Revised and Carefully Corrected. by J. A. SPENCER, D. D. 12mo, 359 pages.

II. PRACTICAL INTRODUCTION TO LATIN PROSE COMPOSITION, Revised and carefully corrected by J. A. SPENCER, D. D. 12mo, 356 pages.

III. CORNELIUS NEPOS. With Questions and Answers, and an Imitative Exercise on each Chapter. With Notes by E. A. JOHNSON, Professor of Latin, in University of New York. New edition, enlarged, with a Lexicon, Historical and Geographical Index, etc. 12mo, 350 pages.

Arnold's Classical Series has attained a circulation almost unparalleled, having been introduced into nearly all the leading educational institutions in the United States. The secret of this success is, that the author has hit upon the true system of teaching the ancient languages. He exhibits them not as dead, but as living 'tongues; and by imitation and repetition, the means which Nature herself points out to the child learning his mother-tongue, he familiarizes the student with the idioms employed by the elegant writers and speakers of antiquity.

The First and Second Latin Book should be put into the hands of the beginners, who will soon acquire from its pages a better idea of the language than could be gained by months of study according to the old system. The reason of this is, that every thing has a practical bearing, and a principle is no sooner learned than it is applied. The pupil is at once set to work on exercises.

The Prose Composition forms an excellent sequel to the above work, or may be used with any other course. It teaches the art of writing Latin more correctly and thoroughly, more easily and pleasantly, than any other work. In its pages Latin syno.nymes are carefully illustrated, differences of idioms noted, cautions as to common errors impressed on the mind, and every help afforded toward attaining a pure and flowing Latin style.

From N. WHEELER, Principal of Worcester County High School.

" In the skill with which he sets forth the *idiomatic peculiarities*, as well as in the directness and simplicity with which he states the facts of the ancient languages, Mr. Arnold has no superior. I know of no books so admirably adapted to awaken an *interest* in the study of the language, or so well fitted to lay the foundation of a correct scholarship and refined taste."

From A. B. RUSSELL, Oakland High School.

" The style in which the books are got up are not their only recommendation. With thorough instruction on the part of the teacher using these books as text-books, I am confident a much more ample return for the time and labor bestowed by our youth upon Latin must be secured. The time certainly has come when an advance must be made upon the old methods of instruction. I am glad to have a work that promises so many advantages as Arnold's First and Second Latin Book to beginners."

From C. M. BLAKE, Classical Teacher, Philadelphia.

" I am much pleased with Arnold's Latin Books. A class of my older boys have just finished the First and Second Book. They had studied Latin for a long time before, but never *understood* it, they say, as they do now."

Cæsar's Commentaries on the Gallic War.

With English Notes, Critical and Explanatory; a Lexicon, Geographical and Historical Indexes, a Map of Gaul, etc.   By Rev. J. A. SPENCER, D. D.   12mo, 408 pages.

In the preparation of this volume, great care has been taken to adapt it in every respect to the wants of the young student, to make it a means at the same time of advancing him in a thorough knowledge of Latin, and inspiring him with a desire for further acquaintance with the classics of the language.   Dr. Spencer has not, like some commentators, given an abundance of help on the easy passages, and allowed the difficult ones to speak for themselves.   His Notes are on those parts on which the pupil wants them, and explain, not only grammatical difficulties, but allusions of every kind in the text.   A well-drawn sketch of Cæsar's life, a Map of the region in which his campaigns were carried on, and a Vocabulary, which removes the necessity of using a large dictionary and the waste of time consequent thereon, enhance the value of the volume in no small degree.

Quintus Curtius :

Life and Exploits of Alexander the Great.   Edited and illustrated with English Notes.   By WILLIAM HENRY CROSBY.   12mo, 385 pages.

Curtius's History of Alexander the Great, though little used in the schools of this country, in England and on the Continent holds a high place in the estimation of classical instructors.   The interesting character of its subject, the elegance of its style, and the purity of its moral sentiments, ought to place it at least on a par with Cæsar's Commentaries or Sallust's Histories.   The present edition, by the late Professor of Latin in Rutgers College, is unexceptionable in typography, convenient in form, scholarly and practical in its notes, and altogether an admirable text-book for classes preparing for college.

From Prof. Owen, of the New York Free Academy.

"It gives me great pleasure to add my testimonial to the many you are receiving in favor of the beautiful and well-edited edition of Quintus Curtius, by Prof. Wm. Henry Crosby.   It is seldom that a classical book is submitted to me for examination, to which I can give so hearty a recommendation as to this.   The external appearance is attractive; the paper, type, and binding, being just what a text-book should be, neat, clear, and durable.   The notes are brief, pertinent, scholar-like, neither too exuberant nor too meagre, but happily exemplifying the golden mean so desirable and yet so very difficult of attainment."

Select Orations of M. Tullius Cicero :

With Notes, for the use of Schools and Colleges. By E. A. JOHNSON, Professor of Latin in the University of New York. 12mo, 459 pages.

This edition of Cicero's Select Orations possesses some special advantages for the student which are both new and important. It is the only edition which contains the improved text that has been prepared by a recent careful collation and correct deciphering of the best manuscripts of Cicero's writings. It is the work of the celebrated Orelli, Madvig, and Klotz, and has been done since the appearance of Orelli's complete edition. The Notes, by Professor Johnson, of the New York University, have been mostly selected, with great care, from the best German authors, as well as the English edition of Arnold.

From THOMAS CHASE, *Tutor in Latin in Harvard University.*

" An edition of Cicero like Johnson's has long been wanted ; and the excellence of the text, the illustrations of words, particles, and pronouns, and the explanation of various points of construction and interpretation, bear witness to the Editor's familiarity with some of the most important results of modern scholarship, and entitle his work to a large share of public favor."

" It seems to us an improvement upon any edition of these Orations that has been published in this country, and will be found a valuable aid in their studies to the lovers of classical literature."—*Troy Daily Whig.*

Cicero de Officiis :

With English Notes, mostly translated from ZUMPT and BONNELL. By THOMAS A. THACHER, of Yale College. 12mo, 194 pages.

In this edition, a few historical notes have been introduced in cases where the Dictionary in common use has not been found to contain the desired information ; the design of which is to aid the learner in understanding the contents of the treatises, the thoughts and reasoning of the author, to explain grammatical difficulties, and inculcate a knowledge of grammatical principles. The Editor has aimed throughout to guide rather than carry the learner through difficulties ; requiring of him more study, in consequence of his help, than he would have devoted to the book without it.

From M. L. STOEVER, *Professor of the Latin Language and Literature in Pennsylvania College.*

" I have examined with much pleasure Prof. Thacher's edition of Cicero de Officiis, and am convinced of its excellence. The Notes have been prepared with great care and good judgment. Practical knowledge of the wants of the student has enabled the Editor to furnish just the kind of assistance required ; grammatical difficulties are removed, and the obscurities of the treatise are explained, the interest of the learner is elicited, and his industry directed rather than superseded. There can be but one opinion with regard to the merits of the work, and I trust that Professor Thacher will be disposed to continue his labors so carefully commenced, in this department of classical learning."

The Works of Horace.

With English Notes, for the use of Schools and Colleges. By J. L. LINCOLN, Professor of the Latin Language and Literature in Brown University. 12mo, 575 pages.

The text of this edition is mainly that of Orelli, the most important readings of other critics being given in foot-notes. The volume is introduced with a biographical sketch of Horace and a critique on his writings, which enable the student to enter intelligently on his work. Peculiar grammatical constructions, as well as geographical and historical allusions, are explained in notes, which are just full enough to aid the pupil, to excite him to gain a thorough understanding of the author, and awaken in him a taste for philological studies, without taking all labor off his hands. While the chief aim has been to impart a clear idea of Latin Syntax as exhibited in the text, it has also been a cherished object to take advantage of the means so variously and richly furnished by Horace for promoting the poetical taste and literary culture of the student.

From an article by Prof. Bahr, *of the University of Heidelberg, in the Heidelberg Annals of Literature.*

"There are already several American editions of Horace, intended for the use of schools; of one of these, which has passed through many editions, and has also been widely circulated in England, mention has been formerly made in this journal; but that one we may not put upon an equality with the one now before us, inasmuch as this has taken a different stand-point, which may serve as a sign of progress in this department of study. The editor has, it is true, also intended his work for the use of schools, and has sought to adapt it, in all its parts, to such a use; but still, without losing sight of this purpose, he has proceeded throughout with more independence. In the preparation of the Notes, the editor has faithfully observed the principles (laid down in his preface); the explanations of the poet's words commend themselves by a compressed brevity which limits itself to what is most essential, and by a sharp precision of expression; and references to other passages of the poet, and also to grammars, dictionaries, etc., are not wanting."

Sallust's Jugurtha and Catiline.

With Notes and a Vocabulary. By NOBLE BUTLER and MINARD STURGIS. 12mo, 397 pages.

The editors have spent a vast amount of time and labor in correcting the text, by a comparison of the most improved German and English editions. It is believed that this will be found superior to any edition hitherto published in this country. In accordance with their chronological order, the "Jugurtha" precedes the "Catiline." The Notes are copious and tersely expressed; they display not only fine scholarship, but (what is quite as necessary in such a book) a practical knowledge of the difficulties which the student encounters in reading this author, and the aids that he requires. The Vocabulary was prepared by the late William H. G. Butler. It will be found an able and faithful performance.

Germania and Agricola of Caius Cornelius Tacitus:

With Notes for Colleges. By W. S. TYLER, Professor of the Greek and Latin Languages in Amherst College. 12mo, 193 pages.

Tacitus's account of Germany and life of Agricola are among the most fascinating and instructive Latin classics. The present edition has been prepared expressly for college classes, by one who knows what they need. In it will be found: 1. A Latin text, approved by all the more recent editors. 2. A copious illustration of the gram-matical constructions, as well as of the rhetorical and poetical usages peculiar to Taci-tus. In a writer so concise it has been deemed necessary to pay particular regard to the connection of thought, and to the particles as the hinges of that connection. 3. Constant comparisons of the writer with the authors of the Augustan age, for the pur-pose of indicating the changes which had already been wrought in the language of the Roman people. 4. An embodiment in small compass of the most valuable labors of such recent German critics as Grimm, Günther, Gruber, Kiessling, Dronke, Roth, Ruperti, and Walther.

From PROF. LINCOLN, of Brown University.

"I have found the book in daily use with my class of very great service, very practi-cal, and well suited to the wants of students. I am very much pleased with the Life of Tacitus and the Introduction, and indeed with the literary character of the book throughout. We shall make the book a part of our Latin course."

The History of Tacitus:

By W. S. TYLER. With Notes for Colleges. 12mo, 453 pages.

The text of Tacitus is here presented in a form as correct as a comparison of the best editions can make it. Notes are appended for the student's use, which contain not only the grammatical, but likewise all the geographical, archæological, and historical illustra-tions that are necessary to render the author intelligible. It has been the constant aim of the editor to carry students beyond the dry details of grammar and lexicography, and introduce them to a familiar acquaintance and lively sympathy with the author and his times. Indexes to the notes, and to the names of persons and places, render refer-ence easy.

From PROF. HACKETT, of Newton Theological Seminary.

"The notes appear to me to be even more neat and elegant than those on the 'Ger-mania and Agricola.' They come as near to such notes as I would be glad to write my-self on a classic, as almost any thing that I have yet seen."

Lincoln's Livy.

Selections from the first Five Books, together with the Twenty-First and Twenty-Second Books entire; with a Plan of Rome, a Map of the passage of Hannibal, and English Notes for the use of Schools. By J. L. LINCOLN, Professor of the Latin Language and Literature in Brown University. 12mo, 329 pages.

The publishers believe that in this edition of Livy a want is supplied which has been universally felt; there being previous to this no American edition furnished with the requisite aids for the successful study of this Latin author. The text is chiefly that of Alschefski, which is now generally received by the best critics. The notes have been prepared with special reference to the grammatical study of the language, and the illustration of its forms, constructions, and idioms, as used by Livy. They will not be found to foster habits of dependance in the student, by supplying indiscriminate translation or unnecessary assistance; but come to his help only in such parts as it is fair to suppose he cannot master by his own exertions. They also embrace all necessary information relating to history, geography, and antiquities.

Lincoln's Livy has been highly commended by critics, and is used in nearly all the colleges in the country.

From PROF. ANDERSON, *of Waterville College.*

"A careful examination of several portions of your work has convinced me that, for the use of students, it is altogether superior to any edition of Livy with which I am acquainted. Among its excellences you will permit me to name the close attention given to particles, to the subjunctive mood, the constant reference to the grammars, the discrimination of words nearly synonymous, and the care in giving the localities mentioned in the text. The book will be hereafter used in our college."

Beza's Latin Version of the New Testament.

12mo, 291 pages.

The now-acknowledged propriety of giving students of languages familiar works for translation—thus adopting in the schools the mode by which the child first learns to talk—has induced the publication of this new American edition of Beza's Latin Version of the New Testament. Ever since its first appearance, this work has kept its place in the general esteem; while more recent versions have been so strongly tinged with the peculiar views of the translators as to make them acceptable to particular classes only. The editor has exerted himself to render the present edition worthy of patronage by its superior accuracy and neatness; and the publishers flatter themselves that the pains bestowed will insure for it a preference over other editions.

Virgil's Æneid.

With Explanatory Notes. By HENRY S. FRIEZE, Professor of Latin in the State University of Michigan. Illustrated. 12mo, 598 pages.

The appearance of this edition of Virgil's Æneid will, it is believed, be hailed with delight by all classical teachers. Neither expense nor pains have been spared to clothe the great Latin epic in a fitting dress. The type is unusually large and distinct, and errors in the text, so annoying to the learner, have been carefully avoided. The work contains eighty-five engravings, which delineate the usages, costumes, weapons, arts, and mythology of the ancients with a vividness that can be attained only by pictorial illustrations. The great feature of this edition is the scholarly and judicious commentary furnished in the appended Notes. The author has here endeavored not to show his learning, but to supply such practical aid as will enable the pupil to understand and appreciate what he reads. The notes are just full enough, thoroughly explaining the most difficult passages, while they are not so extended as to take all labor off the pupil's hands. Properly used, they cannot fail to impart an intelligent acquaintance with the syntax of the language. In a word, this work is commended to teachers as the most elegant, accurate, interesting, and practically useful edition of the Æneid that has yet been published.

From JOHN H. BRUNNER, *President of Hiwassee College.*

"The typography, paper, and binding of Virgil's Æneid, by Prof. Frieze, are all that need be desired; while the learned and judicious notes appended, are very valuable indeed."

From Principal of Piedmont (Va.) Academy.

"I have to thank you for a copy of Prof. Frieze's edition of the Æneid. I have been exceedingly pleased in my examination of it. The size of the type from which the text is printed, and the faultless execution, leave nothing to be desired in these respects. The adherence to a standard text throughout, increases the value of this edition."

From D. G. MOORE, *Principal U. High School, Rutland.*

"The copy of Frieze's 'Virgil' forwarded to me was duly received. It is so evidently superior to any of the other editions, that I shall unhesitatingly adopt it in my classes."

www.ingramcontent.com/pod-product-compliance
Lightning Source LLC
Chambersburg PA
CBHW060521030726
47498CB00004B/1021